THE INTENDED ONES

The prequel & sequel to Substitute Angel

Timothy Best

TouchPoint Press

THE INTENDED ONES by Timothy Best
Published by TouchPoint Press
2075 Attala Road 1990
Kosciusko, MS 39090
www.touchpointpress.com

Copyright © 2014 Timothy Best
All rights reserved.

PRINT ISBN-10: 0692328122
PRINT ISBN-13: 978-0692328125

This is a work of fiction. Names, places, characters, and events are fictitious. Any similarities to actual events and persons, living or dead, are purely coincidental. Any trademarks, service marks, product names, or named features are assumed to be the property of their respective owners and are used only for reference. If any of these terms are used, no endorsement is implied. Except for review purposes, the reproduction of this book, in whole or part, electronically or mechanically, constitutes a copyright violation. Address permissions and review inquiries to media@touchpointpress.com.

Editor: Taylor Bell
Cover Design: R. Brannon Hall

First Edition

Printed in the United States of America.

For Robin.

"Faith is the art of holding on to things your reason has once accepted in spite of your changing moods."—CS Lewis

1 RECKLESS BEHAVIOR

Black smoke belched out of the apartment building as if each broken window was a view to hell itself. The last of the firemen who had been ordered outside chugged to an exhausted halt in the parking lot. He carried a long-handled ax in his hand and a SCBA — or self-contained breathing apparatus — air bottle on his back. He removed his helmet, then slid off his mask revealing a clean oval of white skin upon an otherwise sooty face. He looked back at the building. The blaze was too hot now. It had gotten into the attic and the captain had abruptly ordered his men to fall back. There was nothing left to do except pour water on it from a safe distance with the two hook and ladders that were on the scene.

Nobody was really sure what caused the fire, but its point of origin seemed to be the second floor apartment on the front right-hand side. In a two-story, eight-unit apartment building that was fifty-one years old, anything could have triggered the blaze: faulty wiring, an iron neglectfully left plugged in, a forgotten lit candle, a burning cigarette, even arson.

What was known for sure was no one was in the building. All of the tenants had left for work, as it was just after 9:00 a.m. on a pleasant Friday in late June. The Charlevoix Fire Department had the opportunity to break into every unit and search each room. A dog, a parakeet and two cats had even been rescued.

Paramedic Wyatt "Doc" Reynolds and his heavier set emergency medical technician partner, Lance Vale, watched attentively, standing at the open rear doors of their ambulance in the parking lot as each firefighter was assigned a new task since the tactics were changing. Like the firemen, they were wearing heavy, brown turnout coats with bright yellow day-glow striping on the sleeves, matching pants with suspenders, and treated boots.

Gone were the off-white shirts that separated the city's medical personnel who drove the town's two ambulances from the firefighters. The town was feeling the pinch of recession, so in a measure to conserve Charlevoix's already stretched budget, the city council ruled any paramedic or EMT on the payroll must also be trained as a firefighter, which is what Doc and Lance had been doing for the past five months. Lance was particularly anxious to do well in training since several of the firemen were already EMTs and he figured he was expendable. This was less so for Doc. Only a couple of the city's firefighters had paramedic certification, and none possessed the medical expertise he did. Doc understood the workings of the human body like an IT whiz understood computers. Again and again in the ambulance he had radioed in a possible diagnosis for patients that had saved both time and their lives. Over and over he had restarted a heart or plugged a bleeding artery when no one else could.

When Doc and Lance had first arrived on the scene, they had assisted with removing the hoses from the trucks, hooking them up to hydrants, then cordoning off a perimeter of yellow caution tape as the onlookers gathered. But because it was still early in their training, there wasn't much actual firefighting they were qualified to do other than help out with small jobs.

"Name a James Bond villain who was a real life Olympic medalist?" Lance asked, never taking his eyes off the blaze.

"Harold Sakata," Doc answered, also watching the building. "He played Oddjob in *Goldfinger* and won a silver medal for weightlifting at the 1948 games in London."

Lance grunted and shook his head, exasperated.

"Isn't that right?" Doc asked.

"Yes," his partner answered. "It's just…I can never stump you with this stuff. It's annoying."

Lance was a 007 aficionado and loved to ask people James Bond trivia questions. It was his social icebreaker no matter the situation. At thirty years old, he was a guy that everybody in the small town seemed to like. With his jovial personality, marshmallow body, kind green eyes, thick wiry hair, and ear for gossip, Doc couldn't have asked for a better partner. He studied the back-stories of each Bond film and tried to keep ahead of Lance on the trivia. It was his way of saying he cared about their friendship.

"I don't like smoke," Doc observed as he watched it seep out of the broken apartment building windows. "Only bad things come from it. Like the Wicked Witch of the East."

"Or that monster on *Lost*," Lance recalled.

"Or the alien spaceships in *Independence Day*," Doc said.

"Or, 'Smoke Gets In Your Eyes,'" Lance retorted, referencing the old Platters' tune.

"'Smoke On The Water,'" Doc fired back, remembering the Deep Purple classic.

"'Smokin' In The Boys Room,'" Lance countered, referencing the Brownsville Station's only hit.

"'Smoke From A Distant Fire,'" Doc volleyed.

Lance looked at him puzzled.

"The Sanford-Townsend Band?" Doc clarified, but Lance still didn't know the tune.

"The point is, you don't like smoke," Lance concluded.

"Right," Doc agreed

"So, naturally, you're studying to be a firefighter."

"Naturally," Doc quipped, knowing neither one of them had any choice in the matter.

While they stood there, a green Subaru came to a halt on the street behind them and in front of the building. Its screeching tires caused both Doc and Lance to turn. A young Asian woman with long, shiny black hair and skinny legs jumped out of the car. She looked at the building, screamed a high-pitched, blood-curdling scream and started running toward it.

"私の赤ちゃん！私の赤ちゃん！"

She kept repeating the same phrase as she ran through the crowd of about thirty people. She was met at the yellow-taped perimeter by a cop with extended arms who placed a firm hand on each of her shoulders to stop her.

"What's she saying?" Lance asked, watching the hubbub.

Doc took a few steps away from the ambulance and peered past the onlookers at the woman's green Subaru sitting in the middle of the street while the woman continued being hysterical in one language and the cop tried to calm her down in another.

After a few seconds, he turned and looked at the woman. She was now pointing to a front corner window on the ground floor, the apartment directly below where the fire probably originated. Quickly looking around, his blue eyes saw an orange snow saucer, the kind kids use to sled with in the winter. It was sitting on a wide shelf in a carport at the left end of the parking lot. He ran to the carport, grabbed the saucer, and then ran back to the ambulance where he strapped on his air bottle.

"What? What is it?" Lance asked.

"She's got a window shade on the passenger side rear window," Doc said. He looked toward the front ground floor apartment. "I think there's a baby in there."

"What? No!" Lance argued. "Our guys checked every apartment. Didn't you hear the captain tell 'em?"

"What do you think she's screaming for?" Doc insisted while putting on his air mask then helmet. "TiVoed episodes of *American Idol?* Those are the screams of a frantic mother."

He slipped on his Kevlar gloves, secured the chin strap on his helmet, grabbed the saucer, and then ran toward the hallway in the center of the building to an outside staircase with front door access to the apartments.

"Doc! No!" Lance called.

Seeing him go, Captain Stubigg yelled, "Reynolds! What the hell are you doing?" The veteran fireman was working a hose with another firefighter. He called a third man to take his place and then grabbed a bullhorn off the back of the nearest fire truck.

"*Doc Reynolds, return to your ambulance immediately!*"

Doc ignored him and disappeared into the already open door of the right side ground level apartment. Stubigg lowered the horn and walked impatiently over to Lance.

"Well?" he bellowed, knowing Lance would have the answer.

"He thinks there's a kid in that ground floor unit," Lance responded.

Stubigg looked at the still screaming woman pointing to the first floor corner window, and then raised his bullhorn to address the onlookers.

"Does anyone here know this woman's language?"

When nobody came forward, he ordered all three active hoses to concentrate on the right hand side of the roof.

"Idiot!" he muttered, watching the roof and knowing what was about to happen.

Meanwhile, inside the ground floor apartment Doc kept the snow saucer raised above his head as chunks of the stucco ceiling plopped down all around him. Orange ashes swirled through the air like angry, deranged snowflakes. The apartment was like a furnace.

The second floor unit directly above was now a raging inferno and he could hear an eerie cacophony of pops, thuds and hisses coming from it. As he weaved through the snaking dark smoke he became unsure of his bearings. Was he in the living room? No, it was the dining room he decided as his thigh bumped into the side of a dining table. Straight ahead, he spotted a hallway and the outline of an open doorway to his immediate left. It was a bedroom.

Carefully walking over and peering inside with the saucer still over his head, he could see it wasn't a nursery. It looked like a guest bedroom with a queen-size bed. The comforter and an open suitcase on the unmade bed was now smoldering from the hot chunks of ceiling that had fallen onto it. Doc turned to continue down the hall when he suddenly stopped and turned back.

"Why was that dresser drawer open?" he wondered. Going into the room and looking into the drawer, he saw it had been converted into a crib. There was what looked like a six-month-old infant laying inside the drawer, ashen and still.

"Jesus," Doc muttered.

He dropped the saucer, scooped up the baby, then unbuckled and unzipped his fire-resistant coat and slipped it inside. Seeing a broken window a couple feet away, he elbowed all the remaining glass he could, stuck a leg outside, then hopped out amidst a thick cloud of smoke and tumbled to the ground. His exit from the building wasn't particularly graceful, but at least it was an exit.

He got to his feet and while still holding the bundle inside his coat and began running. He'd only gotten a few yards when there was a loud explosion behind him. Raining shards of fiery wood, melting shingles, and pieces of glass pummeled him. Doc fell to his knees from the sheer force of the blast, but then staggered to his feet and started to run again.

He didn't know if he was injured. He wasn't concentrating on that. He was focused on the waiting ambulance with its open back doors. He never looked back to see the explosion had come from the attic, or that its flaming rafters had crashed into the second floor apartment where the fire had started, which in turn, had caused the already weakened second floor to collapse into the first floor apartment he had just vacated twenty seconds earlier.

When Doc arrived at the ambulance, Lance unzipped his coat and removed the infant while Doc quickly took off the rest of his equipment. The frantic mother had now gotten past the cop and was at the back of the ambulance. She reached for the baby wanting to hold it, but Doc stepped in between her and Lance.

"Let me do my job, ma'am. Okay?"

The woman didn't know what Doc was saying but she understood his serious tone. She also saw how still the baby was and its grey skin tone.

"O-okay," she agreed.

Doc took the baby from Lance and then stepped up and into the ambulance. As he did, Lance noticed the tear and moist stain in between Doc's shoulder blades on his dark blue T-shirt.

Two hours later back at the fire hall, which was also connected to Charlevoix' City Hall and police department on State Street, Doc knocked on Captain Stubigg's open office door. Donald Stubigg was a wide-shouldered, barrel-chested man from German heritage. His short blonde hair was flecked with white. At fifty-one, he'd been a fireman for twenty-six years, and was known for being good at what he did and pulling no punches. Doc had known Stubigg ever since he was hired as a paramedic by the city nearly a year and a half earlier, but he had never directly reported to him until recently. Harry Stanton, the town's senior paramedic, had always been Doc and Lance's boss. But Harry had been forced to take early retirement after twenty-three years on the job. Another cost-saving measure.

Stubigg waved Doc into his small office as he finished a report on his computer. He sat behind an L-shaped desk, his meaty fingers flying over the keyboard with expert dexterity. The fireman-in-training came in wearing black cargo pants and a dark blue T-shirt that had the initials CFD on the left chest pocket.

"Take a seat," Stubigg said, not looking up from his work. "How's the back?" During the explosion at the apartment building, Doc had taken a five-inch long flying nail right between the shoulders.

"Fine. Couple of stitches. I was lucky," Doc shrugged.

"You were stupid," Stubigg corrected, still not looking up. He stopped typing and referred to his computer screen. "The tenant's name was Patricia Miyako, originally from Japan. Her sister, Mai, is visiting and barely speaks English. Her five-month-old daughter, Ali, was up and down all night. So when Patricia went to work and Mai needed diapers, she let the baby sleep in her makeshift crib. How long did the doctor say she'd been dead?"

"He couldn't say for sure," Doc answered. "But both lungs had collapsed."

"Probably happened early. My bet is the kid was already dead when we did our initial search. That's why nobody heard her."

"The mother was gone a long time just for diapers," Doc noted.

"She doesn't know the town, maybe she couldn't read what items were in the aisles," Stubigg suggested. He swiveled in his chair from the computer screen to Doc. "Anyway, she's got a lot to answer for. To God, her family...just like you've got a lot to answer for to me."

"What do you mean?" the paramedic asked earnestly. "I was

trying to save a life."

"You were saving an infant that was already dead."

"Yeah, but *I* didn't know that."

"But I did," the captain stated flatly. "We'd been on scene for more than thirteen minutes, the fire was spreading exponentially, smoke was everywhere. No child survives thirteen minutes of smoke inhalation. So when the mother showed up and we realized the kid was in there, it was already gone. But *you,* you charged into a burning building without authorization and ignored direct orders to come back. You turned an entire company's focus away from firefighting and put it on you. Then you got injured on top of it all. You probably think you were being heroic. I think you were an idiot who undermined my authority."

The captain folded his hands and looked intently at Doc. The younger man's eyes briefly shot to the five gold-framed commendations from the city on the wall behind him.

"Why do you think I called everyone back to the parking lot?" the senior firefighter asked.

"I don't know," Doc answered honestly.

"Because the building is owned by Bubba Martin. Bubba owns a few buildings in town, and even though he doesn't do it for money, he likes to make homemade moonshine from stills. Stills he's been known to keep in attics. So, when the fire reached the attic—"

"If a still was up there, the top of the building was going to explode like a Fourth of July cherry bomb," Doc finished.

"Which it did!" Stubigg pointed out. "Ol' Bubba's in a lot of hot water. Probably gonna get sued by his tenants and be charged by the city."

"So why didn't you just tell me?" Doc asked.

"Why should I have to?" the captain fired back. "Orders are supposed to be followed, Reynolds. Followed without question. Not explained in an emergency where seconds count."

"Did the still cause the fire?"

"No. It looks like a curling iron in the second story front apartment was the culprit. But we'll know more tomorrow."

Doc lowered his eyes, knowing his superior's chastisement was well deserved.

"I ought to can your ass right now for your reckless behavior," Stubigg said, leaning back in his chair. But then he paused, took a breath and looked Doc over. "But it just so happens you're a very gutsy guy. And a hell of a paramedic. Is that why they call you 'Doc?'"

"No. It's a nickname I picked up in high school...I was supposedly 'an operator' with the girls."

Stubigg made a "humph" noise, and then continued, "You're getting a formal reprimand on your record and I'm taking you off days and putting you on nights. At least, while we still have a night shift. That'll be the next thing the city cuts. If you survive your courses and my wrath, you might make a good firefighter someday."

Doc cracked a small grateful smile and nodded, but Stubigg's pronouncement that he'd make a good firefighter felt just like a jail sentence.

2 Futile Attempt

Summer days in Charlevoix, Michigan, could last as long as an oversized county fair lollipop. In mid-June, the sun didn't set until nearly 10:00 p.m. and traces of orange and red still painted the sky until 10:30. Because of this, most of the shops stayed open until 10:00 p.m., and considering several of them opened at 9:00 a.m., it made for a long retail day. But the shopkeepers on Bridge Street in the heart of downtown loved this. It made up for the slow fall, winter, and spring seasons when the town was just a sleepy little village of 3,100 residents. From Memorial Day to Labor Day, the populous swelled to somewhere between 30 and 35,000. It was the time that Charlevoix, like Provincetown in Massachusetts, or Block Island in Rhode Island, or dozens of other waterfront tourist communities made the bulk of its annual income.

The draw of Charlevoix was that it was on a strip of land sandwiched between two magnificent bodies of water: to the west was Lake Michigan, which was forty some odd miles across depending on the course and destination. To the east was the near perfectly circular Round Lake that fed into the sprawling and deep Lake Charlevoix. A river less than a quarter of a mile long called the Pine River connected Lake Michigan to Round Lake and then to Lake Charlevoix beyond it. Like the town, the Pine River was picturesque and manicured. At ninety feet wide, it resembled more of a dredged-out and steel-walled man-made channel than a natural river.

Stretching across the river near its eastern end where the river widened and turned into Round Lake was the Memorial Bridge, a drawbridge which had been completed in 1949 that had a 14-foot clearance when closed. Many locals and tourists alike considered it the centerpiece of downtown.

Below the drawbridge and Bridge Street, which was the town's main thoroughfare, were sidewalks with iron railings that paralleled the Pine River on both sides. Doc stood on the northern side, the side closest to downtown, with a foot propped up on low railing. He was watching the boats that were lined up in the river and waiting for the two halves of the bridge to rise, which it did on the hour and half hour in season.

Doc was off duty and dressed in an untucked, salmon-colored Polo shirt and blue jeans, but he wasn't alone. It was about 7:00 p.m. and tourists from a dozen states casually strolled the sidewalk that led down past a public beach called Michigan Beach and onto a breakwater made of boulders and concrete that ended with an automated lighthouse extending about 100 yards past shore. It was a great place to watch the sunset over Lake Michigan, although it was still a little early for that now.

As he faced the river and watched the waiting boats. Doc reassessed his future. He liked Charlevoix and believed he was pretty much falling in love with a certain young lady in town, but he didn't want to be a fireman. The city's decision to consolidate services had thrown him a curve. Being a fireman required years of online classes, training, and then an internship. It was a direction and commitment he didn't want. Not that being a fireman wasn't a noble calling, but it wasn't his.

While he stood there listening to Gavin Degraw's "I Have You To Thank" come from the sound system of an idling 30-foot sailboat, his girlfriend, Farren Malone, came down the iron steps from Bridge Street above him to the sidewalk and river level below. She was wearing a gold, blue, and red paisley design cotton dress that she had taken to work that morning then changed into after a day of fueling boats, taking engines apart, forklifting boats out of storage cages, and a dozen other things she did at her family's business, the Portside Marina.

As usual, she looked fit, her sleeveless dress showing off her long swimmer's muscles and her high heels accenting her narrow calves and legs. She stood at 5-feet-5-inches without heels and had been blessed with an inner beauty that made her already cute appearance even more attractive, particularly when she dressed up. She usually kept her thick black hair in a short pixie style that exposed her small ears and left bangs casually hanging off her forehead. But months earlier, Doc had made a comment in passing that he was naturally attracted to women with longer hair—probably because his mom wore her hair long—so Farren was making an effort to grow it out for him. Consequently, her hair these days looked more like a mullet than a pixie cut. She also had round, chocolate brown eyes, full lips, deep dimples when she smiled and small hands with yellow callouses on the insides of them from years of working at the marina. A few freckles on her nose gave her a wholesome girl-next-door look, and in a very real way, that's who she was.

It was now well established in the small, gossip-laden community that she and Doc were a couple and had been for the past six months. The townspeople still remembered the newspaper coverage from the previous winter and the events that had brought them together. Farren, who was somewhat romantically naïve, had impulsively married a newcomer to town named Charlie Huffman. He had told everyone that he was a project manager for a construction company based in Flint, Michigan. But the good-looking, smooth-talking Charlie was really a con man and thief. His meeting and whirlwind romance with Farren was all part of plan where she would eventually be killed and he would inherit her valuable lakefront property where the Portside Marina sat. Charlie would then turn the land over to a loan shark to whom he owed seventy thousand dollars.

The loan shark, named Bartholomew, was also hours away to the south in Flint like Charlie's fictional job. For years, Bartholomew had wanted to own prime real estate in Charlevoix and had chosen Farren's land as the perfect site for a multi-story condominium complex. When attempts to buy the property anonymously through a local realtor generated no interest from Farren, Bartholomew recruited and financially backed Charlie for his more elaborate and deadly plan. Had the scheme been successful, it would have cleared Charlie's marker and would have reaped Bartholomew millions in a legitimate business. But Doc, who was also new to town at the time, had befriended Farren and figured out what Charlie was up to. He stopped a murder attempt on Farren's life that cost Charlie his out in the icy December waters of Round Lake. It also resulted in Bartholomew being arrested after Charlie confessed the loan shark was the mastermind behind the con prior to his death. Several local newspapers had reported the juicy details since it was huge news in the mostly quiet town. But now, the media attention had simmered down, leaving the locals to rightly conclude that Doc had developed feelings for Farren and she for him. This was the story that everyone knew.

But what nobody knew, not even Farren, was that Doc had been given divine help. An angel, Farren's Grandma Clair who died tragically at age twenty-five in 1956, had guided him. They had met last December on a snowy night when a deer ran out in front of Doc's Jeep while he was driving home from work. The deer, who was actually Clair traveling anonymously as an animal, was injured but not fatally. Since there are consequences when angels take physical form, she was confined to Doc's rented house on the shores of Lake Charlevoix for more than two weeks while she recuperated.

That's how Doc learned about Farren and the danger she was in. Clair intended to keep her granddaughter from harm herself but had to recruit Doc because of her injuries.

Possessing the rare knowledge that God, angels, and an afterlife actually existed had a tremendous impact on Doc, and he wasn't sure if he was a better person for the experience. But he didn't question the existence of God anymore and believed there was a certain order to things, even if he didn't always understand that order.

There had been a hundred times during the past half year when he had wanted to tell Farren that her grandmother had been sent back to Earth to protect her, that Clair had stayed with him and, because of it, she had also saved *him* from a lifetime of brooding anger, resentment, and misdirected love over the death of an old girlfriend. He had learned the value of having faith again and that he didn't want to live alone anymore. Keeping the miraculous events he had experienced to himself was the toughest thing he had ever done, but he thought it was the right thing to do. Farren was a Christian woman with a strong sense of faith, but he figured no reasonable person would ever believe his story. He wouldn't have believed it himself had he not actually lived it. He really wanted things to grow with Farren, and he wasn't about to go telling her stories of angels that might make her question his very sanity.

She came up behind him, kissed him on the back of the neck, and then slipped her arm in his. Even though she had kissed him dozens of times, he still loved the feel of her lips on his skin.

"Hi," she said softly. "I heard about what happened with that baby this morning. I'm sorry."

His first inclination was to ask how she knew about what had happened since he hadn't spoken to her since the fire. But he didn't. After a year and a half of living in the tightly knit community, he knew that news traveled faster in Charlevoix than jackrabbits reproducing.

"It was a futile attempt," he smiled politely. "All I *really* did was anger Don Stubigg."

"Would you rather not go out to dinner tonight?" she asked. "We could just go back to my place and I'll make something."

"No," he said. "A date's a date. Let's keep it." He turned and they started to walk back toward the stairs. "You smell great, by the way. What is that?"

"Yamaha engine oil," she chuckled, but she still appreciated the compliment.

They dined at a restaurant on Petoskey Avenue, which sat near a public golf course. They had a view of one of the fairways while the remainder of the day faded into night. After dinner, they headed to Farren's small, round house, nicknamed "the mushroom house" because of its unique shape, for some coffee and dessert.

While Farren made coffee and cut some Dutch apple pie in the kitchen, Doc stood in the living room and looked at the black-and-white photo of Farren's grandfather, Gus Cooper, Clair, and a fourteen-month-old Jackie, Farren's mother, sitting on porch swing. The photo sat on Farren's slightly concave fireplace mantel in a room that had rounded exterior walls. Looking at the picture fondly, Doc couldn't help but whisper, "Hey, Clair," under his breath. He hadn't seen or heard from her since Christmas Eve the year before, but he liked to believe that she could hear him in what she used to call her "other plane of existence."

He was so deep in thought about Clair he wasn't aware of Farren approaching from behind. She gently touched him on the back. He drew a sharp breath and jerked in pain.

"What's wrong?" she asked.

"Oh, there was an explosion at the apartment building," he said. "I had to get a couple of stitches."

"What?" she gasped. As good as the gossip vine was in Charlevoix, she hadn't heard that detail.

"It's no big deal," he shrugged. "It's just sensitive."

"Let me see," she said, concerned. "Take off your shirt."

"Honey, it's no big deal. Really."

"Take off your shirt," she insisted.

He expelled a heavy breath, then unbuttoned and pulled his Polo shirt up and over his head slowly so as not to aggravate the wound.

In their six months of dating, this was the first time she had ever seen him naked from the waist up and—even though he was injured—she liked what she saw. Doc was six feet tall and 172 pounds of firmness, mostly due to his rock-climbing hobby when he used to live in Arizona and then Wyoming. His arms were well-defined and his chest was solid and surprisingly void of hair considering his thick dark brown hair and eyebrows.

Farren tried to ignore his great body and turned him around by gently touching his shoulder. She looked at the square gauze dressing that had been taped in between his shoulder blades. Carefully peeling the tape away, she peeked under the gauze. Her mouth slowly fell open.

"What happened to you?"

"I got nailed in an explosion. Literally."

"This is *not* a couple of stitches," she noted, counting each one. "This is more like—seven! Seven is not 'a couple.' A couple means two. Seven is never a couple."

"Okay, it's three-and-a-half couples of stitches," he said, smiling and turning around to her. "Believe me. I'll live."

"You'd better," she half whispered.

He leaned forward and kissed her for her concern. Their tongues gently caressed while their arms wrapped comfortably around one another and drew each other close. After the embrace, she looked tenderly into his deep blue eyes, and then they kissed again, more deeply and passionately this time. One of the things Doc loved about Farren was her sense of romance. She hadn't done a lot of travelling in her twenty-nine years but she had travelled both time and the continents through the epic romances she read. Consequently, she never took holding hands, walking arm-in-arm or kissing for granted. This had led him to believe that deeper and more passionate times lay ahead.

Maybe this is the night, he thought. *Maybe this time is the right time.*

Ever since they had started to officially date, they knew there was chemistry between them, but there was also a white elephant in the room. Farren's late husband, Charlie, used to do things to her when they were intimate. He liked to be rough and objectify his wife and the relatively sexually inexperienced Farren wasn't prepared for this. For the most part, she timidly went along with this treatment because she loved her husband and wanted to please him. But she also knew how she felt afterward and she didn't like those feelings.

When she learned that Charlie really didn't love her and was, in fact, planning to kill her for her property, she felt violated physically, emotionally, and spiritually. Doc was aware of this and was thoroughly prepared to give her time, but it was a Catch-22. Whenever they were close to making love, there always came a point where Farren could go no further. She'd suddenly feel ill or stifled, and she would ask him to stop. Despite knowing Farren felt guilty about ruining the mood, Doc couldn't help but be frustrated every time things ended like this. He was used to the attention of the opposite sex because of his good looks. So a woman that became sexually turned off by his advances was, to say the least, tough to take. Farren was seeing a therapist, which Doc was happy about, except that he still never knew from situation to situation how far to take things in the intimacy department.

But maybe tonight is different, he thought as he continued to kiss her. Maybe this would be the night that her passion would supersede her fears and they'd finally make love. He was certainly willing to try.

After they finished kissing, he scooped her up into his arms like a child, looked at her lovingly, and headed for her bedroom.

"Is this really good for your stitches?" she asked.

"The doctor said I have to exercise, then lie down," he fibbed. "This is the exercise part." Arriving at the bed, he said, "Now it's time for the lying down part."

She smiled, politely trying to steer him in another direction. "Don't you want your pie and coffee? It's all ready in the kitchen."

"I think it'll keep for a while if you feel comfortable doing something else," he said softly.

She began to squirm slightly, wanting to be put down. "I'd, I'd *like* to...but..."

"Fifty shades of nay, huh?" he joked.

He set her feet back down on the hardwood floor. She slowly put an open flat hand on his bare chest, felt his racing heart, and lowered her head.

"Damnit!" she said, frustrated. "Baby, I'm sorry."

He wrapped his arms around her neck and kissed the top of her head.

"Shush...it's okay," he whispered. "It's okay."

It clearly wasn't okay, but if Wyatt "Doc" Reynolds wanted to have a relationship with Farren Malone, for the time being, it had to be.

"C'mon," he said, taking her by the hand. "Let's go get that pie."

"I'm really sorry, Doc," she said.

"You're doing the best you can. So am I, for that matter."

Once back in the living room, he slipped on his shirt again.

"You going to be alright?" she asked.

"Of course."

"Really?"

"Oh, sure," he smiled. "They say there's more to a relationship than sex. Of course, the people who say that are mostly eunuchs."

She smiled at Doc's quirky wit. Lance had his James Bond trivia. Doc had his Monty Python "I'm-a-lumberjack-and-I'm-okay" sense of humor.

He stayed for another hour eating pie, having coffee, and saying silly things that kept his girlfriend smiling. When he had convinced her that everything was fine between them and the evening's snafu was forgotten, he kissed her goodnight, climbed into his red Jeep Wrangler and drove home past the last of the strolling tourists down on Bridge Street. A warm wind was gently coming in off Lake Michigan. It was a perfect summer's evening.

"Everybody in town is gonna get laid tonight. Everybody except me," he said, noticing everyone he saw on the street was either a couple walking arm-in-arm or holding hands. He looked up through his dashboard at the evening sky as if addressing heaven. "This is payback for some of my shallower adventures, isn't it? That waitress in Flagstaff comes to mind, for example. But for the record, she approached me. Is this your sense of humor? Now that I've grown up, I get the really cute girl but she's as frigid as Barrow, Alaska? This and the platypus are your idea of funny?"

He thought for another moment, pursed his lips, and then lowered his guard. Praying was still a relatively new thing for Doc and it was hard for him to express honest feelings out loud.

"Just—just don't let me screw it up," he said, sincerely. "Don't let me trip over my own feet."

3 Searching For Someone

The people who attended St. Ignatius Catholic Church on Sunday were a colorful lot. At least half of them were tourists so the men wore everything from Tommy Bahama Hawaiian shirts to Perry Ellis plaid shorts, while the women wore choices from Dior pineapple print dresses to Vera Wang white slacks. It was the kind of clothing that belonged in either resort towns or country clubs, but not many other places.

It was just after 8:00 a.m. mass on Sunday and Father Ken Pistole was saying good morning to exiting parishioners and making small talk as folks filed out of the small crucifix-shaped church. He was a portly man in his sixties with a white beard that hid shrapnel scars left over from his days of being a Chaplin in Vietnam. He spotted Gus Cooper out of the corner of his eye. Wearing casual black slacks and a red and blue Tommy Hilfiger golf shirt, Farren's grandfather was standing away from the crowd with his arms folded and leaning up against a maple tree. His face showed no emotion while his brown eyes shifted from person to person.

Gus was in his late seventies but looked ten years younger because, at five-feet-ten, he had remained Paul Newman-lean and was still very handsome. He had distinguishing lines going from his nose to the corners of his mouth, crow's feet around his eyes, and his once black hair was now mostly white like the perpetual two-day growth of beard on his face. But the years had worn well on him like an old leather jacket despite some serious heartbreak along the way. Seeing the last of the parishioners say goodbye to the father and head toward the parking lot, he pushed himself off the tree, rubbed his chin as if disappointed, and then turned to leave.

"Cooper!" the rotund priest called. "Gus?"

Gus turned back and strolled over to the clergyman. These two men had once been pretty good friends, particularly after Farren's parents died in a boating accident when she was seventeen and Gus had given up a teaching position at Central Michigan University and moved back to town to assume the duties of her guardianship. But they had drifted apart over the years, mostly because of Gus. He liked Ken Pistole the person, but had some issues with the profession he was in.

"Hi, Ken," Gus greeted. "How're you doing, man?"

"You finally want to tell me what's going on?" the priest asked.

"What do you mean?"

"Ever since Christmas, you've been coming to church regularly, which is good, the rafters hardly cracked. But even when you're not in church, you're lurking around after the masses like a buzzard waiting for road kill. Who are you looking for?"

"I don't lurk," Gus protested.

"Who are you looking for?" the priest repeated.

"It's you," Gus deadpanned. "Your animal magnetism. I think I'm in love."

"Alright, be an ass," the priest said dismissively. "How's Farren?"

"Fine. I suspect she'll be at 11:00 mass like always."

"With Doc?" Pistole asked.

"With Doc," Gus nodded.

"Good man. I'm glad she has him to lean on," the father noted. "What's going on with that loan shark down in Flint?"

"Bartholomew?" Gus grunted. "Our legal system is moving at its usual glacial pace. But at least he was denied bail and is off the streets."

"I heard you've got some sort of source down there."

Gus nodded. "A former student of mine works for the

Associated Press and covers the criminal court beat. He's keeping tabs on things for me. Dates, motions, that kind of thing."

The clergyman looked around, drinking in the beautiful summer morning. "Hard to believe that murder, or even attempted murder, could happen in such a community," he observed.

"Thank you, Pollyanna," Gus answered. "After two tours in Nam, I'd expect you to be a little more realistic."

"I'm very realistic," the priest said, waving to the last parishioner pulling out of the parking lot. "I know the capabilities of my fellow man. I know people are people no matter how picturesque the setting. Just like I know you're looking for someone you saw once in church. Someone you're hoping to see again."

Gus cracked a trace of a smile. "We should get together and play Parcheesi sometime like we used to," he suggested, changing the subject.

"Anytime you're ready to part with your money," the priest replied, smiling.

"I'll call you," Gus promised, then he turned and headed back to his car parked nearby on the street. As he went, he rubbed the goose bumps off his arms. Father was right; he *was* looking for someone he'd seen in church. But he didn't know he was being so obvious about it.

During midnight mass on Christmas Eve the previous year, Gus had seen the spitting image of his late wife. Even though he'd seen her from a distance, she looked straight at him, smiled, and mouthed the words, "I love you." Ever since then, he'd gone through every possible explanation in his mind to convince himself that he was mistaken. But the more he told himself he had simply seen someone who looked like Clair—or perhaps that he even imagined her—the more his instincts told him he was wrong. He *had* seen her. What he couldn't figure out was why.

Despite the fact he had to open up the marina store at 9:00 a.m. on Sundays because business was now in its peak season, he took a meandering way there. He went in the opposite direction and wound up on the outskirts of town before pulling over and stopping across the street from a 7-Eleven convenience store. Putting his black

Honda Accord SUV in park but not turning off the engine, he looked at the store and began to think back to what used to sit on that property: Stu and Ernie's Mobile Gas Station.

"My God, I worked there more than fifty-seven years ago," he muttered out loud. There were few people in town that would remember the place now. It was back in the day when service station attendants wore brown zip-up overall uniforms with white short-sleeve shirts underneath and black bowties. They also wore eight-point caps with shiny black visors and every customer got the full service treatment of their gas being pumped, their oil being checked, and their windshields being washed. Gas was twenty-one cents a gallon, Dwight D. Eisenhower was in the White House and "Shake, Rattle And Roll" by Bill Haley and the Comets was climbing the charts.

In June of 1954, Marlon Brando was starring in *The Wild One*, girls were wearing bobby socks, boys favored jeans with rolled up pant legs, and Gus Cooper was a twenty-one-year-old mechanic working at Stu & Ernie's. It was a small place with a light brown brick facade and an office that had a large bay window with sixteen glass panels outlined by white wooden frames. It also had two gas pumps with a round white globe on top of each pump that lit up at night. On the opposite sides of each globe was the red-winged silhouette of Pegasus, the logo for Mobile Gasoline. There were two service bays with raised doors that rolled open, and because he was working on cars and didn't interface much with customers, Gus wasn't required to wear a white shirt and bowtie under his brown overalls, which, unlike his co-workers, was usually dirty.

As Gus remembered how he used to look when he was twenty-one, he audibly sighed. He was actually a little taller than he was now with hair that sat like a cresting wave about to break on his forehead. He was smooth-skinned, thick-armed, and about twenty pounds heavier than he was as a senior citizen, but it was all solid.

He didn't recall the exact date, but he knew it was around the middle of June when he first laid eyes on Clair. It was nearly noon when her father, Aaron Sinclair, pulled into the station in his new Studebaker Commander. It was a four-door sedan with a cherry-red body, white roof, and metallic silver striping on either side that cut across the doors and went almost all the way back to the taillights. Gus remembered the car distinctly because it was a new model, but it pulled into the station with steam hissing and escaping from under its closed hood.

"Hey boy," Sinclair called as he climbed out of the car. He was about fifty years old and although not fat, had a little potbelly. He was wearing a green sports jacket, a white shirt with pink diamonds on it, blue tie, white fedora, cream-colored slacks and two-tone shoes. Even for 1954, the collision of patterns and colors was noticeable. But Aaron Sinclair was the kind of man who liked to be noticed with his big house, loud clothes, and a brightly colored car.

"Yes, sir, Mr. Sinclair," Louie, the gas jockey on duty, said. Tipping the shiny brim of his cap and snapping into action, he walked briskly to the car.

"She's hissing like an angry coon," Sinclair said, jerking a thumb toward the steam. "She's only got 400 miles on her. You got a mechanic here?"

"Yes, sir, Mr. Sinclair," Louie said as he smiled in his usual overly eager suck-up way. Then he turned and called to his co-worker.

Gus wiped his hands on a rag as he ambled out of Service Bay Two with a toothpick dangling from his mouth and his overalls unzipped to nearly his naval that revealed he wasn't wearing anything but glistening sweat underneath.

"See what you can do, will ya?" Sinclair said, tilting his fedora back and squinting at the summer sun. "Where's the john?" he asked Louie.

"'Round back, sir. Let me just have a word with my mechanic and get the key for you."

Sinclair grunted and took a handkerchief out of his back pocket to wipe the sweat off his brow as Louie approached Gus. He didn't like Louie referring to him as "my mechanic," especially since he was nearly two years older than the gas jockey, but he let it slide.

"This guy's really rich," Louie whispered. "Treat him right and there could be big tips in it for us."

"Who is he?" Gus asked.

Louie gave him a don't-you-know-anything look. "That's old man Sinclair."

Gus stared back blankly.

"You know, Sinclair Construction?"

Gus nodded as the name registered with him. Sinclair Construction was one of the biggest commercial construction companies in the area. He'd seen the name on pick-ups, dump trucks and bulldozers. He had even applied there for a job once, but nobody had ever responded to his application.

While Louie scurried into the station to get the bathroom key for Mr. Sinclair, Gus stepped over to the Studebaker and popped open the hood. He knew that there was a female still sitting on the passenger side front seat, but he honestly hadn't noticed more than that at the time. He figured she was a wife, co-worker, or a girlfriend. As he waved the steam away under the hood and examined the engine, he heard the passenger door open and then the click-clack of light footsteps in heels.

"Hey boy," he heard a young woman's voice say. "You got a Coke machine around here?"

Gus looked up from under the hook, took a step back, and slowly took the toothpick out of his mouth, pleased with what he saw but trying not to show it.

Standing by the car's red front quarter panel was a beautiful girl with long blonde hair in large naturally curly ringlets pulled back into a thick ponytail. She wore Ray Ban sunglasses and a short-sleeve, off-white button-up blouse with a light pink poodle skirt that flared out from her small waist. She had high, Nordic cheekbones, stood about five-feet-four and was curvaceous and buxom like a Swedish version of Elizabeth Taylor. With her black high-heels and flesh-colored nylons, she didn't look like a bobbysoxer but rather a sophisticated college woman. Probably a snobby sorority girl, he figured, and Sinclair's daughter.

She was fanning herself with a paper-thin square handbag. While there wasn't any doubt that she was strikingly attractive, she also had a rich-girl attitude, had just called him "boy," and looked at him as someone clearly below her station.

"No Coke machine. But there's Vernors ginger ale in the cooler inside," he said, then added, "girl."

She stopped fanning herself for a moment, looked at him as if she might say something, but then turned and walked to the office. Gus stuck his toothpick back in his mouth, admiring the view for a moment, then turned and poked his head back under the hood.

About thirty seconds later, he heard the young lady call out to him again from the propped open front door of the station.

"Hey boy, there's no opener in here."

"On the shelf above the cooler," Gus called back.

"What?"

He emerged from under the hood again, took out his toothpick, tossed it on the pavement, and walked toward the office. As he did, he noticed she had removed her Ray Bans, revealing mesmerizing green eyes. Although he didn't stop in his approach, he slowed down, drinking in all her beauty again. She was now leaning against the open doorway, sunglasses in one hand while lazily swinging the bottle of Vernors from its neck between her fingers in the other. She was likewise thinking that he would probably clean up well, were it not for the dirty brown overalls, grimy hands, sweaty chest, and the assumption that he probably had no more than a ninth grade education.

He came to the open office doorway and stopped. Her leaning in the middle of it prevented him from going any further. He glanced around for Louie, but he was nowhere to be found.

"It's on the shelf above the cooler," he repeated.

Not moving her body, she turned her head and looked inside behind her.

"No boy, it's not," she said, turning back to him.

"Well, girl, let me see if I can find it for you." He took a step toward the doorway, but she still didn't move. "Uh—do you mind?" he gestured, asking for access.

She stepped aside, but only a few inches. Gus mustered a polite smile and squeezed past her. She clearly wanted to play the I'm-better-than-you game but he wasn't going along with it. At least, not like Louie would. He figured in ten minutes or less, she and her father would be out of his life anyway.

The soda cooler was one of those waist high rectangular metallic coolers where customers could help themselves, then pay their dime at the cash register. It used to have a bottle opener attached to its side, but it had broken off long ago. She looked him over while he had his back to her, searching the shelf on the wall for the opener.

"So what's wrong with the car?" she asked.

"Cracked radiator hose," he answered, turning and looking at the desk for the lost opener. "No big deal. I can fix it here, or you can just fill up your radiator with water and your dad can have the dealer fix it. They should probably fix it for free considering it's so new."

"Oh, for my father, they *will*," she said with threatening certainty.

"Okay," he said, agreeing with her to keep the conversation to a minimum.

Unable to find the bottle opener, he extended his hand to her, asking for the ginger ale. When she passed it over he stepped over to the desk, propped the bottle with the edge of the cap on the lip of the desk, and swatted the top of the bottle down with his open hand in one quick move. The cap came off effortlessly. Nothing spilled from the bottle and the carbonated drink didn't even fizz. He silently handed it back to her. It was a slick move and he knew it. A little impressed, she took it.

"Thanks," she said.

"You're welcome."

She took a sip then looked at the bottle. "This is good."

"You've never had Vernors before?" he asked.

She shook her head.

"It's a Michigan original. First brewed by a Detroit pharmacist named James Vernor in 1866."

"Actually read the label once, did we?" she teased.

"No. A book about Michigan entrepreneurs," he answered. He passed by her to return to her father's car, but she had shifted her position in the doorway and the leg of his dirty overalls brushed against the side of her pink poodle skirt, causing grease to smear it.

He didn't notice and continued through the doorway, heading back to the Studebaker. She, however, noticed the stain immediately and gasped in horror.

"Oh, my God! *No!* You *cretin!* This is a brand new skirt!"

He turned and looked back at her, not understanding the outburst until his eyes fell on the smudge near the hem of her skirt.

"Do you have any idea how much this cost?" she demanded. "This is only the second time I've worn it!"

"I'm—uh—sorry," Gus stammered. "I'll pay for the cleaning."

"This can't be cleaned, you idiot!" she proclaimed. "It's *oil!*"

"Well, if you'd of just stepped aside and let me get through the doorway..."

"Oh, so this is my fault? You reject from Howdy Doody! When my father gets back, he's going to have your job!"

"What's going on?" Louie said, suddenly appearing from around the back.

"Where have you been?" Gus asked under his breath.

"Putting paper towels in the ladies restroom," Louie explained.

"Are you in charge of this person?" the young lady demanded.

"No," Gus answered, "he's not. Look, I said I was sorry. I'll buy you another floo-floo skirt. I was only near you in the first place to do something for *you.*"

"What did you call my skirt?" she hissed. "Floo-floo? As in 'floosy?'"

"Why were you near her?" Louie asked.

"Now I didn't say anything like that," Gus fired back, losing his patience. "I only meant, it's the kind of skirt that...you know, gets big at the bottom."

The young woman's jaw dropped.

"Are you saying I have a big bottom? Is *that* what you're saying?"

"What the hell's going on?" Aaron Sinclair asked, now returning from the restroom and hearing the raised voices.

"Daddy," his daughter began with an accusing finger. "This, this *grease monkey* got gunk all over my brand new skirt and then made a disparaging remark about my body."

"I did *nothing* of the kind," Gus retorted. "Look, sir, your daughter asked for help at the soda machine. I came in, helped her, brushed by her skirt accidently, got a little oil on it, and offered to have it cleaned. Anything beyond that is her imagination."

"Oh, so now I'm a liar?" she asked combatively.

Aaron Sinclair knew his daughter had a tendency to be dramatic and a princess. After all, she had always been indulged. He examined the bottom of her skirt and knew the truth instantly.

"What's wrong the car?" he asked, ignoring his daughter's accusations.

"Cracked radiator hose," Gus answered. "It happens sometimes when cars just come off the line. It's an easy fix. I can do it here for about five bucks, but your dealer should do it for free because the car's so new."

"You fix it here and I don't pay," Sinclair decided. "Call it a cleaning bill for the stain."

"Daddy!" the daughter protested.

"Shut up!" Sinclair barked, wanting no more nonsense. He turned back to Gus. "Do we have a deal?"

Gus could see that Sinclair believed his story, but he could also see that he was trying to get something out of him for nothing. He was about to answer that he'd have to call either Stu or Ernie about giving away a radiator hose, when Louie jumped into the conversation.

"Deal, Mr. Sinclair! Absolutely no problem! Why don't you and your lovely daughter step into the office and have a complimentary ice-cold soda from our machine. Just the thing for a hot day like today, eh Mr. Sinclair?"

Louie dipped a hand into his pants pocket and pulled out the bottle opener that was supposed to go on the shelf above the soda machine. Gus stared at him incredulously, but then remembered the staff needed the bottle opener to pry open the paper towel dispensers in the bathrooms since the keys had been lost some time ago.

As Sinclair and his daughter started to head into the office, the payphone inside on the wall next to Service Bay Two began to ring. Louie ignored it and went straight to the soda machine until Gus realized it wasn't the payphone hanging on the wall in his hall of memory, but the cellphone hanging on his belt in reality. He grabbed his iPhone and unlocked it.

"Hello?"

"Hey, Gus, you coming to let us in?" It was one of the summer help at the marina that he and Farren always hired during peak season.

Gus looked at his wristwatch. It was 9:15 a.m.

"Yeah. On my way," he said.

He hit the end button, set the phone on the passenger side seat, put the Accord in drive, and pulled away, glancing back at the 7-Eleven through his rearview mirror.

4 Therapy

The following morning, a Monday, was the first day Doc was supposed to switch from working days to nights. The night shift was skeletal and used only four men in total: two medical personnel and two firemen. His new hours would be from 6:00 p.m. to 8:30 a.m. the next morning. But he wasn't yet acclimated to the new schedule and wound up at the fire hall around 11:00 a.m.

Donald Stubigg saw him talking and joking with Lance and some of his fireman buddies and motioned him into his office. When Doc got there, the senior fireman was already situated behind his desk.

"You wanted to see me, Captain?"

"Got something for you, Reynolds," Stubigg said. He pointed to a chair in a corner of the small square room. Sitting on the chair was a life-size female dummy, complete with a black curly wig that had been glued on its head and a button-up faded yellow and green housedress. Her eyes were open, her lips were slightly apart and her legs were bare and shoeless. Frankly, Doc's first impression was that it was a sex toy.

"No thanks, Captain. I have a girlfriend," he joked. "But it's very thoughtful that you'd want to share."

"This is Gertrude," Stubigg said, leaning back in his chair. "She's your new best friend. From now on, you don't go anywhere without her."

"What?"

"If you're out in your Jeep running errands, Gertrude goes with you. If you're at home, she's sitting on your sofa. If you're eating here at the fire hall, she's sitting at the table. If you're taking a class online, she's sitting right next to you. She's always with you unless you're out on a call."

Doc looked at the doll, then at Stubigg.

"To what purpose?"

"Some Native American cultures believed that if you saved a life, you were responsible for it. You disobeyed my orders and tried to save that Miyako infant. Now your responsibility is Gertrude."

"That doesn't even make sense," Doc protested. "In the first place, I didn't save the Miyako baby. In the second place—"

"In the second place," Stubigg interrupted, "Gertrude weighs about sixty pounds. After carrying her around everywhere you go for a few weeks, I bet you'll think twice before disobeying one of my orders." The senior fireman leaned forward in his chair and picked up a pen turning to some paperwork. "That'll be all."

Doc looked at his captain, then at Gertrude, then sighed and picked her up. With some effort, he flung her over his shoulder like a sack of potatoes and carried her through the station with her arms dangling behind him. As he went, his coworkers began to whistle and shout out a variety of catcalls. Everyone in the fire hall knew about Gertrude. Everyone that was except Doc.

"Hey, Doc? Farren know about her?" Lance called.

"The perfect woman," another firefighter observed. "She doesn't shop, eat, or talk back."

While the comments continued, Doc smiled facetiously.

"Perfect. Wonderful. Thank you all very much, losers," he muttered as he carried Gertrude through the hall, past the ambulance and fire trucks and headed outside to his Wrangler.

Meanwhile, just three blocks away on a tree-lined street with quaint Victorian house and large porches, Farren was sitting down in her therapist's office. Dr. Judith Herriman was seventy years old and had never married. Farren thought it a little odd that she spent each Monday talking about very personal sexual issues with an older unmarried woman, but she was the only therapist in town who specialized in the field.

They sat in the downstairs parlor of an old wooden 1930s house that had been converted into office spaces. It had a nice fireplace with a tile hearth, comfortable furniture, and acrylic paintings on the walls of seagulls, and sand dunes chosen to illicit calm and tranquility. Patients entered and exited the parlor through a pair nicely varnished pocket doors.

Dr. Herriman was a handsome, willowy woman who usually wore her long grey hair up in a bun and dressed casually. Physically, she reminded Farren of Jane Goodall, the British primatologist. Personality wise, she reminded her of an older Katherine Hepburn, full of spunk and Yankee frankness. She sat in her leather club chair with a notebook that she would occasionally write in. Mostly though, she just listened to Farren on the sofa with clear, empathetic hazel eyes.

"At our last session," she began in her quiet, steady voice, "you shared certain things that Charlie used to do to you when you were intimate that either hurt or made you feel uncomfortable: pulling your hair during love-making, having his hands around your throat, smacking your rear, picking times and places for lovemaking that you thought were inappropriate."

"It wasn't lovemaking," Farren corrected. "It was just sex. Rough sex for Charlie's sake. I know that now."

"And you told Charlie about your disapproval?"

"Yes, but probably not as much as I should have. I didn't," she paused, and then continued, "I didn't want to be disappointing to him. Can…can we not go over the details anymore, please?"

"Of course," Judith smiled. "And now, whenever things become heated between you and Doc, whenever it seems like sex is inevitable, you manifest physical difficulties: breathing problems, nausea, claustrophobia…"

"'Transference,' yes. We talked about that last week," Farren recalled.

"I said it was *possibly* transference," Herriman corrected. "Have you ever talked to Doc specifically about the things Charlie used to do to you and how that made you feel?"

"Not specifically, although he probably has a general idea," she said, nervously brushing her bangs aside. "Once, I tried to get specific when we were driving back from Traverse City. I...I was pretty upset at the time. I'd just caught Charlie in a couple of whopper lies and was realizing my marriage had some serious problems. I started to ask Doc about his old girlfriend, Julia. I wanted to, well, to ask him about how he 'was' with her, but the words never came out," she said self-consciously. "I suppose I was trying to compare one man's personality and preferences to another's. But the conversation never happened."

"Why not?"

"Well, for one thing, it would have been very inappropriate. I was still married at the time and, up until that day, I thought happily."

"And you haven't tried to talk to him about it since?" Herriman asked.

"What? And inhibit an already inhibited situation?"

The therapist thought and paused. "Okay," she said, changing the subject, "let's talk about your parents for a moment."

"What about them?"

"What kind of marriage did they have? Were they openly demonstrative with one another?"

"Sure. They often held hands when they walked. My father also used to sometimes steal kisses from my mom when she was cooking in the kitchen. When I was a little girl, I liked to get up in the morning and crawl into bed with them and cuddle. Most of the time their bedroom door was open. But sometimes, it was closed and locked." She smiled her dimpled smile. "I didn't figure out why until years later. So, yeah, I'd say they had a healthy, normal marriage."

"Who decided to open the marina?" Herriman asked. "Your mom or your dad?"

"I'm not sure...but my dad ran the business. I mean, he did the books, ordered the merchandise for the store, and had most of the relationships with customers."

"Sounds like it was your dad's dream."

"Well, Mom worked there too."

"Full time?"

"No. Mostly in the summers when we were really busy."

"And you worked there too when your parents were alive?"

"Yes, since I was fifteen."

The older woman wrote something down in her notebook, then continued, "After high school, you never went on to college. How come?"

"I inherited my parents' business."

"But your grandfather was there, wasn't he? You told me after your folks died he moved back to town from Mount Pleasant to help you with the marina."

"Help me, yes, but he was still new to the business. I actually knew more about running the marina than he did."

"Hmm," Herriman mused, writing again.

"What?" Farren asked.

"Well, it's just that when your grandfather moved back to town, he left a teaching position at a university. As an educator, I'm surprised he didn't insist upon you finishing your schooling."

"I intended to go to college. I mean, Grandpa and I talked about it, I just wasn't ready to go right away. But then, one year turned into three, three turned into five, and after a while there didn't seem much point to spending tens-of-thousands of dollars to get a degree just to return to a business I already owned."

"I see," the grey-haired woman said. "Let's pretend your parents hadn't died in that storm out on Lake Michigan. Let's pretend you went to college or were going to go back now. What do you think your major would be?"

"I don't know," Farren shrugged, brushing her bangs aside again. "I like to read. I read a lot, especially in winter. Maybe I'd try majoring in creative writing, or journalism, something like that."

"Do you do any writing now? Just for fun?"

"I have a journal, but I don't write in it every night. I write poetry sometimes."

"Let's get back to Doc," Herriman suggested. "I know you have very strong spiritual convictions. I want to be sure that your sexual hesitancy with Doc is not a morality issue."

Farren smiled faintly and shook her head.

"What initially attracted you to him?" the therapist asked.

"Well, we both liked Jane Austen, and he's handsome, and he's lived in fascinating places like Sedona, Arizona, and Jackson Hole, Wyoming."

"But, I think you told me he's originally from Michigan, right?"

"Yes. Ann Arbor."

"Can you identify for me some of the differences between your late husband and Doc?"

"Oh, there are several. Charlie was gone a lot. Gone to a pretend job I thought he had but he was really seeing another woman over in Traverse City. Doc stays pretty close. I always sensed Charlie was a man of secrets, even before I actually knew he was. Doc doesn't talk much about himself, but if you ask him about his past, you'll get a straight answer. Charlie didn't have a lot of empathy for others. Doc cares about people, I mean, just by virtue of his job. He's also got this very dry sense of humor. He likes to say odd things, left-of-center things, just to see how people will react. But I guess the biggest difference between them is Charlie tried to kill Doc, and five minutes later, after he'd fallen through the ice on Round Lake, Doc tried to save Charlie."

"Do you love him?" Herriman asked.

Farren blushed a little. "I've only been a widow for six months, Judith."

"You're going to consider proprieties about a man who tried to murder you?" she questioned. "Your heart probably already knows. Do you love him?"

Farren's brown eyes began to get moist. "Based upon everything I know about him right now? I'd say, yes, I'm falling. But after Charlie, I'm being more–"

"Have you ever told him?" the older woman interrupted.

"We...we seem to understand we're both headed in the same direction. I mean, we use the usual endearing names, we hug, kiss, walk arm in arm, and he's been totally supportive and patient during this 'thing' I'm going through."

"That doesn't answer my question," the therapist pointed out.

"Have you ever told Doc that you loved him?"

"No," she said, leaning forward and reaching for a tissue on the coffee table.

"Has he ever said that he loved you?"

"Well, I think he thinks of us in the long term," she rationalized, dabbing her eyes.

"That's not an answer."

"No...he's never used those three specific words."

"And this is the man that gives you straight answers, right?"

Farren looked at her therapist and squinted slightly, trying to determine where she was taking the conversation.

"Charlie wasn't a native of Charlevoix and neither is Doc. Why do you think you were attracted to men who weren't locals?" Herriman continued.

"Probably because they *weren't* locals," Farren chuckled. "There's great comfort in coming from a small community, but there's also the feeling of sameness. I guess I just liked the fact that they were different. They were people I hadn't seen since childhood. People who didn't know I chipped a tooth in first grade or accidently wet myself in second."

The grey-haired woman nodded and wrote more notes in her book. Farren was very curious to know what those notes were. She wanted answers so she could move on with her life and hopefully be with Doc.

5 Chemistry

Ever since he'd moved to town Doc had been living in a cabin off Boyne City Road. The turnoff from the county road was an old gravel lane filled with potholes that snaked through a serene forest of white pines and then split off into three long drives that eventually led to summer homes. The homes sat on the scruffy banks of Lake Charlevoix, one of the largest and deepest inland lakes in the state.

Everyone referred to Doc's place as a cabin because it had a cedar log exterior, but actually it was quite comfortable. Built in the 1980s, it would've been considered a luxurious two-bedroom vacation home when it was new. But now it was dwarfed by four and five bedroom homes on either side about fifty yards away that could be bought for prices in the upper six figures and even more before the recession.

It was a little after 5:00 p.m. and Doc was in the kitchen making himself a sandwich before going to work when his cellphone rang. Unclipping the phone from the belt of the black cargo pants, he saw it was Farren calling.

"Hi," he answered cheerfully.

"So, I hear you've been seen around town with another woman," she teased.

"You know about Gertrude already, huh?" he asked, turning to the curly-haired dummy sitting at his kitchen table.

"Charlene called me about a fitting for her bridesmaids' gowns and told me all about it."

Charlene Rogers was engaged to Lance Vale. After more than a decade of dating, Charlene and Lance planned a July wedding. It was going to be a small affair, just a hundred or so people, and Farren had been asked to be of one the bridesmaids.

"Stubigg really wants to slap me down," Doc said, explaining Gertrude. "Instead of trying to save someone, you'd think I'd run over them."

"You said it yourself," she reminded him, "the city's making a big investment by converting you and Lance. Online courses, training at the fire hall, an internship—the Captain just wants to be sure you're committed."

"Converting? You make it sound like I'm joining a church."

"Well, cops and firemen *are* a little cult of their own."

"I guess that's true," he chuckled. "How was your session?"

"Okay...but I don't get where Judith is taking things sometimes. We wander around from topic to topic."

"Well, I wouldn't worry about it until she starts drawing parallels between your family and the one on *Here Comes Honey Boo Boo*."

She giggled, then asked, "You ready for the night shift?"

"Ah, yes. I can't wait for that first drunk tourist to throw up on my shoes. How 'bout you? What're you up to tonight?"

"I'm taking dinner over to Mrs. Mitchell, then I'm going to read to her. We're right in the middle of *Emma*." She was referring to Ellen Mitchell, an elderly and nearly blind woman that Farren often visited. For the past half year, she'd been reading her Jane Austen novels.

"You're a good lady, an 'Intended One,'" he said, recalling what Clair had called her. "The kind of compassionate soul God always meant for us to be."

"No I'm not," she dismissed. "Hey, how's your back today?"

He smiled to himself at the notion that Farren didn't think she was compassionate, yet she was always concerned about others.

"It's a little sore. Itchy."

"Do you want me to drop by the fire hall later? Bring you some antiseptic cream? It might help."

"Of course I want you to drop by the fire hall. But you'd better not. I'll be much too busy doing demeaning jobs until I'm out of the doghouse with Stubigg."

"Okay," she said lightheartedly. Then she changed tone. "Hey– you, you know how glad I am you're in my life, right?"

"Yes I do, as a matter of fact. And you know how important you are to me, right?"

"I do. Yes...I—uh—I'm just sorry I'm so emotionally screwed up. I wonder sometimes why you even put with me."

"Because even on your most emotionally screwed up day, you're still more fun and selfless than any other woman I've known."

"Except for the sex," she laughed, self-deprecatingly.

"Hence my subscription to *Penthouse*," he added without dropping a beat.

She smiled, knowing he was kidding.

"Call me later."

"Okay."

The Portside Marina sat on a point of land where Round Lake fed into Lake Charlevoix. With views to the west of downtown Charlevoix and the Memorial Bridge, and a sprawling view to the east of Lake Charlevoix, it was one of the best pieces of real estate in the city. It was little wonder why Bartholomew had tried to get ahold of it through Farren's late husband, Charlie.

In the fall and winter, Farren and Gus could run the marina by themselves and were home shortly after 5:00 p.m. But in the late spring and summer, the hours were much longer and the staff was beefed up to ten. Most of the additional help were college students who helped run the store and pump gas out on one of the front docks. There were also boats that needed cleaning or staining, propellers that needed refitting, and sailboats that needed rigging. Since several customers stayed right on their boats tied up in rented slips, Farren and Gus kept the marina store open from 9:00 in the morning until 9:00 at night. The store sold everything from sunscreen to night crawlers, potato chips to soda, and outboard engines to ski ropes.

At about 9:15 p.m., Gus pulled into the driveway of his house on West Upright Street. It was a bright yellow two-story, three-bedroom place built in the 1940s with a front porch that wrapped around the right side of the house. The rooms were small and efficient following the construction boom of post-World War II, but it had a full basement. One of the advantages of living in a small town was that Gus had a boyhood friend whose family built the house and he actually hung out there in his youth. By the time his daughter Jackie and son-in-law Paul bought it, Gus had moved three hours south and was teaching Theology of Western Religions at Central Michigan University. After Jackie and Paul died when their sailboat capsized during a sudden storm on Lake Michigan, Gus moved back to become the legal guardian of Farren. He had moved into Jackie and Paul's place so his granddaughter didn't have to be uprooted from the only home she had ever known. Considering he'd been in the house long before Jackie was even born, he saw a certain symmetry to this. He'd now been living in the house for twelve years and had continued to stay after Farren had moved out four years earlier. He'd even done some extensive updating of the kitchen and bathrooms since she'd been gone.

Walking from the detached garage, he was greeted on the three wooden steps leading up to the back door by a meowing, scrawny black cat.

"Hi, Harry," Gus smiled, "escaped again, huh?" He picked up the animal and then called to the house next door, which was only about twenty feet away across his driveway. "Hey, Collins, your cat got out again...

Collins? You hear me?"

Getting no response, he carried Harry into his house. The animal was usually an indoor pet and had had its claws removed, so Gus didn't want it wandering around outside.

He came into the small kitchen, clicked on the lights, kicked the back door shut with the heel of his Sperry Docksiders, and then set the cat down. Going over to a stainless steel refrigerator, he opened it up and retrieved a longneck bottle of Moosehead beer. Twisting off the cap and tossing it on the granite counter, he took a long drink then looked down at Harry who was circling around his ankles and still meowing up a storm. He set down his bottle, got a quart carton of milk out of the fridge, then stepped over to a cabinet, took out a small salad bowl and poured his guest a drink.

"I think you escape just for my two percent," he muttered as he set the bowl on the floor. The cat silently began to lap up the milk while Gus put the carton away. The old man then grabbed his beer and wandered from the kitchen, through the darkened dining room with its mission-style table and chairs and into the living room.

Once in the living room, he turned on the reading lamp that sat next to a light-colored fabric sofa, but the bulb didn't cast much light. Through the front window he saw some kids still playing outside and enjoying the extended daylight of summer. Then he turned around to face a painted white built-in bookcase next to a small fireplace. Sitting on one of the shelves were four framed photos. One was of Jackie in her youth, one was of Jackie and Paul, one was of Farren's high school graduation, and the other one, a black-and-white photo, was of Clair. She was sitting on a large boulder by the water's edge on a spring day and smiling at the camera.

He stepped over to the shelf and picked up Clair's picture. He looked at it for a long moment before he spoke.

"Hi, baby," he finally said quietly. "We were busy today at the marina. Everybody wants to get out on the water." He set the picture back and walked over to a rocking recliner and sat down, sinking deeply into it. He took another long drink of beer, then repeated "the water" under his breath as he closed his eyes and began to remember...

It was a sunny June day back in 1954—just a few days after their first encounter at Stu and Ernie's—when Gus saw Aaron Sinclair's daughter again. He was lying on his stomach on a blanket at Michigan Beach, next to where Lake Michigan fed into the Pine River, wearing swim trunks and tortoise-shell sunglasses. He had his nose buried in a book when he recognized her voice and looked up to see a group of people walking toward him.

She was with three other girls and two young men all about the same age. Everyone was dressed for the beach and carrying either totes or towels. Gus didn't know them by name, but he'd seen them all stop for gas at Stu and Ernie's at one time or another. But it was his day off, so he turned his attention back to his book and didn't give the approaching group much mind, other than noting they were being louder than they needed to be, no doubt to draw attention to themselves.

"Well, if it isn't the boy who loves to ruin women's skirts," the Sinclair girl said after she'd recognized him. She was wearing a cover-up with a strapless navy and white stripe maillot underneath. It wasn't too provocative, but it definitely highlighted her curvaceous figure. Her long blonde hair with the curly ringlets wasn't tied back this time and it spilled all over her white shoulders wild, windblown, and perfect.

Gus looked up from his book and lowered the glasses on his nose. "If it isn't the girl who likes to exaggerate and say things that aren't true."

"Hey, buddy," growled the larger of the two young men with her, "did I just hear you call this lady a liar?"

Gus shifted his eyes from the girl to the guy. He was handsome in a thick-necked jock sort of way. But his black hair had so much Brylcreem on it, he doubted that even a 90-mile-an-hour wind rolling in off the big lake would move it. It was at this point he also noticed his bloodshot eyes beneath a prominent forehead and the smell of whiskey.

"Nnnaw, daddio," Gus smiled, refusing to be chided into anything. He turned back to the girl. "We're just funnin', aren't we, Miss Sinclair?"

She was actually impressed that he hadn't bitten on her friend's bait and been reeled in by a line of machismo.

"Sure," she agreed. "Just funnin'."

She raised her sandaled foot to tilt the cover of the book he held toward her. "What're you reading there?" A second later, her perfectly manicured red toenails had positioned the cover for her bright green eyes. "*Twelfth Night?*" she said with a laugh. "A grease monkey who reads Shakespeare?"

"Oh, don't worry. I've got my copy of *Hot Rod Magazine* here too," he said, patting a picnic basket next to him on the blanket.

"Shakespeare?" the larger of the two men recalled. "Wasn't he that English fairy who wrote a lot in rhyme with a bunch of 'thees' and 'thous'?"

"Yes, Derek," she agreed. "Thou doth have it."

"Only pansies read that stuff," he said, challengingly. But Gus just smiled and slid his glasses back up his nose.

"Let's get some ice cream," one of the girls said.

"Oh, God, if I have ice cream, I'll puke," noted the smaller of the two guys who had also been drinking like his buddy.

"C'mon, Clair. I want ice cream too," chirped another girl. It was the first time Gus had heard the blonde-haired Sinclair girl mentioned by her first name.

"Clair Sinclair?" he asked, amused by the repetition.

"It's short for Clarissa. But I prefer Clair."

"Well, it's easy to remember," he agreed, turning back to his book.

"'A fool thinks himself to be wise,'" she quoted, eying Gus.

"'But the wise man knows himself to be a fool,'" he answered, looking back up and completing the verse. "That's a good one, but it's not from *Twelfth Night*."

She looked at him trying not to act impressed.

"Can we go now, please?" one of the girls whined.

"Yeah, let's get out of here," Derek said, weaving slightly. He pointed a finger at Gus. "I'm watchin' you, Grease Monkey," he warned. He kicked a little sand in Gus' direction as the group left, but the book-reading mechanic remained unruffled. It wasn't that he was afraid of a conflict, quite the contrary, he felt very confident that he could beat up a half-drunken guy. But that was the point—he was half drunk. Besides, he liked to think he had outgrown schoolyard bravado.

Clair and her friends spread out and settled on a couple of blankets about twenty yards away. For the next half hour, it appeared as if Gus still had his nose in his book, but he was really watching Clair.

Although he certainly didn't approve of her superior attitude, he found it difficult to take his eyes off her. Maybe it was just his imagination, but it seemed as if she were shooting the occasional furtive glance his way as well. Meanwhile, her friend Derek kept blabbering on and on about nothing interesting whatsoever and stealing sips of whiskey from a silver flask he and his other male companion shared. Since they were both over twenty-one, their drinking wasn't illegal. But Gus didn't deem it appropriate at a public beach where young kids were playing.

Eventually, Clair's girlfriends went and got some ice cream from a sidewalk vendor and dragged the reluctant smaller guy along with them. Then they spotted some other friends, one of which had a new Chevrolet Bel Air, and went off to admire it. That left Clair and Derek sitting alone on their blanket. But within a few minutes, Derek closed his eyes and fell asleep. So Clair simply tied her hair back into a ponytail like when Gus had first seen her, then began to lather her skin with suntan oil. About the third time she looked in his direction while rubbing her pale shoulders, he knew that his observations were not his imagination. She *was* looking to see if he was watching her. But since he was wearing sunglasses, she couldn't tell if he was returning the glances, or simply reading about Sir Toby Belch, Viola, and the rest of Shakespeare's cast of characters from the early 1600s.

Eventually, Clair got bored with her dozing companion and MIA friends. She rose and stretched, loosened her hair again now that her shoulders and back were oiled, then turned and headed toward the water just as some distant radio began to play "Secret Love" by Doris Day. At first, she just waded into the water up to her waist, running her hands over the surface and getting her body acclimated to the still cool Lake Michigan temperature. But then, like a shot she bravely dove headlong into the lake and started to swim away. From his vantage point, Gus could no longer see her, so he put his book down and sat up.

Within another minute, Clair had swum out further than all of the other people in the water. Gus stretched his neck to keep his eyes on her, and seeing that he had changed his position, she was now certain that he was watching. So, she did what she did best—she began to show off.

She lay on her back, fluttered her arms silently at her sides, and stuck a shapely leg straight up in the air like she was doing a water ballet in an Esther Williams musical. Gus grinned as her body disappeared below the surface, then her leg slowly descended into the water like an erotic periscope. Even her painted toenails were pointed straight up as they went down. She did this maneuver with one leg swimming in one direction, and then turned and repeated the process with the other. Next, she started to breaststroke even further out into the lake, turning back occasionally and leisurely squirting water at him through voluptuous lips. He had to admit, he'd never been so turned on by someone swimming before.

Suddenly, a little boy about two years old took a tumble to the ground behind him and started to cry. Gus turned and looked at the toddler, but his mother was there almost instantly. He watched the mother soothe her son for a few seconds, then he turned back to the lake. When he did, he couldn't see Clair. She was gone.

The smile on his face quickly faded as his eyes darted left, then right, scanning the water's surface. He rose, took off his sunglasses, dropped them to the blanket and started walking quickly toward the shoreline. Suddenly, he saw Clair's head burst above the water and try to yell for help before she disappeared beneath the surface again. Gus burst into a full run and within seconds was up to his ankles, then knees, then waist, before he dove into the water. He noticed instantly how cold the lake still was for June but ignored it and swam as fast as he could to where he'd last seen Clair. When he was almost to where he thought she should be, her head broke the surface again and she yelled, *"Crap!"*

But Gus knew that was just the water in her mouth. He knew she was really trying to say "Cramp!" Michigan's big lakes were slow to warm during the summer months and were notorious for causing muscles to painfully seize up. There was also undertows that could quickly carry an unsuspecting swimmer away.

Diving under the water, he spotted her about four feet below the surface, trying to rub her left calf muscle, tread water, and brush her floating hair out of her eyes all at the same time. He came up behind her, slipped his hands under her armpits, and then scissor kicked his way back up to the surface where her hair-covered face gasped for fresh air a few seconds later. He began to sidestroke back toward shore with her in tow on her back until he could feel the rippled sandy bottom of the lake beneath his feet. Next, he scooped her up in his strong arms and carried her to the beach. By now, half a dozen people had rushed to where Gus was bringing her out of the water, but ironically, none of them were from Clair's original party. Derek was still sleeping and snoring on his blanket and her other friends were still seventy or so yards away admiring that new Chevrolet and oblivious to the drama on the shoreline.

As Gus knelt down on the beach and gently set Clair on the sand, the people gathered around them were all talking at once.

One asked, "What happened?"

Another ordered, "Give her room."

Another said, "Is anyone a doctor?"

And still another announced, "That's Aaron Sinclair's girl."

After Gus had leaned her forward and administered a couple of forceful slaps on her back, she finally started to cough and spat out a mouthful of Lake Michigan. About ten seconds later, the coughing subsided. As the color started to return to her face, Gus began to firmly rub the left calf muscle that had given her so much trouble.

"I'm fine," she finally said, in between deep breaths to those around her. "I'm fine. Thank you everyone. It was just a really bad cramp."

As the onlookers began to slowly disperse, she brushed her thick, wet hair off her forehead and looked at Gus still rubbing her leg.

"How's that feel? Better?" he asked.

She looked at him for a moment as if she might say something about him taking such liberties with her body, but then her face softened.

"Yes. But I need to stand on it and walk it off."

He rose, extended a hand and helped her to her feet. Then he pointed to his blanket where he offered her a waiting towel. She nodded and started walking in that direction, although gingerly and with him holding her arm.

"Thank you," she said sincerely. "For a moment there, I thought I was in real trouble."

"You were never in serious trouble," he assured. "I was watching you."

She smiled appreciatively. "I don't even know your name."

"Gus Cooper. But you can still call me 'Grease Monkey,' if you want."

She looked at him and, for the first time, realized how truly handsome he was with his dark hair, brown eyes, nicely cut arms and abs, and a skin tone more conducive to tanning than hers. The fact that he was dripping wet only seemed to make him sexier.

"I'm Clair, but I guess you know that. I'm sorry I was so horrible to you the other day. I'll be the first to admit, I can get quite an attitude going sometimes."

"Really? I hadn't noticed," he politely lied.

"Yeah, I bet," she responded, wanting him to know that she was really sorry.

They arrived at his blanket and he gave her a white terrycloth towel. She dried herself off, and then offered it to him and he did the same.

"What high school did you go to?" she asked.

"CHS," he answered, which was short for the Charlevoix High School Rayders.

"Really? I don't remember you. How old are you?"

"Twenty-one."

"Oh, that explains it," she figured. "I was two years ahead of you."

"Would you like something to drink?" he asked, gesturing to his basket. "I've got some Vernors. It's warm but it's wet."

"Thanks," she said.

They sat down on his blanket as Gus retrieved a bottle of Vernors and an opener from the basket.

"Do you remember me?" she asked. "I was a cheerleader for the football and basketball teams."

"Sorry," he said, opening the bottle, "I didn't pay much attention to the local sports scene. Most Friday nights I was usually working somewhere in town." He handed her the ginger ale then looked over at Derek, who was still asleep on her blanket. "Let me guess, quarterback from the high school football team?"

"No. High school and college baseball star."

"Boyfriend?"

"I don't know," she said, throwing a glance in Derek's direction. "I haven't decided yet." She turned back to Gus and looked him over. "So, you work a lot and you read Shakespeare. How did a mechanic get interested in the bard?"

"'Mechanic' is not a lifestyle," he answered. "But I've always been good with engines. I like all kinds of things and read all kinds of books. In fact, I'm just a couple of credits away from getting my teaching degree."

"Really?" she said, genuinely surprised.

"Correspondence college. You can do it all through the mail now. I've already done my student teaching over in East Jordan. Sociology."

She looked at him, intrigued. "Shakespeare, engines, sociology—you're a person of many layers."

"I bet you are, too," he reasoned. "You're not defined just by poodle skirts and guys who can't hold their liquor, are you?"

"I hope not. But be careful," she warned, "I *do* like poodle skirts and he *is* my friend."

"Loyalty," he observed. "See? That's an unseen layer and a great quality right there." He looked at Derek, then back to her and smiled. "No offense intended. Really. I'm just trying to get to know you."

"Why?"

"Because you're the prettiest girl on this beach," he said honestly. "And because you were flirting with me out in the water. And because I'd bet twenty bucks there's other layers to you worth getting to know."

She raised a suspicious eyebrow. "Lines like this work for you?"

He casually gestured toward the lake. "So that water ballet was for Derek? 'Cause if it was, he's out. He's cold. He's as stiff as his hair."

She blushed and took another sip of warm Vernors.

"Okay. I just got my nursing degree last month from Ferris State University. I've applied for a job at the hospital and I expect something to open up soon. They're about to move into that new building so that'll mean more staff. I'm particularly interested in being a surgical nurse and working in the OR."

He looked at her and his smile widened. "I knew it. I knew you had a heart."

"What makes you say that?"

"You wouldn't be a nurse if you didn't," he reasoned.

"How do you know I didn't get the degree to marry some rich doctor?"

"Did you?"

She looked at him and smiled teasingly, not wanting to give him a direct answer. She liked that he was interested in her, but a lot of guys were. Clair Sinclair had the looks and upbringing that attracted young men like bees to flowers. But she'd never intentionally flirted with a boy whose father didn't belong to either a yacht or country club before, and Gus excited her. She also even liked that he was younger, although she was about to say the exact opposite.

"Forget it Romeo," she purred, shaking her head. "I'm two years older than you."

"Good, "he smiled, "then there's less to explain."

She looked at him. "About what?"

"Attraction. Chemistry. When it's there, it's there."

She looked at him calculatingly while holding her bottle, then brushed some more of her long wet hair off her shoulder. She shook her head slightly dismissing his observation and smiled again. But it was a girlish smile. An inviting smile. The kind of smile with sparks in the corner of the lips that ignited relationships and burned hearts to the ground.

"Hey, Cooper," a male voice called.

Gus opened his eyes back in his living room. His half-drank Moosehead sat on a coffee table next to his recliner. He looked around then realized someone was knocking on his front door.

"Gus?" the voice called again. "You got my cat in there?"

6 Things Hanging

    It was a bad accident. It happened on old US 31 near Nine Mile Point off Little Traverse Bay at about 10:51 p.m. A nineteen-year-old girl in a Ford Focus was texting a girlfriend when she went over the center line. A Toyota in the oncoming lane reacted by swerving off the road and going into a stand of trees. Although the texting teen was unharmed, the driver of the Toyota slammed into a large pine with thick, low-lying branches. One long branch, about four inches in diameter, broke in half on the windshield while the jagged other half went through the windshield and impaled the driver between the lower sternum and navel. What made the accident worse was its isolated location. It took precious time for the ambulance, fire truck, and county sheriff's cruisers to arrive on the scene.

    It was Doc's third evening on the night shift. The first two nights had been surprisingly quiet, which allowed him to get to know his fireman EMT partner and ambulance driver, Ken Kelly, who everyone called KK. At thirty-two, he was the same age as Doc and had been a fireman/EMT for nearly seven years. He had short dishwater-blonde hair, a circular face and was in excellent shape like Doc thanks to his hobby of long-distance swimming. He could also empathize with his new partner having to lug Gertrude around. He had also "dated" her as he called it when he was in training.

    The ambulance was the first to arrive on the scene. The teenage girl was in shock, and was pacing back and forth behind her Ford parked on the shoulder of the road while talking to her mom on the phone. She kept saying, "Oh-my-God-oh-my-God" very quickly as if it were a medicinal chant that would somehow heal the other driver. After lighting flares and putting them on the road about thirty yards ahead of and behind the ambulance, KK went to the girl while Doc ran to the Toyota that seemed to be half-swallowed by the large pine that had stopped it.

The man inside was darker skinned and Doc guessed he was Hispanic or maybe had roots in the Middle East. He was about the same age as Doc and KK, and like them, in good physical shape. Good, except for the tree branch that had gone some six inches into his stomach. Remarkably, the man was still conscious, although very weak and shuddering occasionally. As Doc approached, he could see that the driver's side window was down.

He maneuvered under the pine branches and opened the driver's side door with one hand while holding a flashlight in the other. As soon as he did, trickles of blood oozed over the floorboard of the car and started to seep down the car's lower exterior. The patient's light yellow T-shirt was soaked in blood as well as the vinyl driver's side seat. The carpeting on the side of the seat where the blood had dripped down was so drenched it could hold no more.

Doc knew the human body held six quarts of blood and that someone could survive losing two. Problem was, it looked like the driver had already lost that much and ambulances weren't equipped to carry extra pints for transfusions.

"Hey, buddy," he began gently, "looks like you've had a rough night." Sometimes, Doc would say a wisecrack or tell a joke as an opening line to test a patient's alertness and put their mind at ease about their injuries. But not tonight. The blood loss was too great.

"W-where's the fire?" the driver slowly asked, noticing Doc's brown fireman's turnout coat with the day-glow striping.

"I'm a paramedic," Doc explained. "What's your name?"

"You wanna know what's funny?" the man said between nearly clenched teeth while his shoulders quivered as if he were cold. "My name is Bob. Now, I'm 'shish kaBob'...get it?"

Doc smiled faintly. "My name's Doc. What happened?"

Bob nodded his head toward the teenage girl, struggling to keep a sense of composure. "Her name is Karen, same as my wife. She...she came over to see if I was okay, but then threw up when she saw my new body piercing," he said, joking about the branch. "So watch where you step. She was texting and weaved over the centerline. I went off the road to avoid her."

Doc turned and yelled in the direction he had just come. But as he did, the fire truck and two sheriff cars arrived and their approaching sirens blocked out his call.

"*KK, I need Saline. All we got!*"

"I was a medic in Iraq," Bob said, shaking his head, his teeth now bathed in red. "Seven...seventeen major engagements and not a scratch. Now, I die by text. Go figure."

"Not on my watch," Doc said, pulling a stethoscope out of one of his large pockets.

"Y-y-you can't fix this with Saline, morphine, or Captain Crunch," Bob said, coughing slightly. "I wanna be coherent as long as...as longaspossss..." His voice was fading with his strength.

A fireman and officer jogged toward the Toyota. *"I need Saline!"* Doc yelled through the branches. The fireman stopped, turned and ran toward KK. The officer kept coming until Doc held up a hand to stop his advance. Understanding, the cop stopped just outside the tangle of greenery where the car sat.

"Bob, you gotta let me try, man," Doc urged. He put the ends of the stethoscope in his ears, then raised Bob's blood-soaked shirt and listened. The patient's heart was racing erratically, trying to make up for the great loss of fluid.

"Tell my wife I love her," Bob moaned, swallowing hard. "Tell her personally...p-p-promise."

A dying patient relaying a message of love to a spouse was one of the last things most people said. Doc used his flashlight to re-examine the puncture wound and blood loss. Blood was everywhere. He knew Bob was right. Saline wasn't going to help.

"You have my word," Doc said earnestly.

Bob's eyes started to fill with tears. "My God," he said, looking through the windshield, the shuddering of his body now stopped.

"I—I sssee someone."

Doc closed his eyes and rubbed his forehead with the tips of his fingers, anticipating an answer he'd heard many times before. "Is it a guy in a long dark overcoat? Kind of thin? Long, slicked-back white hair? Looks like he washed his face with a cheese grater?"

"Nnno..." Bob said, his breathing now in short bursts. "It's my mom," he half smiled. "But...but she's young...and beautiful. There's light everywhere. Sh-she...wants me to come."

Doc looked at him, closed his eyes regretfully again, then reopened them.

"Then, I guess you better go," he said softly. "It's okay, Bob." Doc took one of Bob's hands as the patient's eyes fluttered. He let out one final breath and his head slowly sank to his chest. Doc checked his pulse and then listened to his heart one more time with the stethoscope. After thirty seconds, he stopped listening just as KK came maneuvering through the branches with the Saline. Doc took the ends of the scope out of his ears, put them on his neck, and lowered his head.

"Dear Lord," he whispered, "I commend this man's soul to your care. I didn't know him, but you do. Please accept him into your kingdom and watch over the loved ones he left behind."

KK raised his flashlight and examined the messy interior of the Toyota. Reacting to all the blood now would be moot. Instead, he muttered, "Sorry Doc."

Doc nodded and slowly rose. He took the stethoscope off his neck and slipped it back into his turnout coat pocket. "Yeah," he simply said. He weaved through the tangle of branches and over to the waiting cop. "When you get the address from his license, I'd like to go with you to his house. I promised to deliver a message personally."

Nine and a half hours later, Doc sat on the edge of his aluminum dock. His cabin stood about thirty yards away behind him. It was a beautiful northern Michigan morning. Bright blue sky, no wind, and he could see a couple of smaller boats with fisherman out on Lake Charlevoix. They sat on the glass-like water as if glued in place. Besides the still boats, the only other activity was a flock of geese flying in "V" formation far off and a floating empty can of Bud Light about fifteen yards from Doc's dangling bare feet in the water. Three or four yards behind it was another empty floating can. The third can was still in Doc's hand and half full. Three more sat on the dock next to him, not yet separated from their plastic collar. Minnows nibbled at his toes as he heard the heavy "thump-thump-thump" of someone walking down the dock behind him. He turned to see Gus wearing his usual marina work clothes of Sperry Docksiders, a golf shirt, and jeans.

"Gus, what brings you out this way?" he asked, surprised. The older man got to the end of the dock and observed the floating cans. "Launching a fleet, eh?" he observed. "I've launched a few, myself."

"Care to christen one?" the paramedic asked, jerking a thumb to the remaining beers.

Gus looked at his wristwatch. "It's 9:30 in the morning, man," he protested. Then he thought for a moment and shrugged. "Okay."

He slowly sat down on the dock, which was a long way down for a man of his years. He sat next to Doc although facing toward land in the opposite direction and pulled a beer out of its plastic collar.

"What brings you out this way?" Doc asked. "Why aren't you at work?"

"Need to talk to you 'bout somethin'," the older man said, popping open his beer. "But first, why are we drinking our breakfast?"

Doc scanned the quiet lake thoughtfully. "You know, I've been thinking about it, and all I am is in the shipping business."

"Shipping business?" Gus asked, taking a drink.

"I'm like FedEx only without the Superbowl commercials," Doc said, likewise taking a drink. "I just package up the sick and wounded—or *try* to—then ship 'em off to someone who makes a difference."

"Oh, I think what you do makes a lot of difference," Gus observed.

"And then there's all these things left hanging out there," Doc continued.

"Things hanging?" Gus asked, rubbing the white stubble on his face.

"The wife who has to learn to live without her husband…the teenager who has to live with their mistake…the mother who goes to the grocery store and then finds her baby dead in a drawer."

The old man raised his eyebrows, more or less understanding his friend's chain of thought considering his profession, although he didn't know the particulars of each situation.

"They're not things hanging out there, Doc. Sounds to me like you're talking about consequences people have to live it. Believe me, I know all about living with consequences. People can find strength they didn't know they had."

Doc looked at him and nodded appreciatively. Sitting next to him was a man who had lost his wife when she was only twenty-five, who had raised a daughter by himself and then lost that daughter when she was an adult along with his son-in-law to Lake Michigan, leaving him to raise a teenage granddaughter.

"Yeah, I'd say you do," he said as he finished his beer. He leaned forward and dropped the can into the water.

Gus was anxious to discuss what he came for, but he also knew Doc had things on his mind, so he waited. Patience was one of the few benefits that came with age.

"I don't want to be a fireman, Gus," Doc finally said, "but I can't continue to be a paramedic in Charlevoix unless I become one. And I don't want to move because of Farren."

Gus took a drink of his beer. "Well," he sighed, "you gotta like what you do for a living. That's for sure. What *do* you want to be when you grow up?" he joked.

"I want to be a doctor," Doc answered. "I should've been. Ten years ago, I was accepted to Wayne State Medical School but never went. That was a mistake. If I'm a doctor, I won't be in the shipping business anymore. I'll be in the healing business. Maybe I can even help with some of the things left hanging."

Gus thought for a moment before responding. "Those are admirable thoughts, but ambitious."

"I've been talking to Bob Lancaster about it for some time now," Doc revealed. Bob Lancaster was a doctor over at the local hospital and a friend who had always admired Doc's medical expertise. "I've already retaken my MCAT," he continued, "got my college transcripts, gotten letters of recommendation and reapplied to Wayne State. So I've been doing more than just thinking about it."

"I guess you *have*," the old man said, impressed.

Doc hopped into the water barefoot but still wearing his black cargo-style pants from work. The water wasn't deep, just barely to his knees. He picked up the beer can he had just deposited into the lake, then started heading out into the chilly water for the other two.

"Farren know about this?" Gus asked, slowly spinning around to face the water.

"Not exactly. I mean, she knows I'm not happy with the changes at work and that I've been doing a lot of studying. But she probably assumes it's all been about being a fireman."

"Why haven't you told her?"

Doc plucked the second can out of the water. "Three reasons. One, I may not get accepted. If I don't, why worry her about us being separated? Two, I haven't figured out how we're going to keep things healthy between us. Wayne State is more than five hours away and long distance relationships rarely work. Three, thanks to Charlie, things aren't exactly healthy already. Farren's got some emotional issues to work on and I don't want her thinking if I left town it was because of those issues. Quite the contrary. She's a big part of the reason why I want to do more with myself."

Gus took another swig of his beer while Doc retrieved the last can. He was now a good distance from the dock but his butt still wasn't wet. "How shallow *is* it out there?" he called.

"It drops off pretty fast in another ten yards or so," Doc answered.

"Yeah, I knew she was seeing a shrink," Gus said, returning to the subject. "But I haven't asked her much about it 'cause I was trying to respect her privacy."

"If I did get into Wayne State," Doc said, wading back, "the idea is, I'd come back and practice here and hopefully we'd have a future. But I'm thirty-two now. Four years of medical school, then two, three or more years of residency depending on my specialty—I could be forty before I got back to town. What's she supposed to do? Wait?"

"Get married," Gus suggested. "Not that I'm trying to be pushy, you understand."

Doc smiled at the idea that Farren's grandfather would accept him as a member of the family.

"You saying that means a lot to me, Gus, it does. But the truth is, we're not there yet. She doesn't feel safe with a man right now. She can't..." he stopped himself, not wanting to discuss intimate details. "Anyway, her livelihood's here. You're here."

Gus was about to say that Farren staying in Charlevoix for his sake wasn't enough of a reason for her to stay, but Doc spoke first. "So, what'd you want to talk about?"

"Oh...I've got a former student who's a reporter down in Flint. He's been keeping an eye on the court proceedings against that loan shark, Bartholomew."

"Good," Doc nodded. "Has a trial date finally been set?"

"Just the opposite," Gus answered, setting his unfinished beer on the dock. "The case was thrown out."

The younger man stopped dead in the water. *"What?"*

Gus slowly got to his feet.

"He's on the street again, Doc. And I'm fearful for my granddaughter."

7 Precautions

A half hour later, Doc and Gus were sitting in the office of the Charlevoix Chief of Police. Meaning, Doc was right back at work since the fire hall, police department, and city hall were all in the same building. Everybody called the chief BJ, and although Doc didn't know him well, he had spoken to him a few times about calls he'd been on. Like Captain Stubigg, he'd been with the city for years, but whereas Don Stubigg was fifty-one, the chief was easily twenty-five years older, a fact he tried to conceal by dying his hair, but he always had very noticeable white roots so it wasn't very convincing. He was also quite overweight. Stubigg was merely barrel-chested, but BJ was just plain waddling fat. Some of the guys in the Fire Hall joked that his stomach arrived at an accident or crime scene about thirty seconds before the rest of him did.

While they sat in the chief's office — an office that was exactly the same dimensions as Stubigg's — Gus explained his understanding of the events in Flint. The police had originally questioned then arrested a known loan shark named Gordon Bartholomew because Charlie Huffman had confessed he was the mastermind and financial backer of the scam to get the land where the Portside Marina sat. Incriminating evidence was also found at Bartholomew's office, most notably a portfolio case containing artist renderings of a multi-story condominium complex that left little doubt the condominiums were supposed to replace the marina. Bartholomew was also implicated in a murder Charlie committed in Mount Pleasant, but after six months, it had been determined that the portfolio had been improperly seized so it couldn't be used in court. And although a college student named Daniel Minter *had* disappeared in Mount Pleasant six months earlier, and friends of his *had* stated to the police that Daniel admitted to owing a loan shark, there was no direct connection to Bartholomew. There was also no body so there was no evidence of foul play. The bottom line was Daniel had simply disappeared.

Since the cops in Flint knew Bartholomew and his unsavory ways, the district attorney had tried hard to tie the loan shark, Daniel, Charlie and the events in Charlevoix together. But it now seemed as if Bartholomew had slipped through the cracks of the judicial system.

"Shame about those artist drawings being improperly seized," the chief agreed, his voice was low and gravely from years of drinking Scotch. "Rookie mistake. So, what do you want me to do about it?"

"I want police protection for my granddaughter," Gus answered.

"Has this Bartholomew personally made any threats against Farren?"

"No. He just recruited a con man to court her, make her fall in love, marry him, and then he tried to kill her and have it look like an accident," Gus answered, sarcastically.

"Allegedly," the chief reminded him.

"Allegedly my ass and you know it!" Gus snapped impatiently.

"I was there when Charlie confessed the whole story," Doc added. "He thought Farren was moments away from dying, so he had nothing to lose by talking to her. Why would he tell her about Bartholomew if it wasn't true?"

"He was a con man, son," the chief said. "He made his living by lying and who knows why con men do what they do?" The big man leaned back in his squeaky chair. "Look, fellas, I understand where you're coming from. I'm not trying to defend this loan shark. I've no doubt he's pond-sucking scum. I'm just trying to show you the other side of things. His case was dismissed for a reason. Now, the guy is in a city five hours away, he's made no threats against Farren, and if anything *did* happen to her, God forbid, he'd be the prime suspect. Why would he risk that? Doesn't make sense."

"Why would he spend thousands of dollars and recruit Charlie to con Farren over several months?" Gus answered. "There's a lot of land for sale around here. Don't you see? He didn't want just *any* piece of land. He wanted Farren's!" Gus turned to Doc. "Didn't Charlie say he was sort of obsessed about it?"

"Words to that effect," Doc agreed.

"And now he's been in jail for six months," Gus continued, "out of circulation, not able to make loans. Seems to me if a guy like Bartholomew had all that taken away from him, he'd be pretty pissed."

"Fellas," the chief said, holding up a hand indicating he didn't want to hear anymore. "We're in a recession. Short on resources. The city's consolidating." He looked at Doc. "You know that better than anyone. It's the middle of the tourist season and I'm understaffed as it is. I can't spare manpower on paranoia. I need hard, cold facts."

Gus took offense that he was being called paranoid. "How about when I deliver my granddaughter's hard, cold body on your doorstep?" he hissed. "Will you believe me, then?"

"Hey, don't give me that infamous Cooper attitude, old man," BJ warned, now taking offense, himself. "I *am* the chief of police."

"Who shoulda retired about fifteen years ago," Gus retorted. He glanced at the chief's hair. "Nice roots, BJ."

"Chief," Doc said, hopping in before things got too heated and off track, "what if we hired some of your guys freelance as body guards when they're off duty?"

"It's your money," the old cop shrugged. "I've got no problem with that."

"Well, thanks 'chief,'" Gus said, still not happy that his concerns weren't being taken seriously. "You've been loads of help."

"We're done here," BJ said rising to his feet. The visitors did likewise. Doc was nearly out the door when the chief called out to him.

"Hey, Reynolds. Don't forget Linda Lovelace."

Doc looked at Gertrude sitting on the floor behind his chair, rolled his eyes exasperated, picked her up and flung her over his shoulder, all the while Gus and BJ threw daggers at each other with their hard-edge looks.

Once they were outside and while Gertrude's arms dangled lifelessly behind his back, Doc turned to Gus.

"What was all *that* about?"

"Aw—he's an idiot," Gus said, brushing the chief's comments away like a fly. The two men had driven separately so Gus could go directly to the marina and Doc could go home and get some sleep, although they were parked right behind the other on the side of the street.

"You know, he does have a point," Doc observed. "Bartholomew would have to be crazy to come after Farren."

"So why did you come with me?" Gus asked, now at his black Accord and holding his keys.

Doc rubbed his forehead with the tips of his fingers then looked around as if he didn't want to share what he was about to say. Meanwhile, his rescue dummy was now starting to attract the attention of some tourists walking across the street.

"Because you could be right," he admitted. "If Bartholomew was crazy enough to launch an elaborate con and the con didn't work and he went to jail, yeah, he *could* be pretty pissed off. And I don't want to take that chance with Farren."

Gus nodded and asked, "Did you mean what you said about hiring off-duty cops to watch her?"

"Yes, but that's going to get expensive really fast, and it's not like I'm Bill Gates."

"Me, neither," the older man agreed. "But I do have some money in the bank."

"It might be good if she moved back in with you for a while," Doc suggested, rounding his Jeep to put Gertrude into the passenger seat. "We'll tell her it's just a precaution, which it is."

"Movin' in with me isn't gonna be much help," Gus answered.

"Why?" Doc asked, opening the passenger side door.

"I'm seventy-eight years old. What am I gonna do? Pelt bad guys with stool softener? Gum 'em to death? Besides, thanks to Charlie, if Bartholomew knows where Farren lives, he knows where I live." He suddenly looked at Doc, who had just placed his rescue dummy into the Wrangler, shut the door and was coming around to the sidewalk again. "But Bartholomew or his lackeys wouldn't know where *you* lived."

Doc looked at Gus with a deadpan expression. "You want your granddaughter to move in with a man who's crazy about her and would like nothing better than to—" he stopped himself, remembering who he was talking to.

"Get into her pants?" Gus finished. "Poke her pantry? Do the horizontal bop? I kinda assumed you two were there already?"

Doc continued to look at him straight-faced. "That topic is...complicated. And if you don't mind, off limits."

Gus nodded and fought back a smile, admiring Doc's discretion. "Fair enough. But she'll still be safer with you than me. 'Sides, wouldn't it give you two more time to work out those 'complications?' Not to mention, you've still got to tell her about medical school. She's likely to feel more a part of the future if she's living in your house."

Doc thought for a moment, his face lightening. He hadn't considered that. But Gus could've been wrong when he said Bartholomew or his lackeys didn't know where he lived. Six months earlier, the loan shark sent two of his men to Charlevoix at Charlie's request. Charlie feared that Farren's friendship with Doc would ultimately interfere with his plans and he wanted the paramedic out of the way. So the two men, named Stanley and George, jumped Doc one night and nearly beat him to death. True, they attacked him away from his house, but they might've already known where he lived. The only reason why nobody knew about the attack was because Clair had "absorbed" Doc's injuries and healed him that same night.

Although Bartholomew's people might know where Doc lived, the paramedic decided he'd have to take that chance because he *was* more capable of protecting Farren than was her grandfather.

Ten minutes later, Doc and Gus were at the Portside Marina

standing on one of the three concrete docks in front of the marina store. The store had a sandstone veneer with a slight "A" frame to it, and with its two large windows overlooking the docks from ceiling to floor, it looked more like a fine restaurant than it did a retailer of nautical necessities. In fact, it had been a restaurant back in the 1960s and early '70s.

The concrete docks were about twenty-five feet apart and boats of every description sat tied in their slips parallel to the docks, making the place look like a floating parking lot. There were cabin cruisers, fishing boats, cigarette boats and seagulls sitting atop mooring posts squawking and looking for food. Farren was busy overseeing the cleaning of an eighteen-foot Catalina sailboat. She was wearing a black bikini top, short denim cutoffs, and rubber lake shoes while one of her summer helpers scrubbed the fiberglass hull and another was retrieving packed and bagged sails from below. They were getting the boat ready for an owner who was coming in from Chicago.

"Hey, darlin'," Gus called, "got a minute?"

"Hi," she said, smiling broadly. "Be right there."

Doc didn't know which was better, Farren wearing a bikini top and short cutoffs, because he'd never seen her so undressed before, or the scenic point of land where the marina sat because he'd never been out on the one of the docks before. He glanced to his right and saw the view of downtown Charlevoix and the Memorial Bridge, then looked left and saw a seemingly endless vista of Lake Charlevoix.

"My two favorite guys," she said, stepping off the boat and onto the dock. She looked at her boyfriend. "But shouldn't you be home sleeping?"

"We need to talk to you about something, kiddo," Doc said.

"Anything wrong?" she asked.

"Naw," Gus said, masking his concern.

"No. No," Doc emphasized. "But there's been a little development."

"Development? With what?"

"Bartholomew's been released," Doc shrugged, trying to

minimize it. "Apparently, the case against him was thrown out because of inappropriately seized evidence."

"What?" Farren said, her brown eyes widening. "What does that mean? Should...should I be worried?"

"Naw," Gus repeated, still masking his concern.

"No. No," Doc reemphasized. "We just spoke to the chief of police and we all agree the last place Bartholomew wants to come to is Charlevoix."

"You spoke to BJ?" she asked, her anxiety increasing.

"Precaution, honey," Gus said.

"Strictly a precaution," Doc agreed. "But, uh, we were thinking maybe it'd be a good idea if you weren't alone in your house right now. So, I'd like you to consider staying at my place. Just for a while. Just until we've—y'know—verified that Bartholomew isn't going to cause any more trouble."

"And how exactly are you going to do that?" Farren asked, raising her dark eyebrows.

"We're probably overreacting here," Gus lied. "In fact, I'm *sure* we are. But for the time being, you should take a little break from your normal routine. Don't go to the bookstore every Monday. Don't always go to the same mass. Don't be alone in the evenings."

She furrowed her brow and put her hands on her hips, not really sure how concerned she should be, but seeing holes in this freshly minted plan.

"If I stay at Doc's, I'll still be alone. He just got switched to nights."

"Yeah, but that won't be forever," Doc reminded her, "and—uh—we're probably going to have someone watching the cabin at night."

"What? You mean like police?" she asked, the tension in her voice mounting again.

"Just off-duty cops," Doc shrugged again. "People you know. My poker buds. And—hey—wouldn't it be nice to spend some more time together?"

"Let me get this straight," she said, still with her hands on her hips and suspicious. "You both came down here because you want me to move in with Doc, be protected by off-duty cops at night, change my routine about where I go and when—but there's *nothing* to worry about?"

"Exactly," Gus said

"These are just—precautions," Doc shrugged.

Farren looked at one and then the other, not knowing how much she should be scared, but she was.

8 Logic & Shotguns

Aaron Sinclair and his family lived off M 66 about three miles outside of downtown Charlevoix. The house had a long driveway of nearly eighty yards before it emptied into a circular turn-around that featured colorful flowers and an impressive but gaudy fountain featuring a peeing cherub in the middle of the turn-around. The house itself was a two-story, four-bedroom antebellum-style mansion with four tall white pillars in front that would've been more appropriate south of the Mason-Dixon line. But since Aaron Sinclair liked to make statements, and since he owned a construction company, he could make any architectural statement he wanted.

It was a cloudless summer's day in early July of 1954 as Clair drove up the drive in her light blue Chevrolet Corvette convertible, a graduation present for nursing school. She had the clamp-on top off, her Ray Ban sunglasses on, and the Crewcuts were singing "Sh-Boom" on the radio. Going into the circular turn-around, she saw her sister's yellow 1950 Nash Rambler Coupe sitting in the driveway right behind her father's red and white Studebaker. Her only sister was a precocious sixteen year old named Jessie, and the two girls couldn't have been more different. Clair was a stunner and had an hourglass figure; Jessie was more plain and lean. Clair wore her curly blonde hair long. Jessie also had thick blonde hair but favored a Gamine-style haircut. Clair liked to wear dresses and the newest fashions, while Jessie liked T-shirts and dungarees. Clair wanted to be an OR nurse, but Jessie didn't think any further into the future other than what was coming to the local drive-in.

The foyer of the Sinclair house was just as impressive as the outside. It featured a high ceiling and was open and light with a wallpaper pattern of honeysuckle flowers and a wide curving staircase that led from the foyer to the second floor. It also had a rounded mahogany table in its middle where mail, hats and car keys could be deposited. Clair came into the foyer wearing an off-white summery cotton dress while removing a red scarf to keep her hair in place. Simultaneously, Jessie was just coming out of her father's study. She smiled slyly at her big sister and stuffed a five-dollar bill into her jeans pocket, then hurried upstairs. But Clair really didn't pay her, or what she was doing, much mind.

"That you, Clair?" she heard her father's voice call.

"Yes, Daddy," she answered, putting her sunglasses and car keys on the foyer table.

"C'mere for a second," her father called.

She walked across the twelve-foot wide foyer carrying her red scarf; her high-heels clicking on the imported Spanish tile floor as she went.

Aaron's study was a typically masculine room. It was paneled in oak and featured several paintings of the English countryside with men on horseback during a foxhunt. The riders wore red coats, black hats and tall dark boots. Each painting also featured a pack of hounds in pursuit. The shelves in between the paintings were stacked with books that Sinclair had never read, but the room also held some trophies for skeet shooting that he had actually won. The centerpiece of the room was an ornate wooden desk with two wingback leather chairs in front of it and the entire ensemble sat on a thick oriental fringed rug. Although it was perhaps a predictable looking room for a man who wanted to make a statement that he was wealthy, it was tastefully done, unlike Sinclair's usual wardrobe.

"Come on in, baby," he said, standing behind his desk and rolling up some blueprints. He was a tall, fair-skinned man with thinning blonde hair. Were it not for his horrible taste in clothes and slight potbelly he might even be considered handsome. He was wearing a yellow short-sleeve shirt and seersucker pants. "Where ya been?"

"Hanging out with some friends," she answered, sauntering in.

"'Friends,'" her father questioned, "or, one friend in particular?"

"One friend in particular," she smiled.

"But that friend wasn't Derek Worthing, was it?" Aaron asked, already knowing the answer. "It was that mechanic again."

She turned and looked toward the foyer, figuring out her sister's newfound wealth,

"Have you been paying Jessie to spy on me?"

"Absolutely," Sinclair admitted, unapologetically.

"Why?" she asked, irritated.

"How many times have you seen him in the past two weeks?"

"I don't see how that's any of your business. I'm over twenty-one."

"But still living under my roof!" he reminded her. "Answer my question."

"I don't know," she said, defensively. "I haven't counted."

"Well I have! Today makes six times that I know of. Six times versus one date with Derek during the same time period. And that wasn't really a date because our families had dinner together at the Shooting Club."

"Daddy, why are you spying on me?"

He looked at her, lowered his voice and gestured to a chair. "Sit down, honey." He rounded his desk and headed to the wet bar in the back of the room. On it was a Waterford Crystal decanter holding some port. "I want to discuss a little business with you."

"Business?" she asked, sitting down in one of the leather wingback chairs.

"You know our neighbors up the road, the Harrisons, right?"

"They live about a half mile away," she answered, leaning over the chair to face him, "so I'm not exactly sure that makes them neighbors, but yes, I know who you mean."

"You know their house is for sale, right?"

"Is it? I hadn't noticed."

Sinclair poured himself a drink, put the glass top back in the decanter, and strolled over to her. "The post war boom is over, Clair. The boom that mostly built this house. Haven't you noticed more and more businesses on Bridge Street have closed? Fewer boats are tied to docks downtown? Fewer tourists are on the sidewalks?"

She shook her head.

"The town is in a recession. Tourism is down, the local economy is hurting, people who have lived here all their lives are moving away because they can't make a living anymore."

She thought for a moment. "Do you think that might have something to do with why the hospital hasn't called me yet?"

"Could be," her father answered, taking a sip from a small snifter then sitting down in the chair next to her. "The city council has been feeling the effects of this for quite some time, and they've decided to do something about it. They want to give all the storefronts down on Bridge Street new facades. Dress it up. Give it more of a charming, village-like feel. This is going to be a major contract for somebody. There's even talk of a new waterfront hotel tied to the project. You know we own one of the larger construction companies in the area. If we won this contract, it would keep us busy for quite some time. Maybe a couple of years if they decide to do the hotel. Meantime, Derek's family owns the largest building supply company. Now if our two families were merged, no other company could touch us for the job."

Clair's mouth dropped open slightly. "Are you saying you want me to marry Derek Worthing so you can win a construction contract with the city?"

"I'm saying we're in a recession and I need this contract. In order for you to enjoy this lifestyle, I haven't saved a lot of money. Remember that semester you took off so you could travel around Europe last year? I want you to look at things squarely. Logically. You do *like* Derek, right?"

"Well...yes."

"And he's crazy about you. His father told me so. You're also twenty-three. You know your mother and I were married at twenty-one."

"Yes, but Mommy never wanted to work. I've got a degree in nursing–"

"And there's absolutely no reason why you can't still use it once you're married," her father interrupted. "*If* your husband wants you to work. But with Derek, you wouldn't have to. You two are cut from the same cloth, come from the same type of background. Compare that with Gus Cooper's people."

"What do you mean?"

"Do you know what his parents do?"

She shook her head.

"His father works in a tool and die shop and his mother cleans houses."

"You checked up on them?" she asked, becoming irritated again.

"It's a small town, Clair," he shrugged. "It's not exactly international espionage."

"And what's wrong with what they do?" she asked, still bristling.

"Nothing's wrong with what they do," Aaron assured her. "Not a thing. It's just curious that after six dates, he hasn't volunteered the information."

"Or maybe we've just got better things to talk about, like *his* future. Gus is just a couple of credits away from getting his teaching degree, you know."

"And I'm sure he'll make a fine auto shop teacher somewhere. Look, all I'm asking you to do is think. Think of where your best chances for happiness lie. Think of where you're most likely going to enjoy the lifestyle you've spent a lot of your life in. Think of how you might be putting those chances in jeopardy by tweaking Derek's nose with this other fella."

Clair furrowed her brow and leaned back in the chair. She didn't like her father spying on her or checking up on Gus' parents. But she couldn't exactly argue with his logic, either. She and Gus *were* from very different backgrounds and Derek wasn't. Sinclair saw he was getting through to her.

"It's time to think about the future, Clair. Not a summer fling."

She thought for a moment, her green eyes searching for

alternatives. Then, she lowered them, fiddling with her red scarf. "I—I really like this man, Daddy. He's not like anybody I've ever met."

"I like *I Love Lucy*," her father shrugged, "doesn't mean I want to marry Lucille Ball."

She looked at him exasperated. He could see the traces of defiance in her eyes. She got his logic, but he feared she was on the verge of liking Gus even more simply because he didn't want her to. So he decided to change tactics.

"Alright," he said, raising a conciliatory hand, "if you *really* like this boy, maybe I should get to know him a little better."

"Really?" she said, her face brightening.

"But don't write off Derek either, Clair. He really does like you. There's nothing wrong with playing the field. And if you come to feel the way he does about you, there's also nothing wrong with doing something that would help my business."

"Okay. Fair enough," she agreed.

The next day, Gus pulled his 1947 sea-green Chevy pick-up into the white gravel parking lot of the Traverse Bay Shooting Club. The club was an impressive 4,000 square foot two-story log structure that sat right on the shore of Lake Michigan and about ten miles outside of Charlevoix heading toward Petoskey. It had been built four years earlier by none other than Sinclair Construction. It was a "gentlemen's club" where members could play cards, skeet shoot, target practice, get their guns oiled and cleaned, have a drink, and tell each other exaggerated adventures of hunting and fishing. Wives and children were allowed only on Saturdays.

Gus walked through the propped open double front doors with his hands in his pockets wearing a dark red short-sleeve button-down shirt and faded but clean navy blue slacks with grey Hush Puppies. The first thing he noticed was a huge chandelier hanging down from the large central room that was made entirely of deer antlers.

"Gus," Aaron called as he hopped off a stool at the bar to the right of the room and came toward Gus, maneuvering around leather club chairs and green felt poker tables. He was wearing light tan slacks and a dark green safari shooting jacket with brown leather patches on the shoulders.

"Nice of you to come," he said, extending his hand.

"Good afternoon, Mr. Sinclair," Gus greeted, shaking his hand. "Thanks for the invitation."

"Ever been to the Shooting Club before?"

"No, sir," Gus answered, looking around. He heard the distant "pop-pop- pop" of someone firing a handgun in quick succession. His eyes paused momentarily at a moose head with large antlers mounted behind the bar.

"Would you like something to drink? A beer perhaps?"

"A beer would be great. Thank you."

Sinclair spotted a black waiter and snapped his fingers. The waiter, wearing a buttoned-up white serving jacket, came immediately over with raised, inquisitive eyebrows.

"Beer," Sinclair ordered.

The waiter nodded and headed toward the bar. Sinclair began to lead Gus through the central room. It consisted of a bar, club chairs with end tables and lamps, eating and poker tables, and pine crossbeams above the antler chandelier. The moose head wasn't the only mounted prize on the log walls. There was also a ten-point buck, a buffalo, a Canadian elk, an African water buffalo, and two very tall elephant tusks on stands on either side of the front doors. Ernest Hemingway no longer lived in the area. But if he did, he would have loved the wood, whiskey, and gun oil smell of the place.

"This club is my refuge," the older man said, "from work, complaining foremen, my girls, everything. You a hunter?"

"I've done a bit," Gus said, which was an understatement.

"Good! Then you know your way around guns."

"Well, 'gun.' My grandpa had a double-barrel Remington 12-gauge he passed down to my dad. Now it's mine."

"Perfect for birds, but not much good for ground game," Sinclair noted. "For deer, you'd want something more precise with more punch."

"Well, sir, if it's all you've got, it's all you've got."

Like the double front doors, there were four glass-paneled patio doors that were propped open to let a nice lake breeze through the club. As Sinclair led Gus through one of the open doors to the flagstone back patio, the guest paused admiring the azure blue water.

"Beautiful," Gus said.

"Yeah, not bad," Aaron agreed.

The waiter came up behind them with a pilsner glass of beer on a tray. Gus took the beer and thanked the waiter.

"You're not having one, sir?"

"Little too early for me," Sinclair answered. It really wasn't too early, being about 4:30 p.m., but it made Gus feel self-conscious that he was drinking and his host wasn't.

"Buck," Sinclair called, "got a couple of double-barrels over there?" He was speaking to a bearded man wearing a shooting vest who was standing behind a table about ten yards away to the right. Lying on the table were half a dozen rifles.

"Yes, sir," the man answered.

"Ever shoot any skeet?" Sinclair asked Gus.

"Do cans thrown up in the air count?" Gus asked, taking a sip of his beer.

"Same principle," Clair's father said and gestured to the table. "Wanna give it a go?"

"Okay," Gus shrugged.

The men stepped over to the table where Buck produced an open box of Dupont Peters high velocity shotgun shells. Sinclair grabbed a handful from the green and red box and slipped them into the large side pocket of his shooting jacket. Gus set his beer down and stuffed some shells into one side of his pant pockets, then more in the other until his hips resembled full chipmunk cheeks.

"I appreciate this opportunity to get to know you a little better," Sinclair said, looking over the choices on the table. He finally selected a double-barrel Winchester.

"Well your timing was perfect. Today's my day off," Gus said, scanning the table to see if they had a Remington. They didn't, so he selected a WW Greener, manufactured in England.

"You've been spending a lot of time with my oldest girl," Sinclair noted. "How's that work with your job?"

"My regular hours are from 7:00 to 4:00. So that leaves the late afternoon and evenings open unless we've got an emergency."

"And how are you two getting along?" Sinclair asked, slipping a shell into each barrel.

"Except for that first time we met, great."

"Ah, the grease on the skirt," Clair's father remembered, clicking the barrels of the Winchester shut so they lined up with the stock and shoulder rest. He stepped over to a large black rubber mat on the ground, faced Lake Michigan, and then called to a man who was manning the skeet launcher near the water's edge. "Ready, Eddie?"

"Yes, Mr. Sinclair," a young man waved back who was no older than Gus.

Sinclair took a shooting stance and then put his shotgun to his shoulder.

"Yeah, Clair can have a short fuse. No question about that. Pull!" he called.

Two clay pigeons sprang high into the air from Eddie's position and soared across the water. Taking his time, Sinclair blasted the first pigeon to bits and a moment later, the second one. The blasts from the shotgun echoed across the water as the tiny remnants of shattered clay scattered over the lake's surface.

"She probably gets that from me," he continued, opening the smoking barrels and shucking the shells. "You've got to watch that with her. She's got a hair-trigger temper."

Gus loaded his Greener. "Except for that one time, I haven't really seen that side of her." He closed the gun as his host stepped off the rubber mat and he stepped on.

"Just tell Eddie to pull whenever you're ready," Sinclair said, reloading his gun.

The younger man nodded then took a firing stance. "Pull!"

Two more pigeons soared into the blue sky over Lake Michigan. Gus pulled one trigger and then the other. Both pigeons continued on their flights unscathed. After firing, Gus quickly lowered the rifle, winced in pain and put a hand on his shoulder.

"Yeah, that Greener kicks like a mule, don't it?" Sinclair grinned.

He called over to Buck. "Get our guest a couple of bar towels for his shoulder, will ya?"

The bearded man smiled patronizingly at Gus and went into the clubhouse. As he did, Gus opened his shotgun and shucked his shells, although with some difficulty because of his now bruised shoulder.

"You picked a very powerful and expensive weapon," Sinclair noted. "It's a lot different than an old Remington. Gotta be careful when you reach for things that are beyond you."

"I'll keep being careful in mind," Gus smiled politely, knowing that Sinclair was talking about more than just guns.

"Good," the older man replied.

Gus stepped off the black rubber mat while Aaron took his place back on it.

"One reason why I wanted this chance to talk to you, Gus, is to let you know I have specific plans for Clair." He raised the shotgun to his shoulder. "Pull!"

Two more clay pigeons soared into the air. Four seconds later, the first pigeon was shattered followed soon after by the second.

"Good shot," Gus acknowledged. As he did, Buck came up behind him with two bar towels. He thanked him, placed them over his right shoulder, and then dropped fresh shells into his gun. "What plans are those?"

"For quite some time she's been seeing a young man named Derek Worthing," Sinclair explained, stepping off the mat and shucking his shells. "You know him?"

"We've met," Gus answered flatly.

"I've done business with his father for years. Now, Clair's a single woman and, understandably, enjoying her summer like any young person. But in the end, it's the wish of both her parents that she be with Derek."

Gus closed his gun. "So that's why I'm here? To be told you don't approve of me? What about Clair's wishes?"

The older man smiled. "Certainly you know Clair well enough by now to know she has her amusements. New clothes, new car...but the novelty eventually wears off and deep down inside she knows what's important for her future. I just—well—wouldn't want you to get hurt."

Gus took a moment to absorb Sinclair's words, then he stepped onto the rubber mat, took his firing stance and raised his shotgun.

"Pull!"

Two more clay pigeons streaked into the air. Taking his time, Gus fired, shattering the first pigeon, and then aimed for several moments and fired again. He hit the second one just inches before it plunged into the lake.

"That's better," he said, lowering the weapon. "The towels helped. I just needed to adjust my sights. Thanks." Sinclair cracked a faint smile as Gus stepped off the mat. "You're not very subtle, sir," he said, cracking open his gun.

Sinclair loaded his Winchester then closed it and stepped onto the mat. "I'm in the construction business, son. The men I work with aren't the world's most educated. I can't afford to be subtle. Pull!"

Two more pigeons sprung into the air. Sinclair raised his gun, blasted one pigeon and then shot and struck the other in neat and quick succession. Although the two men didn't realize it yet, a few other members of the club were now watching their shooting competition from the clubhouse behind them.

Sinclair stepped off the mat and cracked open his gun while Gus, now reloaded, closed his and stepped back onto the mat.

"So now what?" Gus asked. "You invited me out here to tell me your wishes. I've heard them. What happens next?"

"We shoot, you finish your beer, then you go home," the older man mused. "A wiser but gracious loser."

Gus took a firing stance. "Pull!"

Two more pigeons were hurled over the lake. Getting a bead on them, Gus fired, splintering one, then fired again disintegrating the other.

"But I haven't exactly lost, have I?" Gus observed. "I wouldn't be here unless you were concerned." While the younger man opened his gun and shucked his shells, the older one looked at him, half amused, half annoyed.

"You challenging me, son?"

Gus stepped off the rubber mat while Sinclair reloaded then closed his rifle.

"With all due respect, sir, I think Clair's old enough to decide things for herself. You may think she views me as some sort of summer fling, or amusement, or whatever, but I don't think so. And I sure don't view her that way."

The corners of Sinclair's mouth slid back with smugness. "Load three, Eddie," he called as he stepped onto the mat and poised his rifle. "You're not going to tell me after only two weeks this is 'love,' are you? Pull!"

Three pigeons soared into the air. Sinclair disposed of all three quickly, firing both barrels in rapid succession. As the older man opened his smoking barrels and stepped off the mat, Gus stood there, clearly impressed.

"That's, uh, wow..." he admired, then he returned to the matter at hand. "I don't know what I'd call it yet. But I'm not going to call it quits just because you say so." He looked at Eddie. "Three," he said.

"Wanna put it to a bet?" Sinclair asked. "If I miss first, you can keep on seeing her. If you miss first, you're done."

"You're missing the point," Gus answered. He loaded his gun then stepped onto the mat, "Even if I miss, Clair will still want to keep seeing me."

He turned to the skeet launcher. "Eddie, make it four."

Sinclair humphed, amused, then turned toward the clubhouse and noticed the members now gathered inside and watching them through the open glass-paneled doors.

Eddie waved that he was ready and Gus took his firing stance. "Pull!"

Four flung pigeons sailed across the water. Just like Sinclair had done a minute earlier, Gus took quick aim and fired in rapid succession. At first, he wasn't even sure that he had hit anything. But a second later, he heard the "ooos" and even applause from those inside the clubhouse.

Lowering his smoking Greener, he turned to his host. Pursed lips had now replaced the older man's smugness.

"Pretty good shooting," Sinclair admitted, although it clearly pained him to say so.

    Gus stepped off the mat, shucked his shells, and walked over to the table where Buck stood. He laid the open shotgun down, removed the bar towels from his shoulder and likewise put them on the table, then picked up his beer that was still sitting there.

    "It's northern Michigan, man," he said, turning and tipping his glass to his host. "Any schmuck with a gun can shoot." He took another sip of beer before setting his drink on the table. "Thank you for the invitation, sir." Then he turned and left.

9 First Night

It had been seven days since Farren had moved in with Doc at his rented cabin on the shores of Lake Charlevoix, and even though their schedules were opposite, when they did talk to each other, which was often by phone, they seemed to slip into having the same conversation over and over again.

It began with Farren asking for the umpteenth time if Doc thought she was in some sort of danger, and Doc would always reply no and assure her that her staying with him was merely a precaution. Then she'd ask if Doc and her grandfather knew something about Bartholomew that they weren't telling her, and again he'd say no. Then, she'd ask about the logic of why she was staying with him to break from her normal routine, but was still very predictably going to work every day? Then Doc would answer that there were always people around her at the marina and reiterate that staying with him was just a precaution. Next, she'd ask how long was she supposed to stay with him and he'd answer that he didn't know. Then, she would say something about how having an off-duty cop roam around in the woods at night near the cabin made her feel inhibited, and he'd suggest she pretend she was a rock star or royalty where security was simply a fact of life. Round and round they'd go because there were no definitive answers. There was only Gus and Doc having unconfirmed suspicions.

But there was a bright side to this nebulous scenario, too. Farren and Doc took to cohabitating and adjusting to each other's schedules very well. In the mornings, they'd sometimes pass and wave to each other on Boyne City Road as she drove her new blue VW Beetle to work and he was driving home in his red Jeep Wrangler with Gertrude. Always following behind Farren was one of the off-duty policemen that had been parked out in front of the cabin for the night. When Doc arrived home he'd find a note and a snack waiting for him.

By the time Farren arrived home—always with another off-duty cop following—it was usually 6:00 or 7:00 p.m. and Doc was already at work. Frequently, she'd find a fresh flower in a vase on the kitchen table and dinner warming in the oven, which she usually shared with her bodyguard. After dinner, she always did some sort of parish or community service work, calling people about an upcoming blood drive, organizing the next cleaning day at St. Ignatius, or chatting with Ellen Mitchell over the phone since visiting and reading to her had to be temporarily suspended. When Doc was at home and wasn't sleeping or doing laundry, he was taking his online classes for fireman certification. Their schedules were a bit grueling, but even after a week and despite having the same conversation several times, they knew one thing for sure: they liked sharing the same space. Gus had been right, living together prompted both of them to more seriously consider the other as a part of their future.

On the eighth day, both Doc and Farren had the day off, so they spent it quietly at the cabin sunning on the dock and reading. That night, they had dinner with Lance and his fiancé, Charlene at the Weathervane Restaurant. Lance and Charlene had befriended Doc when he first came to town and Charlene had even tried to hook Doc and Farren up for a blind date before Charlie came into her life, but it never happened. Lance was not only Doc's EMT day shift and James Bond sparring partner, he was also his closest friend in town. But Doc had to be careful what he said to Lance and Charlene because of their love of gossip. So he and Farren decided not to tell them about her staying at Doc's. They figured they'd probably find out sooner or later anyway but they didn't want to volunteer the information in the interim.

Lance and Charlene had dated since high school and were ideally suited to one another. She was twenty-nine—the same age as Farren—short, pudgy and had an exuberant personality. Charlene was the kind of woman who would coo and fuss over a high school friend becoming pregnant, then tell everyone in town about the birth date, sex, and baby registration. With her frosted blonde hair and big, puffy bangs, she looked like she came straight out of the '80s. And even though she was twenty-five pounds overweight, it was obvious that in her day she was a looker in a Snookie on *Jersey Shore* kind of way.

At six feet, Lance was the same height as Doc and but more overweight than his intended. He was an anchor to her bubbly personality. Also like Doc, he was a city employee in transition and wary about his future. On the weekends, he did the books at his parents' wine store. Charlene was the manager of a fudge store down on Bridge Street but occasionally also answered phones at her sister's nail salon. After a dozen years of dating, they were now just a little more than a week away from getting married.

The Weathervane was one of the better dining establishments in town and sat picturesquely on the Pine River. Diners could watch boats of every kind glide up and down in the river, or see the larger boats waiting for the drawbridge to open. Originally, the restaurant had been a gristmill.

Doc, Farren, Lance, and Charlene sat at a table overlooking the river seated across from one another. The men were dressed in casual dress shirts and slacks while both ladies wore light summer dresses.

"A toast to the bride and groom," Doc said, raising a glass of white wine. Everyone clinked glasses and drank while a Shawn Colvin song played on the Muzak system.

"Eh, since you're out in public, shouldn't Gertrude be with you?" Lance queried.

"She's in the Jeep," Doc answered. "I'm not going through the embarrassment of having her sit here at the table."

"If Stubigg finds out, there'll be hell to pay," Lance warned.

"I'll risk it. Besides, she always orders the most expensive thing on the menu," Doc deadpanned.

"And I don't like to share him," Farren chimed in. "So, where are you two going for your honeymoon?"

"London," Charlene smiled. "Neither one of us have ever been to Europe. The tickets were a gift from Lance's parents. And then we're going to spend some time in New York on the way back."

"You think there's a James Bond museum over there?" Lance asked.

"I wouldn't be surprised," Doc replied.

"I'm so excited!" Charlene gushed. "I've never traveled so far. We're going to take a tour of Buckingham Palace. You should see the outfit I bought for it."

"You can tour Buckingham Palace?" Farren asked.

"During certain months and only certain rooms, but yes."

"You bought a special outfit to tour that overgrown outhouse?" Lance asked.

"Why not?" Charlene countered. "You never know who you might run into."

"What? You think you're going to run into Prince William?"

"It could happen," Charlene replied. She turned to Doc. "You've done a lot of traveling, Doc. Ever been to London?"

"Nope," he answered, then he looked over at Farren. "How about you, hon?"

She shook her head. "I've only been in like five or six states."

"Well, maybe someday," Doc said. "You never know, things are always changing."

"I think there's a big one coming with me," Lance said.

"Oh, I guarantee it," Charlene answered, referring to the wedding.

"No, I didn't mean marriage, although that'll be great. I was talking about work."

"Oh, you're not going to start with that paranoid stuff again, are you?"

Doc asked. He looked at Farren to explain. "He doesn't think he's going to make it as a fireman. He thinks Stubigg's going to let him go."

"I did a stadium run yesterday," Lance explained, "where trainees run up and down the stairs at the high school stadium carrying a fire hose. I was huffing and puffing like I was ninety! Stubigg said I had the worst time of anyone in the department."

"So you're a little overweight," Doc shrugged, "you can fix that. I can workout with you if you want."

"I'm *forty pounds* overweight," Lance emphasized. "They let Morris go, remember?" He was referring to another heavy-set EMT who had been consolidated.

"Morris was about a *hundred* pounds overweight," Doc reminded him.

"The fire department already has plenty of EMTs, I'm not doing that well with the online tests...I just don't think Stubigg's gonna keep me."

"There's always your parents' idea," Charlene suggested.

"What's that?" Farren asked, taking another sip of wine.

"His folks have asked him about taking over their wine store. They're thinking of retiring."

"That could be cool," Doc said. "I mean, if you want to do it. You've been doing their books for years."

"It might be an option," Lance said. "I can see ways to expand the business. Sell some cheeses and crackers, maybe imported chocolates. But, I don't know. I'd miss ridin' with my partner," he said, referring to Doc. "I'd miss helping people."

"Providing a product that people enjoy is helping too," Charlene reminded.

"Well, if I can help with anything, either class stuff or working out, just let me know," Doc said.

"Thanks," Lance said. Then he changed thoughts. "Hey, what James Bond film holds the record for the most car flips ever filmed?"

"Casino Royale," Doc correctly answered.

Charlene rolled her eyes and looked at Farren. "If he makes me visit the grave of Ian Fleming while we're in England, I swear I'll divorce him."

Lance pretended to write a note to himself on a cocktail napkin with an imaginary pencil. "Cancel day trip to Swindon," he said, as if talking to himself.

"The fact that he even knows the town where Fleming is buried is pretty scary," Doc observed.

"So what about you two?" Charlene asked, bringing her wine glass to her lips. "Anything big on the horizon?"

"Pushy, pushy," Lance muttered under his breath.

Charlene took a sip of wine and gulped it down. "No, it's not," she defended. "I mean, everybody *knows* they're a couple. And Farren and I are the same age." She looked across the table at her friend. "Tick-tick-tick, girl."

"She's so subtle," Lance said, leaning into Doc. "Just like a nuclear bomb."

Doc put his elbow on the table, his chin in his hand, and gave Farren an amused look, curious to see how she was going to answer a question that he, himself, had no intention of answering.

"Uh, no big plans on the horizon," Farren smiled. "We're still kind of in the working-things-out-and-getting-to-know-each-other phase."

"What's there to work out?" Charlene persisted. "You guys are crazy about each other, right?"

"Well–" Farren said, turning a little red, "I'm awful glad he came along. He's been a savior in more ways than one."

"Yeah, but she snores," Doc fibbed. "And sleep walks. And steals things in her sleep. You know that old wheelbarrow that disappeared from the front of Harpers Antique Store?" He subtly jerked a thumb in Farren's direction.

"No, she didn't," Charlene smiled, brushing her big puff of bangs aside. "Everybody knows that smart-alecky Brewer kid took the wheelbarrow. It's just that neither BJ nor the guys at the police department have been able to..." and just like that, Doc had successfully deflected one of Charlene's famous interrogations. Farren recognized instantly what he had done and flashed him a little smile of gratitude.

After a wonderful dinner of wine, Caesar salads, and grilled seafood, the couples said their goodbyes and went their separate ways. Lance and Charlene walked through downtown the four blocks back to Lance's apartment, while Farren and Doc rode in his Wrangler over to the marina store to pick up the night deposit from one of the summer help and drop it off at the bank before they headed back to Doc's. This would actually be the first night both of them would be staying at the cabin together and Doc was anxious with anticipation, though it was a limited anticipation. Farren had been sleeping in the guest room next to his all week and he didn't truly expect there to be a deviation in routine just because they were going to be sleeping there at the same time. Still, he couldn't help but be hopeful.

The layout of Doc's rented cabin was small but efficient. Everybody entered from the back door opposite the lakeside entrance that led into a kitchen with pine cabinets that had glass-paneled doors, an "L" shaped Formica counter, overhead track lighting, and a small round wooden dining table with four chairs. Off the kitchen was a small laundry room with a stacked washer and dryer, and through the laundry room was an even smaller half bath.

The kitchen floor was linoleum, the rest of the cabin had wood floors. The living room featured a fieldstone fireplace to the left with an Elk's head mounted over it and two worn but comfortable leather sofas with corresponding end tables and lamps that faced each other in front of the fireplace. Beyond the stone of the fireplace was a writing desk and chair against the same wall. There was a rectangular area rug between the sofas that featured a Native American design, and sitting on the rug between the sofas was a wood-plank coffee table. When people sat on the sofas and looked one way, they saw the fireplace and Elk's head. If they looked the other, they saw a thirty-two inch flat screen TV on a stand with two doors on either side. The door to the right led into Doc's bedroom and the door on the left was a guest bedroom. The two bedrooms were connected by a Jack-and-Jill full bath.

The far side of the living room, opposite the entrance to the kitchen, had a writing desk against the same wall as the fireplace, then two curtained windows on the farthest wall with a side table in between them. On the right-hand side was also a door leading out to a screened-in concrete slab porch with wicker furniture that the windows overlooked. Beyond the porch was thirty yards of scruffy sea grass and weatherworn low-lying shrubbery that was too ornery to be killed off by the harsh northern Michigan winters. In the middle of it was a path that led to a nice man-made piece of beach. At the water's edge was the aluminum dock and the brisk but shallow water where Doc and Gus had chatted over a week ago.

Farren breezed into the kitchen with Doc following and laid her purse on the counter. It was about 9:45 and the sun would soon be completely down. Since Doc was there at the cabin with her this particular evening, he'd given the freelance cop who would usually be watching her the night off.

"A lovely evening," she said. "I'm not sure agreeing to drive over to Traverse City with Charlene to get lingerie for her honeymoon was a good decision, but I couldn't think of a gracious way to get out of it."

"Don't you like shopping for lingerie?" he asked.

"It's our busiest time of year at the marina," she explained, going into the living room and passing a locked glass gun cabinet on the wall opposite the kitchen. She turned on a lamp sitting on one of the end tables next to a leather sofa. "A trip to TC will take the better part of a day."

"Think of it this way, she could've asked her maid of honor, her sister, but she didn't. She asked you."

Farren shrugged and nodded, understanding that she should probably feel complimented. "I'm going to go get out of this dress. Be back in a few."

"Okay."

She walked through the living room and disappeared into the guest bedroom, closing the door behind her. Doc sunk his hands into his pants pockets and looked around, not knowing exactly what to do next in his own home. Should he turn on the TV? Turn on some romantic music and light some candles? Should he make some coffee and invite Farren to sit on the front porch and enjoy the evening? He usually felt very comfortable around her, but tonight was different. Tonight they were going to be sleeping under the same roof at the same time and he didn't want to do anything that would make her feel inhibited or be interpreted that he was being pushy about sex. On the other hand, he wanted things to move forward and, being a man, sex was never far from his mind. There was also the underlying current of celestial strangeness to the situation. Farren was now living with him, just like her twenty-five-year-old grandmother had done six months earlier. They were both sitting on the same furniture, eating off the same dishes, using the same bathroom. And yet, Clair had been deceased for over half-a-century and nearly thirty years before Farren was even born.

"This is so weird," he whispered under his breath. "What am I supposed to do Clair?" he asked. "Are you watching this? Do you know how much I want your granddaughter? Did you know about the emotional scars Charlie was going to leave behind?" He breathed out a heavy breath as his eyes almost instinctively glanced toward the ceiling. "I probably shouldn't even be talking to you, huh? I should be talking to God. And I *have*, I mean, I've asked for patience and understanding about what she's going through. But you're the only dead person I've ever met, so...it's just—since you were sent here once before—I'm assuming you can still intercede on her behalf. I don't want to screw things up with her, y'know? I want her—both of us—to be happy. I'm not even sure I'm supposed to *be* with her romantically. I mean, maybe I was just supposed to help her but not actually wind up with her, y'know?"

He continued glancing around at the ceiling. "Feel free to hop in anytime here. Any. Time."

He was interrupted by Farren emerging from the bedroom wearing a T-shirt and cut-offs. She hadn't bothered to comb her hair and her now shaggy pixie cut was spiky, giving her a bedhead but sexy look.

"I'm going to go swimming in a few after the sun goes completely down. Wanna go for a dip?"

"Actually, I think I'll pass. It's still a little cold for me. But I'll make some coffee or build a fire while you're swimming if you like."

"You don't get out on the water much, do you?" she asked.

"It's not that I don't like the water. Maybe it's because the last time I was in it, I was almost a 'Docsickel.'"

He was referring to a night the previous December when Charlie had tried to kill Farren and, after the attempt failed, both he and Charlie wound up in icy waters of Round Lake. Charlie drowned and Doc would have too had Clair not saved him. And even then, he was hospitalized for two days.

"We're going to have to do something about that," she said.

"Usually, when I'm home in the evenings, I jog down the lane to the road. It's close to a quarter mile, so if I do it four times, it's about a mile. I'm actually getting pretty good at navigating the potholes in the dark."

She looked around the cabin a little and then at him. "It's kind of odd isn't it—both of us being here at the same time, huh? I mean, it's *nice*, but strange that after a full week, this is our first evening together. So what would you like to do? What would you like to talk about?"

He jingled the change in his pockets a little. "You're not going to ask me if your grandfather and I know something about Bartholomew that you don't, are you?"

"No," she smiled faintly. "I've prayed about it and put it all in God's hands. Speaking of which, can I ask you something?"

"Anything."

"Since Charlie's been gone, you've done quite a transformation about going to church. Don't get me wrong, I'm glad about it. But I hope it's not just to appease me."

He nodded. "I can see why you'd ask that. And I don't deny you're a part of the reason. But, no, there's more to it for me."

She smiled again, came over, and gave him a quick kiss. "Good, I'm glad."

He wrapped his arms around her waist. "I know you've got to feel funny about all this. But we'll get your life back to normal again soon. I promise." He leaned in to give her a more serious kiss but she pulled back and put her hand on his chest.

"Uh, before we start something that I can't finish, why don't you change into your jogging clothes, get your run in, and I'll go swimming."

He thought for a moment. "I'm not sure it's wise for you to go swimming alone."

"What? You worried about the treacherous Giant Muskie of Lake Charlevoix?" she joked. "Actually, I'd *like* some time alone. I feel like I've been living under a microscope with cops following me to work, following me back here, hanging around all night..."

"I understand," he agreed. "Okay. I'm going to go change." He headed for his bedroom while she headed for the bathroom to get a beach towel.

"Use bug spray," she reminded him. "The mosquitoes in these woods are the size of Buicks."

"I always do," he answered.

As he changed, the more Doc thought about Farren swimming alone, the more he wondered if it was a good idea. True, there wasn't really anything in the lake that could harm her, but the whole point of her staying with him was so she wouldn't be alone, and here he was, about to leave her alone. On the other hand, she did express a wish for some private time, so he decided to split the difference. He decided to watch her while she swam, but not have her be aware of it.

After he had changed, he went through the cabin and out the kitchen door opposite the lake side. Then, instead of jogging down the lane, he veered off to the left and went into a stand of trees about thirty yards wide that separated his place from his next-door neighbors. This particular piece of woods was much thicker than the usually more open white pine forest on either side of the lane because there were no pines near the shoreline and they usually prevented undergrowth.

Since it was nearly dark, he stepped on and broke a few small branches, and then shuffled through some leaves, causing some noise. But as his eyes adjusted to the evening, he moved more slowly and stealthy toward the water's edge. When he finally pushed the last maple branch aside, making sure he was still partially concealed by some wild raspberry bushes, he couldn't believe what he saw.

Twenty degrees to his left, Farren was wading out into the dark water completely naked. There was just enough orange-red light in the sky for him to see that her beach towel, shorts, T-shirt, and bikini—which she must've been wearing under the shorts and T-shirt—were lying in a heap on the pale silver end of the aluminum dock. And because the water was so shallow for several yards, her descent into it was slow and lingering.

"What the hell is she *doing?*" he whispered to himself, knowing that if he could see her, so could his neighbors. He turned and looked as best he could through the woods at the house to his right. Luckily, it seemed to be dark, meaning the owners were either already in bed or out for the evening. Then he looked to his left at his neighbors on the other side. It seemed to be dark as well. He concluded that between the houses being dark and the distance they were from his dock, plus the fact that night was quickly falling, Farren must've figured she had this portion of the lake all to herself. He could see the red and green lights of a boat off in the distance, but Lake Charlevoix was so big, it was nearly a half-mile away.

Turning his eyes back to her, he became spellbound by the beauty and eroticism of what he was witnessing. Farren was out in the lake far enough where the water was just over her knees. Her tanned skin was as smooth and clear as the water she was moving through. Her hands were in the water and her fingers were slightly open, feeling the liquid pass between them. Her arms were also slightly extended and, since she was slender to begin with, her shoulder blades were clearly pronounced and looked almost like small angel wings folded into her skin. Her butt was chalk white from where the skin hadn't tanned because of her cut-offs. It was narrow, firm and well-rounded as the dark water slowly lapped to the base of her cheeks to meet it. As he watched it disappear inch-by-inch into the water with each slow, progressing step, he could likewise feel his jaw slowly dropping. Once or twice during the past six months, he'd wondered if Farren with the few freckles on her nose, short hair, church-going ways and goody-two-shoes attitude toward others was even capable of being a sensual temptress of a woman. But as he now watched—even in near darkness—such thoughts were obliterated. He hadn't even seen her naked up close, or a front view of her, but he already wanted this woman to have his children. He wanted it so much that he actually physically ached.

"God," he uttered under his breath, "*nice* work!"

It was the most sincere prayer he had ever said.

10 Mileage

That night, Doc didn't run a mile up and down the lane leading to the county road—he ran three.

11 The Challenge

Even in 1954, the 1932 Ford Roadster Coupe was already considered the definitive hot rod, and it also happened to be the car Derek Worthing drove. It was a stripped down convertible, midnight black with wider wheels in back than it had in front and round chrome hubcaps. It also had a flathead V8 under the hood that could blow most other cars off the road.

It was a humid Friday night and Derek was parked at the Dog 'N' Suds Car Hop surrounded by three other guys who were standing in the parking lot talking to him while he sat behind the wheel of his Deuce Coupe. As usual, Derek's black hair was pelted down with hair cream like he was going to his grandma's for Easter dinner. He was taller and thicker than Gus, so button-down shirts sat snuggly on him and made him look intimidating.

While Derek and his buddies chatted and passed around Derek's silver whiskey flask, waitresses in sleeveless white blouses and short, satin rust-colored skirts with white lace aprons tied around their waists hurried here and there delivering burgers, hot dogs, and foamy glass mugs of root beer. The food sat on trays that fit snuggly into the rolled down windows of the cars parked in the lot. Since the guys were all in their twenties, still hanging out at the same drive-in they did when they were in high school was maybe a little sophomoric. But then again, choices where the locals could hang out and avoid the tourist trade were limited in Charlevoix, especially in the 1950s and in the middle of a recession.

When Gus and Clair pulled into the parking lot in Gus' '47 Chevy pickup, one of Derek's pals standing in the lot noticed them immediately. It had been about a month since Gus had come to Clair's rescue on Michigan Beach, and although Clair was following her father's advice and was still seeing Derek, it was occasional. She'd only seen him four times in the past month as opposed to nearly every other day with Gus.

"Hey Derek, ain't that your girl over there?" asked the buddy who had spotted them.

"Sure don't look like his girl anymore," a second friend observed.

"Ooo, looks like a fox has gotten into the henhouse," a third chided.

A slow burn of anger crept across Derek's face as he took a quick sip from his flask and glared at Clair and Gus. He noticed that she was sitting in the middle of the cab's bench-style seat to be closer to the driver. They pulled into a parking space where there was a menu bolted onto a pole. Jo Stafford sang "Make Love To Me" on the outdoor speakers coming from the restaurant while the two engaged in conversation, oblivious to the gallery watching them.

"So why won't you tell me about what happened with my dad at the Shooting Club?" Clair asked in the middle of an interrogation. She was wearing a nice light brown summer dress with a cream-colored flower print on it.

"Ancient history," Gus said, perusing the menu on the pole. Like Derek, he was also wearing a button-down shirt and jeans. "That was, like, two weeks ago."

"But you haven't said anything about it," she reminded him.

"Ask your dad," he suggested.

"I *have*. All he said was that you guys met, had a beer, and he got to know you a little better."

"Well, that's pretty much what happened," Gus replied. He had decided some time ago he wasn't going to tell Clair about what had really transpired. All that would do was pit him against her father and put Clair in the middle, and he didn't want to do that. For being only twenty-one, Gus Cooper knew how to play chess.

"Details, boy! I want details!" she insisted, half joking, half serious.

"I can't," he answered solemnly. "It's a man thing."

"Man thing?"

"A sacred bond. Goes back centuries. We don't show pain, eat vegetables or discuss what goes on in a 'Gentlemen Only' club with women."

She squinted at him disapprovingly.

"Okay, I might be lying about the vegetable thing," he admitted.

She continued to squint, not liking his lack of cooperation.

"Why is this such a big deal to you?" he asked. "You're looking for something really unsensational. We met, we drank, we talked, and he said he was glad I came. What else am I supposed to say?"

She relaxed her face a little, beginning to believe him. "It's just — my father's never asked for a private meeting with one of my beaus before. He can be pretty authoritative sometimes. Intimidating and cagey all at once."

"I didn't sense any caginess in our conversation. I understood perfectly what he was saying."

A waitress who called everybody "toots" came over and asked if they were ready to order. Gus ordered some chili fries and a root beer. Clair decided on a chocolate malt.

"I know why this is so important to you," he said after the waitress was gone. "You want your dad's approval 'cause you're really startin' to fall for me."

"You think?" she said. She leaned over and playfully flicked the wave of hair dangling over his forehead. "What an incredibly arrogant presumption," she proclaimed, but not very convincingly.

"Problem is," he conceded, "I don't have the kind of bank account that would impress a father. At least, not yours."

"Ohhh, that's not important to me," she dismissed.

"It should be though," he said seriously. "Look, Clair, every time we're together, I fall a little deeper for you. It's like I'm in 'Clair quicksand.' One of these days, I'm not going to be able to climb out. I'm going to make a fool of myself and say that I can't live without you — or, some such thing — and you're going to have to think about what that means, what I bring to the table. I'm a guy who's good with engines, likes Shakespeare, and aspires to teach in a high school. Maybe college. That's a lot different than Corvettes, expensive poodle skirts, a big house on a hill, and shooting clubs. But that's the package. That's all I'm ever gonna be. You gotta think about that."

"I don't live on a hill," she corrected.

"You get my point, though."

"Yes," she said. "I get your point."

"Look, I know you see this other guy, sometimes, this Derek Worthing. He's not a better man, but he's got better circumstances. You should maybe, maybe think about that, before..."

"Before what?" she asked softly.

"Before I'm totally screwed here," he laughed, but clearly fearful for his heart.

She leaned back in the front seat, genuinely interested in his feelings and point of view. The Jo Stafford song ended and "Little Things Mean A Lot" by Kitty Kallen began to play over the drive-in's speakers.

"Gus, we've known each other for about a month. How could you possibly feel the way you say you do so fast? I mean, I'm in a little quicksand here myself, but—"

"It's not your looks," he cut in. "I mean, it *is*—you're incredibly beautiful—but it's also your spirit. Your intelligence. Your desire to have your own career despite the silver spoon. It's your self-deprecating honesty that says, 'Yeah, I know I can be a princess,' that makes you anything but," he paused and looked at her. "It's chemistry, Clair. I know it sounds stupid but my heart beats stronger and the world seems better when you're by my side."

She looked deeply into his brown eyes, moved by his conviction.

"It's not stupid," she half whispered putting her open palm on his cheek. "It's not stupid."

Nearly forty-eight hours later, at 10:00 p.m., Gus was working late at Stu and Ernie's. He was in Service Bay One with his nose buried in the engine of a Dodge station wagon that had a work light hanging from the lip of the open hood. His boss, Stu Franklin, shut the front door of the office and flicked a switch on the wall, turning off the pole sign outside as well as the white globes that sat on top of the gas pumps with Pegasus on them. Stu was in his late thirties, a little overweight from too many beers and bags of potato chips, and had seen a lot of action during World War II, particularly on the island of Midway.

"That's it for me," he called, poking his head through the doorway that led from the office into the service bays. "We're buttoned up for the night."

"Okay," Gus called, still working under the hood.

"Thanks for staying late, Gus."

"Mrs. McCoy's got three little kids and no husband. She's needs her car."

"You want me to hang?"

"Naw, I'm almost finished."

"You're a good man. Okay, see ya tomorrow."

"'Night."

Within another twenty minutes, Gus had finished with the car, washed his hands, and had gone out the front door of the station. Checking the door to make sure it was locked, he unzipped his dirty brown overalls a few inches to cool off, then turned and headed for his pickup parked at the far end of Stu and Ernie's property.

He noticed Derek Worthing standing in the lot, leaning with his back against the hood of Gus' Chevy and holding something in his hands. As Gus came closer, he saw it was a baseball bat.

Just about the time he was going to ask what Derek wanted—although he had a pretty good idea already—he heard movement behind him. He turned to see two of Derek's buddies coming out of the night shadows. These were two of the three guys that had been with Derek at the Dog 'N' Suds.

Then, he spotted another one coming from across the street and yet another one approaching from behind the station to his left. This was the shorter friend who had been with Derek that one day at Michigan Beach. He was totally surrounded.

Derek's four friends kept walking until they were all about seven feet away with Gus in the middle.

"You boys looking to start a little league team?" he asked, knowing better.

"You stop seeing her tonight," Derek announced, pushing himself off the hood of Gus' truck. He took his baseball bat, turned to the truck, then took a powerful swing and smashed the left front headlight.

"*Hey!*" Gus called angrily. He bolted after Derek but was soon restrained by one guy coming up from behind and grabbing an arm, then another quickly grabbing the other. Meanwhile, the other two closed in until they were only intimidating inches away and Gus. Still lurching forward, he could feel their alcohol breath on his face.

"You'll never see her again," Derek said, calm and in full control. "'Cause if you *do*—" he turned and took another expert swing at the truck. With an explosion of glass, the right headlight was now destroyed. "It'll be more than headlights that get broken. It'll be your knee caps!"

"What are you, like, twelve?" Gus yelled, still pulling against the other two guys holding him back. "Is this how the big men on campus settle things?"

Derek slowly walked over to the greasy mechanic. "There's nothing to settle, Cooper. Clair is my property. My personal piece of ass. If you see her again, talk to her again, even put gas in her car, I'll kill ya."

Gus looked at his rival with steely eyes. "Big words from an asshole with four friends and a baseball bat. C'mon, Derek, you wanna play? Put the bat down, tell your friends to back off, face me like a man and let's play!"

Derek smiled smugly, then looked at his surrounding friends. He could see that they thought Gus' proposal was reasonable. But he didn't want to be reasonable. Even though he was taller and had twenty pounds on Gus, the mechanic might still beat him in a fistfight. So he formulated another idea.

"You a betting man, Grease Monkey?" he asked.

"Only about your limited future."

Derek smiled again, knowing Gus was going to run the gauntlet he was about to propose.

"You were just asking if this is how college men settle things, and the answer is no. Not if the gentlemen are men of their word." He looked at the two guys holding him. "Let him go, boys," he ordered.

The two guys on either side loosened their grips and Gus jerked his arms free.

"I propose a contest of courage, strength and skill," Derek said. "I propose we jump the Memorial Bridge. First one into the water gets Clair, the loser backs off."

Derek's four friends looked at one another with slightly opened mouths, realizing what he was suggesting. But Gus didn't get it.

"What're you talking about? Jumping from the drawbridge into the Pine River?" This didn't make much sense to him, since that was only about a 14-foot jump.

"That's exactly what I'm proposing. But see, we jump off the edge of the bridge *as it's rising*. At night, say, after it's higher than a 30-degree angle."

"What?"

"We jump when the two halves are separating and opening. When the two halves are higher than 30-degrees, we run past the posts that close off the street traffic, run up the same half of the bridge as it's rising, climb over the edge and drop into the water. Easy as pie! First one to hit the water wins Clair."

Now that Derek had described it, Gus recalled how two summers earlier, two other young men had tried to do the same thing at night. One of them succeeded, escaped the authorities and was never identified. But the other, a boy named Tommy Boil, was killed when he got to the edge of the bridge, lost his nerve, and hesitated to jump. He tried to hang on by locking his fingers into the steel mesh roadway, but as the leaf rose higher and higher, he couldn't keep his grip. He fell backward down the length of the raised leaf and into the bridge's massive counterweight pit. The locals still called it both the most outrageous and dangerous of youthful stunts. Anybody in any town could scale the local water tower and paint graffiti on it. But to scale then jump off the edge of a rising drawbridge in the dark? That was something unique.

Gus noticed the way Derek's buddies were smiling and figured out instantly who the unknown youth was from two summers earlier. He also had a better understanding of why Clair's father liked him. Besides their socioeconomic status, both men had reduced Clair's future—a future neither one actually controlled—to a bet.

"Are you insane?" Gus asked. "Th-that's *crazy!*"

"Oh, so you're conceding then, right?" Derek verified, using the bat as a pointer to everyone there. "In front of all these witnesses. You're giving up Clair now because you're too chicken."

"Why don't we just let Clair decide—"

"Why don't you just shut up!" Derek interrupted. He lurched forward and thrust the head of the bat into Gus' stomach, sucker-punching him. Gus painfully doubled over and dropped to his knees. Derek leaned over him and spoke quietly, but still loud enough so everyone else could hear.

"You do this, Grease Monkey, or me and my friends will catch you alone at night again and again and again. You do this, or maybe we'll catch your pop one night. Or your mom. You do this, or I swear to God you'll be looking over your shoulder for the rest of your life."

Just at that moment, a car on the street in front of Stu and Ernie's rolled to a stop. The driver, a man in his sixties, yelled through his open window at the gang of youths.

"Hey, what're you kids doing there!"

"Move along, Grandpa!" Derek yelled. He walked determinedly over to the stopped car raising his bat until the driver sped away. Then, while his friends were laughing, he turned and walked back to Gus' truck, losing his patience and self-control.

"Say yes, Grease Monkey!" he ordered, taking a swing at and then destroying the driver's side-view mirror.

Gus tried to climb to his feet, but as he was rising, one of Derek's buddies slammed a right jab into his cheek that sent him back to his knees.

"Say yes!" Derek ordered again. He took another swing at the truck. This time, the bat landed squarely on the front windshield,

sending a spider web of cracks in all directions.

"Yes!" Gus moaned, figuring he couldn't afford any more damage to his truck. *"Yes!"*

Derek smiled at his friends. "You're all witnesses. Grease Monkey here has agreed to my challenge to jump the drawbridge. If he doesn't, he loses Clair. If he does the jump but loses the race, he loses Clair. If he wiggles out of any part of this deal, if he goes to the cops—"

"Just tell me where and when?" Gus spat out between gritted teeth, trying to climb to his feet again.

"Tomorrow night, under the bridge. Meet me there at 11:15."

Gus nodded.

"And, ah, Grease Monkey, better wear dark clothes," Derek suggested, flashing an evil smile.

12 Lioness

Behind the Portside Marina store was a large red aluminum rectangular storage barn that was one hundred feet long, forty feet wide and thirty feet high. It had two large airplane hangar-like doors that slid open on tracks and was where many of the marina's customers stored their boats in winter. Its large doors were usually kept open during summer business hours since Farren, Gus, or any one of their seasonal help could be in and out of there numerous times during the day.

The back wall consisted of storage cages stacked on top of one another in pairs with rubber wheels lining the bottoms and sides so boats of up to fifteen feet in length could be slid in and out of them by a forklift with long rubber-sheathed arms.

The barn also featured a lighted workbench area where engines could be torn down and a detail area where boats could be cleaned, buffed, or varnished. The detail area included portable lights on tripods, shelves of paint, sanding masks, electric buffers, and lacquer thinner. There were also some sealed fifty-gallon barrels of used engine oil sitting against the wall awaiting eco-friendly disposal.

Throughout the barn were miscellaneous empty boat trailers positioned here and there just waiting until the cooler weather rolled in and they were needed to be rolled out.

The building was very much the nuts and bolts side of the marine world, and it was Farren's favorite place. Like her grandfather, she enjoyed tinkering with engines and didn't mind getting her hands dirty.

Charlene came down the gravel lane leading into the marina's parking lot going much too fast in her Hyundai, her tires sending little pieces of rock flying haphazardly everywhere. Screeching to a stop outside of the barn, she burst out of the car calling for Farren. When she heard her respond, she turned and followed her voice, running through the barn's large open doors.

"Over here, Charlene," Farren called, standing on a step stool at the back of a Pro Line center council fishing boat that had its engine cowling removed. She was in the middle of unclogging a fuel line with greasy hands when she heard Charlene's feet skittering toward her on the concrete floor.

"Got your message," she said, still working on the motor. "So what's so urg—" She looked up from her work and stopped because Charlene was wearing a bright yellow rain slicker with the hood pulled over her head. It was the same type of coat a fisherman might wear in foul weather.

"Is it raining outside?" she asked, turning her eyes toward the barn's open doors and the beautiful late afternoon.

Charlene lowered the yellow hood teary eyed. Her normally straight, highlighted blonde hair was now platinum white and very curly. She looked like a plump version of Shirley Temple with mascara running down her cheeks.

"Oh my Lord!" Farren gawked, nearly losing her footing on the stool. "What happened?"

"I was perming my hair for the wedding—just giving it a little oomph—when Sharon McCormick called. She had all the inside scoop on that trailer trash Bo Dupree's been seeing on the side. Do you know she's only twenty-two but has already been divorced twice? Twenty-two! Not only that, but if she's twenty-two, that makes her thirteen years younger than Bo! And Carrie Sue still doesn't know a thing about it. Half the town knows Bo's got the moral backbone of a sponge, but she—"

"*Charlene?*" Farren interrupted.

"Well—that's *exactly* what happened. I got so caught up in what

Sharon was saying, I forgot I had the solution and curlers on my head." She looked at her friend as her lip started to tremble from being so distraught. "What am I going to do, Farren? I'm days away from my wedding and I look like an albino poodle!"

Farren wiped her hands on a rag resting on the back of the boat and stepped off the stool. "C'mon, honey. We've got to get you to a hair salon fast!"

Forty minutes later, Charlene was sitting in a swivel chair at New Creations Hair Design down on Bridge Street staring at herself in a mirror with an open mouth. Her hair that used to lay over her shoulders with big bangs was now a short pixie cut like Farren's used to be before she decided to grow hers out. Charlene's chopped hair and exposed ears made her already youthful face appear even younger.

"I look like a twelve-year-old boy with C cups," she moaned. "And ten pounds heavier too!"

Unfortunately, she was right. The shorter hair drew more attention to her pudgy figure.

"It had to be done," Simone, the hair stylist, said, standing behind her and addressing her in the mirror. "You committed first-degree hair murder."

"Shorter hair's really comfortable," Farren added, standing next to Simone and trying to put the best spin on it possible. "It's cool in the hot weather and you don't have to curl or straighten it. Just run a comb through it and go."

"My lioness locks," Charlene lamented, still distraught.

"Your what?" Simone asked.

"That's what Lance calls them. I'll be a lioness going on her honeymoon without her locks."

Farren and Simone glanced at one another. Then Farren looked at Charlene in the mirror and smiled supportively. "It'll be okay."

"Maybe you could wear a nice wig for the wedding," Simone suggested.

"No," Farren disagreed. "Lance loves you for *you*. The hair will grow back."

Charlene looked at herself tentatively in the mirror, and then raised her right hand from under her barber's smock like a claw. She did a low growl, tossing her head seductively as if some long, unruly, imaginary hair would spill across her face.

"No," she sighed, depressed. "It's not going to be the same."

Simone and Farren glanced at one another again, concerned for their friend, but also amused.

13 The Bridge

The Memorial Bridge got its name from the twenty-two Charlevoix area servicemen who died in World War II. Construction began in May 1947, and the bridge was dedicated in July 1949. It was a bascule-type bridge, and each of its two halves, or "leaves," were forty-five feet long and consisted of a see-through steel mesh roadway, which made a distinct hollow sound when cars drove over it like a sudden whirlwind that would start, then abruptly stop, then start again as the next car drove over the bridge. Steel girders painted a bluish-green framed the structure and gave it an attractive under arch.

The bridge raised and lowered through a series of weights and counterweights that were situated in deep, concrete-walled pits at both ends. Electric motors, operated by a bridge keeper in a control house at the bridge's north end, powered these weights. When the leaves were completely open, it was a sixty-foot drop into the ninety-foot-wide Pine River.

The bridge operated from 6:00 a.m. to 11:30 p.m. for boats wanting access into Round Lake and Lake Charlevoix from one way or Lake Michigan in the other direction.

On one of the sidewalks paralleling the river, Gus stood in the shadows underneath the bridge waiting for Derek Worthing. Although he had no way of knowing it, he stood not very far from the spot where his granddaughter would meet her boyfriend for dinner in future decades. But on this particular summer night in 1954, he wasn't thinking about grandchildren or even children for that matter. The only future he was interested in was his own and surviving the night.

He couldn't believe he had agreed to such an idiotic challenge. He wasn't even completely convinced that running and jumping off a rising drawbridge could be successfully done. There were too many variables. He looked up at the iron girders supporting the mesh leaves. They looked like the mouth of a monster, a monster that roared momentarily to life every time a car passed above. Then he looked down at the river. It was black, foreboding, and deep. Ninety feet across looked like a pretty wide stretch of water from the ground level, but it probably only looked like a stream that got continually smaller from a piece of roadway that was reaching for the open sky.

What if he got over the edge of the leaf but fell onto the undercarriage girders? If he were knocked unconscious, nobody would ever find him in that inky water. What if he couldn't bring himself to go over the edge? Then he'd clutch onto the mesh roadway until he eventually tumbled back down the rising leaf into the counterweight pit and to certain death like Tommy Boil did. Or, if he and Derek were spotted by the bridge keeper, the keeper could also just start to lower the bridge as he and Derek were racing out to its edges. If either tried to go over the edge in this scenario, one or the other could be crushed by the leaves coming together. Then there was just the plain and simple risk of being arrested. After Tommy Boil's death from a couple of years earlier, the cops weren't likely to have a sense of humor about this.

"Well, I gotta give you credit for having the guts to show up," Derek said, walking toward him. He was wearing black slacks, a long-sleeve lightweight black jacket, and black tennis shoes. As usual, his hair was stiff and shiny. He eyed Gus who was likewise wearing a black T-shirt, blue jeans, and navy blue tennis shoes.

"Why are we wearing dark clothing again?" Gus asked.

"Makes you harder to spot in the water from searchlights if the cops show up."

"Oh."

Derek reached into his jacket pocket and pulled out a can of Kiwi Black Shoe Polish. "Here. Put some of this on your face," he instructed.

"Because...?"

"Makes you harder to recognize. Geez, Cooper. Don't you know anything?"

"About being an overgrown juvenile delinquent? No, I guess I don't." He opened up the can of shoe polish and started to apply it on his forehead.

"You do this kind of thing a lot?"

"I don't know what you're talkin' about," Derek said, likewise taking a large dab for his face.

"What about that kid who died a couple of years ago," Gus asked. "Friend of yours?"

"I don't know nothin' about that," Derek repeated, smearing the polish over his cheeks.

"So this idea just sort of 'came' to you, huh? Why couldn't we simply duke it out like everybody else does?"

"'Cause you might've beaten me," Derek admitted honestly. "But you won't beat me at this."

Gus finished applying the polish to his face while another couple of cars crossed the bridge above. He looked up and down the river. There wasn't a soul in sight.

"Look, how do we even know the bridge is gonna open?" he argued. "We need a big boat. It's 11:20 at night. I mean, if there isn't a big enough boat in the riv..." his voice trailed off as he heard the low putter of an outboard motor and saw the shadow of a tall, two-mast wooden sailboat glide from Lake Michigan, past the breakwater and automated lighthouse, and into the river.

"Right on time," Derek smiled.

"Friends of yours?" Gus asked.

Derek put another dab of shoe polish under his chin to complete the Al Jolson effect, then tucked the Kiwi can into a pocket. "C'mon, Grease Monkey." He started walking to the stairs that would take them up to street level.

"No matter what, we don't rat on each other," Derek instructed in a whisper. "Understood?"

"Agreed," Gus said.

"You take off down that bridge before I tell you to, you forfeit."

As they quietly climbed the stairs, Gus thought of something. "What if we start running down the bridge, but the bridge keeper sees us and just starts to lower it again?"

Derek shook his head. "He won't be expecting us. It's the last opening of the night, he's been on duty for hours, he'll be tired and his reactions will be slow. It'll be fine."

Gus looked at his opponent with calculation as their heads poked just above the street level near the top of the stairs. Derek crouched down and waited, so Gus did the same. "You've thought of everything, haven't you?"

"Like I said, Grease Monkey, you won't beat me at this. My buddies on the sailboat will have a bird's-eye view of who hits the water first. And just in case it's close, they know I'm wearing long sleeves."

"Oh, I thought they'd recognize you from the louder splash of your ego," Gus quipped.

"Shh," Derek said. "Get ready."

Through the window of the small controller's house, which was only an eight-by-five-foot concrete structure, the bridge keeper saw the sailboat slowing to an idle in the river about where there was a gristmill sitting off shore on the port side. Hitting a switch on a control panel inside the house, the bing-bing-bing of a railroad-crossing bell went off. Seconds later, thick steel posts that sat flush in the street just before the bridge began to rise up, keeping vehicles from going any further.

"Not yet...not yet," Derek advised, whispering to Gus.

With a whine then a loud clank, the two forty-five-foot wire mesh leaves of the bridge began to rise and separate. Derek, still crouched next to Gus, raised his arm and counted down their takeoff: "Three, two, one, *go!*"

Both young men sprang from the shadows near the top of the stairs and bolted past the raised steel posts and onto the rising half of the bridge, which was like running up a hill that increased in steepness with every step.

As Derek suspected, the bridge keeper was preoccupied and looking in a mirror so he could watch for any oncoming traffic behind him coming down Bridge Street, completely oblivious to what was taking place in front of him.

Being larger and having more muscular legs, probably from his years playing baseball, Derek reached the rising edge of the bridge first and swung his legs sideways over some large iron teeth that connected the two leaves together when the bridge was lowered. They were surprisingly smooth for such a mammoth moving structure, except for one tiny three-quarter-of-an-inch spur of iron. It was an imperfection in the casting, and although it was nothing that would've interfered with the operation of the bridge, it was just large and sharp enough to catch the cuff of Derek's black jacket as he swung himself over the edge. With a sudden jerk, Derek Worthing was now caught on the edge of a continually rising bridge being lifted higher and higher above a black river that was getting smaller and smaller.

Gus, only a couple of seconds behind Derek, hesitated a little before hurling himself over the edge. In that moment of hesitation, he heard the struggling grunts of Derek in between the clanging bridge bells and had the presence of mind to climb over the side, but hang onto the edge to see what had gone wrong. Within three seconds, he saw his rival dangling helplessly by the cuff of his jacket, although he didn't know what had caught him because of the darkness.

Since they were rising at a rate of about five feet per second, there wasn't any time to think, just act. Using the smooth iron teeth like monkey bars, Gus went hand-over-hand to get to Derek.

"My sleeve is caught!" Derek cried between gritted teeth, his muscles literally tearing from his own hanging weight. Gus reached over and with one powerful tug, freed his competitor. Derek tumbled head over heels out of control and hit the water with a loud splash.

With the leaves still rising, Gus waited a few more seconds until he could see where Derek had landed, and then pushed himself off the undercarriage, keeping his arms close to his side pencil-style to avoid striking him. Derek's fall into the water was from a height of about thirty feet. Gus' was from a height closer to forty.

Gus' body went deep into the river and he worried for a moment he was ever going to stop descending. When he finally broke the water's surface, and after gasping for air, he surveyed the scene.

He saw Derek had landed badly in the water. He didn't know how, but his competitor had cut his forehead and blood was pouring down his blackened face and running along both sides of his nose. His left arm, the one that had been caught, seemed immobile. He was conscious, but just barely. Fearing he'd drown, Gus swam over to Derek and grabbed him under the armpits, like he had done to Clair. He pulled him over to a wall of wood pilings lining the side of the river. The pilings were lashed together five at a time by bands of steel just above the water line. Derek was lucid enough to grab onto one of these bands with his right hand.

"Need some help here!" Gus yelled to the people on the sailboat.

Two of Derek's friends who had been with him the night Derek caught up with Gus at Stu and Ernie's stood on the prow of the boat and peered into the river, trying to determine exactly where the call for help had come from. Meanwhile, the bridge keeper had by now realized something was wrong because the sailboat wasn't moving. He came out of the control house and was crossing Bridge Street to call out to the boat from the top of the stairs that led to the riverside sidewalk below.

"Get out of here," Derek moaned to Gus, weak and exhausted. "My friends will pull me out of the drink."

"You're really hurt, man." Gus said, water beading on his black face from the shoe polish.

"My goose is cooked," Derek said. "Save yourself. You wanna go to jail?"

"Derek!" one his buddies yelled from the sailboat above the still clanging bells. He now saw the two dark figures clinging to the wood pilings off his starboard side. "Man, you hit that water hard! I thought you were going to ride that bridge all the way up!"

"A little louder, Willie," Derek called back angrily. "I don't think the people over in East Jordan heard you!"

"Get in here with a life jacket!" Gus ordered. *"He's hurt!"*

At the top of the stairs, the bridge keeper had finally figured out what had happened. He ran back across the street to the control house to call the police and an ambulance.

While Willie reappeared with a life jacket and leaped into the water, Derek nodded for Gus to leave. "All right, Boy Scout," he said, disgruntled and in pain, "I'm gonna be fine now, okay? Get *out* of here!"

Gus let go of the metal tie he was hanging on to, but treaded water while waiting for Willie to swim nearer. Although angry at himself that things hadn't gone the way he hoped, it hadn't escaped Derek's notice that Gus Cooper had just saved his life.

"Forget about the bet, Grease Monkey," he said. "Even though, technically, I won."

Gus looked at his opponent with the black smudges, blood and immobile arm, smiled slightly, and then turned and started to swim away just as the sounds of approaching sirens could be heard.

In July 1954, Charlevoix Hospital was close to downtown on Hurlbut Street, but was only a month away from moving to a new and bigger location closer to Lake Michigan. Two nurses wearing crisp white uniforms with grey-bibbed fronts, white pill-box hats with wide folded back brims, and utilitarian black shoes walked up and down the narrow corridor of the twelve-bed hospital. In one of these rooms, Derek lay in a propped-up bed wearing a white hospital gown that tied up the back. His left arm was in a sling, the black shoe polish had been cleaned off his face and there was a large piece of gauze taped to his forehead. He'd been pulled out of the Pine River nearly an hour earlier. In the room with him was his father, Norman Worthing, and Henry Sutter, Charlevoix' chief of police.

Even though it was now going on 1:00 a.m., Derek's father had arrived at the hospital wearing a shirt and tie, but the tie wasn't long enough to go over his protruding stomach. He was what Derek would be in twenty-five years: a once handsome man now with grey hair and eighty pounds of liquor and red meat hanging around his middle. The much trimmer chief of police hadn't dressed so formally. He'd been awakened at home from a sound sleep, so he was wearing his pajama tops, slacks, and his chief of police cap.

"You're a very lucky young man, Derek," the chief said. "The doctor says some torn ligaments, a concussion, a couple of stitches — could've been a lot worse."

"What the hell were you thinking?" his father demanded. "I'm grooming you to be a partner, to take over my business one day, and you pull this, this stupid high school prank?"

"Sorry, Pop," Derek said. It was about the fourth time he'd apologized to his father.

"You and your buddies on the sailboat are in a lot of trouble, son," Chief Sutter said plainly. "The city's going to bring charges against you. Trespassing, reckless endangerment, plus Tommy Boil's parents have been waiting for two years for some additional information about their son's death. Information I bet you have."

"I don't know anything about that," Derek announced defensively. "I wasn't even here. I was attending college back then."

"In early August?" the chief asked, suspiciously.

"Now, Henry," Norman said, "if the boy says he doesn't know anything about that episode of a couple of years ago, then he doesn't know. Tommy Boil's death was terrible. Tragic! But let's stay in the present."

"Okay," the chief said, pushing the brim of his cap back on his forehead. "Who jumped the bridge with you?"

"Nobody," Derek shrugged.

"Bridge keeper said there was someone else in the water with you."

"Willie jumped in and helped me," Derek offered.

"Besides Willie," the cop said. "Somebody else. You were racing with somebody to be the first one over the bridge and into the water."

The cop was simply guessing, but he happened to be right.

"Who said I was racing?" Derek demanded, ready to take revenge on any of his buddies that snitched.

"Did I step on a nerve?" the officer asked. "You jumped the bridge and wound up in the hospital. Did you even win your race? Sounds to me like you got left holdin' the bag."

"Henry, can you please not browbeat my son?" the senior Worthing interjected. "He's already paying for his folly with some considerable pain."

"Your son's a criminal, Norm. He's over twenty-one and he broke the law. What's worse, I believe he's a liar. He knows something about the Boil boy's death. Now, he's gonna go up in front of Judge Levine and he's gonna go to jail unless I get some answers *right now!*"

Derek and Norman looked at each other, then at the police officer.

"Would you mind giving us a minute, Henry?" the senior Worthing asked.

The chief took an exasperated breath, then nodded. "I'll be out in the hall." He turned and exited the room, closing the door behind him.

"You better think *real* carefully about what next passes your lips," Norman warned. "Was anyone else on that bridge with you tonight?"

"No, sir," Derek lied.

"Do you know anything about Tommy Boil's death of two years ago?"

"No," his son repeated, more emphatically.

"You sure?"

"*Yes!*"

Norman looked at his son for a long moment, then nodded. "Why did you try to jump the bridge?"

"I didn't try, I succeeded," Derek reminded him. "It was just a stupid stunt, Pop. No more, no less. If someone else jumps the bridge five years from now, is the chief gonna try to connect that jumper with Tommy Boil, too?"

Norman wasn't 100 percent sure if his son was telling the truth, but he certainly hoped he was. So, he nodded again. "Alright...promise me no more hair-brained stunts. Ever!"

"Yes, sir." Derek winced a little, still in some pain, then asked, "Hey, Pop. Y-you really gonna let him haul me and the guys off to jail?"

Norman glanced toward the closed door leading out in the hall. "Henry Sutter's going to be ramping up his re-election bid for chief of police in a few months. I think I'm about to make a substantial campaign contribution. But you gotta keep your nose clean, Derek. I mean it!"

"I get it. Thanks, Pop," the youth smiled.

His father looked around the room. "They want to keep you here for a day or so. You, you need anything? Want your mother and me to call anyone? Clair Sinclair? Let her know where you are?"

Derek thought for a few moments about the offer.

"No," he finally uttered. "I'm through with her."

Norman looked at his son, surprised. "I thought you were crazy about her. The way Aaron Sinclair talks, you two are already halfway to the church."

Derek looked down at his sheets, self-consciously. "Yeah...well...the truth is, she hasn't been spendin' a lot time with me. If she felt about me like I feel about her...but, she doesn't. I know that now."

Norman looked at his son empathetically. "A false start can be a good thing. Makes you appreciate true love even more when it comes along. You know, her dad's been pushing pretty hard for us to partner up on that downtown refurbishing project. I think maybe he's over extended and really needs it."

"The Collier Brothers over in Traverse City do work just as good," Derek noted.

"Yup," his father agreed. "They do. And since they're not local, we can probably negotiate a better percentage on our end since we've got the home-court advantage."

Derek thought for a few seconds, then looked at his father coolly.

"Screw Sinclair."

14 At The Aladdin

Gordon Bartholomew wasn't just a loan shark, he also had his hands in a variety of legitimate Michigan businesses; a bar in Hamtramck, a trailer park in Mount Pleasant, a carwash in Taylor, and the Aladdin Meat Processing Company in Flint. All of these businesses helped to fuel his loansharking.

There was a part of him that wanted to leave the criminal life, but it wasn't a desire to right his wrongs and contribute to society. It was ego—self-entitlement. He considered himself above the collectors who broke the kneecaps of clients that were delinquent on loans or the Mexican mules he occasionally employed to run drugs for relatives in Eastern Europe. He was also a man of contradictions. In order to go straight, he'd have to give up life-and-death power over people and keep his bipolar personality in check, neither one of which he was particularly willing to do.

He had always thought that a big real estate investment worthy of his time would be his exit from loansharking. Building then overseeing something beautiful and classy would allow him to reinvent himself in another town. Had Charlie Huffman successfully disposed of Farren in Charlevoix, the condo complex he had envisioned on her land would have been just the investment. But it didn't happen, and he had spent the last six months in jail with denied bail while the city prosecutor tried to build a case against him because of it. So Gordon Bartholomew wasn't in a good mood, and hadn't been for quite some time.

He was a self-educated man who had to quit school to help raise siblings when he was thirteen, and, consequently, was sensitive about his lack of formal education. He was therefore a prodigious reader, particularly biographies of the leaders of industry: Iacocca, Gates, Turner, Jobs, and so on. He loved to sprinkle conversations with words that required others to use a dictionary. It was his way of overcompensating for what he felt he lacked.

Two of Bartholomew's regular collectors were Stanley and George. Both were bench-press-made men in their early thirties who looked like former NFL players, but Bartholomew liked his thugs to not dress like thugs so Stanley and George entered the packinghouse wearing dress slacks, shined shoes, and golf shirts. They could have just as easily been going to a Bible study instead of meeting with one of the most dangerous loan sharks in the Midwest.

Stanley had short brown hair, a thick neck, and a flat nose, the result of multiple breakings. George also had brown hair, although longer and lighter than Stanley's, and thick, Buddy Holly-like glasses. The eyewear didn't make him look as intimidating as his colleague, although he was every bit as mean when the situation called for it.

"It's freezin' in here," George said, looking at his wristwatch then glancing around the deserted place.

"It's a slaughterhouse. Of course it's cold," Stanley observed. His description was quite right. "Meat Processing Company" was just a polite way of saying slaughterhouse.

It was about 9:30 p.m., so the employees and cleaning crew were long gone for the day. The inside of the Aladdin Meat Packing Company was all about the efficiency of death and food preparation. It had brick walls and large plain brown tile floors with several grated drains. Like a factory, the place was divided into different workstations. At one station, there was a series of butchering tables where various cuts of meat were made. From there, the meat was sent on a conveyor belt to the second washing station, and then to packaging. But before any of those stations was the knocker room.

Knocker was an industry term for "kill." Cows would be led

from a pen outside, one by one, into the narrow-gated area of the knocker room, then a man would use a device called a stunner that looked similar to a nail gun. He'd put it right in between the cow's eyes and pull the trigger. The stunner shot a metal bolt about the length of an unsharpened pencil into the cow's head, rendering the animal brain dead. The gates would then be moved aside and the cow would be lifted on its rear legs by chains connected to an overhead track. From there it was pushed to the bleeding station. As the name suggested, this was where another worker cut the cow's aorta to bleed it before hide removal. After the hide was removed, it was pushed to the first washing station, then butchering, then the second washing station, and finally to packaging. Because of strict regulations about food preparation, the place looked surprisingly clean and sterile. About two hundred cows a day were processed, making Aladdin a relatively small meat processing operation. There were some operations in the industry that did two hundred cows an hour.

To Stanley and George, Bartholomew's request that they meet him here wasn't unusual. They'd done so before, particularly when there was a body to dispose of. After all, the plant had saws, hoses, drains, incinerators—everything they'd need.

"Where are we supposed to meet?" George asked.

"Over here," Stanley said, pushing some hanging chains from the overhead track aside and walking into the bleeding station.

"Gentlemen," Bartholomew called from a catwalk above that ran the entire length of the building. He descended some metal stairs to meet them. At only 5-foot-5, he was short and stocky with a brush cut haircut and slightly sagging jowls. He was in his mid-fifties and liked to wear tailored clothing. Tonight he was wearing dress slacks, expensive black shoes, a dress shirt, and a blue sports jacket. Although he appeared jovial, Stanley and George both knew that his mood could change in a second. Bartholomew was a sawed-off shotgun of a man with a hair trigger.

"What's new and exciting?" he asked in his gravelly voice.

"Sophia's pregnant again," George answered, referring to his wife.

"Congratulations, George," his boss answered, extending his hand and genuinely pleased. "That's wonderful. Number two for you, isn't it?"

"That's right," George smiled, shaking hands. "She'll be due around Christmas."

"Excellent. Splendid!" Bartholomew said. "No cagamosis here."

"Huh?" George asked.

"An unhappy marriage," the employer clarified. "I don't have any offspring myself, but I know there's nothing more important than family."

"That's right," George agreed.

"So, boss, what're we doin' here tonight?" Stanley asked. "Does somebody need to be 'processed?'"

The short man's jowls slid back in an amused smile while he stuck his hands in his pants pockets. "Tonight's not so much a concilliabule for you as much as it is me looking after my business interests."

"What's a, a con-cill..." George asked, stumbling on the pronunciation.

"'Concilliabule,'" Bartholomew repeated. "A secret meeting of people to hatch a plot. The simple truth, boys, is I've been out of circulation. Festering away in a county jail without any hope of bail while getting reports from my accountant about how my businesses were slowly but surely losing money."

"Nobody's stung us on loans," Stanley said. "Me and George have collected from every client."

"Yes, but you see, that's just the thing. You've collected from every *existing* client. We haven't been getting any *new* ones because I've been incarcerated. And yet, you two have still been on the payroll for doing—what? Certainly not collecting these past six months."

"We didn't know how long you were gonna be held," Stanley defended. "It could've only been a few days, or a week or two."

"You know, if money's tight, boss," George offered, "you don't have to pay me for a while. I'd be willing to work for nothing until you figure we're square."

"Same here," Stanley offered. "Besides, you never told the accountant to take us off the payroll."

The older man nodded, slid his right hand out of his pocket and patted Stanley on his rock hard shoulder. "Thank you, lads. That's a generous offer."

He turned and started to wander around the bleeding station, looking at its two sets of hoses wrapped and hung on wall brackets, and then a collection of large knives laid out neatly on a stainless steel table, as if awaiting some sort of surgical procedure.

"You know what else is important, George?" he said, returning to a previous topic. "Besides family? Honesty. Wouldn't you agree? It's an essential, didactic requirement of a professional relationship."

George looked at Stanley, wondering if they were in some kind of trouble.

"Yeah," he answered tentatively. "Sure."

"Somethin' bugging you, boss?" Stanley asked plainly.

"Well...I've just been in a quandary about something," Bartholomew said, now in front of the stainless steel table where the knives were laid out. "We've been together a long time, us three. You two have always done your job and done it very well. But when I was in jail, I had the opportunity, through my attorney, to study statements—depositions. After all, there wasn't much else of anything I could do."

"I didn't tell anyone anything," Stanley said stoically.

"Me neither," George affirmed.

"It wasn't what you two didn't say," Bartholomew mused, running his finger down the blade of an eight-inch carving knife still lying on the table. "It was what other people said."

He turned away from the table and addressed his employees directly.

"Now you take this paramedic, Wyatt Reynolds, for example. I believe everybody calls him Doc? He was the one who surprised Charlie when he was about to do away with his wife. He and Charlie both wound up struggling in the winter waters of Round Lake. As a result of this, Charlie perished. Now what confuses me about this is, you two told me on the day before this happened you'd gone to

Charlevoix at Charlie's request and had nearly beaten this Doc Reynolds to death."

"That's right," Stanley verified. "We did."

"You okayed it," George reminded his boss.

"But there's the paradox," the short man in the sports jacket said with a pointing finger. "How could you beat this guy nearly to death if he was fit enough to interrupt Charlie at his most critical moment? Then he and Charlie have a tussle in freezing water? He lives? Charlie dies? You see what I mean? Something's not adding up."

Stanley and George looked at each other again, surprised by this revelation. What none of these men knew was that Doc had somehow regained consciousness after Stanley and George had practically left him for dead. He dragged himself into his Jeep and miraculously made it home that night where his pulverized body finally collapsed into Clair's arms. He awoke the next morning to discover he'd been totally healed. It was one of the advantages of having an angel as a houseguest.

"I—I don't know what to say, boss," George said, pushing his glasses back on his nose then shrugging with open hands. "The guy looked like ground hamburger when we left him."

"Is he a prevaricator?" Bartholomew asked, directing the question to Stanley.

"I don't know what that means, but we did our job," Stanley confirmed.

"Could you have gotten the wrong man?" the employer suggested.

"Case of mistaken identity?"

Stanley and George looked at each other again, and after a long moment, Stanley shook his head. "No. It was the right guy. He even told us he was a paramedic."

Bartholomew looked down at the tiled floor for a moment, and then nodded slightly to himself as if making a decision. "This is an enigma, gentlemen. And I don't like enigmas. Don't like them at all. Something's going to have to be done about it."

There was a sudden, short sound like a subtle burst of wind. "PHITT," and George quickly doubled over. Before Stanley had a chance to react, there was a second "PHITT." He quickly brought his open right hand to the side of his neck as if swatting a mosquito. Two seconds later, blood began spurting in between the fingers of his hand.

"Lads, you've just received two mortal wounds from a very good mechanic," Bartholomew calmly said, gesturing to the shadows of the catwalk above. "You, George, have been shot in the liver. You'll bleed to death in about ten minutes. You, Stanley, just had your jugular vein split open. You've got about five. The blood's just literally going to pump right out of you."

Stanley quickly brought his other hand up to his neck and applied pressure, but blood just kept running down his neck and gushing through his fingers. George, meantime, dropped to his knees, wide-eyed and mortified.

"Because you two didn't do what you were supposed to do," Bartholomew continued, "Charlie Huffman was interrupted from killing his wife. Because he didn't kill his wife, I didn't get her land. Because I didn't get her land, I lost a real estate investment in a town I dearly love and the opportunity to run a legitimate business worth tens-of-millions of dollars. I also lost the seed money that I invested into Charlie's con, plus the money he originally owed me. I lost the time it took to run the con, not to mention six *more* months while I languished in jail. Then there are the losses my business interests suffered including this place because I wasn't around. And attorney's fees on top of that. *And all because you two didn't do your jobs!* If you tell me the truth now. I may let your families live."

Stanley screamed in anger at Bartholomew, outstretched his arms and took a couple of steps toward him. A third "PHITT" blew off his right kneecap and he tumbled to the ground, screaming in agony.

"You didn't think I was going to keep you guys around forever, did you?" Bartholomew coolly asked above Stanley's screams. He turned and walked back over to the stainless steel table holding the knives and slipped off his sports jacket. "I'm trying to eventually go straight here and the simple fact is, you two know too much."

While blood continued to flow out of George and Stanley, both of whom were more or less in fetal positions, their employer neatly folded his jacket, put it on the table, and then stepped over to a pair of faded yellow rubber zip-up overalls hanging on a peg on the wall. Next to the overalls was a pair of olive rubber boots. Both of the injured men watched helplessly as Bartholomew slipped off his shoes, stepped into the overalls, zipped them up, and sat down on a bench and picked up the boots.

As this was happening, a man with a hook nose, narrowly set eyes, grey goatee, and a face as creased as a peach pit slowly descended the metal stairs. He wore a flat-brimmed cap and his shirt, pants and shoes looked foreign like he was a Polish potato farmer trying to dress up. He carried a Russian-made Dragunov sniper rifle with a twenty-four-inch barrel and a six-inch silencer. Its walnut stock wasn't solid but "skeletal," with an open rectangle in the middle of the shoulder rest to reduce recoil. Like Bartholomew, he was a man in his mid-fifties, although five inches taller and considerably leaner than the man putting on the rubber boots.

"Ah, this is my cousin, Yuri," he said to the dying men. "He's from Moldavia. When I was a boy, my father used to send me there in the summer. Yuri learned shooting and I learned explosives. I bet you two didn't know that about me, did you? That I started out in pyrotechnics?"

Throughout all of this, Bartholomew's voice had remained calm and conversational. He knew he was in total control.

"Bastard! Bastard!" Stanley half screamed, half moaned. He had one hand on his knee and another back up to his neck, but this was a futile attempt to stop the spilling of blood. He was now feeling light headed and was struggling to stay conscious.

"We did our job!" George likewise yelled, unsuccessfully trying to push himself up with his left arm. *"I—I—I—used a bat on the guy! Yyyou can't do this!"*

"Even if you're telling the truth," the man in the rubber overalls said and now zipping up his boots, "I can't undo this."

"Bassss-tard!" Stanley spat out, losing control of his faculties. He looked at his killer, blurry-eyed. "He'll do you, too," he warned.

"Yuri? No, he's family," Bartholomew answered rising to his feet. "Besides, when his work here is done, he's going home."

Bartholomew walked over to one of the hoses sitting on a wall bracket and lifted it out. He dropped the hose to the floor, then turned on a nearby spigot. On the head of the hose was a spray trigger. Pulling it, he doused Stanley with a steady stream of water, then began to direct his blood to the nearest floor drain.

"As your life is literally being washed down the drain, Stanley, do you still want to stick to your story?"

Stanley's eyes were still open, but he was too weak to speak now. He just lay on the tile floor in a pool of water and blood, waiting to die.

"How about you George?" Bartholomew asked, turning the water to him. "Anything to tell me?"

Through his water-beaded, thick glasses, the other of the two collectors looked at his employer disbelievingly. "You can't do this," he groaned. It was now becoming difficult for him to speak. "My wife's going to have a baby."

"Not for long," Yuri replied unemotionally with a thick Eastern European accent. He raised the rifle to his shoulder and took aim at George's head. A second later: "PHITT."

The European man looked at his cousin still manning the hose.

"Look in the inside pocket of my sports coat," Bartholomew said, not taking his eyes of his victims.

Yuri walked over to the table, put his rifle down, and dipped a hand into the jacket. A moment later, he produced a folded up piece of paper.

"That's the address of Farren Malone in Charlevoix, who is at present the bane of my existence. It's a little over a three hour drive."

"You want me to go see her?" Yuri asked.

"I want you to go kill her," Bartholomew confirmed. "She lives in a small, rounded house made out of boulders. She's twenty-nine, short hair. I'll get you money, identification, a car—I want it done tomorrow."

The taller man with the flat-brimmed cap and goatee looked at his cousin, knowing that if anything happened to Farren, the police would immediately be on Bartholomew's doorstep.

"You caught lucky break to get out of jail," Yuri reminded in broken English. "You sure?"

"Tomorrow!" Bartholomew insisted. He said it behind gritted teeth that hid a seething anger. An anger that proved Gus and Doc's suspicions were well-founded.

15 Deceits

In July 1954, construction was underway in Anaheim, California, for Disneyland. Italian actress Pier Angeli, who would later go on to date James Dean and marry singer Vic Damone, was on the cover of *Life Magazine*.

Proctor & Gamble was testing a new toothpaste called Fluoristan, which was later changed to Crest. And Charlevoix's local hospital was on the verge of closing its doors on Hurlbut Street and moving to a new location on Lake Shore Drive.

The new facility would more than double the hospital's size, meaning a lot more staff. Clair Sinclair had applied at the hospital weeks ago but hadn't heard from them. So it was confusing to her when she ran into an old friend from nursing school downtown who told her she'd just been hired at the hospital. The friend had just moved to Charlevoix from Gross Pointe near Detroit, Clair had graduated with a higher GPA, was a local girl, and had applied long before her friend had. She genuinely didn't understand why nothing had happened with her application. So the following day, she climbed into her blue Corvette and drove to the hospital to meet with Helen Taylor, the director of nursing.

"I don't understand, Mrs. Taylor," Clair said, sitting in her office where evidence of packing was already taking place. She was wearing a nice red circle-skirt dress with small white polka dots on it and a wide white belt. "I applied nearly two months ago. There couldn't possibly have been anything wrong with my transcripts or references."

"No, dear, there wasn't," Helen replied. She was in her fifties and wore the same white uniform with the grey-bibbed front and white pillbox hat with the wide folded back brim that all the other nurses wore.

"So, can you tell me why Cindy Gallagher just got hired but I haven't heard from you? Was there something I said or did in my interview? Because if there was, I'd certainly like to apologize for—"

"You need to talk with your father, dear," the older woman suggested.

"I beg your pardon?"

Helen folded her hands together and had a self-conscious look on her face. "I suggest you go home and have a talk with your father."

"What? Why?"

"There wasn't anything wrong with your application, Clair," the hospital administrator admitted. "Your grades were good and your references excellent. But your father is friends with our CEO. I believe they belong to the same shooting club. And I was told to…" her voice faded uncomfortably.

"Told to what?"

"Well—to shelve your application."

"What?" Clair asked, stunned.

"I suggest you go home and talk to your father," the hospital official repeated. "I'm sorry, dear."

Sixteen minutes later, Clair was pulling into the circular drive in front of her parents' house. Her younger sister, Jessie, was lounging on the front porch furniture in cutoffs and a T-shirt reading a movie magazine about Kirk Douglas.

"Where's Daddy?" she asked, climbing out of her car and slamming the door.

"Inside somewhere," Jessie answered, not looking up from her reading.

Clair took off her Ray Ban sunglasses, tossed them into the passenger side seat, and then stormed into the house.

"Daddy!" she called after bursting through the front door. "Daddy! Get out here immediately!"

Her father appeared in the doorway of his study with a newspaper in his hand. He was wearing light-colored slacks and an off-white shirt with a small maroon square pattern as well as a maroon bow tie. Simultaneously, Clair's mother, Portia, appeared at the top of the winding stairway that emptied into the foyer. Unlike her husband with the small pot belly and thinning hair, Portia had retained her beauty and figure. At forty-nine, the blonde-haired, blue-eyed woman was still one of the finest looking woman in Charlevoix, which pleased her husband to no end although he took her for granted. Portia always wore dresses. In Clair's entire life there had only been a handful of occasions when she had seen her mother in pants. She vacuumed in a skirt and pearls, did laundry in a skirt and pearls, and her hair was usually in a bouffant style that required a lot of hairspray.

"What's all the commotion?" Aaron asked innocently.

"What did you do to my application at the hospital?" she asked, tossing her car keys and purse on the circular table in the foyer.

"Huh?"

"Did you sabotage my application to be a nurse at the hospital?"

"Did you sabotage my partnership with Worthing Building Supply for that downtown contract?" he immediately shot back.

"What?"

"I *told* you that contract was a big deal," he answered, accusingly. "I told you Derek was crazy about you. I told you I needed that partnership to happen. And what did you do? You blew him off for that, that *nobody!* You didn't even go see Derek in the hospital after his accident."

"Accident? Is that what you and your friends are calling it? I call it a stupid ass stunt!"

"Clair, your language!" Portia called from the top of the stairs.

"Do you know what he's done, Mother?" she asked, looking up at her. "He arranged for my nursing application at the hospital to be trashed. And all so he can get some construction job."

"Now wait just a minute, miss," her father said, coming out of his study. "Derek Worthing happens to be a man who can keep you in your lifestyle. He's going to inherit a multi-million-dollar business and he liked you long before this refurbishing job ever became a reality. All I did was to clear the path so nature could take its course with you two."

"By me not working?"

"By you having the time to *be* with him. And yes, if something developed and a business partnership also happened, what's wrong with that?"

"You're manipulating my life!" she declared angrily.

"All parents manipulate their children's lives," Sinclair bellowed. "They just call it 'guidance.'"

Seething, Clair turned and marched upstairs heading toward her room.

"You're done seeing this mechanic," Aaron ordered as she went. "You understand? You patch things up with Derek, young miss. *You hear me?*"

Clair passed her mother at the top of the stairs. Portia watched her storm into her room and slam the door, then she silently descended the stairs, giving a disapproving look to her husband all the way down.

"Oh, don't be hypocritical," he growled. "You wish she would have chosen Derek, too."

"But she didn't," his wife reminded him. "And if you've prevented her from getting a job at the hospital when she's been trained to be a nurse, what were all those years of schooling for?"

"Oh, I didn't ruin her chances of anything," Sinclair grumbled, annoyed. "It's a phone call fix, okay? A phone call fix!" He looked at his wife seriously. "We need this contract, Portia. I didn't get the hospital job and how many big jobs in a town this size do you think there are? I haven't bid on anything in two months. Nobody's doing *anything!* You wanna lose all this? You'd better turn around, go upstairs, and have a talk with your daughter."

"What do you want her to do, Aaron? Sleep with Derek?"

"If only she *would*," he muttered.

Portia put her hands on her hips, not appreciating her husband's sense of humor, if in fact, it was humor. Simultaneously, Jessie came through the front door holding her movie magazine.

"What's going on? I can hear you guys outside even over the peeing angel."

"Jessie!" Portia warned, not liking her language.

"Jeepers creepers, Mom, that's what it *does*," she defended.

"Call the Worthings," Sinclair ordered his wife. "Invite them to go boating with us this weekend."

"They cancelled our Wednesday bridge game, Aaron. I think they're probably aware Clair's no longer interested in Derek."

"Really?" Jessie asked, her face lighting up with the wattage of fresh gossip.

Just then, Clair came out of her room and hurried down the stairs. She was wearing a pair of jeans, shoes with no heels, and a button-up short-sleeve, light-green blouse. Her hair that had been pinned up when she went to the hospital now bounced loose and free over her shoulders.

"Excuse me, are those my dungarees?" Jessie asked.

Clair didn't answer and picked up her keys and purse off the table in the foyer.

"You're going out like that?" Portia asked.

"Why not?" Clair defiantly answered. "It's not like I've got a job to go to."

"I'm not finished with you, Clair!" her father barked. She ignored him and left through the front door.

A few minutes later, she pulled into Stu and Ernie's where Gus and Louie were sitting in old wooden chairs outside the office enjoying the mid-morning sun. Both men noticed that the clamp-on top had been attached to Clair's car when she pulled in, as if she were going on a trip.

"Hi, Miss Sinclair," Louie said, standing up and tipping his cap. "Need any gas?" He was aware that Gus and Clair were spending time together but still sucked up to her because of her father's wealth.

"No thanks, Louie," she said, giving him a polite smile. She turned to Gus, who had also risen out of his chair. "I've got to get out of town," she announced.

Gus, who had his usual toothpick hanging out the side of his mouth, slowly removed it, seeing how upset she was. He turned to his co-worker.

"Don't you have a couple of cases of motor oil to unpack?"

"Uh...sure," Louie answered, understanding. "Excuse me, Miss Sinclair," he said, tipping his cap again. Then he went inside and disappeared into Service Bay One.

"Where are you going?" Gus asked once they were alone.

"I don't know."

"What happened?"

"That day you went to my father's club, he told you to stay away from me, didn't he?"

"Well..."

"Don't be polite, Gus," she said, knowingly. "He did, didn't he?"

"What happened?" he repeated.

"I've got to get out of town," she repeated, shaking her head. "Clear my head."

He looked at her for a moment, then made a decision. "You want some company? If you don't, I understand."

"Can you?" she asked, liking the idea. "What about work? Where's Stu and Ernie?"

"Ernie's helping his mom move a washing machine and Stu's running errands in town. We're not busy today. Matter of fact, when Stu gets back, he'll probably send one of us home."

"But, you're the mechanic."

He pointed to the empty service bays.

"Well, if you think you can."

"Just give me a couple of minutes to get out of my monkey suit, wash up, and talk to Louie."

She nodded and walked back her car while he went into the office. As she went, she saw his truck parked on the corner of the property and noticed its smashed windshield and broken off driver's side mirror.

Within another five minutes, a cleaned-up Gus walked out of the station and headed over to Clair's Corvette where she was waiting behind the wheel. He wore high-top black tennis shoes, a clean white T-shirt, and he carried a lightweight red jacket.

"All set. Where we headed?" he asked, climbing into the passenger side seat and brushing the breaking wave of black hair off his forehead.

"That wasn't a deer, was it?" she said, looking at his truck. "You said you hit a deer, but it wasn't a deer, was it?"

"Clair—" he started to say.

"Why is everybody lying to me?" she asked. "Deceiving me?"

"Where would you like to go?"

"Out of this town. Off this planet," she lamented.

He thought for a moment, then hit upon an idea.

"I can arrange that," he said.

She looked at him, not understanding.

16 Confiding

It was another Monday morning and Farren sat in Dr. Judith Herriman's parlor staring at a painting of seagulls suspended in flight that was hanging on a wall. The therapist sat as usual in her brown leather club chair with a pad and pencil in hand and her grey hair pinned up in an efficient bun.

"So," she began, "nine days ago you moved in with Doc. How's that going?"

"Good," Farren answered. "Good. I mean, we don't see each other much. I work days and he works nights, but good."

"So, it would be good, then," Herriman verified, noting that she had used the word three times in three sentences.

"Yes, it's good."

"Any evidence of this loan shark coming to town?"

"Bartholomew? No. And no one really expects him to. Me staying at Doc's is just a precaution."

"So you said last week," the therapist remembered.

"You haven't said anything to anyone, have you?" Farren asked, a little concerned. "About me staying at Doc's?"

"Of course not. What you tell me is in confidence. Besides, if it's a precaution for your safety, the fewer the people that know about it, the better."

"Actually, I want your advice about that," Farren said. "We've got a couple of friends, Lance and Charlene. We haven't said anything to them yet, but I'm afraid it's just a matter of time before they find out."

"Lance Vale and Charlene Rogers?" Dr. Herriman asked.

"You know them?"

Judith smiled, already understanding Farren's concern. "I know them."

"They're great people with generous hearts. But they *do* love their gossip."

"And you're worried if they find out you're staying at Doc's, they'll start telling people?"

"Either that, or be angry we didn't take them into confidence."

The older woman thought for a moment, considering an idea. "Then maybe you should take them into confidence. Make them allies."

"But you just said the fewer the people—"

"Sometimes when a dog is running toward you and growling, the best thing to do is whistle for it to come," the older woman interrupted. "It's called diffusion. Knowing secrets is having power. So, if you gave Lance and Charlene a secret and asked them to keep it, if they didn't, they'd be giving away their power. Logically, why would anyone want to do that?"

"You think diffusion will work?"

"Well, humans aren't always logical," Herriman smiled. "But in the case of Lance and Charlene, I think it's worth a try."

Farren nodded, considering it.

"So, you're not concerned about the loan shark?" the therapist asked, leaning forward in her chair and intently interested.

"Well, of course, I don't *like* that he's out of jail. But I can't live my life in fear, either. I think I'm taking reasonable precautions. And after a certain amount of time, if everything remains status quo, then I'll go home."

"How long is a certain amount of time?"

"I don't know," she shrugged.

The therapist wrote something on her pad. "And you and Doc are sleeping separately?"

"Yes."

"Do you want to?"

Farren fixed her eyes on nothing in particular. "Not necessarily," she said quietly.

The older woman wrote some more notes. "So, you and Doc aren't sleeping together, you're on different schedules, and nothing in particular of a sexual nature has transpired in the time you've been staying with him?"

"Yes. No," Farren corrected, "that's not entirely true. We went out to dinner Friday with Charlene and Lance. Doc had the night off. And when we got home, I decided to go swimming and he decided to go for a run even though it was nearly dark. But he didn't go for a run. He rounded the cabin and wound up in some woods near the water to spy on me."

"How do you know he was spying on you?"

"Because I heard him thrashing around in the undergrowth. We're not talking James Bond, here," she smiled. "I'm sure he figured I needed protecting. And just before I got into the water, I—I took my swimsuit off. I was naked."

The therapist leaned forward even more. "He saw you naked?"

"Yes, as I was wading out into water." She cocked her head with a bit of a naughty smile. "At least, I sure *hope* it was Doc. He does have neighbors."

The therapist leaned back in her chair and reached for a bottle of water on the end table next to her. "Why did you want Doc to see you naked?"

"I don't know. Maybe I thought if he saw something he liked, he'd hang in there a while longer."

The older woman took a drink of water then screwed the cap back on the bottle before setting it down. "Don't you think you're worth waiting for?"

"C'mon, Judith. He's a good-looking grown man who has needs. He wants to take our relationship to the next level. What would you do if someone said they wanted you and you said you wanted them, but then every time you were close to making love, you felt like you were going to vomit, or have some imaginary walls crush you, or die?"

"Did you feel that way when he was watching you? When there was distance between you?"

The patient thought for a moment. "Uh—no—actually," she said, surprised.

"How did you feel?"

Farren looked at nothing in particular again, trying to figure out her feelings. "I don't know...I guess I felt okay about it. Otherwise, I wouldn't have done it, right? What does that mean?"

"Sorry to give the obvious therapist retort, but what do *you* think it means?"

"That I'm comfortable with intimacy so long as there's a physical distance? What does *that* mean? That I'd be good at phone sex?" she joked.

"Maybe," the doctor smiled kindly. "It's a thought. Try it if you want."

"I don't know about that," Farren mused. "I say that a lot these days, don't I? 'I don't know.'"

"It's okay if you don't know everything," Herriman smiled again. A lot of life is us just fumbling around trying to figure things out. We do the best we can. But you want to find some answers for you and Doc, and frankly, I think you're getting close to finding some."

Farren smiled, hoping what Judith was saying was true.

Two hours later, Farren and Charlene were in Victoria's Secret in Grand Traverse Mall in Traverse City, Michigan, some fifty miles north of Charlevoix. With a population of more than 14,600 compared with Charlevoix's 3,100 permanent residents, Traverse City, or "TC" as many called it, had much better boudoir building options.

As they roamed around the store, Charlene was very self-conscious about her new shortened white locks and moaned every time she caught herself in a mirror. Farren kept reinforcing that she looked fine, which in fact, she did. While her hair was now shorter than Farren's, it wasn't a total Sinead O'Connor shave. Still, the unanticipated style change was hard for her friend to adjust to.

"Not sexy enough," the bride-to-be said, running her fingers over a black silk teddy on the sale rack. She looked around disheartened at the pictures of the models on the walls, all of whom were younger and slimmer.

"Remember when Victoria's Secret had truly provocative stuff? They're going for cutesy now. Catering to teenagers. This place is like Claire's, with thongs."

Farren smiled, noticing a Claire's directly across the mall. It was chain that sold inexpensive jewelry and bobbles and had a huge teen clientele.

"This is nice," she said, plucking a red sheer teddy off the rack. "It's your size too."

"Not sexy enough," Charlene repeated, losing interest and heading over to another rack.

"Well, what exactly are you going for?" Farren asked, following her.

"Oh, a Dream-Girls-meets-Stevie-Nicks kind of thing."

"I have no idea what that means."

"A woman capable of both leather *and* lace," Charlene answered, referencing an old Stevie Nicks song.

"Right," Farren agreed, still not understanding.

"Well, what does Doc like?" the bride casually asked, looking through the rack and ready for some frank girl talk.

"Doc?"

"Yeah. What do you wear for him?"

"Um, not much."

"You mean, he likes floss underwear?"

"I mean, I don't wear anything for him." Even as the words left her mouth, Farren wondered if she was giving away too much information.

"All the experts say that packaging keeps things fresh, interesting,"

Charlene shared. She caught her pudgy reflection in a glass display, saw her short hair, and sighed again. "I lost eleven pounds for the wedding. Eleven pounds! You'd think it would at least show."

Farren decided to take a chance with Charlene and confide in her a little. Maybe Dr. Herriman was right. Besides, she figured, she wanted the input of someone her own age who was in a relationship.

"What I mean is...we haven't gone that far yet."

Charlene stopped plucking through the clothing rack and gave her friend a disbelieving look.

"Really? Wow...I just assumed after six months...but I guess I understand with you being such a church-going girl and all."

Farren paused to look at a panties and bra combo, "It's not that." She was now at the point where she either had to jump in and take Charlene into confidence, or not. She decided to leap. "The truth is, after I found out about Charlie, it affected me emotionally. I can't 'be' with a man that way right now."

Charlene stopped looking at merchandise and turned to Farren. "Oh my God. I never thought of that. Of course his deceit would take a toll on you, you poor thing!"

"And there's actually more to the story," Farren volunteered timidly. "You remember that loan shark Charlie owed so much money to?"

"Bartholomew?"

"Well, he's not in jail anymore."

"What?"

"So, for the time being, I've been staying at Doc's. Just as a precaution."

Charlene's eyes we're as big as salad plates. She looked around the store, and then took Farren by the hand.

"C'mon."

"Where're we going?"

"Coffee break."

For the next half hour, Farren and Charlene sat at a table in the mall's food court in front of a Chic-fil-A and talked. Farren spoke more about her sexual hesitancy, seeing a therapist, staying with Doc, and even her concerns about Bartholomew being out of jail, although she truly believed nothing would come of it. She thought that taking Charlene into confidence would be hard, but it wasn't. It was really the first time since Charlie's death that she'd unburdened herself to someone who wasn't a grandparent, therapist, or boyfriend and the unburdening felt good.

"Wow!" Charlene finally said, after everything had been laid on the table and she'd taken a final sip of her unsweetened ice tea. "You've really been dealing with some stuff, haven't you?"

"My problems aren't as bad as others," Farren said diplomatically, "but, yeah, I've had some challenges lately."

Charlene leaned forward and took her friend's hand. "Thanks for telling me, Farren. I know I'm a blabbermouth sometimes. But this is serious stuff. And if you want me to keep quiet about it, I swear to God I will. I won't even tell Lance."

"No," Farren assured her, "you two are friends of ours. Tell Lance, but I'd appreciate it if it didn't go beyond you two."

Charlene closed her mouth tightly, brought a hand to her lips and made a key-locking motion.

"Thanks," Farren smiled genuinely believing her girlfriend might actually keep the confidence.

Charlene looked at Farren and made a decision. "You know what I think? I think we ought to march right back into Victoria's Secret and you should get some sexy stuff too. Real sheet burnin' stuff!"

"Oh my," Farren laughed. "Yeah, that's me. The Rihanna of northern Michigan."

"No, I mean it," Charlene reiterated. "You can't let anything Charlie did to you affect how you are with Doc. Charlie was a pig! If you let him run around in your head, then he's won."

"Won? My emotional condition isn't a game," Farren said, slightly defensive.

"It was to Charlie," her friend reminded her. "It was never anything but. Isn't that what con men do? Manipulate, scheme, make a game out of other people's emotions? Charlie played you, girl. Recognize it, then let it go. Simple as that. Otherwise, you'll be in therapy until you're as old as Judith Herriman."

"It's not that simple," Farren lamented, nervously brushing her bangs aside.

"Why? Why can't it be that simple, honey?"

Farren looked at Charlene and opened her mouth to speak but was stumped for an answer. Clearly, Charlene had glossed over a lot of details in her logic, like Charlie's specific actions, or Farren's naivety, or the total betraying of vows, or even how this was just the latest in a line of other catastrophic events in Farren's life, for example the sudden and unexpected death of her parents. Yet, at the end of it all, Charlene had boiled things down to their simplest common denominator and was right: Farren *had* to get past this or the fallout from Charlie and Bartholomew would just go on and on. It was as if Charlene in her own way had flicked some kind of switch in her friend's head. She was the outside objective point of view Farren needed to hear.

"You're right," Farren said quietly. "What am I *doing?*"

"You're not sleeping with the best-looking guy in town," Charlene said plainly. "Ready to go back to Claire's-With-Thongs?"

The women did go back to Victoria's Secret, but Farren didn't buy anything, saying she actually had several pieces of lingerie back at her house that she could pick up once she and Charlene got back to town. But then on the ride home, she remembered a promise she made to both Doc and her grandfather that she wouldn't go to her house under any circumstances. She thought it a little dramatic of Doc and Gus to have her make such a promise, but Farren Malone didn't break promises.

"No problem," Charlene said after Clair had told her. "Tell me what you want, where it is, give me your key, and I'll swing over to your place and pick up a few things and put them in a nice, discreet zip-up tote. Then I'll give it to Lance and he'll leave it at the fire hall in Doc's locker to take home."

"Won't Lance be curious about what's in the bag?" Farren asked.

"Not if I tell him it's feminine hygiene stuff," Charlene smiled.

The plan sounded reasonable to Farren, so she agreed.

The women returned to Charlevoix at about 5:00 p.m. When Charlene dropped Farren off at the marina, her first instinct was to hurry to Doc's cabin so she could spend some time with him prior to his going to work. But as soon as she walked into the marina, one employee asked her about this, then another about that, then a customer complained to her about the power outlet near his slip not working, and before she knew it, she was consumed by marina business and didn't get to see Doc at all. Meanwhile, he went to work, taking Gertrude with him, and Charlene and Lance had dinner that night with Charlene's parents and sister.

It wasn't until after 10:00 p.m. that Charlene and Lance finally drove over to Farren's house. On the way, Charlene filled her fiancé in on what she'd learned earlier.

"So, she's been staying with him for more than a week?" Lance asked, as he drove his GMC pick-up. "Doc never said a thing to me about this," he confessed with a little hurt in his voice.

"Except for dinner, he hasn't seen you since he's been working nights," Charlene reminded him.

"That's not the point. We're partners. Best friends. At least, I *thought* we were. If I didn't have so many cousins, he'd be one of my groomsmen, y'know."

"Well, you know *now*. And Farren is one of my bridesmaids. And he will be working days again so you'll still be partners. And he has offered to help you with losing weight and getting your certification. So lighten up. He does consider you his best friend."

"I just don't like being the last one to know these things," Lance grumbled. "I mean, her therapist, the freelance cops–"

"People who *had* to know," Charlene chimed in. "We're the only ones who know strictly out of friendship."

"Well..." Lance mused, but he began to see his girl's reasoning and feel better about the situation.

The exterior walls of Farren's small, rounded "mushroom house" consisted of thousands of stacked and mortared boulders, all about the size of a watermelon or a little bigger. A wide-base chimney that got narrower as it reached for the sky made the house look like a place where Bilbo Baggins could reside, and the thick wooden shingles on the roof did indeed resemble a mushroom cap.

Lance pulled his pickup over to the side of the street in front of the house, put the truck in park, and turned off the engine.

"You wait here," Charlene said. "I'll just be a minute."

"You don't want me to go in with you?"

"No. I'm getting girl stuff. Maxi pads, a Barbara Streisand CD, things like that," she fibbed.

"Okay," Lance said leaning back in his seat. "Hey, speaking of Barbra Streisand, name the connection she has to the James Bond franchise."

"I haven't the vaguest idea," Charlene answered wearily. "She sang one of the theme songs, right?"

"No. She married James Brolin. One of the few Americans who actually screen tested to play Bond."

"If you could only make money from this," she quipped, opening her door.

"Hurry up," Lance said. "It's been a long day and I've still got studying to do."

Once Charlene was in the house, she snooped around a little having the privacy and opportunity to do so. She opened some kitchen cabinets, peeked into the fridge, and then inspected a new sofa covering Farren had told her about in the living room. After a few minutes, she started to look for the lingerie, but it took longer than she expected because she started searching in the guest bedroom mistaking it for the master bedroom. Farren had simply said the lingerie was in the bottom drawer of her dresser and Charlene went through all five drawers in the guest bedroom weeding through Farren's winter clothes. She was interrupted by the cellphone ringing on her belt.

"Hello?"

"What's taking so long?" Lance asked. "You okay?"

"I'm just collecting a few things."

"You're being nosy," Lance correctly guessed, knowing his girlfriend. "I'm getting old waiting out here."

"We've been dating for twelve years. You really wanna talk to me about waiting?"

"Ah...er..." Lance stammered.

"Think of another James Bond question," she smiled, hanging up. "Like I care," she added, after she knew the call was disconnected.

Finally giving up in the spare bedroom, she walked past the house's only bathroom and into the correct bedroom. Once the lights were on in the master bedroom, she paused, looking around.

"Where's the dresser?" she asked out loud. "There's no dresser in here?" She walked back down the hall and looked in the spare bedroom again, then walked back into the master bedroom. Putting her hands on her hips, she looked around until she spotted the closet and walked over to it. Opening the door, she saw there was a dresser inside to better utilize the limited floor space. "Ah-ha," she said, and opened up the bottom drawer. Spotting the lingerie, she started to sort through it. Some of the things were pieces Farren had gotten and others were items Charlie had given her. One by one, she started to make her selections. As she did, her cell rang again.

Taking the phone off her belt and seeing it was Lance, she clicked a button and started talking. "I'm coming, I'm coming."

"What were the only James Bond films that Jack Kennedy saw?" Lance asked.

"I don't know. The first couple?" she guessed, still making selections.

"That's absolutely right," Lance said. "*Dr. No* and *From Russia With Love*. In fact, Kennedy saw *From Russia With Love* just three nights before Dallas."

"You are *so* going to stop drinking this Kool-Aid after we get married," she said while holding up a pair of panties and looking them over. "Cute," she said approvingly.

"Thank you, honey," Lance said. "You're cute, too. You wanna know which parts I think are the cutest?"

"Hang onto your jet pack, Double-0 Seven. Be out in a minute," she said and disconnected the call. She began looking around for a tote bag with a clasp or zipper that she could put everything into.

Within another minute, she had found a bag and packed everything up. Then, she used the bathroom and turned out the lights. In total, she'd been in the house close to thirteen minutes.

Seeing her come outside and throw the deadbolt on the front door, Lance playfully speed dialed her number one more time.

"Really?" Charlene queried, hearing her cell ring for the third time in less than eight minutes. She could look across the short front yard and see Lance smiling and holding his phone. She reached with her left arm across her chest for the phone hanging on the right side of her waist. As she did, she felt a sudden, sharp sting in her upper left arm, about four inches below the shoulder. The sting had a punch to it, and nearly knocked her off the doorstep.

"*Ow!*" she cried, dropping Farren's key. She looked down at her arm and saw a hole about the circumference of soda bottle cap with blood rapidly running down from it. She looked up at Lance who had seen her jerk from the impact.

"Hey..." she said, calling to him. Then she dropped the bag she was carrying in her right hand and sunk to her knees on the concrete doorstep.

"*Charlene?*" Lance called out. He burst out of his truck and ran across the lawn. She was lying on her side by the time he reached her.

"Baby?" he asked, now on his knees and leaning over her.

"I, I think I've been...shot," she sputtered disbelievingly. Her eyelids started to flicker and she fainted.

Lance threw his body over her in case there were other shots and reached for his cellphone.

About a mile away at the fire hall, Doc sat in the dining area with five playing cards in his hand. He looked at Gertrude sitting across the table from him. She also had five cards sitting face down in front of her. He was in the middle of a pretend poker game.

"Stay?" he asked the mannequin in the housedress with the curly black hair, bare feet, and slightly open mouth. "You sure?" He looked at his cards, then at her. "The dealer takes two."

Just then, KK stuck his strawberry-blonde head around a corner. "Goin' for a run."

"Got a walkie?" Doc asked, not looking up and taking two cards.

"Yeah," KK replied, before disappearing around the corner again.

"Okay," Doc said and turned his attention back to the game, rearranging his cards.

He looked at Gertrude again as if she had spoken. "Raise me?" he asked. He glanced at his cards, then at the dummy. He rubbed his chin and mulled things over, taking his time. "I think you're bluffin'. I'll see your raise and raise you two more." He took four toothpicks and added them to the ten already sitting in the middle of the table between them. "I call."

He lay his cards down on the table face up, then reached over and turned over her five.

"Damn," he said, disappointed. "You weren't bluffin', were you?"

Just then, he heard an alarm followed a few seconds later by a female dispatcher's voice over the intercom. There had been a gunshot victim. When he heard the address, he recognized it instantly.

Doc sprang up and ran out of the dining area and into the garage. He didn't bother to step into his fireman's outfit. Instead, he leaped into the driver's side of his ambulance and turned the key. It was a warm night and the tall station doors were already open. The siren started screaming before he rolled out of the garage. As he was pulling out of the drive, he could see KK to his left running down the sidewalk returning to the fire hall. But he didn't wait. He turned right and sped away, knowing his partner could catch a ride in the fire truck that would follow.

KK arrived at the driveway just in time to see the boxy back of the ambulance speed down the street, running every stop sign it came to and disappearing into the summer night.

17 Beaver Island

Thirty-two miles away from the tourists who shopped on Bridge Street in Charlevoix lay a green emerald isle in the deep blue, white-capped water of Lake Michigan. Beaver Island was the largest island in the lake and in the 1800s was a fisherman's paradise. In 1954, it was nearly a two-and-a-half-hour boat ride or a forty-minute flight on a Douglas DC-3, and on this particular July day, that's how Gus and Clair were getting there.

They hitched a ride on a transport carrying groceries, mail, and other supplies for the island's 300 or so residents. The pilot happened to be a friend of Gus' named Glen. It was a beautiful day and the sky was mostly blue although there were some darker clouds a few miles away to the northeast.

"Boy, when you said you could get me off this planet, you weren't kidding," Clair said. She spoke loudly to be heard over the drone of the twin Rolls-Royce Dart engines in the sparsely appointed but crowded fuselage.

There were twelve worn fabric passenger seats, two on each side of the plane with an aisle in between. Immediately behind them were wooden crates and cardboard boxes with thick straps holding them in place and no curtain or wall separating the passengers from cargo.

Clair wore a leather jacket with a thick lamb's wool collar over her blouse. She looked lost in the outer garment. It was a loaner from

Glen who knew, even in summer, the air at 14,000 feet would be cold.

"Ever been to Beaver Island before?" Gus asked, likewise speaking loudly. He had his lightweight red jacket on and zipped all the way up.

"No," she practically yelled. "Isn't that funny? I've lived here my whole life and have never done what some tourists take for granted. You?"

"Yeah," he said and jerked his thumb toward the pilot. "My buddy Glen has hired me a few times to fly over and unload cargo. It's a good way to pick up some extra cash."

She nodded and glanced out the window at the flat island with its green treetops. It was thirteen miles long and anywhere from three to six miles wide, depending on where you were.

A century earlier, the Mormons had tried to farm there and there was still some farmland where a living could be scratched out. But it was fishing that kept most of the locals fed, combined with tourism, although the number of visitors to the island had dwindled significantly in the past year. There were pristine beaches, unspoiled woodlands, hiking trails, campgrounds and good hunting for deer and turkey, but Beaver Island was rustic, so it took a special kind of tourist to appreciate it; a no-frills-make-coffee-on-a-campfire kind of tourist, which wasn't the usual more affluent kind of Charlevoix visitor.

"Did you know there was once a king on the island?" Gus asked while the plane circled to land on a dirt runway.

Clair shook her head.

"In the 1840s, a Mormon who had broken off with the main church named James Strang brought his followers here to live undisturbed by outside influences. He proclaimed himself king in 1850, not of the island, but of his church. There was a formal coronation and everything. From what I understand, though, he ruled with a pretty firm hand. He had five wives and fourteen children."

"Religions help some, but warp others," Clair opinioned.

Gus cracked a smile as the ground came closer and closer until the wheels kicked up a cloud of dust and the plane touched down.

Once on the ground—and after thanking Glen who advised them to be back in three hours or earlier if a reported storm front moved in—they got some ice cream cones at a general store and then walked along the shoreline. It was laden with millions of smooth rounded stones, each about the size of one's palm and most were perfect for skipping. There were black stones, white stones, speckled and even rust-colored ones. They were left over from the glaciers and once prized by Ottawa Indians for ax and arrowheads. Because the water was crystal clear, the quarry of colors could be seen for dozens of yards as it descended deeper and deeper into the lake.

"He had no right to manipulate my life that way," Clair said, talking about her father and the arrangements he'd made with the hospital CEO.

"He does like things done his way," Gus agreed, but still trying to be non-judgmental in his tone.

"God, this is beautiful," she mused, pausing to look at the water then up at a few billowy clouds that had arrived. She turned her attention back to the conversation. "It's time for total truth between us. When you went to the Shooting Club my father tried to buy you off or something, didn't he?"

"He might've indicated other desires for your future besides me," Gus hesitantly admitted.

"Why didn't you tell me this sooner?"

"Because this isn't high school and it's not us versus them. I didn't want to be a wedge between you and your dad."

"And what happened to your truck? It was Derek, wasn't it?"

"I didn't want to be a wedge between you and your friends, either. Look, Clair. I'm not trying to deceive you. I want to be in your life because that's what *you* want. Not because you're angry at this person or are trying to show up that person."

"Give me a little more credit, Gus."

He stopped walking, scanned the horizon for a moment, and then turned his eyes to hers. "Okay. Your dad told me at his club that he had plans for you and wanted you to be with Derek. Derek and his friends wrecked my truck, sucker-punched me, and then threatened both me and my parents if I didn't run some stupid race with him off the Memorial Bridge while it was opening. So I ran the race. It was at night and very dangerous. He wound up in the hospital and got found out by the cops, and I didn't. There ya go."

She looked at him for a long moment, her jade-green eyes searching for something appropriate to say. But in the end, all she did was take his hand and they continued walking along the picturesque shoreline.

For the next hour they didn't talk about their relationship or those who had tried to sabotage it. They talked about themselves and their expectations out of life. Clair called herself, "Two opposing personalities in one body." On the one hand, she had been brought up with money, had been treated like a princess, and knew exactly how to play the diva. On the other, she wanted to be a nurse, work in an operating room, care for the sick and reassure the frightened.

"My upbringing and professional desires don't quite make sense, do they?" she said as they walked. "Is there any such thing as a tiara-wearing-bedpan cleaner?"

He likewise spoke of his opposites. He admitted there probably weren't a lot of men who worked at a service station but read Shakespeare. He prided himself on being levelheaded and more mature than a lot of his peers, but then he was chided into a schoolboy challenge on the Memorial Bridge that most sensible people would have turned down.

"I guess there are contradictions in both of us," he concluded. "But I think that's the way of most people."

While they walked and talked, the clouds above grew dark and moody as a storm front moved in from Wisconsin. Feeling the wind pick up, Clair looked up at the sky then turned and looked behind her.

"We'd better start back," she said.

"Yeah, I've kind of lost track of time," he admitted.

They turned and headed back to the island's only small village, but they had been walking for more than an hour by now and the incoming storm overtook the island within fifteen minutes. The Great Lakes were notorious for fast-changing weather.

Feeling the first raindrop on her forehead, Clair became concerned. "We're going to get clobbered," she said.

"C'mon," Gus said, heading inland, "let's see if we can find someplace."

They picked up their pace and moved off the stony beach, across a dirt road, and into a stand of tall white pines. At least the overhead canopy would deflect some of the rain, Gus figured.

Just about the time a sheet of rain rolled across the lake and was splashing its way toward shore, Clair spotted something in the distance.

"Over there," she pointed, looking through the trees.

About fifty yards away was a small structure in the woods. They couldn't make out much detail because of the pines in front of them, but a rumble of thunder quickened their steps.

As more and more rain began to pierce the pine canopy above, Gus could see the building was a small clapboard hunter's cabin with a small, curtained four-pane glass window on either side of the wooden plank door. It also had a piece of black stove pipe coming out its side instead of a chimney. Arriving at the door, Gus tried the latch and, as he expected, found it locked.

"It's probably a weekend place for hunters," he said, the wave of black hair on his forehead now flattened because of the rain.

"I'm getting soaked!" Clair complained.

"Right. Stand back," he said, getting ready to kick in the door.

"Wait!" she said. "Step aside."

Moving away from the door, Gus realized he was standing on an old rubber mat that she wanted to look under.

"Clair, nobody's going to hide a key under a mat. I mean, that's the *first* place somebody who wanted to break in would—" he stopped as she produced an old brass key.

"This is an island," she reminded him. "People here know how quick the weather can change and that someone might need emergency shelter." She inserted the key into the lock and the door clicked open.

The inside was sparsely appointed. There was no electricity in the one-room cabin, but they did spot a gas lantern and a box of matches on an old wooden table.

Leaving the door open for light, Gus walked over to where the lantern and matches sat. He opened the box, struck a match, and then lifted the glass on the lantern and fired it up. Meanwhile, Clair shut the door to keep the rain from blowing in.

Looking around, they examined their humble surroundings. There was a wooden floor, a table with two chairs, a cedar chest, a bunk bed with mattresses and pillows but no bedding, some homemade shelves with non-perishable food items, and a small, pot-belly wood-fire stove with two grated cooking places on its top and a door on its rounded face for fuel. There was no running water, bathroom, insulated walls, screens for the windows, or any place else to sit beside the chairs at the table.

"Yeah," Clair said sarcastically, "I can see why burglars would love this place."

Gus ran his finger over the tabletop, looking at the dust. It was obvious the cabin hadn't been recently used. Then he noticed how wet Clair was. Her white bra could be clearly seen under her light-green blouse that was now clinging to her just like his red jacket was clinging to him. Her long hair with its naturally curly ringlets was also limp and stringy.

"Let me see if we've got some towels or blankets or something," Gus said, just as a loud boom of thunder rolled across the sky.

"I'll see about a fire," Clair replied, eying some kindling in wicker a basket with some old rolled-up newspapers next to it.

There was a third small, curtained four-paned window in the rear cabin wall just above the cedar chest that was next to the bunk bed. Gus brushed the thin curtain aside and looked out the back.

"There's an outhouse," he announced.

"Mmm, just like home," Clair joked.

Gus opened the chest while she opened the stove door. "Hey, this isn't bad," he said, poking around the chest. "Sheets, blankets, pillow cases and—thank God—towels. There's even a couple pair of long johns. Looks like one large, one small."

"You think this rain is going to last long?" she asked, feeding some wood into the stove.

"I don't know. But if there's thunder there's probably lightning. So I'm hoping Glen isn't taking off anytime soon. It's still an hour's walk back to what little civilization there is."

He took two towels and the folded winter underwear and put them on the table, then inspected the shelves while peeling off his wet jacket.

"A tin of kerosene, crackers, peanut butter, soup, dried beef jerky, a glass gallon jug of water...we're not going to starve." He saw a rolled-up piece of quarter-inch rope that was looped at both ends. He picked up the rope, searching around at the cabin walls. Sure enough, as he suspected, he saw a small metal hook in one wall and another on the opposite wall. He put one looped end on a hook, then unrolled the rope as he crossed the cabin.

"What's that?" Clair asked, now finished with the wood and putting a rolled newspaper into the stove.

"Clothesline," he said, hooking up the other end. He took his wet jacket and hung it on the rope followed by his T-shirt.

"What're you doing?" she asked.

"Getting out of these wet clothes," he answered.

She looked at his taut bare chest with hesitation.

"We *have* seen each other in swimwear," he reminded her.

"I didn't say anything," she responded, as another clap of thunder crackled.

He plucked a towel off the table, rubbed his hair, and then started to dry off his chest while she turned her attention back to the stove and struck a match.

"Is there a flue for the stove?" he asked.

"I didn't see one," she answered.

"Look the other way for a moment," he said.

She did as he requested, knowing he was taking off his pants. There was a part of her upbringing that told her his getting undressed without asking her permission was inappropriate and presumptuous. But another part of her reasoned, what were they supposed to do? Stay in soaking wet clothes? Besides, in the weeks that they had been keeping company, Gus had never been anything but a perfect gentleman.

She listened to the rain on the roof and pretended to fiddle with the fire crouched in front of the stove door until he came over and offered her the other pair of smaller folded long johns and a towel.

She turned and rose. He was now wearing the larger white long johns and his damp hair was wild and askew.

"Comb your hair," she laughed. "You look like a wooly mammoth." She turned and headed for the door.

"Where are you going?"

"If I'm going to get into some dry clothes, I'm going to keep my wet ones on until I use the facilities."

"Oh, yeah," he agreed. "I hadn't thought of that." He turned and took his red jacket off of the clothesline. "Put this over your head. It's not much but it'll help." He turned to the shelves looking for a roll of toilet paper.

"I'll be fine," Clair said, knowing what he was looking for. She spread his jacket over his head, then opened the door to the outside, where it was raining harder than ever.

While Clair was using the outhouse in back, Gus decided to run out to the nearest tree in front. He took off his dry long johns, put his wet Hanes briefs back on, and hurried outside barefoot in only his underwear. While he was peeing, he heard the familiar drone of two Rolls-Royce Dart engines above and caught just a glimpse of a DC-3 in between the tops of the pines.

"Oh, no," he said, knowing they'd now be stuck on Beaver Island until the following morning.

By the time Clair came running back to the cabin with his jacket still stretched over her head. He was back into his long john bottoms and was once again drying off his bare chest.

"You okay?" he asked, as she came into the cabin thoroughly soaked.

"That's maybe the nastiest smelling place I've ever been," she said plainly, her hair, clothes and his jacket dripping everywhere. She noticed he was shirtless again.

"I changed into my wet underwear and used a tree out front," he explained.

"Ah, the advantages of having a penis," she noted. It was the first time he had ever heard her speak so bluntly about the male anatomy. But then, he figured, she was a nurse.

"Get out of those clothes," he said, turning his back to her and pulling on his long john top. While he heard her wet clothes coming off, he made small talk.

"I, uh...I hate to tell you this...but when I was outside, I think I saw...no, I *know* I saw our ride flying back to Charlevoix."

"Yes, I heard it too and figured it was our plane. Your friend's probably trying to get ahead of even worse weather."

"Which means we're stuck here until tomorrow. I'm sorry about the inconvenience. When it lets up, we can walk back to town. There's a phone at the general store and you can call your folks."

"I don't need my folks' permission to stay out," she said, a little defensively.

"Of course not. I just thought you might not want them to worry." He had a comb sitting next to his wallet that was drying out on the table, which he used to put his wet hair back in order. By the time he was finished, Clair had changed.

"Eh—I don't think these are going to work for me," she said.

"What's wrong?"

"This long underwear is made for, like, a twelve-year-old boy."

"Meaning?"

"Meaning it's kinda tight."

"You want to wear my top? There's also a blanket in the cedar chest."

"Just, just don't gawk too much. Okay? This is really embarrassing."

He slowly turned around to face her. As she had warned, the outfit was very snug and short on her. The sleeves came to a stop four inches above her wrists while her braless thirty-two D-size breasts hung loose and were pretty clearly outlined. Her erect nipples were obvious. Meanwhile, her long john bottoms hugged the outline of her rounded thighs and voluptuous pear-shaped butt and her calves continued a good six inches beyond the ribbed ends of the fabric's legs. All in all, it looked like the long johns had been painted on her.

He saw that her wet, stringy hair was causing her shoulders and neck to get wet, so he temporarily ignored her immense woman-of-the-wild attractiveness, went over to the cedar chest, pulled out a blanket, and then stepped over to her and wrapped it around her shoulders.

"Here," he said softly, gently pulling her hair out from under the blanket. "No sense in getting these clothes wet too."

The awkward moment was over. He had seen the total outline of her body, which didn't leave much to the imagination, and had handled it gallantly. He had taken off work for her, given her his jacket to go outside, and had tried to find toilet paper so she could be more comfortable. He had endured intimidation from her father and physical violence from Derek to be with her. Above and beyond all this, he'd risked his life at least in part for her on the Memorial Bridge. It was at this exact moment that Clair Sinclair knew for certain she had fallen in love with Gus Cooper.

"Thank you," she smiled. She looked around the cabin while another crack of thunder rattled the windows. "Now what?"

Gus looked over at the shelves and saw a box of Bicycle playing cards.

"Know how to play Gin Rummy?"

For the next hour-and-a-half, they played cards at the table. They laughed and joked and spoke of everything from favorite books to favorite foods. A little to Gus' surprise, Clair claimed to be a decent cook. He likewise spoke of particular dishes that he made. Being an only child, his mother had taught him some family recipes, like five-alarm chili and the Cooper's famous spaghetti sauce.

By the time they finished, the rain had lightened up, but it was still falling, so they decided to have something to eat. They had chicken noodle soup, peanut butter on crackers, and water. Clair asked if Gus had spoken to his parents about her and he responded that he had. He also said that they wanted him to bring her over to the house for dinner. He told her his parents were in a different financial bracket than her family and that she shouldn't be put off by his modest home. But he was also quick to point out he wasn't ashamed of his parents' lack of money. In fact, he admired how they could stretch a dollar and how he enjoyed a childhood that may not have been full of material possessions, but was full of love.

By 8:15 p.m., the rain had finally stopped. Gus wasn't sure how late the general store in the village stayed open but he knew of a hotel that had a phone a couple of doors down and volunteered to walk there and make a call on Clair's behalf, since her clothes were still quite wet. But she said no. Partly because it was an hour's walk there and back and the rain could start up again, and partly because she was still angry at her father and she figured she didn't owe her parents a call if she wanted to stay out all night. She also didn't want to be left alone in someone else's hunting cabin on an island she'd never been on before.

"Okay, then," Gus said, after asking her to turn around while he changed back into his damp clothes. "While we've got a break in the weather, I want to gather some more wood for the stove. It might be a little smoky 'cause it'll be wet, but it'll be better than freezing." He was overstating it, but she knew what he meant. Even in summer, the nights in northern Michigan could drop down into the fifties. So while she was turned in the opposite direction and he was changing, she inspected the night by looking out one of the front windows.

"I think it's still pretty cloudy up there," she said, looking at the sky.

"Hard to tell with the trees, though. It's also weird, being on this island but not seeing a single soul except in the village."

"There's more island these days than there are people," Gus said, slipping off his bottoms. "Your dad's right about one thing, there *is* a recession going on. Some people say it's the worst since the 1930s."

As he spoke, he wasn't aware Clair was unintentionally seeing his naked reflection in the glass of the window. The sight of his fit form excited her tremendously.

"Yeah, I think I'll change too, after you're done, and use that aromatic outhouse again."

"Well, if all you're going to do is pee, you don't have to go out back," he suggested. "You could just find a place out front and squat."

"No," she said, self-consciously. "I couldn't do that."

"Why not? The smell of urine will keep the bears away."

She suddenly turned to him as he was buttoning up his shirt.

"There are bears?" she asked seriously.

A slow smile crept across his face. "No." Then he drank in the site of her.

Her long blonde hair was now dry, frizzy and unruly, framing her dark eyebrows and high cheekbones. With her rounded breasts, shapely hips, and legs that looked longer than they were because of the children's size clothing she was wearing, she looked like a pin-up girl for Fruit Of The Loom.

"You are so incredibly beautiful," he said quietly.

She smiled. "I'll give you an hour to stop with the compliments."

They looked at each other for a long moment, then he pointed to the door.

"Firewood," he reminded himself.

She smiled again as he went out the door.

He was gone about fifteen minutes and purposely gathered firewood far enough away from the cabin where Clair would have privacy if she chose not to use the outhouse. When he returned with an armful of wood, she had just finished making the bunk beds.

He stood in the open doorway a little surprised that the beds had been made. She noticed his reaction.

"Did I do something wrong?" she asked. "Aren't we going to be spending the night?"

"Yes, we are. It's just—" he looked at his wristwatch, "it's still early, there's still light in the sky, and I thought the whole sleeping thing might be a little awkward for you."

She shook her head with a knowing smile. "No. There's no awkwardness with you. Not anymore."

"Good. Then I call dibs on top," he said and shut the door. He placed the branches he had gathered on the floor side-by-side in a corner of the cabin. "These will dry out a little faster if they're not all jammed together in the basket."

They played cards again for another hour and talked for a little more afterward. When the sun finally disappeared around 10:00 p.m., the kerosene lamp was turned off and they climbed into their respective bunks, she on the bottom and he on top. Neither one was particularly tired, but there wasn't anything else left to do in the small cabin, except for the night to evolve into an evening of passion, which frankly, both of them were thinking about.

As their eyes adjusted to the darkness, the flicker of the flames in between the closed seams of the stove's iron door danced on the wooden walls with slivers of light giving the bare place a warm, even romantic look.

"So who do you think uses this cabin?" Clair asked, looking up at the bunk above her.

"Based on the size of your long underwear, I'd say a father a son," Gus quietly answered. "I'm sure they use it for hunting."

"Do you want to go hunting with your son someday?" she asked, really trying to find out whether or not he liked children.

"Absolutely," he said. "I'm actually pretty good with a shotgun. And being out in the woods brings a father and son together."

She smiled, liking his answer.

"What about religion?" she asked.

"What about it?"

"Do you go to church? Believe in God?"

"Yes. I do."

After a moment, she responded. "Good."

"You?"

"Yes. I like to think there's a greater intelligence guiding us, helping us."

"Good."

Then they were quiet, each thinking about how much they wanted the other, but worried about what the other might think if those feelings were exposed. In the interim, they noticed the tree frogs outside had begun to sing, a good sign that the foul weather was behind them.

"Gus?" she finally asked, breaking the silence.

"Mmm?"

"Why haven't you kissed me since we stepped inside this cabin?"

"Why haven't I—" he stopped in mid-sentence and hopped out

of his bunk. Once on the floor, he slowly squatted down until he was level with her.

With her bright green eyes, inviting lips and long blonde hair spilling over her pillow and shoulders, she was a vision.

"Because I'm trying to be a gentleman," he answered softly. "And with you, that's not always easy. If we start kissing, particularly with the wonderful way you look right now, I'm not going to want to stop. But there will come a point tonight when you'll want me to. So, why endure the torture?"

She mustered all her courage to say her response, "How do you know I'm going to want you to stop?"

His eyes sparkled with desire at her answer. He started to slowly move toward her, but then paused.

"If we do this," he half whispered, "that's it for me. I'll be a goner. Far as I'm concerned, it'll be forever."

She smiled and slowly opened her arms.

"Then, let forever begin."

18 Aftermath

Michael O'Hearn was a tall, big-shouldered cop who stood at six-feet-two and worked out a lot. He played poker every couple of weeks with Doc, Lance, and some other guys from the fire hall. The game always rotated from one player's house to the next and the only person who participated that wasn't a cop or fireman was Gus, who Doc had brought into the game. Most of the guys knew Gus from the marina so they knew he'd be a good addition. They liked his wry sense of humor and observations of life from a mature perspective. They also knew he could be opinionated and downright feisty. So when Michael saw Gus' Honda SUV speed down the street then screech to a stop in front of Farren's house, he took a deep anticipatory breath. Even as imposing as Michael was physically, he didn't want to rile Farren's grandfather.

Her mushroom house looked like a crime scene right out of a CSI show. Three of the city's five police cars sat in front of Farren's place with their bubble lights blinking and cutting through the night. Both neighbors and tourists watched from a cordoned-off perimeter of yellow caution tape. Some in the crowd talked about a shooting. Others recognized that the victim had been Charlene Rogers. A photographer took pictures of Farren's bloodstained front step, the flash from his camera exploding in the night for a second at a time like a miniature bomb blast. BJ, with his unmistakable protruding stomach silhouetted in profile and another cop stood in the front yard talking about a probable trajectory for the shot. The cop talking with BJ was pointing east, past Farren's front yard and down to the corner of another street about sixty yards away. A fire truck with its blinking lights and throaty diesel engine idling was also there. KK, still in his running shorts and dark blue Charlevoix Fire Department T-shirt, spoke in a huddle with the two other firefighters of the night crew who were ready to help with everything from directing traffic to interviewing neighbors.

Seeing Gus approach through the crowd with determination and heading straight to the perimeter tape, Michael walked over to him and held out an arm, trying to stop him, or at least slow him down.

"Whoa, hang on there, Gus!"

The old man didn't say a word, he simply grabbed the yellow plastic tape with both calloused hands, broke it, and then continued walking.

"You can't do that Gus!" Michael called. "This is a crime scene! *Gus?*"

Seeing him come up the lawn, BJ told the officer he was talking with to give him a minute. The officer walked away as Gus arrived.

"Where's your granddaughter?" the chief asked.

"Doc's cabin with David Wright," Gus answered. David was the off-duty cop who was guarding Farren this particular night. "He practically had to tie her into a chair to keep her from going to the hospital."

"Anything new on Charlene?" the old cop asked.

Gus shook his head. "You'll order twenty-four-hour protection for my granddaughter. Heavily armed protection."

"Don't dictate to me what I will or won't—"

"You'll order it *now*," Gus demanded.

BJ looked at Gus' lock-jawed, razor-steel expression. As chief of police, he wasn't used to taking orders from a civilian. But then he remembered that he worked for civilians and that Gus had seen this threat coming all along. He locked his thumbs into the belt loops under his huge gut, demonstrating an unusual moment of contriteness, and nodded.

"Alright."

Without speaking further, Gus turned and started to return the way he came.

"You know, it could've just been a random shot," the chief called. "There's three times more guns in this county than people. Somebody coulda been celebratin' a birthday or anniversary."

"But it wasn't, Sherlock!" Gus called as he strode back past Michael.

An hour and twenty minutes later in the small waiting room at the hospital, Doc held a Styrofoam cup of coffee while sitting next to Lance. Since Lance was off-duty when Charlene had been shot, he was wearing a short-sleeve shirt and old some jeans. His thick, steel wool-like hair was at present a little unruly from him nervously running his fingers through it. It was now after midnight and both men were emotionally spent. Since Doc left the Fire Hall without KK, Lance had acted as EMT for his own fiancé. In fact, a large smear of her blood was still on his arm. He looked down at it and gently put his hand on it. It was a caress that didn't escape Doc's notice.

"I'm done," Lance said quietly. "I'm through with blood, and pain, and death...when Charlene recovers, we're gonna get married and I'm going to take over my parent's wine store. The only red stain I ever want to see on my clothes again is from a spilled glass of rose."

"Don't make any big decisions tonight," Doc advised, taking a sip of coffee.

"No, I mean it," Lance said, "I'm through. I'm not even going to ask stupid James Bond trivia questions anymore. I'm not going to celebrate someone who kills people."

Doc opened his mouth to remind his friend that James Bond wasn't even real, but saw Lance wasn't in a state of mind to be argued with, so he decided to pursue another thought.

"You sure you don't want to call Charlene's parents? Her sister?"

Lance ran his fingers through his hair again. "No. Charlene's mom is even more high strung than Charlene. She'd just be pacing up and down here, bawling her eyes out and adding a level of stress that isn't helpful. When we have a definitive prognosis, then I'll tell both sets of parents."

Doc nodded and took another sip of coffee.

"I, uh, know you wanted to keep the news about Bartholomew being released from jail contained," Lance said, "but, I don't know how I can sit on this."

"I understand," Doc agreed. "You know, Lance, if I could've taken that bullet for her..."

"It's not your fault, man," Lance answered. "Anyway, thanks for getting on the scene so fast. I think you set a new land speed record."

"And you don't know what she was picking up for Farren?"

"She just said 'girl stuff.' That bag for her is still in the back of the ambulance, by the way."

Dr. Bob Lancaster coming into the waiting room interrupted them. Lancaster was thirty-four years old, lean and fit, and a crackerjack emergency room physician. Doc thought the city was lucky to have him and he considered himself especially lucky that Lancaster happened to be working the late shift tonight. He came into the waiting area wearing his usual surgical scrubs and a skullcap. Like Lance's arm, his clothing was blotched with Charlene's blood. The sight immediately caused Lance's anxiety level to skyrocket. Both Lance and Doc hopped to their feet as he entered the room.

"Hey guys," the doctor said, sounding a little tired. "First things first. She's going to be fine."

"Thank God," Lance and Doc both said at the same time.

"But we've still got work to do," Lancaster continued. "The humerus was shattered by the bullet. I had to put it back together using a couple of steel pins, and the muscle tissue in the forearm was pretty messy too. Even with rigorous physical therapy, I think there's going to be some motion loss."

"How much?" Doc asked.

"Depends how successful the therapy is. Best case? She might regain eighty percent use."

Doc and Lance exchanged concerned glances. Seeing this, Lancaster felt the need to say more.

"Guys, she's incredibly lucky. If she hadn't turned her body to reach for her cell at that exact moment, she'd be dead. The bullet would've gone right through her heart."

Tears started to well up in Lance's eyes. Doc put a reassuring arm on his friend's shoulder.

"That hole in her arm was huge," the paramedic noted. "What caliber bullet was it?"

Lancaster reached into the breast pocket of his surgical scrubs and pulled out a partially flattened, blood-soaked slug about an inch long. "You tell me?" he said, handing it to Doc. "I'm no forensics expert, but I've taken my share of bullets out of people and I've never seen one like this." The surgeon paused for a moment, changing subjects. "Is Farren safe? I mean, you guys were talking when you brought Charlene in about how that loan shark was back on the street and that this could have been meant for her."

"She's safe," Doc answered, examining the bullet then handing it back to the doctor.

"It was probably the hair," Lance realized. "Charlene was coming out of Farren's house, she has short hair like her now, the outside front light was off, they're the same age..."

"That makes sense," Doc agreed.

"Dude, you should go be with Farren," Lance urged.

"I'm on night shift," Doc reminded him.

"In all probability, someone tried to kill your girlfriend tonight," Lancaster said. "Not even Stubigg could argue with that. Lance is right."

"Somebody might need me," Doc protested.

"Somebody *does* need you," Lancaster agreed. "Look, I'll go out with KK myself if he gets a call. Charlene's the only patient in-house tonight, your shift's already half over, so go."

"Well..."

"Take the ambulance back to the fire hall, tell KK I'm covering for you and go."

"In the meantime, can I see Charlene?" Lance asked.

"She's not going to wake up for a while," the surgeon warned.

"That's okay," he replied as he turned to Doc. "Go take care of your own. I'll let all the relatives know in the morning."

Doc nodded, but felt the need to apologize some more.

"It's okay, man," Lance assured him. "I know. I know." He cracked a polite smile, and then headed for the ICU.

Lancaster held up a finger for Doc to hang for a moment after Lance had gone.

"This probably isn't the night to ask, but, have you heard anything from Wayne State Medical School?"

"No," Doc said, glancing down at the floor.

"How long has it been?"

"Long enough," Doc said as he shook his head. "They're not going to accept me, Bob. Either I'm too old, or a bad risk because I was accepted ten years ago but didn't go, or my MCATs were too low, or, I don't know what?"

"You're a natural-born physician, man," Lancaster reinforced. "I've never seen anyone with the gift like you."

"Doesn't matter," Doc shrugged.

Lancaster looked at him for a moment. "How many bones in the adult human body?"

"What?"

"How many bones are in the adult human body?"

"About two hundred six," Doc answered.

"How many bones are in a newborn?"

Doc looked at Lancaster, not wanting to take a test to prove his medical expertise at this particular moment, but he answered anyway.

"More than two-seventy."

"How can that be if there are only two hundred six bones in the adult body?" the surgeon asked.

"A newborn's bones aren't entirely fused together yet," Doc correctly answered, rubbing his forehead wearily.

"A fifty-six-year-old man goes and sees his physician for an annual check-up," Lancaster continued. "The doctor asks how he's feeling. The man says fine except when he gets up in the morning and urinates his stream isn't as strong as it is the rest of the–"

"Enlarged prostate," Doc correctly diagnosed.

Lancaster cracked a small smile, and then went on, "A woman, forty years old, two hundred sixty pounds gets off a plane after a flying non-stop across the country. She has a sudden onset of chest pain and shortness of breath. An on-scene EMT thinks she's having a heart attack. Is she?"

"It could be that," Doc agreed, "but it could also be a pulmonary embolism."

"And what would you do for that?" Lancaster asked.

"Blood thinners," Doc answered.

The physician's smile widened. "Average paramedics don't know stuff like that, Doc. Believe me, you've *got* the gift."

"Maybe," Doc admitted, "but the application's been made. It's all in God's hands now."

"God helps those who help themselves," Lancaster reminded him.

Doc patted his friend on the arm. "I appreciate everything you've done...I gotta go."

Twenty-two minutes later, Doc's red Jeep Wrangler turned from Boyne City Road onto the dirt and gravel lane that wound through the woods leading back to his cabin. As he was turning, a uniformed officer wearing a bulletproof vest and carrying a shotgun stepped out of the darkness of the woods about ten yards down the lane. Seeing it was Doc with the ever-present Gertrude in the passenger side seat, he waved him on.

A quarter of a mile later, after twisting and turning through the white pine woods on either side of the lane, he arrived at his cabin. A police cruiser sat in the turn-around behind Farren's blue VW, and another uniformed officer wearing another bulletproof vest stood outside near the back door. As Doc rolled to a halt, he saw yet another figure step out of the shadows around the lake side of the cabin. It was David Wright. Months earlier, Officer Wright had been shot and wounded by Charlie as he tried to escape from the authorities after Doc had foiled his attempted murder of Farren. But he made a full recovery and was now a better cop for the experience. His Beretta semi-automatic pistol was clearly visible on the belt of his blue jeans as he strode toward the Jeep.

"This is like a scene out of *The Godfather*," Doc quipped. Seeing that everybody else was carrying, he reached over to his glove compartment, opened it, and took out his snubnosed Smith & Wesson 38-caliber revolver.

He also picked up the bag Charlene had gotten for Farren.

"Hey, Doc," Wright greeted as he climbed out. "The chief's ordered 24/7 protection for Farren until further notice. So with the other two guys here, I guess that means you don't need me for freelance anymore."

"No, you're still on the payroll," Doc verified, slipping the revolver into his front cargo pants pocket. "Right now I want Farren to have all the protection she can get."

"How's Charlene?" the other uniformed cop asked.

"Lancaster thinks she's going to lose some movement in her arm," Doc answered.

"A lot?" Wright asked.

"He hopes not," Doc replied.

The three men looked at one another with short, serious glances. It was a silent reaffirmation to both protect Farren and get the shooter that had done this to Charlene. Since both the fire and police departments shared the same building, most of the guys in one department knew the wives and girlfriends of the guys in the other. It was hard not to take what happened to Charlene personally.

"Oh, thank God, you're home," Farren said, hurrying out of the kitchen door and still clearly upset about Charlene.

All three men quickly stepped over to her.

"Uh, let's get back inside, honey," Doc said, hastily hugging her then turning her around.

"Yes, I think that's best," the uniformed cop said.

"Please, Farren, back inside," Officer Wright encouraged.

"She looked at all three men puzzled at first, but then understood the additional risk of her being out in the open at night. She went back into the cabin without argument followed by Doc.

"I'll be back near the water," Wright said as Doc nodded then shut the door.

"How'd you get off work early?" she asked as he threw the deadbolt.

"Bob Lancaster's covering for me," he answered.

"How's Charlene?"

"She's going to live. Lancaster thinks she'll lose some use of her arm."

"Oh, no!"

"Actually, Lancaster says she's lucky. Lance was calling her when it happened. If she hadn't of turned to reach for her phone..." he looked at her and didn't have to finish the sentence.

"My-God-my-God-my-God," Farren repeated, quickly and regretfully.

"Here," Doc said, handing her the zipped-up bag. "I guess Charlene was getting some stuff for you?"

She nodded, stepped forward and gently took it. "Did you — do you know what she was picking up?"

"No," he said honestly. "What?"

"You didn't peek inside?"

He shook his head. "Lance said Charlene told him it was girl stuff."

She smiled sadly, unzipped the bag and looked inside. "She was getting lingerie for me. She bought some for her honeymoon today in Traverse City, and we got talking about sexy clothes and I thought I might try to..." her voice faded, just like their chances of being intimate tonight, given the circumstances.

Doc was surprised, even pleased, he supposed, with Farren's effort. But he couldn't help but wonder if tonight's events would actually further damage his girl's emotional fragility. He didn't quite know what to say. Instead, he simply drew her near and gave her a reassuring hug. It helped for the moment, but both of them were now scared and uncertain about the future.

Three hours later, a little after 4:00 a.m., a phone rang in one of the last still-functioning phone booths in Flint. It was in a dingy rural area near a vacant General Motors assembly plant and was in front of a twenty-four-hour convenience store. The phone booth had been spray-painted by a gang to mark its local territory. Bartholomew got out of his white Cadillac Escalade, looked around, then stepped into the booth. Using a public phone was always more preferable than a cell when discussing potentially incriminating matters, and he and

Yuri had worked out this arrangement before Yuri ever headed north.

Picking up the receiver, the loan shark didn't even say "Hello."

"Was the delivery made?" he began.

"There was problem," Yuri's voice answered in his broken, heavily-accented English.

"'Problem' is my least favorite word," his American cousin responded.

"There was mistake. Someone who looked like customer got damaged. Not fatal, but damaged."

"You left a witness?"

"No. No witness. Just wrong person in wrong place."

"How do you know this?" Bartholomew asked.

"I was in crowd afterward. There were police. Many people standing around. Some couple knew the girl. It wasn't our customer. Next time, you should give me photo instead of just description and address."

Bartholomew lowered his head and expelled a frustrated breath. "This is unbelievable. I imported you so there wouldn't *be* any mistakes!"

"Shit can occur," Yuri said, meaning to say: 'Shit happens.' "But I will fix."

"Yes, you do that," Bartholomew answered, trying to control his anger.

"You fix it! Don't come back until you do!"

19 Mid-air

It wasn't until 1:00 p.m. the following day that the DC-3 from Charlevoix was scheduled to return to Beaver Island. That gave Gus and Clair plenty of time to get up the following morning, walk back to the village with their laundry from the cabin, go to a Laundromat, and get the sheets and long underwear washed and dried. A man at the Laundromat who knew where the cabin was promised to return the items and once again leave the key under the mat. He understood why Gus and Clair were forced to use the cabin and appreciated their efforts to put everything back the way it was. But he also noticed some stains on the sheets prior to laundering and winked at Gus knowingly.

Glen was all apologies about stranding them, but as Clair had correctly guessed, he wanted to get back to the mainland before the storm got worse. Now in the air and flying over the occasional iron ore freighter and sailboat on another cloudless, magnificent day, Clair rested her head on Gus' shoulder wearing his lightweight red jacket with a contented smile on her face.

"Are you okay?" he asked.

"What?"

Are you okay?" he asked more loudly because of the engines.

"Fine."

Are you warm enough?" he practically yelled. "Can I get you anything?"

"Gus, that's about the tenth time you've asked if I'm okay," she said loudly. "I lost my virginity last night. Not my left lung!"

Glen, in the cockpit, smiled to himself from behind his dark aviator glasses, having also heard Clair's pronouncement.

Gus patted her leg. "I just want to make sure you're alright."

"I'm perfect," she half bellowed.

"Yes, you are," he agreed. "What do you think's going to happen when we get back to town?"

"You mean, besides my father's head coming off?"

"There's bound to be talk."

"So there will be talk," she replied, not caring.

"What do you want to happen?" he asked loudly.

"What do *I* want?" she asked as she thought for a moment. "I want to begin the next chapter of my life. I want to be an OR nurse. I want my father to leave me alone and realize I'm a grown woman. And I want to spend as much time with you as possible," she said, giving him a peck on the neck.

She was sitting in the seat next to the window and Gus was sitting next to the aisle. He suddenly got up, turned to her, knelt down on one knee in middle of the aisle and took her left hand.

"Then please do me the honor of marrying me," he said loudly.

"What?" she cried, astonished.

"Clair, I love you!" he said more loudly than ever since he was now further away from her than when he was sitting next to her. "I couldn't love another human being more. I'm sorry that I don't have a ring. I'm sorry that I don't have the kind of lifestyle you've been brought up in. I'm even sorry that this is happening in mid-air. But ever since I've met you, that's where my heart's been—in mid-air. After last night, I can't go back to just dating. I can't go back to not sleeping with you. Your parents are never going to say yes to me. So let's say yes to ourselves. Beginning right here. Right now. I know a chapel in Petoskey where you get can a license, ring, everything. I've got almost 5,000 dollars in the bank and Mr. Kirkland, the principal over at the high school, doesn't think the sociology teacher's coming back in the fall. I can be hired on a probationary basis while I'm finishing my degree. What do you say? Do you *really* want the next chapter of your life to begin?"

Glen looked over his shoulder from the cockpit and back at Clair to see what she'd say.

Her green eyes were flooding with tears.

"Oh, Gus," she smiled, "that's the nicest proposal anybody's ever yelled at me."

20 Signs

At 9:00 a.m. the morning after Charlene had been shot, a police cruiser pulled into one of the back garage doors of the fire hall and into the space where Doc and Lance's ambulance usually sat. After the garage door was shut, two officers wearing bulletproof vests got out, one of them opening the door for the slender figure in the backseat. It was Farren wearing a long sleeve light grey hoodie pulled up over her head despite the fact it was already in the high seventies outside. She was likewise wearing a bulletproof vest.

Walking across the clean concrete floor to meet them was Doc who had driven separately under the advisement of the cops and had arrived a few minutes earlier. He was carrying Gertrude under his arm. Both he and Farren were pretty dragged out. Neither one had gotten much sleep, although he was trying to keep her in a good humor.

"Not everybody can wear one of those and get away with it," he said, gesturing to her vest, "but on you, it works."

"I feel stupid in this," she said, pulling off her hood. "Was it really necessary?"

"Better safe than sorry," one of the officers replied. "'Sides, we never get the chance to use this stuff."

"C'mon," Doc said, "BJ's waiting for us."

They walked from the garage area down a narrow hall, past the dispatcher and Captain Stubigg's office to BJ's. After the rescue dummy had been put on the floor behind their chairs, Doc helped Farren off with her vest.

Half a minute later, BJ's protruding stomach came through the office doorway followed by the rest of him carrying a mug of coffee that said "Chief."

"Good morning," he said, looking the tired pair over. "You two look like I feel. I guess nobody got much sleep last night."

"No," Doc said.

"Not much," Farren added.

"Anything new on Charlene?" the chief asked, settling into a squeaky chair.

"Not that I know of," Doc said. "But I wouldn't be surprised if they start her on physical therapy this morning."

"Yeah, they're doin' that earlier and earlier these days," BJ agreed.

"You two want some coffee?"

"No thanks," Farren answered.

"I'm good," Doc said.

The big cop took a sip from his mug then set it down. "Well, I'm sure you both want to know what we've accomplished thus far. About an hour ago, the Flint Police showed up at Gordon Bartholomew's condo to question him. They rousted him and his girlfriend out of the sack, which I'm sure they loved doing. Unfortunately, Bartholomew's got an airtight alibi for last night. He and his girlfriend were hosting a dinner party for eight guests, including his attorney and a former state representative. There are suspicions by the police down there that the former representative is a gambling client of Bartholomew's, but that's unsubstantiated."

"If the shooter wasn't Bartholomew, then it was certainly someone sent by him," Doc concluded.

"That's a fair guess," BJ said, "and we're working under that assumption. But, so far, we've got no shell casing, no witnesses, no tire tracks, we *do* have the bullet removed from the victim, but it's covered with yours and Bob Lancaster's fingerprints."

Doc rubbed his forehead with his fingertips, embarrassed. "Uh, yeah. Sorry 'bout that."

"We'll run ballistics, but I gotta be honest with you two, we don't have a whole hell of a lot to go on at the moment. What we need is a significant lead."

"And you can't tell your people to be on the lookout for strangers," Farren concluded, "because ninety-five percent of the people in town are strangers."

"Exactly," BJ nodded, picking up his coffee and taking another sip.

"So, what can we do?" Doc asked.

"Three things," BJ replied. "First, we'll see what ballistics turns up. It looks to me like the round could be foreign made, but that's just a guess. Second, Miss Farren, if you'd like to be a guest of the city, we can probably fix up a holding cell for you. We may not be the Ritz Carlton, but you'd be very secure."

Farren grimaced at the prospect. "What's the third thing?" she asked.

"Get out of town. Take a vacation. Give us some time to try and find a respectable lead."

"I'm not going to run away just because you don't have a lead," Farren said, getting irritated.

"If that shot was meant for you and a professional's behind it—well—I'm sorry to say this, but it's likely he'll try again."

The chief's comment should have put the fear of God into Farren. But it didn't. Instead, she got angry.

"Stay at Doc's but nobody knows for how long. Stay here but nobody knows for how long. Get out of town and give you time. Maybe Bartholomew's after me. Maybe he's not. How much time do you need chief? A week? A month? A *year?*"

"Calm down," Doc suggested, patting her hand.

"I don't want to calm down!" she said, hopping to her feet. "I didn't ask for this! And I didn't do anything wrong! I've got a life! I'm entitled to live it! So if you'll excuse me, gentlemen, that's exactly what I'm going to do!"

She started to walk out of the office. As she did, BJ rose from his chair.

"Now just hold on there, young lady!" he ordered. "Where do

you think you're going?"

"I'm going to go visit a friend in the hospital. Then I'm going to work. I'm not basing my life on 'maybes' anymore!"

"That isn't very wise," the old cop advised. "In fact, it could be downright dangerous."

"Come on, honey," Doc urged. "We're just thinking about your safety and trying to get your life back to normal."

"Normal?" she asked, becoming the angriest that Doc had ever seen her. "In all the time you've known me, nothing in my life has been normal! I've been a mark, a sucker! A perpetual victim! Of loneliness, of Charlie, of an assassin, of God Almighty who stole my parents! Y'know, most kids get to go shopping with their mom for a prom dress. But not me! Most kids get to have their parents there for high school graduation. But not me! Most brides get to have somebody walk them down the aisle. Most wives aren't choked on their honeymoon by their husbands while he's, he's..."

She stopped herself, realizing she was revealing too much. She wiped hot, angry tears off her cheek and tried to get control of herself.

"D-don't talk to me about 'normal,'" she finally said. Then she turned and stormed out of the office.

BJ followed her out the door and found the two officers that had brought her in, ordering them to stick to her like glue no matter where she went. Doc knew that she couldn't be directed or held against her will, so he picked Gertrude up with one arm and his girlfriend's bulletproof vest with the other and walked down the hall, discouraged, fearful and even embarrassed for her.

"Reynolds?" he heard Stubigg's voice call as he passed his office. He closed his eyes painfully and slowly turned back to the captain's office, not wanting any more grief this particular morning. He appeared in the doorway loaded down with Gertrude and the vest.

"Sorry about what happened last night," Stubigg said, sitting behind his desk. "I'm not even going to chew you out for going out on a call and leaving your partner stranded, although I should."

Doc just looked at him knowing he was right, but being too tired to even try and mount a defense. Stubigg saw this and continued,

"Look, if you need to take some time, get some things in order..."

"Lance is probably going to call you this morning," Doc said, "He's the one who needs the time. He might try to quit. Don't accept his resignation."

"I already have," the chief answered. "He called from the hospital about twenty minutes ago."

Doc's heart sank. He didn't know what to say.

"Take some time off," Stubigg suggested. "But keep up with your online classes. That's something I can't stop."

Doc nodded slightly, then turned and continued down the hall. By the time he reached the garage, the cruiser was already pulling out with Farren in the backseat, presumably heading for the hospital. Doc knew she needed her space and didn't particularly want him around at the moment, so he decided to go home and get some much-needed sleep.

Once in his Jeep and heading through town with Gertrude in the passenger-side seat, he began to pray.

"God, please keep Farren safe today. Please let the cops find something that'll lead us to the shooter," then his prayers changed recipients, "and Clair, if you can hear me, ask the boss if you can come back. I think your granddaughter is in more danger now than she's ever been. I can't protect her without you're help. I, I'm just a small town paramedic. So please!" He looked over at Gertrude and sighed. "I might as well be talking to you...Prayers are just an excuse for people to talk to themselves."

Once back at the cabin, he fell into bed and slept for the next seven hours. At 4:30 that afternoon, the piercing organ notes that kicked off Sarah McLachlan's "Sweet Surrender" came over his clock radio, waking him. Slapping the top of the device with his hand, he thought about whether or not he wanted to take Stubigg up on his offer and take some time off work or go in for his shift at 6:00 p.m. Whatever he was going to do, he figured he'd have to make a decision quickly if a nighttime replacement was going to be found.

He rolled out of bed, opened the bedroom door leading out into the living room, and called for Farren. Hearing nothing, he assumed she went to work and wondered how in the world she ever got through the day with so little sleep.

He wandered back through his bedroom and into the Jack-and-Jill bathroom that connected the cabin's two bedrooms. He urinated, washed his face, put on a clean CFD navy-blue T-shirt, a clean pair of black cargo pants, shoes and socks, and a burgundy long-sleeve shirt over the T-shirt because he felt a little chilly. He walked into the kitchen feeling more awake and made himself a cup of instant coffee in the microwave. Taking his mug of coffee, he walked from the kitchen, back through the living room, past the two leather sofas facing each other in front of the fireplace and through the doorway leading onto the screened-in porch. He walked through the porch and out its screen door, then went down the small path that cut in between the sea-grass and scrub heading for the beach. He looked up at the sky and out at the lake. There were several boats out on the water and the waves were one to two feet. He checked his wristwatch and decided since he was dressed for it, he might as well go to work. If there had been any kind of problem with Farren during the day, he would have heard something by now.

He stepped up onto the aluminum dock and slowly wandered down it, thinking about two days earlier and how incredible Farren's naked backside looked. Then he thought about whether or not he and Farren were ever going to have a life together, a married life. It seemed far away, even if they got past her current danger, because what if he got accepted into medical school? But then again, that didn't seem very likely at the moment.

As he wrestled with all of his uncertainties, he looked up and saw a Grebe, a freshwater bird that could dive into the water for food, circling in the sky. The Grebe swooped down over the water like it was going to make a dive, but then veered away, apparently deciding to go after its prey from a different angle. Doc took a sip from his coffee watching the bird line up its supper. After a few more seconds, the Grebe stiffened its body, dove at a ninety-degree angle and splooshed into the water about twenty yards off the end of the dock in front of him. Doc watched the ripples in the lake where the bird disappeared, expecting it to re-emerge at any moment.

Five seconds went by, ten seconds went by, and then, just about the time the paramedic started to lower his coffee cup with concern, a figure suddenly popped out of the bluish-green water where the Grebe had disappeared. It was a human figure—a totally naked female figure. It was Clair.

She tossed her long, wet, naturally curly blonde locks to one side and rubbed her green eyes. She smiled at him, but then, realizing she was naked, quickly plopped back down in the water until only her face and neck showed. Doc's mug of coffee slipped out of his fingers and broke on the dock.

"Hey!" she called. "Got a towel?"

"Holy shit!" he muttered under his breath.

"Really?" she called. "I traverse dimensions as God's messenger and being profane is all you've got?"

"Sorry," he called back, not thinking that she heard him. "I–I was just—"

"Besides," she cut in, "that particular expression's never made any sense to me. I mean, think about it. Who has holy feces anyway?"

"Pope?" he asked. "Jesus? I mean—y'know—when he was a guy?"

She looked at him not amused. "Have you got a towel or not?"

He took off his long-sleeve shirt, hopped into the water with his shoes and socks still on, and started to wade out to her. As he did, a speedboat with some high school boys cruised in toward shore.

"Here," he said, offering her his shirt.

"Thank you. Turn around, please," she asked.

Doc obeyed and turned around, but not before spotting the boat that was veering off and passing them nearby.

"Those guys can't see you, right?" he asked.

As Clair stood up to put the shirt on, he suddenly heard a burst of *"Woohoo!"* and *"Yeah, baby!"* from the boys on the boat.

"Guess they can," he said to himself.

"Okay," she said a few seconds later, "you can turn around, but don't look too closely. I need a towel. Things are kind of 'clinging.'"

They started wading in toward the dock with Doc keeping his eyes focused on her face.

"I'm really glad to see you, Clair. *Really* glad! I've never been so glad to see a dead person in all my life!"

"Only the flesh is dead. That's not the whole, or even the most important, part of the package."

"Well, I'm really glad to see you in *any* package: bird, deer, llama–"

"How's Gus?" she asked.

"Good. I mean, worried about Farren, we all are, but good."

"Well, let me get dried off and into something, then you can tell me all about it."

They bypassed the dock and walked straight onto the beach. Once there, Clair turned her dripping self around and looked at the near perfect but cooler summer's day.

"Glorious," she said under her breath. "Simply glorious! What's the date?"

He looked at her, a little surprised that she didn't know.

"July 1st."

"Feels like July," she agreed, turning and heading toward the cottage.

He followed her down the path and then inside and let her use his bedroom. He still had some of the clothes and make-up he had bought for her from six months earlier and told her where she could find them in his closet. She thanked him then disappeared for what seemed like a long time. While Doc was changing his pants, shoes, and socks, he even heard the hair drier whining in the bathroom. When she emerged, it felt like deja-vu. Her hair was dry and brushed, she had make-up on, and she was also wearing a pair of jeans and a white sweatshirt with "Charlevoix Yacht Club" in gold lettering spelled out on the chest.

"You saved all my things?" she asked, coming out of his bedroom and into the living room.

"Yeah. That way I know what happened *really* happened," he said, standing in front of the fireplace. "I call them my holy relics from Kmart."

She ignored the joke, interested in something else. "I see another woman's things in the bathroom. Hairbrush, deodorant, eyeliner..."

"Your granddaughter's," he said. "You, you do know what's

happening, right?"

"I'd like to hear it from you," she said. She walked over to the sofa in bare feet to sit down, but became momentarily distracted while she looked around the cottage with a half-smile. "Nothing's changed. The Christmas tree and snow are gone but, other than that, everything's the same."

"It's only been a little more than six months," he reminded her.

She looked around the room again, a little mystically.

"Time...it's so important to us while we're here. When really it's just..." she decided to abandon the introspection and turn her mind back to business.

"So tell me, what's been going on?" she asked as she sat down on the leather sofa nearest the writing desk and tucked her feet up and under her.

"Okay," he said, sitting down on the edge of the sofa opposite her and a little curious that he would have to spell things out for an angel. "You remember Bartholomew, right?"

"The loan shark in Flint," she answered. "Of course."

"After Charlie died, he was arrested. The district attorney in Flint was trying to build a case against him. But it got thrown out on a technicality and now he's back on the street."

"Oh, dear," she said.

"Gus came up with the notion that Bartholomew might want to take revenge on Farren. After all, she cost him a lot of time and money."

"He's a smart one, my Gus," she nodded.

"So as a precaution," he continued, "she agreed to temporarily move in here with me. But yesterday, a good female friend of ours, who's got short hair and could pass for Farren at a distance in the dark, was shot while coming out of Farren's house. She had just stopped by to collect a few things to be brought out here. There's very little doubt it was a case of mistaken identity."

"Your friend," Clair asked, concerned, "how bad was it?"

"Fortunately, she was turning and reaching for her cellphone when she was shot. So not as bad as it could've been."

"Thank God for your technology."

"But Farren's still in danger. We found out this morning that Bartholomew has an airtight alibi. So you can bet the farm he hired a professional who's going to come after her again."

He stopped talking, waiting for his celestial guest to say something. Clair looked at him inquisitively for a moment.

"Is that all?" she asked.

"Isn't that enough?"

"It certainly should be—but I have the feeling there's more."

Doc looked down at the floor, then rose and stuck his hands into his pockets as he started to wander around the living room. He looked at his wristwatch, being mindful of the time and that he still had to go to work.

"Doc?" Clair asked again.

"If you really want full disclosure, there's a problem with Farren and me."

"What kind of problem?"

"Charlie messed up her mind. He apparently did things to her when they were intimate—rough things, mean things—and now she can't feel safe with another man. She's in therapy, but our relationship is kind of stuck at the moment. On top of all this, I might be moving out of town."

"Why?"

"You really don't know?" he wondered, again surprised by her apparent grasp of the facts.

"You think we sit around on clouds all day and watch our relatives like watching episodes of *Gunsmoke*? There's only one being I know who is all-knowing and seeing."

"Okay, whatever," he said. "I've reapplied to medical school."

"Really?" she smiled, clearly pleased. "That's wonderful!"

"Well, I've got to get in first, which is kind of a long shot. Probably a real long shot. I mean, I think I would have heard something by now. But if I *did* get in, I'll be living away from Charlevoix for years. And no one has to tell you that separation and loneliness isn't good for a relationship."

Clair's green eyes drifted away for a couple of moments thinking about Gus, but then she regained her focus.

"Got any Vernors?" she asked.

It wasn't the response Doc was looking for, but he exercised patience. "I, uh, I don't know. Let me look." He headed for the kitchen, while she eyed the elk's head over the fireplace.

"So what are you going to do about all this?" she called while he was in the other room.

"I was hoping *you* could help with that," he answered. "Oh, I'm sorry. I'm out of Vernors. Would you like something else? Lemonade? Coffee?"

"No, it's okay. Thanks."

He came back into the room, anxious for her input.

"Sorry, Doc," she said. "I can't help this time."

"What do you mean you can't help? This is the future and safety of your granddaughter we're talking about. You know, an Intended One?"

She shook her head and rose from the sofa, now suddenly irritated. "Boy, you're unbelievable."

"What're you talking about?"

She started to pace behind the sofa with arms folded. "You, better than anyone, should know by now the power of faith. You, better than anyone, should know by now how to read the signs."

"Signs? What, you mean like cryptic little messages that could mean anything to anyone because they *want* them to?"

"No. I'm talking about signs that you should be smart enough to see. I'm talking about doing what you think is right, but also praying about it and being open to a change in direction if necessary."

"I *have* been doing that!" he said defensively.

"Really? Then why am I here?"

"*Because I need help!*"

"So does the mother with the terminally ill child. So does the couple trying to have a baby but can't. So does the man who's out of work and has a family to support. So does the soldier who finds himself in a firefight far from home. So does the student who needs help in school. How about one who just lost their father? Or the wife whose husband just came home and announced he doesn't love her anymore? What makes *you* so special, Doc, that every time things get tough, God has to prove that he's there? That he's listening? Especially since he's already given you so much!"

He was taken off guard by her lack of empathy and harsh attitude. He opened his mouth to fire back a response, but he wasn't sure what to say.

"By the way," she added, "my relationship with Gus survives! No, our years of separation haven't been easy. But the love survives. Even if he had married again which, frankly, I wish he had, it survives!"

"You ever ask God why?" Doc asked quietly.

"Why what?"

"Why he took you so young?"

Clair stopped pacing and looked at him seriously.

"If he hadn't, Gus would've never gone to Central Michigan University and taught hundreds of students, because I wanted to live my life here. He wouldn't have sat on a financial aid committee that helped one needy student become a doctor and another become a world-renown chemist. He wouldn't have inspired thirteen of his students to become teachers, three more to become theology writers and still another to become a member of the clergy. If God hadn't of called me, then Gus might not have been available to take care of Farren after her parents died. He wouldn't have maintained engines and boats at the marina that have kept dozens of families safe out on the water. If he hadn't, Gus wouldn't have his suspicious inclinations. He wouldn't have come out here and had a beer with you on the dock and shared his concerns about Bartholomew being back on the street. Yes, Doc, I've asked."

"So, you *do* know the score," he realized.

"Which is more than I can say for you," she fired back.

He felt both embarrassed and a little humbled by her answer. Just at that moment, the microwave in the kitchen beeped, announcing that something he had put in there was ready. But he hadn't put anything in the microwave. He turned toward the kitchen confused.

"I can't come back here anymore, Doc," Clair continued, softening her tone. "In fact, I'm not really here now. You're going to have to figure things out. Please tell Gus that I love him."

He turned and looked at her, but then the microwave beeped again so he turned back toward the kitchen. When he turned back to the living room, his visitor was gone.

"Clair?" he called. *"Clair?"*

The sound of his own voice woke him up. That, and the alarm clock beeping on the night stand next to his bed. It was 4:30 p.m. He'd been sleeping for the past seven hours. Slapping the top of the device with his hand, he thought about the vividness of the dream he'd just had. It was one of those dreams where he remembered every detail and wished it hadn't been a dream. He slowly tossed back the covers, put his feet on the floor and sat on the side of his bed for nearly a minute. Then he thought about whether or not he wanted to take Stubigg up on his offer and take some time off work, or go in for his shift at 6 p.m. Whatever he was going to do, he figured he'd have to make a decision quickly if a nighttime replacement was going to be found.

21 Dinner At The Regency

The Regency was a popular downtown restaurant in 1954. Tourists and locals alike enjoyed the black-and-white-tiled floor, the clean off-white walls with photos of Great Lakes freighters in ornate gold frames, the waiters that wore black pants, polished black shoes, sharply ironed white shirts and aprons, and the legendary food that was delivered under silver warming trays whether you ordered a bowl of soup or a twenty-five-ounce, ten dollar sirloin.

It was the kind of restaurant that Leland and Mary Cooper went to on only special occasions, like a birthday or anniversary. So when their son, Gus, called after having not come home the night before and asked them to meet him there for dinner, they were surprised. They were also surprised by his not going to work that day and him not calling the evening before. But when he did finally call, he explained the situation. He apologized for worrying them and said he'd gotten stranded on Beaver Island the day before and had no access to a phone because of a storm. Knowing how remote some areas of the island were, not to mention their son's integrity, his folks accepted the explanation. As for him not going to work, he said he'd explain everything when he saw them at dinner.

As they waiting for Gus to arrive, they also wondered about how he could be dressed for the jacket-and-tie place when his mom had last seen him wearing a T-shirt and jeans for work at Stu and Ernie's. The speculation ran rampant in their minds. They thought it might have something to do with a promotion at the station, or getting his teaching degree, or maybe even getting a teaching job. But then they decided it was probably about meeting this girl, Clair Sinclair, who their son had been seeing.

"Dinner reservation for Cooper, please?" Leland asked the maître d'. Leland was a tall and slender man, forty-four years old, who was wearing the only suit he owned, a blue pinstripe, seven years old, and just a little out of fashion. Like his son, Leland had dark black hair but he also had bags under his eyes and prominent wrinkles on his forehead from smoking Camel unfiltered cigarettes since he was a teenager. The suit he wore was mostly brought out for weddings or funerals and although he looked nice, he wasn't used to such clothing. He was a hard-working, good-natured man who had worked in the same tool and dye shop for seventeen years and never had a sick day, even when he was really sick.

After the Japanese attacked Pearl Harbor in 1941, twenty-nine-year-old Leland volunteered for the army, but by then he already had a wife and eight-year-old son, so he was passed over. He loved his son more than anything and had it not been for Mary needing a hysterectomy, he and his wife would've had more children.

Mary Cooper had fallen in love with Leland when he used to be a lifeguard on Michigan Beach. She herself was still a good-looking woman. She had light brown hair, a slender figure like her husband, and was wearing a peach-colored dress with a delicate-looking feathered hat on her head. She had no particular career aspirations other than being a good wife and mother. Two days a week she cleaned houses for people who mingled with the Sinclair family and this extra income afforded the Coopers a small camper. The family loved to go camping whenever they could and Leland and Gus probably had their best bonding times when they were out either hunting or hiking in the woods.

"Now remember, Lee," she whispered as they were being led to a table. "Don't order the most expensive thing on the menu. This is Gus' treat."

"Don't worry, Mother," he said, surprised to see that they were being taken to a table with six chairs and that two of the six chairs were already occupied.

The couple already seated was just as surprised to see the Coopers as the Coopers were to see them. They were a nicely dressed couple, except that the man was wearing a loud tie that didn't match either his shirt or his suit jacket.

"Excuse me, is this right?" Mary asked the maître d'.

"Yes, ma'am," the maître d' answered. "Reservation for Cooper."

"Our reservation was in the name of Sinclair," Aaron said, sitting with an open menu and a martini already in front of him.

"Yes, sir," the maître-d' replied. "That is also correct. I was instructed to seat both the Sinclairs and Coopers at the same table."

The four people looked at one another awkwardly for a moment until Portia finally stood up and extended her hand.

"Hello, I'm Portia Sinclair. This is my husband, Aaron."

Portia and Mary shook hands while Aaron rose to meet Leland.

"Oh, this is starting to make sense now," Mary smiled. "I think our kids have been plotting something. I'm Gus' mom, Mary, and this is Leland."

The two men shook hands and said hello to each other, then everyone sat down.

"Well, this is very unexpected," Aaron said politely, but not enthused. "By the number of chairs, we knew others were going to be joining us, but we weren't quite sure who." He eyed Mary's hat and forced a smile, thinking to himself a more sophisticated woman would know better than to wear a hat to dinner.

"Did your daughter invite you here tonight?" Mary asked.

"She did, and she was rather mysterious about it," Portia answered.

"We thought it was to apologize for a stunt she pulled last night," Aaron added.

A waiter came over and asked the Coopers if they wanted a cocktail. Mary ordered a glass of white wine. Leland ordered a beer.

"What stunt was that?" Mary continued, after the waiter was gone.

"She didn't come home last night," Aaron said. "I mean, she's over twenty-one, but she scared her mother and I half to death."

Didn't even call!"

"Now, Aaron, she explained that," Portia said. "She couldn't get to a phone once the storm set in."

Leland and Mary looked at one another, Aaron noticed the exchange instantly.

"What?" he asked.

"Beaver Island?" Leland asked.

Aaron and Portia looked at one another. It only took a moment to figure out that Clair and Gus had spent the night together.

"Oh, no," Aaron said, reaching for his martini. "Hell, no!"

Portia looked at Mary, concerned but still very polite.

"Didn't Gus come home last night, either?" she asked.

"Now there's no need to worry," Mary assured. "I'm sure Gus was a perfect gentleman. They were just caught up in circumstances beyond their control."

"What were they doing over on Beaver Island in the first place?" Aaron asked.

"They just got caught in the storm," Leland agreed. "This dinner is their way of apologizing for frightening the mothers. Besides, Gus has been saying he wants us to meet Clair, so that's what this is, everybody getting together and meeting everybody."

"Yes, that's what it is," Portia agreed. "Isn't this nice."

"Why?" Aaron asked, still disgruntled.

The waiter returned with the drinks for the Coopers. As he was leaving, Gus and Clair came into the restaurant. Gus was wearing a dark sports jacket, slacks, dress shoes and socks, a red tie and a smile as wide as the Memorial Bridge. Clair came in with her hair pinned up and wearing a nice satin cream-colored dress, nylons, and high heels. She was also carrying a small bouquet of daisies. Even as they were coming over to the table, both mothers noticed the rings on her left finger.

"Oh, my God," Portia said, under her breath, concerned.

"Oh, my God," Mary exclaimed with delightful surprise.

"Where'd he get those clothes?" Leland asked.

"Oh, no," Aaron exclaimed.

"Hi, everyone," Gus smiled, arriving at the table. "Thanks for coming. I'm glad you're all sitting down."

A smiling Clair raised her left hand to show off a small diamond ring and inexpensive, 10-percent, white gold band. "I changed my name to Cooper today!" she beamed.

There was a suspended moment of silence where everybody waited for somebody to say something. Finally, Leland stood up with a dazed smile and said, "Well, can I maybe meet my new daughter-in-law?"

Clair, Gus, Mary, and Portia all laughed and starting talking simultaneously. Gus introduced his parents to Clair, Portia stood and introduced herself to Gus, Clair gave her new in-laws a big hug, and Aaron simply sat still open-mouthed.

As everyone was taking their seats, Aaron took a big gulp of his martini then set his glass down. "Excuse me, but, is anyone here besides me just a little pissed off by this!"

"Aaron, your language," Portia hushed.

"My language? *Their actions!*" he said loudly.

"Calm down, Daddy," Clair said. "You're not going to spoil this."

"Oh, okay," Aaron said. He called the waiter over and ordered another martini. While he was doing so, Leland asked about Gus' new clothes and Gus explained that he took some money out of the bank and they both bought new clothes prior to getting married in Petoskey. After the waiter was gone, Aaron looked at Clair calmly but was seething on the inside. "You say you don't want me to spoil this. Then maybe you can explain why you two decided to sneak off like thieves in the night? Did you think you were doing something wrong? Why did you put us through a night of worry? Perhaps you can also explain to your mother why you've denied her the right to see her oldest daughter get married? Something she's dreamed about for years."

"We didn't sneak off like thieves in the night," Clair responded.

Aaron looked at Gus. "What you did, young man, was incredibly selfish and disrespectful!"

"Now hold on," Leland said, holding up his palm but still polite. "We would've liked to have seen our only child get married, too. But

I'm sure there's an explanation for everything happening the way it did. Let's give the kids a chance, eh?"

"Kids!" Aaron grumbled. "Truer words were never spoken. Pretty unthinking, immature kids, if you ask me."

"Well nobody did," Portia said. Then she turned to Clair. "Honey, tell us how and why you two came to this decision. Help us understand."

The waiter coming back with Aaron's drink interrupted them. He asked if anyone was interested in an appetizer.

"Get lost," Aaron ordered.

Clearly put off by Aaron's gruff words, the waiter left. Clair looked around the table and smiled somewhat timidly. "I know this is a surprise to everyone. And yes, there is an explanation."

"Oh my God, you're pregnant," Aaron assumed.

"No, Daddy. I'm not. But getting on with things and wanting to have a family did have something to do with our decision. Look, we love each other. We can all sit around and debate whether or not it happened too fast, but in the end, we love each other and we were anxious to begin our life together."

"We're sorry that we didn't call anyone last night, but we couldn't," Gus said. "We honestly couldn't."

"What were you doing over on Beaver Island?" Mary asked.

Gus shot a glance at Aaron before answering. "Clair showed up at Stu and Eddie's yesterday and was pretty upset about a job she was hoping would materialize at the hospital. But things didn't work out. She wanted to get away for a little while and I volunteered to take off work and go with her. We hitched a ride on Glen Chamberlin's plane. We had no idea a storm was going to roll in. A few-hour trip turned into twenty-four hours, and again, we're sorry for causing any worry."

"Where'd you stay?" Portia asked.

"We found a hunting cabin," Clair answered.

"Weren't there any hotels?" Aaron asked. "Hotels with separate rooms?"

"Not on the part of the island where the storm caught us, no," Clair explained.

"And you two just got up this morning and said: 'Hey, let's get married?'" Leland asked.

"To be perfectly honest about it, Dad," Gus said, "when I asked Clair to marry me, we knew it would be without the support of Mr. Sinclair. And although I sure hope that changes, I also hope you and Mom understand we couldn't invite one set of parents who would be more accepting of the marriage but not the other. The fact remains we wanted to start a life together. So I called in sick at work today, and we got married over in Petoskey." He looked around the table earnestly. "We weren't trying to cheat anyone out of anything or be selfish. But we weren't going open up a subject for discussion that was clearly only our decision." He looked at his new father-in-law. "You *do* deserve respect, sir. No question about it. That's what I tried to give you at your club. But you didn't want anything to do with it."

Mary looked at her husband. "What's he talking about?" Leland shook his head, not understanding the reference, either. Aaron took a drink from the fresh martini the waiter had brought him, downing about half of it.

"I see. This is all *my* fault. Clair being angry and running to Gus...Gus feeling that I had rejected him a suitor..."

"Uh—you did," Gus reminded him.

"It's all *my* fault," Aaron said, his voice getting louder, "for wanting the best for my little girl. A life where she didn't have to worry about groceries, utilities, mortgage payments or work. A life where she had a prominent place in the community."

"Those are the challenges every young couple has to face, Daddy," Clair said. "I said that being anxious to start a family was part of the reason we eloped. Another was—and I'm sorry to have to say this—I was leery of a parent who's tried to manipulate my destiny without my permission because he thinks it's good for business."

Insulted and hurt by the comment, Aaron flung the remainder of his martini's contents into his daughter's face. Gus jumped to his feet and was over to Aaron so fast he was almost a blur, grabbing him by both lapels and dragging him to his feet.

"Gus, *no!*" Clair pleaded, her face still dripping with gin and vermouth.

Gus looked at her, then turned to her father. "Only because she asked," he hissed. Then he dropped a stunned Aaron back into his chair.

Everyone in the crowded restaurant stopped. The air was thick with tension. Portia took her napkin and dabbed off Clair's face. Gus glared at Aaron for a moment, then turned to his dad. "We're going to need a place to stay."

Leland took his napkin off his lap, set it on the table and rose. "You and Clair come home with us. Your room is still your room." He looked at Aaron, trying not to be disgusted while Mary also stood.

"Well," she said, with an uncomfortable smile, "I, uh, I'm sure we'll all be seeing each other again." She turned to Clair, "Come on, dear."

Clair rose and handed her mother her flowers. "I'll call you tomorrow, Mom."

Aaron regained his composure, or tried to, and noticed that all eyes in the restaurant were on him. He likewise rose.

"C'mon, Portia," he said, tossing a twenty dollar bill on the table. "We're leaving."

His wife looked at him steely eyed, then slowly got out of her chair with as much dignity as she could muster.

22 On The Lake

Farren returned home from work at about 6:20 the evening after she stormed out of BJ's office. Her visit to Charlene in the hospital was both tearful and full of apology but her short, white-haired friend was gracious and surprisingly understanding about what had happened. Farren was terribly guilt-ridden but Charlene reminded her that nobody was to blame for what had happened except the assassin. She even urged Farren to put the lingerie she had gotten for her to good use.

"I can honestly say, I risked my life for your love life. So get on with the lovin'!" she said. Lance was also at the hospital with both his and Charlene's parents, but he steered everyone out of her room to give the two friends privacy. He also did it so Farren wouldn't be inundated with questions that she couldn't answer about the trouble she was in.

When the police cruiser rolled into the turn-around in front of the cabin's kitchen door, she was surprised to see Doc's Jeep still parked outside next to her VW. An officer wearing a bulletproof vest got out of the cruiser, knocked on the door, and spoke with Doc before letting Farren out. When the officer was sure the coast was clear and Farren climbed out, both cops that had been riding with her this day huddled closely behind her, blocking any access to a possible shot. Watching from inside the kitchen, Doc couldn't help but be grateful for the protectiveness of the Charlevoix Police

Department.

Coming into the kitchen, Farren looked at him a little puzzled. "What're you doing here?" she asked, brushing her bangs aside and eyeing his street clothes.

"Stubigg offered me some time off, so I took it. I—ah—I wasn't entirely sure you'd come back here after work."

She looked at him, still with the trace of anger from that morning, but she was more in control of it now. "Where else am I gonna go?"

He started toward her to give her a hug, but contained the urge, wanting her to have her space if she needed it. "So how's Charlene? How was work?"

"You know Charlene. She was kind and smiling and said all the right things to make me not feel guilty—"

"But you still felt guilty," he concluded.

"Terribly! I didn't stay too long, though. Her parents were there, Lance's parents were there, cops were with me—it was quite the circus. Fortunately, no parent said anything to make me feel worse than I already did. People are surprising, sometimes."

"Yes they are," Doc agreed.

"As for work, I never left the storage barn and my shadows made me keep the big doors closed. So I feel very antsy. Closed in. Guess I've got cabin fever."

"So, naturally, here you are in a cabin," he joked.

"Like I said, where else am I gonna go?"

"Where would you like to go?" he asked. "I'll take you anywhere it's within my power to take you."

Her face lightened, "You mean it?"

"Absolutely."

Three hours later, Doc walked down a wooded gravel lane toward a main county road in another part of town. Although it was still light, the day was definitely fading. At the end of the lane closing it off was a police cruiser and a replacement team of two new officers for Farren also wearing vests like the earlier shift. As he approached, the cop behind the wheel lowered his window.

"Everything okay?" Doc asked.

"If somebody followed us, it's a mystery to me," the officer said. "You know, she's really not supposed to be leaving like this. We could get into a lot of trouble with BJ."

"She's feeling claustrophobic," Doc said. He reached into his back jeans pocket and pulled out his Remington snubnose revolver. "I've got this and if you guys just keep monitoring channel fourteen, we should be cool."

"We won't be able to get you quickly," the cop said. "I hope you're right."

"Me, too," Doc smiled. He thanked both of them for all their efforts and headed back down the lane.

The lane wasn't like the one that led to Doc's cabin. It was only about thirty yards long before it emptied out onto a driveway and a large, dark green manicured lawn with an expensive, modernistic split-level house. The house had a flat roof and large windows that overlooked the lawn one way and Lake Michigan the other. The waterfront property belonged to a CIO from Kalamazoo who was a customer of the Portside Marina. He was kindly lending his dock out front to Gus who had a waiting Criss-Craft Corsair 36 idling at the end of it. Farren was already below in the bow cabin at her grandfather's insistence.

As Doc rounded the yard to the lake side, he couldn't help but be impressed with the boat. It looked like a traditional inboard motor speedboat, only one on steroids. It was over thirty-eight feet long including the aft end swimming platform, was mostly blue fiberglass with red and white trim, and had a deep bow cabin that featured a dinette area, combination head and shower, and galley seating for six that could also be converted into a stateroom with a queen-size bed. With stainless steel hardware, cherry veneer cabinetry, a teak wood deck, and seating for eight behind the bridge, it was the perfect weekend getaway boat—that was if one could afford a 450,000-dollar getaway.

As Doc came aboard, Gus was on the bridge, giving all the gauges the once over.

"Hey, Doc," he called, "I think you're all set. There's food in the galley, you've got full tanks, fifty gallons of fresh water, and the weather tonight should be clear and calm. Ever drive a boat this big?"

Stepping onto the bridge, the younger man eyed the gauges, dials, and instrumentation illuminated in blue light. "I've never driven a boat *half* this big."

"Okay," Gus said, not particularly concerned.

"Whose is this, anyway?"

"A deadbeat's," Gus grumbled. "He owes us six months storage, four months of slip rental, and an engine overhaul."

"What happened?"

"The recession," Gus said, sadly. "I think the owner has just abandoned her. We expect the bank to show up and repossess any time."

"What about your money?"

"We've spoken to our attorney about it, but I'm not very optimistic."

"And meantime, possession is nine-tenths of the law?" Doc figured.

"Actually, taking her out after an overhaul is part of our service agreement. We're just honoring the agreement," Gus grinned.

Just then, Farren came up from below. She was wearing skinny jeans, lake shoes, her black bikini top, and the grey hoodie she had worn earlier.

"Thanks for arranging this, Grandpa," she said. "And thanks for not trying to talk me out of wanting to get away for a while."

"Been there, done that," Gus said, referring to a certain trip to Beaver Island many years ago. "But you should be wearing the vest the police gave you."

"We'll be in the middle of nowhere in ten minutes," she reasoned.

"How long you figure to be gone?"

"We'll be back tomorrow morning," Farren replied.

He nodded and looked at Doc. "The police are going to monitor your CB?"

"Channel fourteen," Doc nodded.

"Okay. Keep her safe," Gus said.

"You know I will."

Gus looked at them, then back at the house and grounds. "Alright. You two better get out of here. Her being out in the open like this makes me nervous."

"We'll call with our ETA tomorrow," Farren said, kissing her grandfather on the cheek as she stepped behind the wheel.

Doc and Gus left the bridge and cast off the lines. Doc untied the stern while remaining on the boat and Gus did the bow line from the dock. Farren clicked on the red and green running lights and the big Criss-Craft slowly rumbled away from the dock with its twin Volvo V8s impatient for open water.

Within another forty seconds, Doc had joined Farren on the bridge and was seated next to her.

"You ready to run?" she asked.

"Let 'er rip," Doc said.

She wrapped her delicate hands around the two side-by-side silver throttles and pushed them forward. The Volvos below roared to life and the nearly instant G-force threw both of them back. Not being particularly experienced with Great Lakes watercraft, Doc felt like he was strapped to a rocket.

"Oh my God!" he yelled with delight. *"This is awesome!"*

Farren looked over at his thick brown hair laying straight back from the wind and smiled. She was pleased that she could share this part of her life with him. "Don't get too used to this," she called loudly. "This is a pretty expensive ride."

"No! I *want* to get used to this!" Doc yelled happily. "At least, some version of it."

"You're going to have to be a really highly paid fireman," she said.

"Actually, I wanna talk to you about that," he answered.

"About what?"

"About being a fireman."

"Oh, I already know about that," she said. "Lance told me at the hospital that he resigned this morning."

He looked at her and nodded, but that wasn't what he meant. He was talking about his medical school application, but he quickly decided he didn't want to get into that right now. For the moment, he just wanted to enjoy the wind in his face, the setting red sun before them, the endless horizon and the rhythm of the Criss-Craft as it flew over the calm water.

Farren kept the throttle open until they were about six miles off shore and they could just barely see the lights on the shoreline behind them. The sun off the bow was no more than a sliver of crimson on the water's surface, and in another sixty seconds, it would be gone.

Farren eased up on the throttle until the boat was barely moving and then turned off the engines. The world around them was suddenly incredibly quiet and with no other boats in sight and just the sound of the water licking the hull. For the moment at least, it seemed as if Wyatt "Doc" Reynolds and Farren Malone were the only two human beings on the planet.

"Wow," Doc said. "That was *so* cool...now what?"

"Now nothing," she said, drinking in the openness. "We drift. We go wherever the current takes us."

He looked up at the sky noticing all the stars that had seemingly appeared on cue. "Whoa! Look up there! I haven't seen so many stars since I lived in Sedona."

"I'm glad you like it," she said, pleased.

"Being out here, I can understand why you love it so much, why your folks loved it so much."

She looked around at the black, tranquil water. "Not long after my parents died, I used to come out here in the evenings. Not on anything this grand, but an old Lund I had. I used to call out to my parents. Their bodies were never recovered, you know. Sometimes I'd just hop into the water. Just sort of float around...and if it happened that I got tired and went under, that would've been alright."

He looked at her for a long moment before responding.

"I understand what it means to have somebody unexpectedly taken from you. But I didn't know your folks were never found."

"Their sailboat was. It turtled. It was turned completely upside down with the keel above the water and the masts pointing straight down. When the Coast Guard found it, I knew they were gone."

He shook his head, thinking. "You're family seems to have a history of untimely dramatic deaths. Your Grandma Clair, your parents, even Charlie."

"And now an assassin's after me."

"You guys are like the Kennedys," he quipped. "Only without the movie stars and money."

She half smiled, but it quickly faded. "I'm scared, Doc. I'm really, really scared."

"You are *not* going to be shot by an assassin," he assured her. "I promise."

Farren stepped off the bridge and onto the teak wood deck in the middle of the boat, appreciating Doc's promise, but also knowing he had no control to keep it. She jammed her hands into her hoodie pockets and looked up at the stars. The Milky Way was now crystal clear and a shooting star briefly streaked through the constellation of Cygnus nearly directly overhead. Doc followed her onto the deck.

"Baby, I have tell you something. Something that *probably* isn't going to happen, but you need to know about it just in case it does."

She looked at him concerned. "Oh, dear. Is this like when you said I'm 'probably not' in any danger after Bartholomew got out of jail?"

"Yes. No...I don't know...the thing is, I don't want to be a fireman. In fact, I've retaken the MCAT and have reapplied to Wayne State Medical School."

She looked at him surprised. "In Detroit?"

"Yes."

Her eyebrows winced for a second registering hurt, but then she smiled her dimpled smile and tried to mask it. "Doc, th-that's wonderful! Just, just wonderful. You'll be an amazing physician. I know it."

"I'm not very confident about getting in. But if do, it's really important you understand it's because I want to be a doctor. Not because I want to get away from anyone or anything here. I mean, other than being a fireman."

"No, of course not," she smiled, but at the same time her eyes were becoming moist. "I understand you've got a calling and that calling might be 'calling' you away. When will you hear something?"

"Any day now," he said.

"W-w-we ought to celebrate," she said, trying to be happy for him but actually fearing their future would disintegrate, "I think there's some wine in the galley refrigerator."

As she turned and headed for the galley, he caught her by the arm.

"Wait. Just wait a second." He looked at her sincerely. "I'm in love with you, Farren Malone. I have been for a long time, but this is the first time I've actually had the guts to say it. I don't want us to be apart. But if I'm accepted to medical school, I have to go. So we're going to have to figure something out, aren't we? Because you not being in my life is unacceptable. If you're scared about me leaving, we could become engaged as a pledge of my devotion and I'll come back here on as many weekends as I can. Better yet, you could come down to Wayne State and live with me. Or, if I don't get in, then there's no separation to worry about but I *am* going to have to find a new career. If you want to live in Charlevoix, that's fine. If you want to live a thousand miles away, that's fine too. I'll go wherever you want. But any way you cut it, we're *going* to be together. And if we don't make love for a week, or a month, or a year, then that's the way it is. It takes what it takes. Because I love you, and I want to spend the rest of my life with you, and I'm not going to hurt you or do anything with you until you feel safe with me. Period. The end. That's it. Roll credits."

She looked at him with now fully wet eyes, a red nose, and a trembling lower lip. She excused herself and hurried down below to get a tissue. A few seconds later, Doc heard her blowing her nose loudly.

"Is that a yes?" he called.

"Yes to what?" she called back. "You just said a lot of things."

"Yes to all of it, some of it, any of it," he called back.

He heard her blowing her nose again, then there was silence for a few moments. Eventually she emerged from below deck wearing only her black bikini and carrying a beach towel.

"I'm going for a swim," she announced, her emotions now apparently in check. She turned and went to the bridge. With the flick of a switch, six floodlights below the water line illuminated the lake around the boat with a golden-green halo. With another flick of a switch, the radio came on. Shakira was singing "Empires" low in the background.

"You want to go swimming *now*?" he asked. "You do realize the commitment of what I just said, right?"

"Yes," she said. She slowly walked passed him, down the long length of the deck and then swung open an upholstered gate at the stern and took two more steps down to the swimming platform.

"Was that a 'yes' for you want to go swimming now? Or was that a 'yes' to everything I just said."

She smiled, then turned and dove into the water, her slender attractive body silhouetted by the hull lights.

"Whoa, that's cold!" she cried, breaking the surface a moment later. "That'll wake you up!" She swam a little distance away from the perimeter of the floodlights. "Why don't you come on in?" she called. "You can really see the stars from out here."

"What is it with you and swimming in the dark?" he asked. "Are you sure this is even safe? Natalie Wood, Dennis Wilson, Leonardo DiCaprio. That's all I'm sayin'."

"You know what?" she called still unseen beyond the halo of the floodlights.

"What?"

"You saying what you said to me was good. Suddenly, I'm not so scared anymore."

"So...does that mean you were saying 'yes' to everything else I was saying besides saying 'yes' to wanting to go swimming?"

Just then, a wet wad of something landed on the deck. When Doc bent down and picked it up, he could see that Farren's black bikini top and bottom had been tied together.

He rose from the deck to see her swimming back into the halo of light around the Criss-Craft, completely naked.

"Yes, Doc," she smiled, her wet, slicked back hair making the dimples on her cheeks seem even deeper. "That's what it meant.

And I love you too."

Without saying another word, he stripped down to his skin, swung open the upholstered stern gate, stepped down to the swimming platform and dove into the water to join his proclaimed love. They hugged and kissed in the lake, then, a few minutes later, made love in the galley shower while the hot water rained down on them. After that, they made love a second time in their stateroom while the current continued to take them wherever it wanted to go.

23 The Fallen

In late August 1954, a new magazine called *Sports Illustrated* had just hit the national newsstands, *The Lone Ranger* was winding up a twenty-one-year run on network radio, and newlyweds Gus and Clair Cooper had been married for nearly five weeks. The tourist season was starting to wind down in Charlevoix as the evenings were getting shorter. The fudge stores, clothing stores, art galleries, and book stores on Bridge Street were all having sales, trying to squeeze the last few dollars out of the remaining tourists in town. The Labor Day Weekend would no doubt be good—it always was—but 1954 would eventually be recorded as the city's worst season since the end of the war.

Aaron Sinclair had just stopped into the city offices to get a building permit. As usual his clothing was loud, light khaki slacks, a mustard-yellow short-sleeve shirt, long brown tie, two-tone shoes, and a white Stevens straw hat. The large lady seated behind the counter next to the Faygo Soda Pop calendar was no fashion plate herself. She sat with her back to him and wore a yellow and white polka dot dress complete with a beehive hairdo with a pencil stuck in it. She sat in an armless office chair and her thighs hung over the seat's sides like drooping pork chops while she typed in the blank spaces for the permit. When she was done, she pulled the paper out of her Remington typewriter with a loud clacking sound, then rose, picked up her coffee, and stepped over to the counter.

"This is just a little itty-bitty job for you, huh, Mr. Sinclair?" she asked, speaking clearly so her two other co-workers behind the counter could also hear.

"Work is work," Sinclair answered, politely but self-consciously.

"Yeah, but this is really small for a company like Sinclair Construction," she continued. "This ain't no more than, what, a two, three man job?"

"Do you need me to sign something?" Sinclair asked impatiently, taking a pen out of his shirt pocket.

"I just need you to sign here, and here," the woman said, pointing to the places on the permit. "And, uh, let me just move my coffee out of your way," she said playfully, picking it up off the counter. "After all, I don't wanna be wearin' it now, do I?"

Another woman co-worker behind the counter giggled at the joke. Aaron held his tongue and his temper because he needed the permit. He cracked a faint smile and signed. It seemed that every local in Charlevoix over the age of eighteen knew that he had thrown a drink in his daughter's face at the Regency.

The woman behind the counter produced a large, red leather-covered book from behind the counter and plopped it down with a heavy thud. "Now, let me just log the permit number," she said, feeling around in her hair for the pencil. While she recorded the number, Sinclair slid his pen back into his shirt, feeling the glances of the other two people behind the counter who were pretending to act busy.

"Alrighty...there we go," the woman said. She handed him the permit and smiled insincerely. "Thank you, Mr. Sinclair."

The red-faced man took the paper and walked out of the office. After the door was closed behind him, everyone laughed loudly.

"Oh, Lordy," the big woman in the polka dot dressed exclaimed, "How the mighty have fallen."

It was true. During the past five weeks, Aaron Sinclair's life had taken a nosedive. The recession and the fact that he hadn't had a decent bid in months, losing the partnership with Worthing Building Supply and consequently the contract for the refurbishing of the downtown storefronts, and then the incident at the Regency had all taken a toll on him. People didn't want to be affiliated with a man who treated his own family so poorly and had always had an arrogant demeanor in the first place. There was also his savings. Simply put, he didn't have any.

In his haste to build up a lifestyle and flaunt his success, he had never planned for the inevitable slow times. As a result, he was behind in his dues at the Traverse Bay Shooting Club, he'd been late on his last two house payments, Earl Young, the architect, had hired away his favorite foreman, and other business associates as well as Derek Worthing and his father weren't returning his calls. The walls of Aaron Sinclair's world were crumbling faster than he ever imagined and he didn't quite know what to do about it. Now he was doing small jobs like converting carports into garages just to keep the wolves at bay.

As he was driving through town in his Studebaker, he passed Uncle Moe's Great Catch used car lot and suddenly executed an abrupt U-turn after he saw Clair standing in the lot. She was pointing to her Corvette and having a conversation with someone, presumably Uncle Moe.

Aaron pulled into the lot and came up right behind Clair's blue coupe. As he did, his daughter, wearing a nice but simple light-colored sundress, asked the salesperson if she could have a few minutes alone with her father. The salesman smiled and walked toward a small building in the back corner of the lot that wasn't much bigger than a tool shed.

"What the hell do you think you're doing?" Aaron began, hopping out of the car and ready for a fight.

"And good morning to you, Daddy," she answered, politely but not smiling. "Nice to see you after—how many weeks?"

"You're not selling this car, are you?" he asked, getting right to the point.

"Actually I am. The top leaks, there's no cargo room, and it's not very practical for Gus and me."

"I forbid it!" Aaron barked. "I paid nearly three grand for this car! It's brand new!"

"Well it may be brand new and you might have paid for it, but you gave it to me, my name's on the title, and we need something bigger. Uncle Moe is going to give me 1,200 dollars cash and that station wagon." She pointed to a 1951 Willys Jeep station wagon. It was a two-door wagon, maroon with wide whitewall tires, a front grill that was slightly "V" shaped, and a rear bumper that was slightly askew from backing into something. Although it was only three years old, it had a worn look, like it had been used on a farm or maybe by the Forestry Service. The driver's side had several scratches on it like it had gone down some woodsy trails where thick overgrowth had scraped the paint as it passed.

"What?" Aaron bellowed. "That doesn't even look like it runs."

"Well it does. And in case you've forgotten, my husband's pretty handy with engines. We're going to need a practical second car now with me going into basic training."

"Basic...what are you talking about?"

"Didn't mom tell you? I joined the Army Reserve as a nurse."

"What?"

"Since all the positions for OR nurses were quickly filled at the hospital, it was one the only places where I could get surgical experience unless we moved. I'll be gone at Camp Grayling for six weeks. Civilian hospitals favor people who serve their country. Besides, with my GI benefits, Gus can get a cost break toward getting his master's in education. He'll teach at the high school by day then work toward his degree at night. He'll also keep working at Stu and Ernie's on the weekends. So you see? A sports car with no cargo room and a leaky roof isn't going to work for us."

Sinclair smiled smugly, "I know you, girl. You'll never last in the military."

"It's not full time. It's six weeks of basic training, then one weekend a month for the next eight years with two weeks of refresher training every year."

"You'll never do it," her father said, shaking his head. "And who told you that hoodlum you married could save money on education?"

"My recruiter, the department of defense, the GI Bill..."

Aaron was taken aback by all the plans that had been put into action without his knowledge, consultation, or permission. "I, I thought Gus didn't even *have* an undergraduate degree."

"He finishes his last correspondence class this week. In the meantime, he's been hired on a probationary basis by the high school. Since he's used to juggling two career paths anyway, we thought he might as well just keep going to school and get his master's." She looked at him a little puzzled. "Mom knows all this, hasn't she been filling you in?"

Aaron stuck his hands into the pockets of his khaki slacks. "Your mother and I aren't exactly on the best of terms these days," he admitted. He looked up and saw the salesperson watching them anxiously from the small window of his small building. "Got it all figured out, don't you, girl?"

"No, I don't. But at least my decisions are *my* decisions."

He saw the stubborn determination in her eye. *She is definitely her father's daughter,* he thought.

"Fine. Do what you want," he pronounced, as if she wouldn't have done it anyway. He turned and walked back to his car. Clair swept her long blonde hair to one side watching him go and wishing he had said more, like offer an apology for his behavior on her wedding day. But he didn't. And since she was the one who had been publically humiliated, she didn't feel compelled to go after him, although a part of her wanted to.

24 Porch Memories

The last of Father Ken Pistole's pawns had reached home on the Parcheesi game board as Gus slumped back in his chair at the dining room table in his house on West Upright Street. The priest laughed and snatched up two five dollar bills sitting on the table.

"Ha! That's three in a row, Cooper. Want to go again?"

"You're like Jack Sparrow with a collar," Gus moaned, shaking his head.

"I'm glad you called," the clergyman said, who wasn't actually wearing a collar at the time. He looked at his wristwatch then took a final swig from his Moosehead longneck. "It's been too long since we did this. It was fun."

"Yeah, and that's kinda been my fault," Gus admitted. "I'm sorry, man." He gestured to the Father's empty beer. "You want another?"

"No thanks. But if you don't mind, I might just step out on your porch and have a cigar."

"Not at all," Gus said, picking up his still half-full bottle of Moosehead.

The men walked from the dining room with its mission-style furniture into Gus' small living room and then out the front door into the July evening.

It was after 10:00 p.m. so the sun was completely down. The porch was one of the best features about Gus' house since it took up all of the front of the house then wrapped around to the same side as the driveway. Gus sat in a wicker rocking chair with his Polo shirt, blue jeans, Sperry Docksiders, and beer. Father Ken settled into a companion chair and pulled a Hav-A-Tampa out of his Hawaiian shirt pocket and a box of matches from his jeans. After the priest had unwrapped and lit up his cigar, Gus borrowed his matches and lit three candles already thick with dripping wax that were sitting on a round wicker table between them.

"Perfect night," Father Ken observed. "But I have to ask, was Parcheesi all that was on your mind tonight?"

"What do you mean?"

"Oh, I don't know...did you want to talk about why you stalk the church grounds after the masses looking for someone? Or talk about the hit man that might be after Farren? Did you want to talk about Farren and Doc's relationship and her staying out at Doc's place?"

"You know about the hit man and her staying at Doc's?" Gus asked, surprised.

"Well, 'alleged' hit man," Father Ken answered, slowly rocking to and fro. "You know how it is in a small town. People at the 4th of July Parish Picnic spoke of little else. The police are still protecting her, right?"

"Yeah," Gus admitted, also starting to rock. "And Doc's taken some time off work so he can also be with her in the evenings. He took a swig of beer. "I'll tell you what, it's been one weird summer so far."

The priest took a long drag off his narrow cigar and exhaled a cloud of white smoke.

"Do the police have any solid leads on who shot Charlene Rogers?"

"I don't think so."

"You think the guy who shot her is still in town?"

Gus shrugged. "I hope not."

The two men were quiet for a couple of moments, enjoying the evening and taking a break from questions that neither one knew the answers to.

"Is the recession cutting into your business down at the marina?"

the priest finally asked, changing subjects.

"Do you think miracles really happen?" Gus queried, ignoring the previous question.

"Yes, I do," Father Ken answered, wondering what had prompted the query.

"No bullshit, Ken," Gus emphasized. "Do you think they happen?"

"I've been a priest for thirty-seven years, Gus. Yes, I think they really happen."

"Ever see any?" the host asked, taking another drink of beer.

"Yes, I have. I've seen people who were supposed to die make remarkable recoveries. I've seen murderers turn from crime to God. I've seen a grenade land in a foxhole full of men and *not* go off."

"Those are all explainable," Gus dismissed. "I'm talking about something that's truly miraculous, something that couldn't be anything else but."

"Like what?"

"Like seeing a person walking around that you *know* is dead."

The priest stopped rocking in his chair and turned to his friend with a serious expression on his face.

"What're we talking about here? Souls in Purgatory, or..."

"I don't know," Gus interrupted anxiously. "I—I don't know."

"All things are possible with God," the priest conceded. "But you should ask yourself is what you saw *likely*? I don't think miracles happen unless there's a good reason."

"Agreed."

"Who was it you think you saw, Gus?"

The older man stopped rocking, set down his beer on the floor of the painted wood-plank porch, and went into the house. A few seconds later, he returned with the framed black-and-white photo of Clair that had been sitting on the painted bookcase in the living room. He handed it over to the clergyman.

Father Ken studied the picture, taking another slow drag from his stogie.

"This was your wife, right?" he asked.

"Yeah," Gus said, leaning against the wooden porch railing so he was facing the priest, "Clair."

Even though the two men had known each other for years, Gus had spoken very sparingly about his wife or her untimely and tragic death.

"Pretty girl...I wish I would've known her. She appeared to you?"

"During midnight mass," Gus nodded folding his arms. "I saw her standing in church on the opposite side from where I was sitting. She looked exactly the way she does there except she was wearing different clothes. Modern clothes."

The priest handed the photograph back to Gus. "Isn't it more likely you saw someone who simply resembled her? The holidays are the most emotional time of year for people. Especially..." he stopped himself, not wishing to cause offense.

"For elderly people who live alone?" Gus finished. "I thought of that. But she spoke to me, Ken. Well, not 'spoke' to me. But mouthed something from across the church. Something only I would know."

"Which was?"

"I love you."

"A packed church and you're the only one who would recognize the words 'I love you?'"

Gus realized the illogic of what he was saying. He returned to his rocking chair, carefully set the picture down on the porch floor, then picked up his beer and took another drink.

"We had this agreement," he finally said, "'vow' if you like, that we would never end a phone conversation without saying we loved each other. It was something she came up with because she joined the Army Reserve shortly after we got married and was being shipped off to basic training for six weeks. We were still pretty infatuated with one another at the time. Everything was still new."

"Of course," the priest said.

"Three summers into the marriage, August of '56, she was over at Camp Grayling doing her annual two-week training. Her first night there, she called but was being rushed and had to end the conversation abruptly. She hung up without saying 'I love you.' To make it worse, we were kind of in the middle of a fight." He shook his head. "Silly, really...just a stupid, romantic sentiment. A promise that was certainly going to be broken at some point. Except, that was the last time I talked to her. She died the next morning."

Father Ken paused for a moment before asking his next question.

"Farren mentioned it to me once. It was a helicopter crash, wasn't it?"

Gus nodded, stoically. "Korea was over but they were still practicing the delivery of airlifted patients to field hospitals. Y'know, like they used to do on M*A*S*H? This Bubble Bird developed a problem in the tail section. That's what they used to call the ambulance choppers because the pilot was in a Plexiglas cockpit that looked like a big bubble. Anyway, it went down hard, exploded on impact, and threw a fireball right into a surgical tent that Clair was in. They told me nobody in the tent knew what hit 'em. Four people died. I drove over to Grayling that night and made an ID but—" Gus paused to get a better grip on his emotions, "there, there wasn't a whole lot left that was recognizable."

The priest looked at his friend, understanding why Gus was going to church and hanging out after the masses. He was hoping to either see Clair again, or see someone who might've looked like her therefore disproving the theory of a miracle.

Gus picked up his beer, guzzled down what was left in the bottle, and tried to shake off his melancholy. "That's the mercy of God for you. What're ya gonna do, eh?"

Father Ken continued to stare at his host both surprised and empathetic. After several more seconds of silence, he put down his cigar.

"When I was in Nam, I saw good men die and selfish, immoral men win medals. It's hard not to be angry at God sometimes. But you know what? I think unfair things, even what we call 'random things,' are somehow part of the Great Equation. I don't profess to know everything that makes up that equation, but I think God does."

"That's just so you can believe there's an order to things," Gus opinioned.

"I don't think so," Father Ken answered back. "I didn't know everything there was to know about my parents. As their child, I saw only one perspective. But there was unquestionably a lot more to them. I think it works that way with God. If you're going to have a relationship with him, you go in knowing you only get one perspective. Not because he's unfair, but because he's God. He's the parent and you're not."

"Why did he have to kill my wife, priest?" Gus hissed with a flame of anger that hadn't been extinguished in more than fifty-seven years.

"He didn't. A malfunctioning helicopter did."

"Semantics," Gus said.

"Faith is a promise that's bigger than yourself," the clergyman retorted. He rose out of his chair. "Look, I don't know if you saw Clair at midnight mass or not. I can think of a dozen reasons why you probably didn't. But I also know that by you telling me her story tonight, you've kept her memory alive. And that's a good thing because if she's alive in your head, she's alive in there." He pointed to Gus' heart.

The older man looked at his friend and rubbed the white stubble on his cheek, still trying to shake off his sadness. "Well *that* was an incredibly vague bit of comfort. Thanks for nothin', Ken."

The priest smiled. "Anytime." He looked at his wristwatch. "I've gotta scoot. I'm visiting shut-ins early tomorrow. Thanks again for the beer, Parcheesi, and about a half tank of gas," he said, patting his jeans front pocket and rising. "I'll light a candle for Clair, tomorrow."

"Thanks, man," Gus smiled also getting to his feet.

The heavyset priest picked up his cigar and stepped off the front porch, onto the sidewalk, walking the sixteen steps to his car parked in front of the house on the street.

"Goodnight, Cooper," he called.

Gus raised a hand while stuffing the other partially in his jeans pocket. He stood on the porch watching the car drive down the street and turn down the block. He looked out at the night, then over to the picture on the porch floor. He stepped back over to his wicker rocking chair, sat down and picked it up. He gazed at it longingly until his eyes were moist and a tear nearly escaped and ran down his weathered cheek. He set the picture back down and closed his tired eyes.

"Our Father who aren't in heaven..." he quietly whispered. "...I hate your guts!"

25 Family Tradition

    Clair plopped her weekender bag down on the sofa of her and Gus' apartment. It was a furnished but modest one-bedroom place that was actually the second floor of a house. The landlord and his family lived downstairs while the newlyweds lived upstairs in the converted space. They had found the apartment after staying with Gus' parents for less than a week. It had a small kitchenette, bathroom, living room, and its own access stairway in the back of the house. But they were already anxious for another place. The steep back stairs were going to be treacherous when the first freeze arrived, and they had already been spoken to about their squeaky bed and certain sounds that emanated from their bedroom late at night, so the two were keeping their eyes peeled for a house. There were plenty of houses for rent in Charlevoix for tourists, but few that a young couple just starting out could afford.

    "You sure you got everything?" Gus asked as he walked into the living room. He was dressed for work at Stu and Ernie's in his brown zip-up overalls. Even though the high school had hired him as a teacher on a trial basis, he still worked as a mechanic on the weekends to pick up extra cash.

    "I think so," she answered, rummaging through her purse. She was wearing a breezy summer dress and appeared ready for travel. "I mean, the army provides my clothing, boots, socks, helmet, footlocker...all I really need is a toothbrush."

"Are they going to cut your hair?" he asked, touching her natural curls affectionately.

"Not if I keep it pinned up and nailed down," she said, pulling her keys out of her purse.

"Six weeks," he lamented. "We're about to spend more time apart as marrieds than we've spent together."

"Yes, but getting your master's is going to be a fraction of the cost," she said as she disappeared into the kitchen.

"You're not going to be doing much OR training during basic are you?"

"Maybe some," she called. "But mostly I'll also be doing training with firearms, marching, crawling through the mud under barbed wire, you know, soldier stuff." She reappeared from the kitchen holding an open bottle of Vernors. "Where's my sunglasses?"

"On your head," he smiled, seeing her Ray Bans peek out from in between her blonde locks.

"Aw geez," she said, feeling the top of her head. "Eight years! How am I going to do this for eight years?"

"The first part's the worst," he said, picking up her bag. "But yeah, you really surprised me with this one. I never would've thought of you as army material."

"You and my father," she added, and then looked at her watch. "I'm running late, I'd better go."

He grabbed her bag and they walked through the apartment and out their front door—which was really in the back of the house—then down the white-painted staircase that led to her Jeep station wagon and his Chevy pick-up.

He opened the back window of the wagon, which still left the gate up, put her bag in back, and then closed the window.

"Thank you for doing this."

"What?"

"I know you did this so I could continue going to school on the cheap."

"It wasn't just that," she replied. "It's going to look good on an application when something finally opens up at the hospital, I'll get valuable medical training, I'm serving my country—"

"And you're tweaking your dad's nose," he interrupted.

"No."

"Yes," he teased. "You're out to prove you're not the helpless princess he thinks you are."

"No...well...maybe a little."

He put his arms around her waist. "I'm going to miss you more than I can say. Don't ever forget how much I love you."

She likewise put her arms around him. "Then remind me of it every time we talk on the phone. Let's promise to end every phone conversation by saying 'I love you.' Even if we're mad at each other at the time."

"Deal."

She put her hands on his cheeks so his clear brown eyes were looking directly into her bright green ones.

"No, really! Promise me we'll always do that. It'll be one of those family traditions we'll pass along to our kids."

"Or, strange idiosyncrasies."

"Either way, I love you, Gus Cooper. Thank you for giving me a future I never saw coming, but see so perfectly now."

They kissed long and tenderly, then he opened the door for her and she climbed into the station wagon to begin her occasional army life.

26 Discoveries

Al Stanislaus was a customer of the Portside Marina and the owner of a thirty-four-foot Beneteau Flyer Gran Turismo cabin cruiser. Its sleek lines and three elegant portholes on either side of the hull were the exact opposite of Al. At only five-foot-six-inches, he was a Chrome-cologne-wearing gorilla of a man, a hairy-chested, hairy-armed Greek who, ironically, had no hair on top of his head but had a half-halo of black hair encircling the sides and back. In fact, it was hard to tell where the hair on the back of Al's head stopped and the hair on the back of his neck began.

He came into the marina store wearing an unbuttoned double extra-large Hawaiian shirt, Bermuda shorts, noisy flip-flops, and two gold chains around his neck that were expensive but didn't improve his looks. Being fifty-five years old and sixty pounds overweight, he was a heart attack waiting to happen.

He shuffled past the gleaming outboard engines that sat on stands, past the fishing rods, past the ski ropes and coolers of soda pop and beer, and went straight up to Gus who was standing behind the counter clipping snack bags of potato chips into a counter-top display.

"I've had it with that woman, Gus!" Al announced before he had even arrived at the counter.

"Who?" Gus asked, but already knowing the answer.

"Jiggle Jugs in the slip next to me."

He was referring to Lupe Hernandez, a new tenant of the marina just this season. She was a well-endowed red-headed woman from Costa Rica, twenty-eight years old, and the owner of a thirty-three-foot Hunter sailboat, a prize from her recent divorce that was worth about ninety grand. Lupe wasn't a sailor, she was a fisherman. Right now she was trolling for a new husband, using her leopard-skin Brazilian bikini and flirtatious poses and smiles as bait for any man that could put her in a higher tax bracket. The first one to bite happened to be Al. But Lupe threw him back after the first date. He didn't like being rejected and therefore took every opportunity to complain about her.

"Are you talking about Miss Hernandez?" Gus asked innocently.

"Who else? She had a party going on last night until God knows when. I didn't sleep a wink! I nearly called the police."

"Why didn't you?"

"Well, I just assumed somebody else would," Al fumed.

"Funny," Gus said, scratching his stubble. "Nobody else has complained to me about it."

"I thought this was supposed to be a family place," the disgruntled boat owner huffed. "We've got people with kids here and she's out there practically naked!"

"It's a marina, Al," Gus deadpanned. "All the people here are practically naked." Then he lightened his tone. "Look, I'll go talk to her and see if she'd be willing to trade slips with another customer. If she's not, I'll talk to her about the noise. Meantime, go to the cooler, grab yourself a beer on the house, and stop trying to screw women that are young enough to be your daughter."

"What?" Al said, indignant.

"You're a valued customer," Gus said sincerely, "been with us for years. I don't want you having a stroke and dyin' on me. I also don't want a stranger takin' all your money. *I* want all your money."

The fat, hairy Greek got the gold digger implications of what Gus was saying and started to chuckle. "You look out for me, eh, Gus?"

"I try to."

Al nodded and smiled. "Okay. I'll be happy if you can just get her a few slips away." He turned and left the store, his flip-flops slapping the bottoms of his thick feet with every step. Gus watched him go then returned to clipping bags of potato chips.

"Nicely done," he heard a woman's voice say. He looked up again and saw Judith Herriman coming around one of the aisle ends wearing her usual slacks, casual top, and carrying a shoulder bag. Though he didn't know who she was, he liked her hazel eyes and trim figure.

"I was stooped down over there looking at your boat wax to see if you had my brand, but you don't. I didn't mean to eavesdrop but I'm glad I did. You're quite the negotiator."

"I taught at a university for a long time," Gus answered, surprised by her appearance. "There's an old saying: 'College professors really don't teach, they just negotiate tidbits of knowledge.'"

"RD Laing," Judith said, recognizing the words of the noted psychiatrist and author.

"I, uh, didn't hear you come in."

"You were in back getting your box of chips, I think."

Gus nodded and held out his hand. "Gus Cooper."

The grey-haired woman came over and shook it. "Yes, I know. Judith Herriman."

He cocked his head. "Have we met before?"

"I've known you all my life," Judith confessed. "You used to put air in my bicycle tires when I was a kid. You worked at Stu and Ernie's. I don't suppose you'd remember a skinny thirteen-year-old girl with braces?"

"Sorry, no," Gus smiled. "But there sure aren't many of us left who'd remember Stu and Ernie's."

"Not many," she agreed, and glanced over her shoulder toward the door.

"Your friend, Al, didn't get his complimentary beer."

"He's a Scotch drinker. That's why I offered it."

She looked at him and smiled, liking his quick thinking and sense of humor.

"You a boater?" Gus asked. "I haven't seen you in here before."

"My folks use to live in town but now I live down the South

Arm," she replied, referring to the South Arm of Lake Charlevoix. "I have a vintage MasterCraft. I usually get my stuff at a place a little closer."

"What brings you here today?"

"Your granddaughter," she dipped a hand into her shoulder bag and produced a business card. "I'm her therapist."

"Oh," Gus said, taking and reading the card. "I knew she was seeing someone, but I haven't stuck my nose too deep down that well. Therapy is hard enough without having to explain it to your grandpa." He looked at her playfully. "Guess I'm gonna have to watch myself around you."

"Too late," Judith smiled. "Farren's already given me a pretty clear impression."

"Great," Gus said, rolling his eyes. "So much for flirting. Farren's out in the storage barn, the big red building behind this one. You're going to have to get past Starsky and Hutch, though."

"Her police protection?"

Gus chuckled and sighed. "Is there anyone left in this town who *doesn't* know the cops are watching her?"

"I know Charlene Rogers' folks," she explained. "Small town."

"Pain in the butt town, sometimes," Gus grumbled, more to himself than to her.

"Maybe people knowing that someone might be after Farren and she's got police protection is a good thing," Judith suggested. "The more people who know, the more people are on the lookout for strangers hanging around here, or her house, or Doc's."

"Or, the bigger the challenge to a dedicated assassin," Gus countered.

"I sure hope you're wrong about that," she replied. "Farren's something of a landmark with me, you know. First and foremost, I want her safe. But beyond that, she's my last new patient. Soon as she's turned a corner and feels like she doesn't need me, I'm retiring. I'm selling the boat, selling the house, and moving to Florida. I can't take the winters here anymore."

"I've wanted to go south for a long time myself," Gus agreed. "There's this beach in Venice, Florida—"

"Caspersen Beach?" she cut in, knowingly.

"The very one," Gus nodded.

"Shark's teeth wash up there," she said, smiling.

"Yep. Millions of years old. I've often thought that someday I'd like to retire there. I'd spend my days going to the beach, digging around for shark's teeth, watch the dolphins...it's a place where I can be around water and not feel like I'm working."

"So why don't you?"

"Farren's a landmark with me, too. I can't leave until I know she's safe and her life's in order."

The therapist smiled. "You're a good man."

Gus returned a weary smile. "I used to be. C'mon, I'll walk to you to storage barn and get you past the coppers."

"That's okay," she said, "I saw them when I came in. I actually know Andy Bush. His mom and I play bridge."

"Okay...and, uh, sorry I don't remember you from Stu and Ernie's."

The willowy woman walked down the center aisle of the store toward the front door.

"That's okay. No reason why you should. But I remember you. You were my first secret crush."

"Really?" Gus replied, genuinely surprised.

Judith got to the door, put her hand on the push bar, and paused. "Of course, you were taller then." She turned back to him, smiled, and continued out the door.

Meanwhile, inside the storage barn, Farren was in the detailing area surrounded by six-foot high lights on tripods and had just finished buffing the exterior hull of a twenty-two-foot Donzi runabout that was sitting on a trailer. The barn's large hanger-like doors were closed and no one was allowed in without first checking with the officers in the police cruiser out front.

Farren was wearing zip-up blue overalls, goggles, and a mask over her mouth. Her outfit made her look like a cute bug with oversized eyes and a tuft of black hair. She put the buffer on a shelf, wrapped up and put away an extension cord, turned off two of the tripod lights, and then slipped off her mask and goggles just as Carly

Simon's "Attitude Dancing" came on her iPod.

The 70s siren was the favorite singer of her mother, Jackie, and Farren grew up listening to all her songs. Finished with the Donzi and knowing she was alone in the windowless, cavernous barn, she turned off an exhaust fan then started dancing to the song. She shuffled her feet, swung her hips and picked up a couple of paint stirrer sticks and started to beat in rhythm on a fifty-gallon oil drum. She started to sing out loud: "At-it-tude dan-sin!... At-it-tude dan-sin!" She pranced, tossed her head to and fro, shook her butt, then struck a pose and started to dance again. Truth be told, her impromptu performance was both coordinated and downright sexy until she turned and saw Judith Herriman smiling at her.

"Judith!" she nearly screamed, abruptly stopping. "W-w-what're you doing here?" She fumbled for her iPod to turn it off.

"I heard about Charlene Rogers and wanted to make sure you were okay. But, uh, it seems you are."

Farren took out her ear buds and put her iPod on a shelf. Then she unzipped and stepped out of her overalls, revealing a red T-shirt and cutoffs.

"No, I *do* feel bad about Charlene. I pray for her all the time. But, things have changed with Doc and me. Changed for the better. That's why I'm...well...happy."

"You two finally consummated your relationship?"

"Three days ago," Farren nodded, hanging her overalls on a wall hook.

"We were on a boat out in the middle of Lake Michigan."

"Sounds romantic," Judith said.

"It was *very* romantic!" Farren gushed.

"And no fears or memories connected with Charlie?"

Farren brushed her bangs aside, thinking. "No."

Herriman took a few steps and looked around the barn, processing the news. After a few moments, she asked: "Did Doc share any new information with you? Any revelations? Announcements?"

"Yes. A *lot* of revelations. He told me that he didn't want to be a fireman and that he really wanted to be a doctor. He's already taken his MCAT and applied to medical school." Her dimpled smile widened. "He also told me he loved me."

"Those *are* some revelations," Herriman agreed.

"He said that he would continue to be patient about my emotional problem and that if he got accepted into medical school, he'd figure out a way for us to be together. He said that us *not* being together was unacceptable." She smiled again, recalling his words. "He said that if I wanted the assurance of a diamond, we'd become engaged. And he also said he'd live anywhere I wanted to go."

"Sounds like it was quite a night," the older woman smiled. "You two have been sexually active since?"

Farren blushed a little as she put her goggles and mask into a drawer.

"Like nymphomaniacs. He's taken a few days off so when I get home, he's there."

"What's he doing with his days?"

"Well, he still has to keep up with his online classes for fireman certification until he hears from the medical school in Detroit. Y'know, keeping options open. He's afraid he won't get in, but I know he will."

"What medical school did he apply to?"

"Wayne State. He actually applied and was accepted there ten years ago, but never went."

"Why not?"

"Julia, the girl he was seeing at the time, was killed in this horrible car accident. She was on her way home after just seeing him. It messed with his head. Not unlike Charlie messing with mine, I suppose. Anyway, it sidetracked him from medical school."

"Interesting," Judith mused.

"What?"

"That Doc suffered the tragic death of someone close and you did too, the death of your parents."

"So did grandpa, for that matter," Farren noted.

"Yes," Herriman said with a faraway look in her eye, "I remember my parents talking about it when I was a girl. What was her name again?"

"My Grandma Clair. She was in the wrong place at the wrong

time when a helicopter crash-landed at Camp Grayling."

"Clair. That's right...tragic death." The older woman thought for a moment, half leaning, half sitting on an empty saw horse. "Why do you think you and Doc had this breakthrough? What do you think triggered it?"

Farren stuck her hands in the back pockets of her cut-offs. "Like I said, it was a romantic evening. That, plus he told me he loved me. I mean, I thought he did, I hoped he did, but he'd never actually said it until a few days ago."

"Or that he wanted to be a doctor," the therapist added.

"Well that didn't have anything to do with anything. He's always been a caregiver." She paused and looked at the older woman. "You're not suggesting I gave myself to Doc because he, he might be financially successful or something, are you?"

Judith leaned off the sawhorse. "Of course not. But I think it's significant that he's going to Detroit and said that you not being with him was unacceptable."

"What do you mean?"

"Did he mention anything about the possibility of you going with him?"

Farren thought for a moment. "Yes, as a matter of fact."

"Sounds to me like if Doc goes to medical school, you're making a move."

"Well, not necessarily. We could be engaged and still be separated."

"But that's not what he really wants and you know it," Herriman pointed out. "What'd he'd prefer is you going with him. Taking you out of Charlevoix. Taking you away from this business. Significantly changing your life."

Farren nervously brushed her bangs aside again and walked over to the Donzi runabout, feeling its hull and checking her buffing job. "We, we haven't gotten that far in our plans yet. I mean, there's a lot to consider. My safety, for one thing. Then there's the business, and Grandpa. He can't run this place by himself."

"You have staff," Judith reminded her. "I saw some in the parking lot and on the docks."

"Temporary summer help," Farren explained, turning back to her therapist.

"The point is, this place can run without you. It's running without you now. Aren't you locked away in a barn doing things that any high school kid could do?"

"No," she said defensively. "Not just anybody can buff a hull like this!"

"How old were you when you learned?"

"Sixteen, seventeen?" Farren furrowed her brow. "Where are you taking this, Judith?"

The therapist hung her shoulder bag on the sawhorse. "I don't think you're intimacy problem with Doc was because of the way Charlie treated you. Oh, I've no doubt you didn't like some of the things he did to you. But I think real reason you had intimacy problems with Doc was because you don't like your life."

"What?" Farren said, wide-eyed. "That's absurd."

"Is it? This marina was your father's dream, not yours. You admitted you were initially attracted to Charlie and Doc because they weren't from around here. I don't doubt that, but half your customers aren't from around here, so there's got to be more to the story, doesn't there? And there is. You told me you believed Charlie was a man of secrets even before you knew that was true. I think part of you was drawn to those secrets. They represented something different, an element of the unknown, and this was exciting to you. Then Doc comes along, a paramedic with all these life-harrowing experiences who's lived in places like Sedona and Jackson Hole. He finds out Charlie's secrets are dangerous and saves you from him. He wants to help get your life back to normal. But you don't want 'normal.' Because normal means the next forty years are all mapped out, they're right here in this barn and doing the same things you've been doing since you were a teenager. So you pushed him away with all these claustrophobic symptoms. Then, suddenly, something happened. Doc changed career directions. He may leave town. Take you with him. And even if he doesn't go to medical school, he declared he'd live anywhere you want. With those words he became both your security blanket *and* your ticket of escape. And suddenly, boom, you're overcome with passion."

Farren shook her head. "You're wrong, Judith. I love this place and I'd never 'use' Doc as a ticket to anything."

"Not consciously, no you wouldn't. But you once told me that if Charlie had really loved you, you would've given up this land to settle his debt with Bartholomew."

"I was naive," she countered.

"You were hoping for an escape. Look, I've no doubt you're very fond of this place. Prisoners can like their jailers too. But this isn't what you chose, Farren, because you were never given a choice. Think about it, the two men you've fallen in love with are two men who, in their own way, represent escape. One had a lot secrets, and the other lived in—what did you call them—'fascinating' places."

Farren's eyes darted around the storage barn and winced slightly as if Judith's diagnosis was causing her physical pain. Seeing this, the therapist softened her face and tone.

"Of course, the possibility that some madman is out there with a gun and might want to kill you could have something to do with throwing your inhibitions out the window too...I'm sorry. I didn't mean to lay that worry on you."

Farren shook her head and shrugged. "You didn't lay it on me. It's reality. Sometimes it's in the forefront of my mind, sometimes in back, but it's always there. Like someone having cancer, I suppose." She looked around the barn for a few more moments. "Okay," she finally said, "let's say, for the sake of discussion, what you say is true. What do I do?"

"You realize that the only one who can change your life is *you*," Judith answered with a wise smile.

"That's it?"

"I think we've identified where your issues are really coming from. If you know what the cause is, you can do something about it. In the meantime, you've broken down your barriers with Doc, and whether he goes to medical school or not, it's probably time for you to make some changes."

"What kind of changes?"

"That's up to you."

Meanwhile, out at Doc's cabin, the fireman-in-training sat behind the writing desk in his living room working on his laptop wearing a T-shirt and cut-offs. He hit the send button having just completed a test on the most common methods of professional arson. A slight wind was blowing through the open windows that overlooked the screened-in porch and the open storm door leading out to it. He could hear the crank-and-sputter of someone trying to start an outboard engine with a pull starter.

He heard the starter rope pulled once, twice, three times, then a fourth and fifth time. It made him mildly curious, but he didn't want to investigate because he was waiting for the score on his test. But the attempts outside continued. He heard a sixth pull on the engine, then a seventh. It slowly dawned on him that even with the wind blowing just right, that boat had to be close. Really close. Was it just off shore? At his dock?

A yellow balloon popped up on the computer screen that read: "Congratulations. Your score is 91%." The corner of his mouth cracked a smile. But then he heard yet another couple of engine pulls from outside and finally decided to investigate.

He rose from the desk and walked out of the living room through the screen door and onto the porch. About midway through the porch he heard the boat motor finally come to life, then throttle up and start to pull away.

He went through the screen door at the porch's other end and stepped outside onto the path that led down to the beach. In another few steps he could see that an old aluminum rowboat with a twenty-five horsepower, handle-controlled outboard motor was pulling away from close to his dock.

By the time he spotted the boat, it was already ten yards from the end of the dock and the engine was tilted up slightly because of the shallow water. Was it a fisherman who was merely fishing close to shore? Or was it something else?

He quickened his pace as he stepped from the path onto the beach and then onto the dock. He could see that the man at the control handle, who had his back to him, appeared to be middle-aged. He wore a white tank top undershirt and a flat dark cap. There was a fishing pole peeking up from the hull of the boat, but something instinctively told Doc this wasn't a fisherman. For one thing, the man's arms and shoulders were noticeably pale, meaning he wasn't a local. It could've been a tourist in a rental, but rental boats were newer looking and usually had the name and phone number of the rental place painted on the side of the hull. Since the man didn't turn around to look at Doc, he couldn't make out a lot of detail.

By the time Doc had walked out to the end of his dock, the rowboat was fifty yards off and still moving in the straight line away from him. He watched as the operator tilted the engine back for deeper water. Doc had an uneasy feeling in his stomach.

He thought about calling the police. But then, what was he going to say? That he saw a boat close to his dock driven by a pale man on a public lake? He stuck his hands into his cutoff pockets and decided he was overreacting, that he was being paranoid. He told himself that a professional killer wouldn't be casing his place in the middle of the day in an older, rinky-dink rowboat. He looked down at the dock and turned to return to the beach.

On his way back he saw three little beads of water on the aluminum dock's surface, each being about the size of a bottle cap. He knew that water certainly could've splashed up on the dock from a wave. But at the moment, the water was calm except for the deteriorating gently rolling wake of the departing rowboat and that wasn't enough to get the dock wet. Plus, the rest of the dock was bone dry.

Doc spun around and looked toward the boat again, but it was too far away to make out anything else about its mysterious driver.

27 Back From Basic

September in Charlevoix was a wonderful time of year. With most of the tourists gone, the town had returned to its quaint village feel despite the flurry of reconstruction going on with the storefronts down on Bridge Street. The fall colors were also well underway and leaves dotted the lawns and skittered across the streets and sidewalks. Flocks of birds gathered on fences and telephone wires for winter migration, salmon fishermen went out on their boats for large catches, and farmers with tractors pulled their wagons into town selling bales of hay to be sprinkled over flowerbeds and vegetable gardens for protection from the inevitable snow.

School had started once again and Clair's sister, Jessie, and two of her girlfriends from high school pulled into Stu and Ernie's on a crisp but sunny Saturday afternoon. Jessie was riding in the back seat of her friend's Ford convertible with the top down, even though it was a little too cold for it. She was wearing jeans, tennis shoes, and a long-sleeve black turtleneck, as if to defy her sister's more stylish and womanly ways. She looked like something between a bobbysoxer and a starving poet from Greenwich Village.

As Stu walked out of the office and toward the car, Jessie sat up on the top of the back seat and called to Gus, whom she saw working on a Chrysler in Service Bay Two.

"Hey, Gus!" she said, waving and smiling. "She shown up yet?"

Seeing her, Gus called back, "Hey, Stringbean! No, not yet."

"I think it's so cool that you can call our new sociology teacher by his first name," the girl behind the steering wheel said.

"Well, he's my brother-in-law," Jessie answered.

"Who's not back? Who were you guys talking about?" the other girl sitting in the passenger side seat asked.

"My sister. She just graduated from basic training down at Camp Grayling yesterday. My mom, me, and Gus all went, but she stayed another night to celebrate with friends and is driving back today."

"No family chit-chat with Gus today, please, Jessie," Stu said, approaching the car. "Mr. Vandermeer's going to be here any minute to pick up his car." He looked at the driver. "What do you need, dear?"

"Three dollars of regular, please, Mr. Stu," the girl answered.

"Well I think it's admirable that Mr. Cooper is breaking with social norms," the other girl sitting in the front seat noted. "He moves so seamlessly between being a middle-class schoolteacher during the weekdays and a working-class mechanic on the weekends. I call that social adaptability."

"I call it working to save money for a house," Stu mumbled under his breath as he opened the Ford's gas tank.

Just at that moment, Clair pulled into the parking lot behind the wheel of her scratched-up Jeep station wagon. She was wearing a newly issued beige summer dress uniform with her hair pinned-up under her cap.

"It's Clair! She's back!" Jessie announced as she hopped out of the car and ran over to her sister.

"Vandermeer's car is never going to get finished," Stu grumbled, shaking his head while pumping the gas.

"So, are you hung over?" Jessie asked. She held up three fingers as her sister climbed out of her wagon. "How many fingers do you see?"

"Oh, stop it," Clair said, taking off her sunglasses and putting them in her breast pocket. "C'mere and give me a hug."

"So how was it, General?" Stu called from the pump.

"They worked my butt off," Clair called while smiling and hugging Jessie simultaneously.

"Oh, I'd say you still have some butt left," Gus smiled as he came out of Service Bay Two wiping his hands and walking toward her.

"Eeww," Jessie protested.

"Excuse me for a second, honey," Clair said, letting go of her little sister.

She ran over to Gus and their lips locked in a long kiss. It was the kind of kiss that took away the breath of the two girls in the Ford.

"Uh, it's great to see you, General," Stu called, "but I've got a customer named Vandermeer that's gonna be here any minute and–"

"It's done," Gus called, breaking away from Clair's mouth.

"Oh, well, then—uh—as you were." Stu said.

While Gus and Clair resumed their kissing, Jessie walked over to her friend's Ford as Stu was washing the windshield. "You guys go ahead. I'll catch a ride home with my sister," she told her friends.

As the schoolgirls said goodbye to each other and Stu collected his three dollars, Gus and Clair finally came up for air.

"Have fun last night?" he asked.

"I made some good friends over the past six weeks. Girls who are great nurses and one or two even had a job lead in the area. So, thanks for letting me stay another night."

"No problem," he said. Then he started feeling her arms and shoulders. "You feel different. More muscular. I didn't notice that yesterday."

"Marching, calisthenics, and running up and down hills everyday will do that to you."

"Was it terrible?" he asked, wrapping his arms around her waist.

"Eh, it was hard work but nothing I didn't expect, except for the gas mask chamber I showed you yesterday. You go into this room that's full of gas, then you have to take your mask off and find your way out. That was *terrible!* I threw up for an hour afterward."

"Well, I'm sorry you got sick but I'm glad you're back. Six weeks felt like six months."

They kissed again, and then Clair wanted to catch up on all things local.

"So tell me about school? How are you getting along with the kids? You didn't say much about it yesterday."

"Yesterday wasn't about me," Gus said. "It was about you."

"I'm so sick of people saying, 'Oh, Mr. Cooper is sooo dreamy,'" Jessie interjected, answering the question for him as she walked over.

"Is it weird having your brother-in-law teach at your school?" Clair asked.

"Yes!" Jessie answered, with all of the drama of a high school student. "But, I took sociology last year, so, it's okay, I guess."

"Well, thank you, Stringbean," Gus noted. "That'll make me sleep better tonight."

"So Jess," Clair asked, taking off her army cap and starting to unpin her hair that was tightly concealed under it, "what's going on at home?"

"It's pretty strange. Dad's there, but he and Mom aren't...I mean, he's been sleeping in your room. And I hear him on the phone a lot arguing with people at the bank and talking to people about extending time limits for payments. He's had to sell some of his company's trucks and stuff...I think he's in real trouble, Clair."

"Is he doing any work?"

"Little things. That's why he didn't come yesterday. He was working."

"Yeah, I bet," Clair responded, believing that her father might've been working the previous day, but not believing it was his sole reason for him missing her graduation.

"It's nothing like he used to do, though." Jessie added.

"I've been hearing some stuff, too," Gus said. He glanced at Jessie, then back to his wife. "I'll fill you in later."

"Code for 'Daddy's in the crapper,'" Jessie surmised.

"Okay. Thank you, Miss Toilet Tongue. C'mon, I'll give you a ride home." She turned to her husband. "See you later."

"Absolutely," he said, with a hunger for her that was unmistakable. Jessie just rolled her eyes.

Later that night, a satisfied Gus rolled over on his back in bed under the sheets. Seconds later, Clair climbed on top of him, also under the sheets. Both of them were naked except for the army cap she still wore. With her hair now completely down and spilling over

Gus' face and shoulders, it looked a lot sexier than it did military.

"Well, Army Nurse Cooper," he said quietly. "Thank you for taking me on, uh, night maneuvers."

"Thank *you* for standing at attention for so long," she whispered playfully.

They kissed a few more times, then Gus revisited the subject of her training.

"So, you won't have to go through everything you did in basic anymore?"

"Oh, there will be refresher stuff. But nothing I can't handle."

"Except for the gas."

"Except for the gas," she verified.

"Did a lot of the other nurses get sick, too?"

"No, I was the only one."

"Mmm," he mused, "must be because you're a princess."

"Maybe. But I think it was because I'm pregnant."

He looked up at her wide-eyed. She, lying on top of him, looked down and grinned.

"We—we're going to have a baby?" he asked, delighted.

She looked at him and nodded.

They hugged, kissed, then they rolled over in bed so he was on top of her.

"Oh, honey, that's *fabulous!*" Then he realized he was now lying on her. "Is this okay?"

"Of course," she laughed. "If I can climb ropes and crawl under barbed wire, I can have my husband on top of me."

"How far along are you?"

"I figure about six weeks. The doctor on base said I'll be due in June of next year."

"The night before you left," he remembered fondly.

"Is this okay?" she asked. "I mean, I know we wanted children, but there's a lot of things going on with your night school, and two jobs, and–"

"It's perfect," he smiled down at her. "*You're* perfect." They kissed for a long, lingering time. Then Gus was ready to make plans.

"We've got to tell our folks."

"Well, not right away," she suggested. "Let's just keep it between us for a little while. I mean, how many times in life do you get to really and truly hang onto a secret? And a good secret at that?"

"Okay," he agreed, "we won't tell anyone for a while." He rolled off of her and got out of bed. "This calls for a celebration. You hungry? Can I fix you something? Any cravings?"

"Only for you and I'm pretty satisfied at the moment," she smiled.

He looked around the floor and found his boxer shorts. "I feel like an omelet. God, Clair. This is going to great! A family!" He slipped on his shorts and started to head toward the kitchen, but then paused and turned around.

"Ah, what about your dad?"

"What about him?"

"Don't you think it's time you—y'know—made peace with him?"

Clair looked around and found her short silk robe hanging on the closet doorknob. She got out of bed, went over to the closet, and slipped it on.

"I'm not the one who tried to orchestrate a marriage for a business deal. I'm not the one who paid one daughter to spy on another. I'm not the one who tried to scare off his daughter's boyfriend. I'm not the one who made an arrangement with the CEO of the hospital so his daughter wouldn't get a job. I'm not the one who threw a drink in that daughter's face on her wedding day in a crowded restaurant. And I'm not the one who never wrote or called that daughter while she was away at basic training. He didn't even come to my graduation!"

"Well, when you put it *that* way, yeah, it sounds kinda bad," Gus joked.

When he saw Clair wasn't smiling, he continued: "Look, someone's got to take the first step. For the sake of the baby, don't you think it's time to make nice?"

She looked at him with a pouting lip, knowing he was right, but not wanting to admit to it.

28 Believing

"Okay, everybody," the photographer said, "just one more. On three. One, two, big smiles..." The camera flash popped and the seventh and final formal photo of the Vale/Rogers wedding party was finished. The party consisted of three bridesmaids including Charlene's maid of honor and three groomsmen including Lance's best man. The bridesmaids were in tasteful shoulderless light-blue long chiffon dresses and the groomsmen were in traditional black After Six tuxes. All of the groomsmen were first cousins of Lance while the bridesmaids consisted of Charlene's older sister Tabatha, the sister who owned the nail salon, Lindsay, a best friend from college days at Michigan State University, and Farren. Only the wedding party remained in St. Mark's Lutheran Church. The other hundred or so guests stood out front, waiting to douse the couple with flower petals before everyone drove off to the reception.

Charlene looked radiant in a white, floor-length Chapel Appliques Luba's Dress. It was also shoulderless with lace on the torso that smoothed out into cascading layers of sheer fabric. She wore a mid-length veil on her head and her left arm was in a sling made of the same fabric as the bottom half of her dress. Between the veil and the dress, her shorter white hair that she had worried so much about, wasn't that noticeable and it clearly made no difference to Lance. He looked as proud as James Bond being knighted by the Queen.

The Intended Ones

"Great," the photographer said, "now I just want a couple more of the bride and groom, please."

As the wedding party stepped off the altar and chatted, Farren walked over to Doc, who was looking dapper in a dark-grey suit. He was sitting and watching in the third row of pews from the altar. She also spotted the cop in the vestibule who was monitoring the church's front door and there was another officer doing the same at the back door. The cops weren't wearing their bulletproof vests so the guests wouldn't be so apprehensive about their presence, but this tactic wasn't really working. The guests were very aware of their presence and why they were needed at the wedding.

"Was Charlene's mom glaring at me during the ceremony?" Farren asked.

"Not that *I* saw."

"I felt glaring."

"It was shock because Lance is finally making an honest woman out of her daughter," Doc joked.

She turned back to the altar and watched the bride and groom posing and smiling.

"I wish we could go the reception," Farren said.

"The cops didn't even want you to do the wedding," Doc reminded her.

"This is so stupid," she said quietly. "My life is finally turning a corner and I'm so happy, but the circumstances are so awful."

"'It was the best of times, it was the worst of times,'" Doc said. "I know that's totally not helpful, but how many times do you get to quote Charles Dickens in a conversation?"

She looked at him and pursed her lips as the photographer said, "Lovely. Just one more...Hold it...Perfect! We're done. Now, just give me a minute to get outside."

Everyone in the wedding party started to slowly move toward the front door while the photographer and his assistant gathered up their gear and went at a more hurried pace. As they did, Lance and Charlene stepped off the altar and came over to Farren and Doc, who stood up as they neared.

"You're the prettiest bride I ever saw, Mrs. Vale," Doc smiled.

"You're lying, but I'll take it," Charlene grinned.

"I wish you guys would change your minds and come to the reception," Lance urged. "It'll be weird not to have our entire wedding party there."

"It'll be weirder with the police patrolling your reception and making your guests feel uncomfortable," Farren said with a weak smile.

"She's right," Doc added. "Do you really want your guests being frisked?"

"I saw a couple of women in the church I wouldn't mind frisking," Lance quipped. Charlene immediately responded by punching him in the arm.

"Those days are over, dog."

"What time does your flight take off tomorrow?" Doc asked.

"We've got a 1:15 afternoon flight out of TC, then a 4:40 flight from Detroit non-stop to London."

"Hey, c'mere," Charlene gestured to Farren, walking back toward the altar. Farren dutifully followed, wondering if she might be having some trouble with her sling or dress. "Is everything okay with you and Doc?" she whispered. "I mean, have you guys made any progress?"

Farren smiled. "You were right. Just diving in did the trick. Someday, maybe in the not too distant future, you're going to be wearing the bridesmaid dress and I'm going to be the one in white."

Charlene gently patted her wounded arm. "Good! Then this was 'almost' worth it. Although I still hope they nail the son of a bitch." She suddenly remembered where she was and looked up toward heaven innocently. "Sorry."

"C'mon, babe, everyone's waiting," Lance reminded his new bride.

Doc extended his hand and Lance took it. "You're the best EMT I ever rode with. Thanks for being my partner, but more importantly, thanks for being my friend."

"You're just sayin' that to get discounts off wine," Lance noted.

"Naturally," Doc agreed, smiling.

Charlene hurried over to Lance, then the newlyweds joined

hands, waved goodbye, and walked down the aisle heading for the vestibule. As the officer opened the front door for them, the crowd outside cheered and began to throw their flower petals. After the doors were closed, Farren slowly walked over to Doc.

"They looked happy, didn't they?"

"Yes," he agreed. "It was a long time coming."

Farren turned and looked at the altar. "Would you mind...Is it okay if we hang for a couple of minutes and pray?"

"Sure," he said. He looked at the officer in the vestibule and asked if they could be alone for a minute. The cop understood and said he'd wait outside.

Farren and Doc settled into a pew and both knelt down. After nearly a minute of silence, Doc looked over at his girlfriend. "Can I ask you something?"

"Of course."

"When you pray to God, how do you know when he answers you?"

"What do you mean?"

"I mean, he's not the most direct of supreme beings."

"I think he answers us in all sorts of ways; through us developing new thoughts or ideas, through the advice people give, through things you read in the Bible, through the events going on in your life. You just have to pay attention to the signs."

He looked at her, surprised.

"What?"

"'Signs', I've heard that one before. But why does God have to use 'signs?' Why can't He just *speak* to us? I mean, I *know* he exists. I'm absolutely certain of it. So why can't he just talk to us like I'm talking to you?"

"I don't know, honey. Maybe it's because he's on another plane of existence. Or, maybe he knows the way he communicates with us is the best; we learn more if we have to look for the answers. But *I* think he probably communicates with us the way he does because he wants us to have faith. He gives us so many blessings and faith and prayer is what he expects in return.

Doc rubbed his forehead with the tips of his fingers, still

frustrated. "I don't argue with what you're saying but—"

"You still want directness," she concluded.

"Well—*yeah!*"

Farren smiled understandingly and thought for a moment. "After my folks died, I thought I was the loneliest person on the face of the Earth. Every family tradition I'd ever known, everything I ever hoped to share with my parents—high school and college graduation, my wedding, grandchildren—it was all gone in an instant. People used to say to me, 'Well, think of *this* person who just got diagnosed with lung cancer, or *that* person who was just in a car wreck and is now a paraplegic.' You can't compare sufferings. That's a game nobody wins. But I will say this, unless you've lost both your parents as a teenager, you have no conception of what that does to your emotions. I used to pray: 'Dear Lord, I don't understand why you've taken them, but at least let me fall in love with someone who thinks I'm special. Someone I can share my life with completely." She looked at him and smiled. "And see? Here you are."

"Aren't you forgetting the fact that you married another man first?" he reminded her.

"Not at all. If I hadn't of married him, you wouldn't have saved me. I'd say that was a pretty direct response."

"And how do you know I'm the right guy for you?" he asked.

"I'm sure you've prayed about it. Did you get a response?"

"You're not listening," she smiled. "I asked for someone I could share my life with completely. That includes my spiritual life. And here we are, praying together and discussing God. So yeah, I'd say that's another pretty direct response."

She put her palm on his cheek tenderly, then rose. He got up too, thinking about how he had to practice listening more after he prayed and looking for answers that might be right there in front of him.

With the police cruiser following faithfully behind, they passed St. Ignatius church on their way home, just in time for Saturday 5:00 p.m. mass. Driving past the parking lot across the street from the church, Doc spotted Gus sitting in his black Acura SUV wearing a suit. He had the driver's side window down and was watching people head into church like a cop on a stakeout, complete with a toothpick hanging out of his mouth.

"What's your grandfather doing here?" he asked. "Why isn't he at Lance and Charlene's reception?"

"He knows we weren't going, so he probably decided to bail."

"But what's he doing here? Going to mass?"

She shook her head. "It's some sort of vigil thing."

"Excuse me?"

He won't talk to me about it. But I've noticed he's started to go to church again. Not only going to mass, but hanging around outside church either before or after other masses."

"Why?"

"I don't know. Maybe to make up for all the years he didn't go after Grandma died."

Doc thought for a moment. "You've got Father Ken's cell, don't you?"

"Sure. Why?"

"Just a hunch I want to follow," he answered.

Later that evening at about 8:00 p.m., Gus was sitting in his living room watching TV, wearing his usual golf shirt, jeans, and Sperry Docksiders. Harry the black cat was drinking some milk out of a little serving bowl on the floor next to his recliner. After Harry was finished, he hopped up onto the arm of the recliner, then plopped himself down into Gus' lap. The old man smiled faintly and gently stroked the feline's back when there was a knock at the front door.

"Ah...there's your dad comin' to get you," Gus said, grabbing the remote. He turned off the TV and rose in his chair to see Doc casually dressed in a T-shirt and jeans and standing on the porch. Curious, Gus went over to the front door and opened it.

"Somethin' wrong with Farren?" he began cautiously.

"She's fine. She's back at the cabin with the cops," Doc replied, producing a six-pack of Moosehead from behind his back. "This is just a social call."

Gus saw the beer and raised his eyebrows. "Well, you're always welcome, son. But you're especially welcome when you come bearing gifts."

Doc walked into the house and spotted Harry sitting in the recliner. "I didn't know you had a cat."

"I don't," Gus answered as he walked through the living room and dining room and into the kitchen. Doc heard him open up then holler out the back door: "Hey, Collins, your cat's escaped again!"

While this was going on at the back of the house, the younger man peeked out the front window, past the front porch and up and down the street. The sun was just starting its descent and the street was filled with streaks of butter-like light that showed off the hundreds of insects buzzing here and there.

"Yeah, I do that, too," Gus said, returning to the living room.

"Do what?" Doc asked, turning back to him.

"Look out the window for a stranger sitting in a car, someone standing on a corner watching the house...Hell, I don't even know what I'm looking for. Do the police have anything new?"

"The ballistics report came back. The bullet definitely came from a foreign-made, high-powered rifle. They've narrowed it down to two or three possible makes."

"Terrific," Gus moaned, "more uncertainties. It ain't like this on *Hawaii Five-0*."

"That's because they've only got fifty-two minutes, allowing for commercials," Doc deadpanned.

Moving on with his thoughts, Gus plucked a long neck out of the six-pack and twisted it open. "Anyway, it sure was a nice wedding today. How long they been datin'?"

"A dozen years, I think," Doc answered.

"'Bout time he bought the cow after all that milk. Not that I'm callin' Charlene a bovine, you understand," Gus gestured for Doc to sit. "I guess between Lance bein' on his honeymoon and our concern for Farren's safety, our poker game's on hiatus."

"Yeah," Doc said, sitting down on the sofa, "I guess so." He looked around the room and saw the family photos on the bookshelf.

The old man settled back into his recliner with Harry and took a long swig of beer. "So, what's on your mind?"

"Who says there has to be anything on my mind?"

"I do. It ain't poker night, I just saw you a couple hours ago at a wedding and now you show up here with beer. You've got something you want to get off your chest."

"Actually, it's something I want to get off your bookshelf," Doc said, pointing to the black-and-white photo of Clair. "May I?" he asked, gesturing to the picture.

"Sure," Gus said.

Doc got went over to the picture, picked it up and examined it for a moment. "She was so pretty," he mused admiringly. "How'd you get her to marry you? Tell her you were going to inherit millions?"

Gus smiled. "Actually, it was just the opposite. If you think she was pretty there, you should have seen her in person."

"I hear you think you saw her at midnight mass," Doc said.

"Aww, that blabbermouth Pistole," Gus moaned. "Don't I get the sanctity of the confessional, or something? Now you're gonna think I'm losing my marbles."

Doc carefully set the photo back on the shelf next to a picture of Farren's parents, Jackie and Paul. "Nope. I think you *did* see her."

"Oh?" Gus said curiously, taking another drink of beer.

Doc turned to the old man. "Did you tell Father what she was wearing when you saw her?"

"What?"

"Do you remember what she was wearing when you saw her?"

"Sure."

"Did you tell Father Ken?"

Gus thought. "No...I just said she was dressed in modern clothes."

The younger man walked back over the sofa and sat down. "Was she wearing a dark-green raincoat? Black pleated slacks, red silk blouse?"

All of the color nearly drained out of Gus' face. "How the hell do you know that?" he asked, frozen.

"Because I bought 'em for her."

Gus' brow furrowed as his guest nervously popped up again and started to pace.

"Just, just hear me out for a moment...Haven't you ever wondered how I was able enter Farren's life when I did? Just weeks before Charlie tried to kill her?"

"You walked into the edge of a door at the bookstore as she was coming out and had to go to the hospital?"

"But how did I know she was there? At that particular time on that particular day? I had help, Gus. Someone *else* was looking out for Farren."

The older man narrowed his eyes, already not willing to believe what Doc was about to say.

"Last year in early December," he continued, "I was driving home one night after work in a snowstorm. This deer ran out in front of me and I hit it. I didn't kill it, but I banged it up pretty good. But Gus, it wasn't an ordinary deer. It was an angel just arrived from heaven. And it wasn't just *any* angel..." he stopped so his host could process what he was hearing.

Gus took another long drink of his beer, set it down on an end table, put Harry on the floor and slowly rose.

"Doc, I like you. I always have. But whatever you're doing now, it's not funny and it's not appreciated. So I want you to stop it."

"Remember that night last winter at the Crow's Nest when I was asking you and Father Ken about angels? *That's* why!"

"I mean it now, man," Gus insisted, stepping toward him. "*Stop!*"

"Clair was too injured to protect Farren herself," Doc went on, "so I had to step in and be her substitute while she recuperated at my place. She stayed with me for more than two weeks. Actually, I think her getting hurt so I could meet and spend time with Farren was all part of some master plan."

Without warning, Gus threw a right jab that caught Doc squarely on the chin. Doc faltered and stumbled backward, but then recovered and continued, "I don't blame you for that," he said, rubbing his chin. "I wouldn't believe me either. Except what I'm saying is true. Clair had bright green eyes, long slender fingers and large, naturally curly ringlets in her blonde hair."

Furious, Gus threw another right jab. Doc faltered backward again, then added: "But her eyebrows were darker than her hair. She liked Vernors ginger ale and made hot chocolate with a secret ingredient. She thought Barbara Stanwyck was beautiful in *Christmas In Connecticut* and when she wrapped presents, she curled the ribbon with the edge of the scissors."

Gus threw a left hook this time that caught Doc on the cheek. Although no singular punch from a seventy-eight-year-old man was seriously injurious, three in a row—and with Doc doing nothing to protect himself—was starting to take its toll. A small trickle of blood now slid down the corner of his lower lip from the left-hand-side of his mouth. The rest of his face was beet red.

"How could I know all this stuff, Gus?" he continued. "You never told Farren these kind of details about her grandmother, did you? Did you tell her how she liked Rosemary Clooney? Or making snow angels? Did you tell her about the birthmark shaped like a maple leaf she had on her right thigh?"

Gus hit Doc in the face again. This time with a right hook. *"Stop it! Stop it! Stop it!"* he yelled with equal parts anger and tears. *"What the hell are you trying to do to me?"*

The young man put his fingertips to the corner of his mouth, looked at the blood on them, then continued, "Those X-rays you had last year really *did* show a problem with your lungs. A problem that she cured, Gus! She called it 'regeneration.' She did it because she loved you! She was sent back to help me save Farren but also to tell you that she loved you. She didn't get the chance the last time you two spoke and one of the things I've finally got into my thick head about God is he's a guy that's all about second chances, for her, for me, for *you!*"

Gus drew his fist back to throw another right hook. Doc caught his fist with his hand in mid-air, stopping its momentum cold.

"Why would I be saying these things if they weren't true?" Doc asked, still clutching the old man's fist. "What do you think I did this morning? Got up and said, 'Gee, I think I'll alienate and totally piss off a man I admire and respect?'"

With a vicious scream, Gus charged Doc and clung onto him. He began to pound uncontrollably on his back. But within ten seconds, the angry screams turned into the deep, hot sobs of a broken man.

Doc held onto him until his knees finally gave out from under him and both men slowly sank to the floor. Gus' sorrow was inconsolable. It was as if a dike built up from the pain of the past half-century had suddenly burst. He pushed away from Doc and crawled on his hands and knees toward the bottom of the stairs a few feet away. Tears fell from his eyes to the wooden floor as he went and his nose ran sloppily out of control.

When he got to the edge of the stairs, he wept on them with heaving shoulders for what seemed like minutes. Just about the time Doc was worried Gus was going to have a stroke, the old man slowly pushed himself up a little and turned to him.

"S-s-s-she never got to hear her daughter say a complete sentence. S-she never got to see her lose her first tooth, put out cookies for Santa, have a first day at school...She never got to see her have sleepovers, make a snowman, fly a kite. We never even bought a house together. She missed *everything!* God took *everything* from her! Everything from *me!*"

"I can't explain the timing," Doc replied quietly. "But I *do* know she saved your granddaughter's life. And mine. And I hope by me telling you this, yours."

Still leaning on the first step of the stairs, Gus sadly shook his head. "I fell in love forever, but I never dreamed forever meant a lifetime of staring at the stars alone."

He suddenly sat up and looked at Doc with a very worried look in his wet, red eyes.

"W-was she burned? Did she—was she hurt?"

Doc shook his head knowing he was referring to Clair's fiery death. "She was hurt from my Jeep hitting her. The injuries were serious but she healed really fast. Miraculously fast. That's how I knew about the birthmark. I was monitoring her wounds."

Harry wandered over and rubbed up against the old man. Still on the floor but now in better control of his emotions, Gus looked at Doc with resolve.

"Tell me everything. Everything you remember."

Two hours later, it was dark outside. Doc lay on the sofa holding an icepack bottle of half-melted ice on his face while Gus walked from the kitchen back into the living room with a fresh beer in his hand. The six-pack that Doc had bought was long gone.

"So, if she was here for two weeks, and even in this very house to heal me, why did she only appear to me briefly in church?" he asked.

"I guess because you weren't her primary mission," Doc answered, removing the icepack from his face, "Farren was."

"Why was *she* sent back? She never even knew Farren. Why not Jackie or Paul?"

"I asked her that, too. She said she could be more objective about things because she was a generation removed. That, plus it gave her the chance to say goodbye to you properly."

Gus took a drink of beer, picked up Harry who was circling at his feet, then sat down in his recliner, thinking.

"If she needed to say goodbye, then I *was* part of her mission. So why couldn't I see her more? Talk to her?"

"What do I look like, The Answer Angel? How do *I* know? Maybe her having direct contact with you wasn't allowed. Maybe she broke the rules by you seeing her for those few seconds in church. Maybe you were only supposed to see her for a few seconds because you need to take more things on faith."

"Well, it would be nice to know *something* definite," Gus grumbled.

"Welcome to my world," Doc moaned.

"And, and you haven't seen her since?"

"Only in a dream," the paramedic answered. "A dream where she told me she wouldn't be back—and that she loved you."

Gus stared off into space, but continued to gently stroke Harry's fur. "I wonder what she thinks of the life I've led? I haven't been much of a spiritual man...I wonder if she's made up for lost time with Jackie? Gotten to know Paul?"

Doc slowly sat up and looked at his friend. "Can I ask you something?"

"Sure."

"I know you loved Clair, that's a given. But, after a few years..."

"Why didn't I ever marry again?" Gus asked, anticipating the rest of the question.

Doc nodded.

"I don't know," Gus sighed. "I had a daughter to raise, two jobs, grandparents that I wanted her to know and spend time with. Over time, Jackie and I built up this little insulated world and I guess I was afraid to let anyone new come into it. I'm not sayin' there wasn't the occasional soft shoulder to lean on...but they were just stolen evenings here and there. None of them were Clair."

"I understand," Doc said, fiddling with the icepack. "Look, I'm just trying to follow the signs here. Clair appearing to you seems to have done you more harm than good, and I was just trying to give you a little reassurance that you weren't going crazy or imagining things. There are greater forces at work in the universe than we realize."

"Then why is Farren still in so much danger?"

"She's alive and being protected, isn't she?" Doc replied. "You had the foresight to anticipate Bartholomew, didn't you?" He suddenly realized something. "Geez, I'm starting to sound like Clair."

Gus looked at his guest for a moment, started to take another swig of beer, but then decided he'd had enough and set it down on an end table. He leaned back in his chair and sighed. "You ain't boring, kid. I'll give ya that."

Doc rubbed the back of his neck, knowing he had to get home. "So, you believe me?"

Gus rubbed the white stubble on his chin.

"You know things about Clair nobody else could possibly know. You know things about her that, frankly, I'd forgotten. Like that birthmark. And even before I had those X-rays, I knew somethin' was wrong. There was a little blood in my stools, and I'd been losing weight for weeks. So, yeah. I believe you."

29 Busy

By November 5, 1954, snow was already on the ground in Charlevoix. It wasn't a permanent snow—the grass would still reappear—but it was enough of an overture to leave little doubt that the long northern Michigan winter was about to begin its five-month-long engagement. Snow in Charlevoix was usually on the ground from late November until mid-April. In early November, it could still be spotty, coming and going like Mother Nature was playing peek-a-boo, but by the end of the month, chances were it would be a permanent fixture on the ground until spring.

Clair steered her Willys Jeep Wagon down the long drive to her parents' house for the first time in nearly a month. When she arrived, she was disturbed by what she saw. A small semi-truck with the words "Hutton's Used Furniture" on its sides was in the circular part of the driveway pulled up close to the open front door. The cherub fountain in the middle of the circle drive had been turned off for the winter and the fountain trays as well as the flowerbed at its base were empty and bare. The surrounding trees were likewise as bare as the flowerbed. Only a few stubborn brown leaves still clung to branches while others had been gathered in bunches for the squirrel nests that dotted the treetops.

Pulling up behind the truck, she could see that it was filled with several fixtures from her life: her father's desk and the chair that sat behind it, a favorite divan of her mom's, even the furniture from her bedroom. This last sight actually made her heart skip a beat. As it did, two men dressed in blue-grey overalls came out of the open front doorway. One got into the truck while the other closed up its back doors then also climbed into the cab. As she opened the door and stepped out of her Jeep, Aaron appeared in the doorway, a check in one hand, and a whiskey sour in the other. He was wearing a white cardigan sweater with a red shirt underneath. For a change, it actually went well with his dark blue pants.

"Well," he said, grandiosely waving his drink in her direction, "if it isn't the prodigal daughter."

She walked toward him wearing a tan skirt, a dark-green long-sleeve blouse, and red plaid jacket. She wasn't really showing yet and her pregnancy was still a secret. Clair had seen her father tipsy before but never this early in the day.

"I know we haven't been friends for a while, Daddy," she said as the truck engine started up, "but did you have to get rid of my bedroom furniture?"

"We are downsizing," he said, while truck started to slowly pull away. "Economizing. Making ends meet. Some ends haven't met around here in a long time." He spoke in that very pronounced way that half-drunk people do to make sure nobody thinks they're half-drunk.

"I'm sorry you're going through a rough time," she said sincerely.

"Did you think I was kidding when I said I needed that partnership with Derek's father?"

"Can we talk about something else please? I've actually come to extend an invitation."

She passed him in the doorway and walked into the house. The first thing she noticed was that the round mahogany table in the foyer was gone. She could see the open doorway leading into her father's study and everything that used to be on his desk was now on the floor. Even the oriental fringed rug his desk once sat on was gone.

"Is Mom home?" she asked.

"She and your sister have gone to your grandparents down

state," he answered, taking a sip of his drink.

"But she knows about this, right?" Clair asked. When Aaron didn't answer but instead took a second sip of his drink, she repeated, "Right?"

"I do what I have to do to keep going. Do you have any idea what the monthly nut on this place is?"

"Oh, Daddy," she said, disappointed. "Then just sell it!"

"Yes, there are *so* many people in the market for a house like this today," he replied sarcastically. "I'd only lose fifty or sixty grand on the price, then *still* have to pay off a 100,000-dollar-mortgage." He pointed an accusing finger at her. "You could've prevented this! You could've prevented *all* of this!"

Clair tried to shake off the net of guilt her father was casting and get back to her reason for the visit. "I've come to invite everyone to our place for Thanksgiving. We've got a small kitchen so we'll probably be eating off TV trays, but we'll all be together, and besides, you've never seen our apartment."

She smiled hopefully at her father, but Aaron ignored it and started walking across the foyer heading for his study. "Can't make it. I'll be working," he called over his shoulder.

"You'll be working?" she asked disbelievingly. "On Thanksgiving?"

"I'm doing a house remodel with a small crew," he answered, having now disappeared into his study. His voice echoed from the emptiness of the space. "There's a bonus for me if we can finish before Christmas."

She heard the clinking of fresh ice cubes tumbling into a glass. She walked across the foyer toward the study. When she entered, she noticed that not only were her father's desk, chairs, and rug gone, the English hunting pictures on the walls were gone too. Then she saw that one of Aaron's trophies from the Traverse Bay Shooting Club lay in pieces on the floor.

"What happened to your trophy? Did the movers accidentally —"

"My membership has been revoked," he answered, interrupting her and now holding a fresh drink. "Can you believe it? I built the place. *I built it!*"

She looked at him empathetically. "Daddy, this has to stop.

You're angry at me. You're angry at everyone! You're in a slump. It happens to all of us."

"'Slump?'" he hissed. "Is that what you call it? I lost a partnership and contract I desperately needed. I have to sell furniture to cover my monthly mortgage. I'm doing these little piss-ant jobs that I used to do twenty years ago that are *miles* below my expertise! I'm a laughing stock in town! I've been kicked out of a club that I built because I can't pay my dues! The bank is threatening to repossess my car. Your mother and I barely talk let alone sleep together. And you wanna call this a 'slump?'"

He looked at her with contempt, but held what was left of his anger.

"I'm busy Thanksgiving," he simply said instead. "Now if you don't mind, I've got things to do."

"Daddy, I need to tell you something. I'm going to—"

"*I said I'm busy!*" Aaron snapped, cutting her off.

Father and daughter looked at each other for a moment, then she stiffened her back and tugged self-consciously on the bottom of her plaid jacket.

"Fine," she said quietly, turning and walking out of the nearly empty room.

30 Edgar Seward

Two chestnut-haired brothers were lazily trolling for largemouth bass on a sunny July day about twenty yards off shore in front of a thickly wooded area of Lake Charlevoix. The eldest, John, was sixteen and wore a Black Sabbath T-shirt, jeans, white Nike running shoes, and a green John Deere ball cap. His younger sibling, Donny, was fourteen and wore cutoffs, a plain red T-shirt, and lake shoes. Both of them were wearing PFDs, or personal floatation devices, around their waists that resembled blue fanny packs. Each pack had a small cord and pull-handle attached that inflated the PFD with just a tug. They were on their father's bass boat, a low riding 18-foot Ranger with a silver glitter finish and a 150 horsepower black Mercury outboard on the back. It was a special occasion for the boys. John had gotten his boater's license only a week earlier and this was only the second time their father had let them venture out onto the lake alone. They were discovering—as generations had done before them—the feeling of oneness with nature that happens out on the lake. But John was also impatient to do something else, release the Merc's 150 horses out on the open water.

"I shoulda brought some beer," he said, holding his casting rod in one hand while poking around in an open ice chest with the other.

"You don't drink beer," Donny said. Even being two years younger, he knew his big brother was trying to act more grown-up than he really was.

"That's what *you* think," John defended, tugging on the brim of his cap. "I drink it all the time. I sneak a can or two out of the garage fridge when no one's looking. Dad keeps so much in there, he never misses it."

"Better not let him catch you," the younger brother warned. "He'll skin you for sure."

Seeing nothing in the cooler that caught his fancy, John closed the lid and turned his attention back to the lake. He threw out a long cast as the boat slowly moved forward via the trolling motor, but within another minute he became antsy.

"This is bullshit. There's nothing here. Let's go across the lake. There's a cove Dad's taken me to about a mile away over there," John said, pointing in the direction he wanted to go.

"Whoa!" Donny suddenly yelled seeing his pole dramatically bend like a question mark. "Cut the motor! I got something!"

John reached over and clicked off the trolling motor, then looked at the steady arch of his brother's rod. "You ain't got nothin'," he concluded. "Your line's not moving. You're just snagged on weeds."

"No, really!" Donny protested.

"No, really!" his older brother insisted, reeling in his line. He set his rod down in the boat and reached for his brother's. "Here, give me your rod." The younger one handed off his rod and John gave it a couple of unyielding yanks.

"Man, you're really caught. On weeds, maybe a log."

"Well, cut the line then," Donny suggested.

"Cut the line? That's a twenty-dollar lure I gave Dad for his birthday. We ain't cuttin' no line. Go down there and unsnag it."

"What? You mean, in the water?"

"No ass-wipe, I mean climb that tree over there. *Yes, get in the water, follow the line down and unsnag the lure!*"

"I don't want to go in the water. I'll get bit by something," Donny objected.

"We've been trollin' for twenty minutes," John pointed out, still holding Donny's rod. "Have we gotten any bites? There's *nothin'* down there."

"Well, how come *I* have to go?"

256

"Gee, let me think. It's your rod, you're wearing cutoffs and lake shoes, you're the one who got snagged..."

"C'mon, Johnny," Donny whined, "I don't wanna go down where it's weedy."

His older brother looked at him. "Are you tellin' me you're afraid? It can't be more than ten feet deep."

Donny looked over the side of the boat. Even though they were close to shore, he couldn't see bottom.

"I don't wanna go down there," he repeated. "It's your birthday present to Dad. *You* get it."

John became impatient with his sibling. "If you don't get your ass over the side of this boat, I'm going to tell all your friends what a coward you are."

"If you make me go down there, I'm gonna tell Dad you steal his beer," Donny countered.

The two boys looked at one another in a standoff for a couple of moments, then John handed Donny back his rod. "Fine!" he said. "*Fine!* You're really a chicken shit, Donny, you know that?"

The older boy flung off his cap, pulled off his T-shirt, emptied his pockets, and unsnapped his PFD. "Put the anchor over the side, Sissy Boy," he ordered.

"Cut it out, Johnny," Donny said, still holding his rod but moving toward the bow and the trolling motor. He opened up a compartment flush in the floor where an anchor on a fifty-foot rope was stored.

"Ease it over the side. Don't throw it," his brother reminded him, taking off his shoes.

"I know," Donny said, having heard the same instruction a hundred times. He eased the twenty-pound anchor over the side, then let go of the rope, allowing the anchor to free fall.

John glanced around the boat. "Sure wish we had a mask on board. Oh well..." He dove over the side of the boat opposite the side his brother was on. When his head broke the surface he instructed: "Keep the rod steady. I'm gonna follow the line down."

"Okay."

John swam around the bow and past the anchor line to where his brother's rod was still arched, then with a deep breath, his head disappeared below the surface.

Having been raised on Lake Charlevoix, John was fearless when it came to the water. He had dived to the shallow bottom areas on more than one occasion and knew that whatever creatures might live in the weeds, they were much more afraid of him than he was of them. But he also knew those shallow bottoms had drop-offs. At its deepest, the main basin of the lake was nearly one hundred twenty-five feet deep.

Following the line down and pushing a tangle of weaving weeds aside, he soon found the snagged lure, and with the tug and snap of a couple of weeds, set it free. He was just about to head back to the surface, some six feet above, when his eyes caught a glimpse of something in between the weeds about eighteen feet away.

Realizing the bottom was getting deeper as he swam further, he fearlessly brushed aside one armful of weeds then another like an underwater Indiana Jones until he came to a clearing on the bottom that was about twelve to fourteen feet deep. There, in the middle of this clearing, he saw a strange sight. At first he thought it was a sunken Coast Guard buoy, for it stood straight up like one and weaved slowly to and fro in the current. Within another five seconds, however, he realized the gruesome truth. It wasn't a buoy, it was body. A body that was tied to a concrete block.

The arms of the deceased had been secured to the torso with rope to keep them from floating haphazardly. It was an old man, perhaps seventy-five years old wearing dark cotton slacks and a short-sleeve button-down dark-green shirt that was untucked. His body was bloated from being in the water and his skin was greyish white. He had a large cut on the left side of his head near the temple and the loose skin from the open wound likewise weaved back and forth in the current. What little hair he had on his head was white and also weaving in the water. His right eye was open wide and glazed over while the left eye was completely gone leaving only an empty socket. It had probably been a gelatinous meal for some fish. When John fully absorbed what he was seeing, he screamed in horror and made a scramble for the surface with his arms and legs flaying madly amidst a flurry of bubbles. He made it, but just barely because of the large mouthful of water he had swallowed. He clung onto the side of his father's bass boat for nearly thirty seconds, coughing and hacking, before he could tell his brother what he had discovered.

A little more than an hour later, the woods twenty yards inland from the lake were buzzing with activity and people while an officer was talking to John and Donny near their father's beached bass boat. By this time, their dad was now with them, too. He stood on the shore with folded arms and listened intently while the boys gave a formal statement to the officer who was taking notes.

Farther down the shoreline, the retrieved victim lay in a black plastic body bag with a large open zipper. Standing over the body was BJ and Allen Colfax, a co-worker of Bob Lancaster's and also a doctor from the hospital. Eight yards inland from them stood a paramedic and EMT from the fire hall. Since they were merely assisting the coroner transporting a body, they weren't wearing their heavier firefighting clothes, although they both wish they had. Mosquitoes were chewing them up and they were both swatting their legs and arms every few seconds. Behind them, and on the other side of the woods over one hundred yards away, another cop stood on a dirt road where his cruiser and an ambulance sat. Meaning, the paramedic and EMT were going to have to haul the waterlogged body through the woods to get it to the ambulance.

Offshore near where the body was found, two silver Coast Guard Safe Boats with twin Honda 225s on the back of each craft were anchored in the water while divers in the lake with black neoprene wetsuits and scratchy silver tanks searched for more clues, their flippers slapping the water's surface with each new surge to the weedy bottom.

"Edgar Seward," BJ said, looking down sadly at the body and a face he'd known all his life. "When I was a senior he was maybe a sophomore in high school. Skinny kid. Used to run cross-country. Worked at the cement factory until about eight years ago."

Allen Colfax was fifty-three, medium weight, wore bifocals and had a bushy mustache. He also had a lot more experience as a forensic doctor than Bob Lancaster having lived for years in Lansing.

He was also a deer hunter and not easily squeamish. He looked at the body dispassionately, not knowing the victim while chewing a wad of gum.

"Did he have family?" he asked.

"Couple of kids but they both live out of town. One lives out of state, I think. His wife died about three years ago."

BJ waddled his expansive girth a little closer to the water and looked down the shoreline. "He's got a place maybe half a mile that way. It's not much, but he always said his retirement plan was to sell the lakefront property it sat on. Guess he was waitin' 'til the recession got better like a lot of folks."

BJ took off his chief of police cap and scratched the top of his head with its badly dyed hair.

"Why would anyone want to kill Edgar? He didn't have any money, didn't have any valuables...all he had was an old cottage and an old rowboat."

"Well, I don't think he was killed around here, I think he was brought here," Colfax said between chews. "Probably in a boat. There's no sign of a struggle. So, he either knew his killer or was surprised. Judging from the angle of the wound on the head, I'd say he was surprised, like he was turning toward someone."

"Okay. Anything else?"

"He's been in the water anywhere from three to five days. Half the cottages on the lake have foundations made of the cement block he was tied to. Oh, the knots used to tie his arms close to the body were constrictor knots. Nautical knots. So, whoever killed him knows about boating."

"Great," BJ sighed, putting his cap back on. "Considering this state is a peninsula that narrows it right down." He looked at the body again. "If you're finished here, I'll mosey on over to Edgar's place and see what I can find."

Just then, they heard the sound of someone thrashing through the woods and coming toward them in a hurry. It was Chester McGowen, editor of the *Charlevoix Courier*.

"Oh, Lord," BJ sighed. "Press."

The following evening, Gus was coming out of the Winchester

Funeral Home on State Street having just visited Edgar Seward. Winchester was a large old home remodeled to be a business, but it had been a funeral home for so long is was hard to decipher the original home from the refurbishing. The building had a painted white exterior and black shutters on either side of all its windows.

Tan slacks, a long-sleeve burnt-orange dress shirt, and a navy blazer had replaced Gus' usual jeans and golf shirt. As he was coming off the porch and down the three concrete steps to the front sidewalk, he ran into BJ, who was heading inside.

"I wouldn't go in there unless you've got some answers," Gus warned. "Both of Edgar's kids are in there with their kids and they all want to know why their father and grandfather was turned into fish food."

"I didn't know you knew Edgar," BJ said, a little surprised to see him.

Gus shrugged. "Small town. So, *do* you know anything new? According to the paper, you haven't got squat."

"He was attacked outside his home," BJ answered candidly. "We're pretty sure near his dock. Our guess is close to sunset. We're also pretty sure he was surprised. Someone came up from behind and hit him just as he was turning. Based on the angle and bruising of the blow, it was a right-handed male, about six feet, one hundred sixty pounds. He was struck with a piece of firewood, oak to be precise, taken from a woodpile near his house. We found traces of blood on a piece of wood that had been placed in the middle of the pile. Unfortunately though, no fingerprints. There were some loose concrete blocks stashed under his back deck and one of those blocks was tied to his feet to weigh him down. The killer had a knowledge of nautical knots. Nothing was taken from Edgar's house. In fact, the killer probably never even went inside. It wasn't a robbery, either. Edgar had both folding money and his wallet in his pockets. The only thing that *was* taken was an old rowboat with an even older twenty-five horsepower Evinrude on the back, Michigan registration number sixteen-ten. Total worth of the boat and engine was about two hundred bucks. Oh, one other thing, we think Edgar was unconscious but still breathing when he was dumped into the lake.

The blow itself wasn't fatal. The reason why the paper says we don't have squat is because I don't want Edgar's kids reading that their father was murdered for a two hundred-dollar rowboat. I also want the killer to feel like he got away with it because if he's still in the area, he might get cocky, and cocky people make mistakes."

Gus looked at BJ, frankly impressed with all the information. "Okay," he nodded, "fair enough. So why tell me?"

"'Cause when we actually have somethin' to go on, we're a damn fine police department."

Gus understood what the chief was saying. They had nothing to go on when Charlene was shot. They still didn't have any leads and, because of that, Gus had basically guilted BJ into giving Farren round-the-clock protection.

"Could this be connected to my granddaughter?" Gus asked.

"I don't see how," BJ answered. "Murders *do* happen in this county, y'know."

Gus nodded again, neither accepting nor rejecting the old cop's rationale, then turned to continue down the sidewalk. After a few steps, he turned back to the chief.

"Thanks for keeping an eye on Farren," he said.

BJ paused, turned back to him, gave an expressionless slight nod, then turned and lumbered up the steps to the funeral home.

31 Riding Betsy

By the second week of June 1955, things were looking better in Charlevoix from the recession of the previous year. In fact, things seemed to be perking up throughout the entire United States. Stan Musial hit his three hundredth home run, President Eisenhower was the first president to be broadcast on color TV, and the latest Walt Disney film, *Lady And The Tramp*, was about to hit theaters. By this time, Clair Cooper was extremely pregnant and her husband, Gus, had put one full school year of teaching high school sociology under his belt. He was back at Stu and Ernie's for the summer and, on this particular sunny day, was working at the station alone. Stu had decided to go fishing, Ernie was painting his kitchen, Louie was out of town, and Jessie, had borrowed Gus' truck to help a friend whose family was moving.

It was a busy but not frantic day at the station. A steady stream of mostly tourist gas customers came and went, and although Gus wasn't dressed as snappily as Louie would've been with his shiny black visor cap, white shirt, and bowtie, he didn't mind pumping gas and occasionally giving customers directions.

In the meantime, he was working on a special car in Service Bay Two. It was a miniature clown car owned by the local Shriners' chapter that was used every year in the annual 4th of July parade. The engine was actually a ten-horsepower scooter engine that was way overdue for a new spark plug, filters, and lube job. Since it was for a service organization, Gus was donating his time, as he did every year.

Shortly after 1:00 p.m., the payphone on the wall of the office rang. Gus was just finishing with a customer at the pumps and hurried in to catch the phone on its fourth ring. "Rock Around The Clock" by Bill Haley and the Comets was playing on the radio in the service bay area.

"Stu and Ernie's?"

"Gus? It's Portia."

"Hey, Mom."

"Clair was over here visiting when her water broke, so we've just arrived at the hospital. She's going into labor fast. You'd better get over here, dear."

"Jessie's got my truck!"

"Oh, that's right," his mother-in-law remembered. "Her car's at home 'cause Susi brought her over to you. Is there somebody at the station that can run you over?"

"No," he said anxiously, "I'm here alone."

"Well, I can't leave Clair. Maybe you'd better call your folks."

"Okay...okay. Be there as fast as I can!"

"I'll tell Clair you're on your way."

"Okay, Mom. Thanks! Goodbye."

He hung up the phone then stepped out of the office and outside, feeling sure he could get a ride from the next customer that pulled in once he explained the circumstances.

He stood near the gas pumps with his hands on his hips and looked one way down the street in front of the station, then the other. No traffic in sight.

"Perfect," he muttered. "Cars rolled in and out of here all mornin' like Grand Central Station. Now?"

He thought about calling his folks, but he didn't want to lose the time it would take for them to come and get him. He thought for a moment with his hands still on his hips, then turned and looked at the miniature car in Service Bay Two. It was a one-seater convertible with a body not much bigger than a push mower. It was also painted with large purple, yellow, and red flowers. But it could go farther than Gus could run, and the new hospital was clear on the other side of town.

Five minutes later, Gus had called Ernie to tell him he had to close the station and was already a quarter of a mile down the dusty dirt shoulder of the road heading toward the hospital. He hunched over the steering wheel of the miniature car while his knees and folded legs jutted outward on opposite sides like a big brown praying mantis riding a beetle. Every time a car passed, he waved at them to pull over. But considering the vehicle he was driving, people just assumed he was being friendly, until finally, a car came up from behind then slowed down next to him.

"Only authorized members of the Shriners are allowed to drive Betsy," he heard a familiar voice say. He turned and saw Aaron leaning over in his direction from behind the wheel of his Studebaker.

"Clair just went into labor and I've gotta get to the hospital!" Gus announced.

Aaron eyed the toy car with the brightly colored painted flowers. "Then you better stop clownin' around and get in." He pulled over to the side of the road and Gus immediately hopped off his ride and climbed into the Studebaker.

"Thanks," he said, closing the door and noting that his father-in-law was wearing jeans and a blue short-sleeve work shirt as if he'd just come from a job site.

"Why are you driving Shriners' property?" Aaron asked sternly, stepping on the accelerator.

"I was alone at the station working on it and Jessie's got my truck. You call the thing Betsy?"

"Yes. Why does Jessie have your truck?"

"She's helping some friends move," he answered.

"So you just let a seventeen-year-old have your truck?"

"No, I let a family member have my truck," he corrected.

Aaron was silent as he pressed down on the accelerator. "I, uh, I guess I didn't quite realize Clair was so far along."

"Yeah, that'll happen when you don't see or speak to your child for months at a time," Gus responded.

"I've been working out of town a lot," Aaron explained. "Petoskey, mostly. I guess you know by now it's over with me and Portia."

Gus nodded, knowing that Aaron had moved out of the house three months earlier and that the bank had recently accepted a short sale. Portia and Jessie were now living in a nice but considerably smaller apartment in town.

"So, I'm trying to build a new life," Aaron explained.

"Us, too," Gus said. "But we've still got time for family."

Aaron glanced over at the son-in-law he never wanted and chuckled.

"Got it all figured out, do ya? Now that you're married, high school teacher and all."

"Never mind," Gus said. "I don't want to poke the bear. I'm just grateful for the ride."

The two didn't speak again until Aaron pulled into the emergency room entrance at the new hospital. Slowing to a stop, all Clair's father offered was, "Here you are."

Gus paused and expelled a heavy breath before getting out. "Look, park the car, come inside, and be with us. Clair will be thrilled."

The older man ran his hands through his thin blonde hair and seemed tempted at first, but then asked, "Portia in there?"

"Yes. She brought Clair here."

Aaron looked at the entrance doors with narrow, tight lips. "No. I better go back and get Betsy before somebody *else* wants to take her joyridin'."

"Mr. Sinclair—Aaron—" Gus urged, "this is ridiculous! Come inside. *Be* with us."

"Thanks," he muttered. "But, it's complicated. More than you know."

Gus didn't understand what his father-in-law meant, but he couldn't take the time to pursue it now, so he simply nodded and opened the door.

"If you say so," he said climbing out.

"Tell Clair—" he paused for a moment. "Tell her I'm thinkin' of her."

"Will do," Gus replied. Then he closed the door and hurried inside.

32 Realizations & Rescues

It had been nine days since Charlene had been shot, nearly three weeks since Farren had moved in with Doc, and the anxiousness of what might happen next hung thick in the air like the seagulls that trailed the loaded fishing boats coming into port.

At one point or another, Doc and Farren had discussed everything from leaving Charlevoix and taking an extended vacation to the Cayman Islands, to Farren carrying Doc's snubnose .38, which she didn't want to do, to hiring bodyguards more experienced and tactical than the local cops. But at the end of these options, no questions were being answered, and the only facts they had—*truly had*—was that Bartholomew was out of jail and Charlene had been shot. And as unlikely a possibility as it was that a stray bullet fired by some local yahoo who was celebrating something had struck Charlene, it was still a possibility. After all, northern Michigan had its fair share of camouflage-clad survivalists and *Guns & Ammo* enthusiasts. So after days and days of waiting, watching the shadows, and Farren being followed everywhere by her vested boys in blue, she decided she had enough.

Because of her new level of intimacy with Doc, she wasn't ready to move back to her mushroom house, but she *was* ready for her police escorts to return to directing tourist traffic and for Doc to go back to work. He pleaded with her to hang onto the escorts for at least another week and to carry his handgun. She finally agreed, but only if he would return to work and she could do more with her life than spend every day in the windowless, closed-up marina storage barn. She wanted to get involved again with her parish committees, resume reading Jane Austen to Ellen Mitchell, work in the marina store, and start visiting the local bookstore again every week to check out the new titles. Reluctantly, Doc agreed.

During all of this time, however, Doc never spoke to anyone about that old rowboat that came so close to his dock. After all, what could he truthfully say? It was just another festering "maybe" in a situation that cried for concrete facts.

Even though Doc was terribly concerned about Farren, even he had to admit there was a certain comfort in him returning to the fire hall. It was the camaraderie of men and women willing to risk their lives on a moment's notice, the familiar smell of diesel fuel and rubber boots that lingered in the garage, and the fact that any call that came in was a new adrenaline rush. These were things he understood. Constantly looking over his shoulder and waiting for something horrible to happen to the woman he loved were not.

It was about 7:20 p.m. on a Thursday when Gus wandered into the fire hall through one of its large open garage doors. Keb Mo's "God Trying To Get Your Attention" was playing on a radio in the garage sitting on a shelf. Doc and KK were standing nearby and Doc had just finished telling his new partner that Captain Stubigg had told him he didn't have to "date" Gertrude anymore. She was still at his house, but not having to lug her everywhere was something he was obviously pleased with.

"Hey Gus," KK called, spotting him first, "you here for poker?"

"Man, I wish," he smiled with his hands in his blue jean pockets.

"Everything okay?" Doc asked, a little concerned to see him.

"Fine. Just wanted to know if you could chat for a few minutes. Maybe go for a short walk?"

"Sure," Doc said and turned to KK, "I'm going to grab a walkie and take a stroll with Gus."

"Go for it," KK said, turning and heading toward the kitchen.

Gus and Doc wound up just a block away on Bridge Street where the tourist dinner crowd was in full force. People stood with pagers outside of restaurants, others breezed in and out of clothing stores and art galleries and, a half block away, the Beaver Island ferry, the *Michigan Mist*, glided down the Pine River returning day visitors to its dock on Round Lake. With a length of one hundred thirty feet, three levels, and a passenger capacity of nearly three hundred, it was a larger boat than most that used the river and it dwarfed the condos and trees it passed on either shore.

"I don't come down here enough and just look around," Gus observed amidst the busy sidewalk traffic. "I should. I've always liked living in a town that people want to come visit."

"I understand," Doc said. "So what's up? Is this about that guy they found in the lake, Edgar Seward?"

"Not really."

"But you knew him, right? You guys were close in age?"

"Yeah, I knew him."

"You think his murder has anything to do with Charlene or Farren?"

"Doesn't seem so. Seems like it was just a robbery, but not for money."

"For what then?"

"I'm real sorry about Edgar," Gus said impatiently, "but that's not what I want to talk about."

"Okay."

Gus looked around a little secretively. "I, I feel like somebody who just won the lottery."

"What do you mean?"

The old man rubbed the white stubble on his chin and leaned into his young friend. "I mean—God's really *real!*" he half whispered. "Heaven *exists!*" He thought for a moment. "Do I sound stupid? I know billions believe already, but, they're *right*."

"No," Doc smiled. "I know exactly what you mean. It's like finding out there's a Santa Clause after all."

"Did you know that most of the ancient world's largest manmade structures were built for either worship or the afterlife? I've been reading up on it on the Internet. It feels really good to know we were always on the right track, to know there's more than this. To know I'm gonna be with Clair again. See my folks, my grandparents. But, I also feel..."

"Incredibly guilty too," Doc continued, knowingly. "You wished you hadn't been so angry at God for all those years."

"*Yes!*" Gus said in a way that was unusually animated for him. "You understand."

A group of college-age girls passed them going in the opposite direction. One was wearing a T-shirt from Eastern Michigan University where Doc graduated. It made him want to share something.

"There was a girl I once loved in college...I was even thinking about marriage. But she died in a car accident. It rattled my beliefs and I was pretty angry at God for a decade. So yeah, I understand."

Gus slowed their already casual pace and looked at Doc seriously as people continued on around them. "You never told me. I'm sorry, man."

Doc smiled appreciatively. "There was no reason for me to. I'm only telling you now to point out we've walked some similar paths. I really *do* understand what you're feeling: first the amazement, then the happiness, then the guilt, and most of all, the tidal wave of questions that comes after."

"Oh, my God, *yes*," the older man agreed, "no pun intended. The questions that come after! Talk about a Pandora's box! How do you handle it? How do you cope with such knowledge?"

Doc thought before answering. "You accept that you'll never understand it all. That's the gig."

"I wanna know why Clair had to die so young? What's heaven like? It is up? Down? Can Clair see me? Hear me? I was a sociology teacher who wound up teaching theology for years. Which theology was right?"

"I asked Clair once what heaven was like."

"What'd she say?"

"It was nebulous. She said, 'Imagine a choir singing beautiful music. Each member has his or her own personality, joys, fears, likes and dislikes. But for that one song, those few moments in time, everyone is in perfect pitch, perfect harmony, happy with the moment.'"

Gus thought for a few seconds. "And what'd you say?"

"I asked if the choir was naked. 'Cause if they're in heaven, why would they need robes?"

The old man shrugged in agreement. "I've been thinking. If there's a God, then there must be Satan, right?" He looked at Doc who did a double take in response.

"What? You expect *me* to know?" Doc asked.

"You must've thought about these things. You've known about God, the afterlife and angels for months. You must've reached *some* conclusions by now."

Doc came to a bench outside of the fudge store that Charlene managed and sat down. Gus sat down next to him as the passing stream of camera and souvenir toting tourists continued.

"Yes, I've thought about things," he conceded. "If I've reached any conclusions, it's stuff like, 'Try to accept more things on faith...Try to be nicer to people...Give God some time every day...Never eat asparagus with a stranger'...Stuff like that."

Gus smiled at Doc's quirky sense of humor, but he understood what he meant; the larger the concepts that had been revealed to him, the more it seemed like the simpler things of faith, kindness, and love were of primary importance.

Gus glanced around at the people surrounding them. "There's a part of me that wants everybody else to know what I know."

"I know."

"But I also know, if I told everyone, a lot of people would think I'm an old nut."

"I know."

"Have you told Farren any of this?"

"No. I don't want her to think I'm a young nut."

Gus took a deep breath and looked around again. "Actually, people not believing us if we said anything really kind of sucks."

"I know."

Just then, there was a dispatcher call on Doc's walkie. He looked at Gus. "I've gotta go."

The Sippewissett Campground was about seven miles outside of town going in the general direction of Traverse City. It was a place where pup tent campers and people in six-figure Winnebagos lived side-by-side. From the dispatcher, Doc and KK already knew that the call they were responding to was a separated finger from a camper chopping firewood, so before departing, Doc had KK grab a couple extra ice packs in hopes to preserve the separated appendage.

Sippewissett was picturesquely, set back from the highway, and had a winding creek that meandered through the campground. The only paved road was the one leading back to the campground, but before doing so, it passed an office and a shower and bathrooms for guests. The shower and bathrooms were divided between male on one side, and female on the other. The building was made out of concrete blocks but was open-aired about eight feet off the ground. A series of small concrete pillars connected the bathroom and shower walls to the slightly angled roof. On cooler evenings, one could watch the warm steam from the showers escape over the walls, drift into the woods and dampen everything within fifteen feet of the building.

Following procedure, the entire Charlevoix Fire Hall night crew was on the scene, KK and Doc in their ambulance, and two firefighters in a fire truck behind them. Following the pointing fingers and waves of the twenty or so campers, they were led to a campsite with a black 2014 Chrysler minivan, a four-person pup tent, and three men sitting around a lit campfire. All of the men were about sixty-five years old and looked like relics from Woodstock era. One was wearing a tie-dyed T-shirt, jeans and sandals. He had his thinning grey and white hair pulled back into a ponytail and was strumming a Fender guitar with dried blood on his arm. Another man was wearing a Hawaiian shirt with dirty white cut-offs that also had bloodstains on them. His blacker and thicker hair was neat and trim in contrast to the other two. He kept offering sips of Jack Daniels from a bottle to the neighboring campers who had congregated near their campfire. The third man, wearing a Jimi Hendrix T-shirt, jeans, and John Lennon-type wire rim glasses, also wore his salt-and-pepper hair in a ponytail that was longer than his guitar-playing buddy's. His left hand was wrapped in a blood-soaked white washcloth while the right held a joint up to his lips. He was in the middle of taking a deep toke from it as Doc and KK approached the campfire. All of these old hippies were twenty to fifty pounds overweight, which in a way, suited their laid-back demeanors.

"Ah–calvary's here!" the man with the guitar announced, playing a "ta-da" flourish on the strings. He spied Doc carrying a medical kit that looked like a tackle box. "And they brought party favors, too!"

"Where's the fire, boys?" the one in the Hawaiian shirt asked, eyeing the fire truck with its blinking red and white lights. He was the largest of the three and held out his bottle to KK, offering him a sip.

"I want you to know," the injured man said, speaking in a croaky half-swallowed voice while still trying to keep the smoke he had just inhaled in his lungs, "this is strictly for medicinal purposes." Several of the bystanders laughed knowing it wasn't true.

Doc looked at the injured man and smiled sympathetically. "I'm afraid this might affect your violin playing."

The injured man pushed his glasses back on his nose with his good hand that still held the joint and giggled, causing the marijuana smoke to burst out in between his teeth in quick, short successions. "That's funny, man. You're cool."

"Thanks. My name's Doc. What's yours?"

"Carl Segin. That's 'See-Gun.' Not Sagan, like the astronomer."

"Although he does see stars sometimes," the man in the Hawaiian shirt suggested." All three of the campers giggled and snorted at the witticism.

They were like a bunch of college kids, only instead of student IDs they had AARP cards. It was hard not to be amused by them.

"Can you tell me what happened, Carl?" Doc asked.

"Well, you can't chop wood while you're high. That's for sure!" the injured man answered.

"You can't chop wood straight," the guitar-playing man observed.

"That over there is Ray and this big ugly guy is Fast Frankie,"

Carl said. Fast Frankie held up his bottle of Jack and grinned, "Wassup?"

"Yeah," Doc nodded a little playfully, "that whole getting-high-thing does tend to wreak havoc with the manual dexterity."

"Hey, man. You gotta have s'mores when you go campin'," Ray said, "so you gotta have firewood." He stopped strumming his guitar and reached over to Carl for the joint.

"And Jack," Fast Frankie added, holding up his bottle again.

"C'mon, folks," KK said, turning and extending his arms to the bystanders in a shepherding manner. "Please go back to your campsites. And thank you to whoever called." The two other fireman likewise started to encourage people to move on.

"I'm the one who called," Fast Frankie volunteered.

"Why didn't you just drive your friend to the hospital?" KK asked.

"Because they're having too much fun around the campfire," Doc answered, knowingly.

"Yeah," Fast Frankie agreed, taking a swig from his bottle. "We ain't got no designated driver."

"We got Minnie Driver on Blue Ray in the van," Ray offered.

"Carl, can I see your hand, please?" Doc asked.

"Huh?" he said, apparently temporarily forgetting his serious injury.

"Your hand?" Doc repeated.

Resting his guitar on his lap, Ray held up ten fingers. "This is the tenth year of our annual boy's weekend."

"Showoff!" Carl observed. "I *used* to be able to do that."

All three men started to giggle and snort again. KK rolled his eyes while Doc tried to steady Carl's injured hand and examine it. "Hold still for me, Carl, will ya? Let me take a look, okay?"

"It's pretty ugly, man," the patient forewarned.

Doc carefully unwrapped the towel and examined the man's fingers. Thankfully, the severed appendage was a clean stroke of the ax, just below the left hand forefinger knuckle and base of the hand. "Naw," Doc observed, trying to allay any fears Carl might have. "This isn't ugly. Mary Ann Bronner in the tenth grade. Now *she* was ugly."

The men smiled, liking Doc's jovial approach. "So where you from, Carl?"

"Jackson."

"What do you do there?"

"Court stenographer," he grinned. "Recently retired."

All three of the old hippies burst into laughter again. Even Doc laughed at that one. Then he dug into his medical kit. "I think we'd better numb up that hand, Carl. Are you allergic to anything?"

"Just my wife."

The men broke out into laughter again. Ray offered his joint to KK, who took it, but then disposed of it.

"Besides Doctor Jack and Nurse Mary Jane, are you on any other medications?"

"Naw, man."

"Okay. Just to verify, you're not on any medications and you're not allergic to anything other than your wife, correct?"

"Right on."

"How much alcohol would you say you've consumed tonight?"

Just then, a fairly loud scratching and cackling sound came from the wooden box Carl was sitting on.

"What the hell was that?" KK asked.

"Oh, that's Rocky," Fast Frankie said.

"Yeah. Rocky Raccoon," Ray confirmed, playing some licks from the Beatles' song. "He came out of the bushes over there bold as brass and tried to run off with Carl's finger. But we got the son of a bitch."

"Feisty little booger, too," Frankie added, taking another swig of Jack.

It was at this point that Doc noticed the dried blood on Ray's arm wasn't from his friend's accident, but rather he'd been scratched and bitten. The same seemed to be true with Fast Frankie's bloodstained shorts.

"So, the raccoon bit you guys?" Doc asked.

"Just a little," Ray said, still strumming.

"But I smacked him into submission," Frankie noted.

Doc looked at his partner. "We're going to need some information here, please."

KK nodded, understanding. It was time to get complete names, addresses, allergy history and any other type of pertinent medical information from Ray and Fast Frankie who were absolutely going to need rabies shots. Meanwhile, Doc concentrated on Carl while opening his medical kit. He tore open a foil container containing a new syringe and got out a vile of numbing medicine.

"So, Carl, how much alcohol did you say you had tonight?"

"I don't drink, man. Just smoke."

"Any idea what your blood type is?"

"Red, dude."

"How about that wife of yours?" Doc asked, inserting the needle into the rubber top of the small vile and measuring the syringe. "Can you give me a name and phone number?"

"Sandy. Five-one-seven, seven-eight-three, two-two-seven-six. But she won't know my blood type, either."

"That's okay. May we call her in case of an emergency?"

"What? You expect me to have *another* one tonight?"

The three men started to giggle again. Doc smiled. "Well, you've never ridden with KK before."

"You better write that number down," Fast Frankie squawked, diverting momentarily from KK asking about his allergies.

"No, I got it," Doc assured, moving over to Carl and squatting down in front of him. "Sandy. Five-one-seven, seven-eight-three, two-two-seven-six."

"Wow, I can't even remember what color boxer shorts I wore yesterday," Ray said, starting to play a blues riff.

"You didn't wear any boxer shorts yesterday," Carl observed. "You just wore those ratty blue jean cutoffs with some of your junk hangin' out. And I *do* mean it was 'junk.'"

"Gave me nightmares," Fast Frankie agreed.

The three old hippies started to snort in laughter again.

"Okay, settle down here, Carl," Doc instructed. "You're going to feel a little pinch, then burn, but it'll only be for a second." He made the first injection, cutting back on the usual dosage because of the patient's already medicated condition. "Here comes another one," he warned almost immediately after the first. "So what do you really do?"

"I own a fleet of ice cream trucks," Carl answered, wincing a little at the second and then third injection that encircled the bloody hole where his finger had been. "Y'know, those trucks that play that annoying Tinkerbell music?"

"I suggested Ozzie," Fast Frankie noted.

"I like it when all the neighborhood kids come runnin'," Carl smiled.

"That's pretty cool," Doc agreed, ignoring the Ozzie comment and focusing on Carl. "You do something where everyone likes to see you come."

"Except Sandy," Ray deadpanned.

The three men burst out into their loudest laughter yet. Doc grinned at the joke, then elevated the patient's hand to a forty-degree angle.

"Just hold your hand up like that for a few minutes until the medication kicks in. Okay?"

"You got it, Chief," Carl agreed.

"Do you happen to know where the finger is?" Doc asked.

"Rocky Raccoon tried to go back into his room, man," Carl said, referencing Paul McCartney's lyrics. "He had it in his mouth but Frankie grabbed him. He's fat, but he's fast."

"Yeah, but the finger fell between the grating," Frankie announced.

"Grating?" Doc asked.

"The storm grate over there," Ray said, pointing.

Doc looked back toward the paved center road they had just driven down. Along the side of the road was a water run-off drain with an opening big enough for a small animal to squeeze through. Just in front of the drain was the storm grate.

"How long ago did the accident happen?" Doc asked Carl.

"I don't know. Time flies when you're severing body parts."

"The call came in at 7:29," KK remembered. Doc looked at his wristwatch. He knew the sooner he could get the finger on ice and to the hospital, the better the chances were of reattachment, especially if Bob Lancaster was on duty tonight.

"Okay," he said, patting Carl's shoulder and rising. "Gentlemen," he said to his fellow firefighters, "I need your help."

The two other firemen followed Doc over to the grate and the paramedic got down on his hands and knees peering through the grate since there was still adequate daylight. The storm drain was rectangular, five feet deep, and about three feet wide.

"I don't see anything," Doc said. Then he called over to Carl. "You're sure it fell down here?"

"Absolutely," Carl answered.

One of the firefighters stooped down next to Doc with a flashlight and examined the bottom of the drain. "There's an open-ended piece of PVC piping down there," he observed. "Probably a run-off from the showers. It could've rolled into there."

"We've got to be sure," Doc said. "If we can get the finger and it's in good shape, this guy's got a chance of having all ten fingers again."

The three men knew immediately what had to be done. They all rose and Doc stepped aside while one of the firemen ran back to the truck and then returned with two iron rods. Each rod had a handle on one end and a hook on the other. The rods were specifically made to lift and move sewer grates.

Within seconds, the firemen had inserted the rods on either side of the grate, turned them so they hooked onto each side, then lifted and removed the grate. As soon as this was done, Doc scurried down into the storm drain with a flashlight to investigate the connecting pipe. It was a tight squeeze, but he got to the bottom.

"I don't really have a good angle to see into the pipe," he said. "I've got to feel for it." He slowly stuck his hand into the PVC pipe. He reached farther and farther back, until suddenly, he yelled, "Ow!"

"What?" one of the firemen called.

"I think something just bit—ow! *Ow! What the—ow! OW! Damnit!*"

"What's goin' on?" KK called.

"It's a troll!" Fast Frankie proclaimed. He tried to get up, but by now had consumed too much Jack and plopped unceremoniously back down.

"Ow! You little..." Doc yelled painfully.

"Gremlins," Ray decided. "You ever see that movie?"

"Yeah!" Fast Frankie recalled. "Like, when they were all weirding out in that movie theater?" He started chuckling. "You remember that?"

"Oh man, that was a riot!" Ray agreed. They both started giggling while the sounds of Doc yelling and cursing kept coming from the storm drain with increasing intensity.

"Hey! I think it worked!" Carl announced, poking the open bloody hole in his left hand with a finger from his right hand. "I can't feel my finger anymore!"

"That's because it's not there anymore, man," Fast Frankie observed.

"Guys, give me a break!" KK ordered the three jolly campers. "What's going on over there, Dennis? Is Doc alright?"

"I don't think it's 'Rocky Raccoon,'" one of the firefighters called back. "It's more like a Roxanne. 'He's' a 'she' with babies!"

"Rrrroxanne," Ray sang, breaking immediately into the Police song. "You don't-have-to-live-in-the-storm-drain. You-don't-have-to-live-in-the-storm-drain."

"Live-in-the-storm-drain," Fast Frankie joined in. Then they both started singing in unison, "Live-in-the-storm-drain! Live-in-the-storm-drain! Live-in-the-storm-drain!"

A little more than a minute later, Doc slowly returned to the campfire. His hair was a mess, there were scratches on his forehead, cheeks and arms. his Charlevoix Fire Department T-shirt was ripped in a couple of places, and the one arm that had dipped into the PVC pipe had been bitten numerous times, meaning, he, too, was going to need a rabies shot.

"I'm really sorry, Carl," he said wearily. "Reattachment isn't really an option."

He held up what was left of Carl's finger. It looked like a skinny piece of chalk that had been dipped in watery red paint. Most of it had been gnawed to the bone by the baby raccoons.

    Carl looked at his separated finger in open-mouthed amazement, then broke into hysterical laughter as did Ray and Fast-Frankie, who offered Doc a swig from his bottle.

33 Unpacking

It was December 20, 1955, and Charlevoix was covered with a thick blanket of white. Thirteen inches of snow covered lawns and rooftops while large mounds of half-frozen brownish white dotted the corners of parking lots and street corners like the tops of huge snow cones. There was still a horse-drawn snowplow in use by the city back then, and a team of two sturdy black mares pulled a faded red wagon with a plow attached to it past a small single-story house on Sheridan Street. The house was white with yellow shutters and had a wreath on the door made of fresh boughs. It also had a nice wide front porch and on one end of the porch facing its length was a swing on chains that ran through the arm rests and hooked up to eyebolts in the bead board ceiling. At the moment though, the swing was frozen and forlorn with three inches of snow on its slatted seats.

The scene inside was much more cheery and warm. Bing Crosby sang "Jingle Bells" on a table-top radio accompanied by the Andrews Sisters, a decorated five-foot high Scotch Pine Christmas tree sat in a corner with fat, big multicolored bulbs, and cardboard boxes were piled everywhere with wadded-up newspaper strewn along the floor. There was also a stack of books sitting in a chair, pictures leaning up against a wall, and curtain rods were up but there were no curtains. The disarray was evidence of the new occupants that had just moved in.

Clair's mother, Portia, sat on a fabric sofa wearing a nice dress, high -heels, a string of pearls, and a sweater slung over her shoulders. She was holding six-month-old Jackie and talking to the infant in a loving voice, telling her how pretty she was. Clair was also in a dress, although one less expensive than her mother's, and carried a cardboard box into the kitchen. Her figure had returned to its usual curvaceous self because she'd worked hard to lose the extra weight she'd gained from the baby.

Portia stopped cooing with the child long enough to eye the Christmas tree. "Your tree sure is pretty, honey. Jackie doesn't know what she's looking at, of course, but she sure is taken with the big, colorful lights and tinsel."

"It was the first thing I wanted to do," Clair called from the kitchen. "Get the tree up so we could enjoy Christmas in our new home."

"I'm still amazed you got the low rent you did," Portia answered. "Two bedrooms, a living room, dining room, kitchen, and a full bath for one forty five a month? Places like this usually go for two hundred in the off-season and three hundred in-season."

"If the house isn't occupied then the landlord risks frozen pipes," Clair pointed out. "The early snow helped negotiations a lot."

"Has your father seen it yet?"

"No, I haven't seen Daddy in nearly three weeks. He stopped by the old apartment and spent a little time with the baby, but then," she stopped herself, wanting to choose her words carefully, "he, he had to go."

"You mean, he found out I was coming over to take care of the baby and wanted to leave before I arrived."

"Now, I didn't say that," she corrected, coming out of the kitchen, grabbing another box, and then walking back into the kitchen with it. "He had to get back to Petoskey. He's doing so much work there now, he's actually thinking about moving there."

Portia thought for a moment then smiled at the baby still working on her bottle. "Well, I'm glad things are much better between you two."

"Things, are better," Clair called back, unwrapping some glasses, "but I wouldn't say 'much' better. We don't see him that often and he still only tolerates Gus. I can hear it in his voice."

"I'm sure it isn't tolerance so much as concern," her mother clarified. "He worries about you two. You're both working two jobs—Gus at the school and filling station, then you at Dr. Morton's office and the toy store. I think he wishes you two didn't have to work so much. And when you say you don't see him often, remember, he gives Jessie more time because she's younger."

Clair came out of the kitchen with an empty box and put it on a stack of other empty ones. "Even now, you still do PR for him. He never deserved you."

"It takes two for a marriage to fail, Clair. You side with me because your father didn't initially approve of Gus and acted foolishly on your wedding day. But believe me, there was plenty of blame to go around."

Just then, the rotary phone on an end table rang. Clair walked over and picked it up.

"Hello?"

"Hey, baby," Gus' voice said. "What's going on?"

"I'm working on the kitchen and Mom's feeding your daughter. How 'bout you, still going to be home by six?"

"Yep, just got out of the teachers' meeting. Jessie's been waiting for me in the library. She's probably out of her mind by now."

"She's not at school anymore. Mom said she got tired of waiting and got a ride home with Craig."

"Craig Berry? Yeah, I see them walking together in the hall sometimes. You think Jessie's finally decided to like boys?"

"Oh, I think she's liked boys for a while, but now she's got one that seems to like her back."

"Well, I'm glad. When I get home, I'll work on the kitchen with you."

"Can't. Dan at the toy store called. The snow left him short-handed on staff tonight, so I told him I'd fill in. It's extra Christmas money, y'know?"

"Oh," he said, a little disappointed. "Uh, okay."

"Five days before Christmas the store's going to be busy. Besides, Dan says I'm the best gift wrapper he's got. He likes the way I curl the ribbons."

"Yeah," he agreed. "I liked where you placed those three ribbons the other night when we went to bed early."

"Hey, keep it clean. This is a party line," she said, smiling.

"What time do you have to go in?"

"5:30, but Mom will stay with the baby until you get here."

"Okay. I'll see you later tonight. Remember Clair Cooper, I love you."

"And I love you! See you later."

Portia smiled at her daughter still being so much in love. She looked down at the infant in her arms. "I bet it's not too long until you have a little brother."

"So what did you mean there was plenty of blame to go around?" Clair asked after she hung up the phone.

"What?"

"With you and Daddy?"

The older woman's face became a little flushed by the question. She smiled self-consciously and patted the baby.

"I mean, your father made mistakes and so did I. You can't put all the blame on him."

"Daddy was always too dictatorial with us," Clair noted. "And that included you, Mom. He ordered us around like a drill sergeant. He didn't treat you like a partner at all. I sometimes feel like he only married you—" she stopped abruptly, not wanting to hurt her mother's feelings.

"For my looks?" she said, completing the thought. "Don't a lot of men do that? Women too, for that matter?"

"I don't know...It just seemed sometimes like he used you as an ornament for his arm."

"I'm sure he did," she agreed. "One of my assets is my looks, or was," she said self-deprecatingly. "When I married your father, one of the ways I could help him was to—How did you put it?—be an ornament on his arm. He was building a business. We both were."

"Yes, but Gus doesn't treat me, or Jackie, for that matter, like Daddy treated us."

"Your father's a different personality than Gus and came from a background not as loving. I grant you, he's gruff, authoritative and used all of us for his own devices. But we also benefitted from it—a beautiful house, vacations, clothes, your education—opportunities other people don't always get."

"Okay," Clair agreed, going along. "So where's your blame in all of this?"

Portia handed the baby back over to her mother. "I think she's ready to go down, but burp her first."

Clair took the infant and, in a baby's voice, said, "Bye-bye Grandma, see you later," then disappeared into one of the two bedrooms. She returned a couple of minutes later. By this time, Rosemary Clooney was singing "Silver Bells" on the radio and Portia was picking up discarded wads of unpacked newspaper and putting them into one particular empty box.

"Ask Gus to put the changing table together tonight, will you? I can't keep changing the baby on the floor."

"Will do."

"Now, back to you. What's your blame in all this?"

"My goodness, Clair, you're like a piglet obsessed with finding that one last truffle."

"Did you just call me a pig?"

"Of course not."

"Then what?"

"I don't want you thinking ill of me," Portia said, nervously pressing an open hand on her sprayed blonde bouffant hair to make sure everything was in place.

"Mother!"

"The thing is...I—I haven't always been faithful to your father."

"*What?*" Clair asked, astonished.

"I mean, you're right. He does, he *did* act like a drill sergeant. After so many years, I was feeling demeaned, ignored. Both of you girls had your lives at school and he was always working late when things were going good with the business...I know I should've tried to talk to him about it more...but..."

"When was this?"

"Shortly before you graduated from nursing school."

Clair stood there with a still stunned expression on her face. "I...uh, I don't know what to say...Who, who was he?"

"His first name was Grant. I don't think I ever got a last name. He was a tourist on vacation with his son."

Clair's mouth fell open even wider. "He had a family, too?"

Portia shook her head and walked over to the front window with folded arms to look at the late afternoon snow. A few fat flakes drifted through the air like white flower petals.

"He was divorced. He was in town visiting relatives. One night, he'd had his fill of family and his son was spending the night with some cousins, so he went to a bar for a drink. I felt neglected by your father one too many times and wound up at the same bar. We've both been blessed with good genes, Clair. Men have never ignored you and me. Except for the one man I loved the most. Your father."

"You—went to a motel?" Clair asked, trying to piece things together.

Her mother nodded. "It was just for a couple hours. To tell you the truth, even now there's a part of me that doesn't regret it. I felt desirable again," she half smiled, "but I also knew it was a betrayal. So I decided it wouldn't happen again. And it hasn't. It was going to be my little mid-life crisis that I'd take to the grave...But then, I changed my mind and decided to tell Aaron."

Clair looked at her mother for a moment, who still had her back to her staring out the window.

"When was this?" she finally asked.

Portia turned to her daughter. "Shortly after he flung a drink in your face on your wedding day. I knew he hurt you terribly and I wanted to hurt him back. So I told him later that night."

A lot of things from the past seventeen months suddenly clicked into place for Clair: her father's constant anger, his not wanting to be with Clair when Portia was around, the rebuilding of his business in another town. He'd always remember her wedding day as the day of his wife's infidelity. Of course he'd have conflicted feelings.

"Do you hate me?" Portia asked, her eyes welling with tears. "I wouldn't blame you if you did."

Clair paused for a moment, then walked over and gave her

mother a hug. Both women started to cry.

"Well," Clair said, rubbing her hand up and down on her mother's back, "you two aren't exactly Ozzie and Harriet!"

34 The Michigan Mist

"Sir," the mate said, politely but firmly, "this is the second time I've told you. There is absolutely no smoking on board the boat. We'll be docking in about fifteen minutes. Please wait until you've disembarked."

"Fine. Fine!" the tourist said impatiently. He was big guy in his early thirties who looked like he might've been a truck driver or worked on an assembly line, and he certainly didn't like some puny teenager doing a summer job ordering him around. He flicked the cigarette over the top of the retracted gangplank walkway, which left about a 3-foot open space between the edge of the walkway and the roof of the cargo deck. As soon as the mate had turned a corner and gone up some iron grate stairs to the second deck, the tourist pulled out another cigarette and fired it up.

The *Michigan Mist* was the one of the ferries that made the two-hour daily runs to Beaver Island. She was one hundred thirty feet long and had three levels: a cargo level for cars, bikes, small trucks and supplies, then two passenger decks. Made of lightweight sheet metal, she was white with blue trim and had two large, gold "Ms" painted on her short smokestack.

Owned by the Wolverine Transport Company, the recession had taken its toll on this business like nearly every other business in Charlevoix. Staff had been reduced and because of it, maintenance had too. So when the smoking passenger heard someone coming down the stairs again to the cargo level, he unthinkingly flicked his cigarette into a hallway and a small pile of oily rags that normally would've never been there.

    It was nearly seven minutes before anyone noticed the smoke. The boat was slowing down to enter the Pine River for a 7:30 p.m. arrival at the company's dock and ticket office on Round Lake. By then, the fire had reached the temporarily unattended engine room. When a small compressor exploded, which actually posed no threat to the ship's structural integrity but caused thick plumes of rushing black smoke, panic erupted among the ship's two hundred sixty-one passengers. Forty-seven of the passengers were Girl Scout Brownies consisting of little girls between six and nine years old, and their high-pitched screams could be heard all the way to Bridge Street. Meantime, on the bridge, the captain began blasting his loud air horn in short bursts to let the drawbridge keeper know the Memorial Bridge had to be raised immediately so the distressed ship could get to the dock.

    A passenger in his thirties decided to jump over the side of the smoking craft and swim to shore a couple hundred yards away, but he was struck in the water twenty seconds after landing in it by an approaching ski boat that didn't see him. The accident wasn't fatal, but the passenger was critically wounded. As his blood spread throughout the water, there were more screams followed by the splashes of a few other jumping passengers who intended to help the injured man. In the interim, still other passengers screamed for people to stay calm and remain where they were. Between the clanging bells of the rising bridge, the screaming little girls, the air horn blasts from the ferry, people running back and forth on all three decks, the accident in the water and the curling black smoke—it was pandemonium.

    Things had only gotten worse by the time Doc and the three other members of the night crew arrived on Bridge Street. The drawbridge was up and a couple hundred tourists had come out of restaurants or stores and were taking pictures with phones and cameras since there was still at least two hours of daylight left.

    An overwhelmed cop was trying to have the stopped traffic on

Bridge Street back up and get off the main thoroughfare, but the street was packed with a long line of cars so it was easier said than done. The *Michigan Mist* was now in the Pine River and moving at only a few knots. Once in the river, two more people jumped off the boat. One was a strong swimmer and swam to an access ladder on the metal walled sides of the river, but the other, a twenty-three-year-old girl, wasn't so lucky. She landed too close to the ferry and got caught in its undertow. The girl screamed then disappeared under the boat only to be chopped into three separate pieces by the propellers a few seconds later. Seeing the horrific red bobbing mess off the stern, the passengers on the boat and those watching on shore started screaming anew all over again.

"What do we do?" KK asked, now on the scene but watching helplessly from Bridge Street with Doc, the two night crew firemen and a sidewalk full of tourists.

"Call everyone," Doc ordered, the scratches on his face still evident from his raccoon encounter. "BJ, Stubigg, the Coast Guard—everybody comes! Every cop. Every fireman. Then call the hospital. Tell them to get ready for a disaster scenario. They should call the hospitals in Petoskey and TC, too. Put 'em on alert for possible assistance. Especially airlift."

"Doc, even the cops with Farren?" KK asked.

"Get everyone out here, *now!*" Doc said. Then he ran over to the bridge keeper's control house.

"What's the captain say?" he asked, knowing the bridge keeper would've been in radio contact with the ferry by now.

"It's not that bad," the keeper said. "Looks worse than it is. He says he can dock and get everyone off, but the freakin' passengers are their own worst enemies!"

Doc turned, ran back to the fire truck, retrieved a bullhorn, then pushed his way back through the crowd until he reached the top of the stairs on the street level that led down to the riverside sidewalk. From this position both those on the street and the passengers on the boat could see him.

"Ladies and gentlemen, can I have your attention, please! May I have your attention *please!* It's very important that you people on the boat stop screaming and running around. You're only making things more confusing by doing so. So listen up!"

Several of the passengers did stand still to hear what Doc had to say.

"We've been in contact with the captain and the fire is not, I repeat, *not* that bad! It's more smoke than flames. So if you'll just stay clear of the smoke and *remain calm*, we'll get you through the river, back to the dock and off the boat. But it's very, very important that you remain calm! And it's *especially* important that no one jump from the boat. You could be sucked under by the undertow and we've already had one terrible accident. So remain calm, keep clear of the smoke and *stay* on the boat. As the boat nears the dock, I want the men to let the women and small children leave the vessel first. Again, there is *no* immediate danger! But we don't want any kids to get lost or trampled. Okay?"

Then he turned to address the people behind him on the sidewalk and street. "You people need to clear this area so emergency vehicles can get down to the ferry dock. If you're in a car on the street, I need you to back up—way up—down the street." He pointed to the one cop he could see. "That officer is going to tell you what to do. If there are any doctors or nurses who are visiting, I need you to come to the fire truck over here just in case your services are needed."

Doc clicked off the bullhorn and, for a few moments at least, it seemed as if everyone was cooperating. He saw a tourist approach, a young mother with an eight-year-old boy who looked like he was nauseated.

"There are body parts of a young woman floating in the water behind the boat," she said, looking almost as nauseated as her son.

The paramedic looked off in that direction. "Yes, ma'am. Thank you." Then he moved over to KK who had just gotten off the phone with Captain Stubigg.

"We've got to get that severed body out of the water or it'll wind up online as the new tourism poster for Charlevoix."

The two of them hurried down the staircase that led to the sidewalk by the river. The presence of emergency personnel on land paralleling the distressed ferry just twenty or so feet away did seem to have a reassuring effect on the passengers.

When they got to the stern, they noticed that another craft, a seventeen-foot center console Century fishing boat with a Yamaha 150 strapped to its stern, was breaking marine law as it raced down the river way above wake speed. But the engine dropped to a crawl when it came to the bloody part of the water and the floating chunks of torn flesh, hair, and bone that used to be a person. The Century was a rental from one of the marinas that competed with Farren's, and Doc could see its passengers were a concerned-looking Carl Segin, Fast Frankie, still sporting a Hawaiian shirt although a different one from the other night at Sippewissett Campgrounds, and Ray, who was behind the wheel.

"We've got to get that poor soul out of the water!" Carl announced as he cut the engine.

"Young eyes. Young eyes," Fast Frankie acknowledged, spotting the horrified Brownies watching on the ferry with their hands clasped over their opened mouths.

"Be careful, guys," Ray said, as Fast Frankie leaned over the port side to pick up an arm. "That's somebody's daughter. Gently!"

Doc was impressed by the swiftness and compassion of the old hippies. Normally, he would've never allowed citizens to touch the dead body of an accident victim, but these weren't normal circumstances. It was unwise to wait for the Coast Guard when the living needed Doc and KK.

"Thank you, guys," Doc called, then he eyed Carl's bandaged right hand. "Don't get your injured hand wet, Carl. Let Frankie get—" he paused, not wanting to say 'the pieces', "—let Frankie retrieve the deceased."

"Will do, Chief," Carl answered.

Ray eyed a surprised looking KK "What? You think we stay high and drunk all the time?" He pointed to Fast Frankie. "He's an undertaker and I'm an insurance adjuster."

KK nodded acceptingly. "Do you have anything to cover the victim?"

Ray looked around the boat. "We've got a beach towel."

"And this," Fast Frankie said, unbuttoning his Hawaiian shirt.

Doc pointed down river. "Meet us at the ferry's dock once the boat has cleared the river. And thanks again, guys. We've got to get going."

"Go! Go where you're needed," Carl waved with his bandaged hand. "We've got this."

Doc looked at the mess in the water again. The three older men were doing a gruesome service that few others could stomach to perform. He cracked an appreciative smile, then he and KK turned and ran back toward the stairs leading up to the street level.

By the time they got back to Bridge Street, the *Michigan Mist* had crawled its way past the open drawbridge and was now just fifty yards from its dock on Round Lake. All it needed to do was turn right from the mouth of the river and it would reach the loading dock and ticket office.

Although the traffic on Bridge Street was slowly starting to back up and the access road leading to the dock was starting to clear, there seemed to be more people on Bridge Street than ever before—people asking what happened, people waving smoke out of their faces, kids crying because of the blood-soaked river—and it now seemed as if every other person on the street and sidewalks was taking pictures or filming with their cellphones. The picturesque hum and rhythm of Charlevoix was now a crammed flood of careening necks, tear-filled eyes, still occasionally screaming people and plumes of black smoke.

Doc spotted David Wright, the youngest member of the police force, pushing his way through the crowd. Then, he spotted the formidable presence of Captain Stubigg not far behind.

"Get that truck down the access road to the dock!" Stubigg ordered one of the firemen on the night crew. He turned to Doc. "What happened?"

"Fire broke out on the Beaver Island ferry. We don't know the cause but the captain told the bridge keeper via radio it's not that bad."

"Can he get it to the dock?"

"Yes. But the passengers are very antsy. Some have jumped off the boat. One woman jumped into the river and got caught in the undertow." Doc shook his head. "She didn't make it. Her body's still in the river."

"I heard somebody say there was another accident involving a jumping passenger in the lake near the mouth of the river. But that's all we know." KK said.

"Call everybody in," Stubigg ordered.

"Done," KK answered.

"Call the hospitals in Petoskey and Traverse City —" the captain began.

"Done," KK interrupted. "Doc had me do that first thing."

"The corpse in the river?" Stubigg asked.

"Volunteers with a boat are on scene doing retrieval," Doc replied. "One of them is an undertaker."

The captain looked at the paramedic and nodded. "Good. Then get down to the dock. I want you two on board first thing. Get the injured off first, then children, then women. If there are no injuries, keep the exodus organized. Nobody runs off. Everybody walks. Got it?"

"Yes, sir," they both said simultaneously.

"Meanwhile," Stubigg said, looking toward the end of the river on the Lake Michigan side, "I'll see what I can find out about that other jumper."

KK and Doc hopped into the ambulance, then, with the whirr of their siren going on and off again, they maneuvered slowly through the crowd toward the side access street that led to the dock and ticket office.

As they went, Doc thought about Farren. With her police protectors being summoned away, the last place in the world he wanted her to be was somewhere expected. That included his cabin since she had been staying there for more than three weeks, and especially since someone might've been on his dock uninvited.

He reached for his cellphone to call her, but there wasn't the time. As the *Michigan Mist* slowly moved into position at the dock, the passengers on board pressed forward in a mass toward where they knew the bow and stern gangplanks would be lowered.

Tensions rose as did the voices and the pushing and shoving. It was no time to make a phone call.

Even before the mates on board had thrown the mooring lines to their counterparts on the dock, KK and Doc leapt simultaneously from the dock onto one of the now nearly lowered gangplanks. After the easy jump, Doc said to KK, "You organize the passengers down here. I'll do the same on the upper decks."

As Doc made his way through the anxious and sweaty crowd carrying his medical kit, he kept repeating, "Everyone remain calm. The ship is in no danger, it's just smoky. Is anyone injured?" There were several stepped-on feet, some people that had been knocked down and bruised, but nothing that he could see that merited medical attention.

Just as Doc was climbing the stairs leading to the middle deck, a man about twenty-five years old and wearing a tight wine-colored T-shirt and a University of Michigan ball cap was pushing his way through the crowd on that deck in a near panic.

"Angela?" he called. "Angela? If you can hear me, *answer* me!" He was beginning to fear that the young woman who had jumped into the river then had been sucked under and killed might've been *his* girlfriend, who he had not seen since she'd taken a bathroom break. "Angela?" he called again, plowing his determined way past several of the Girl Scout Brownies. One of them, an eight year old who had stepped up onto one of the railings to photograph the Coast Guard safe boats speeding toward them from across Round Lake was knocked off balance. With a scream, she dropped her camera and tumbled head over heels thirteen feet into water.

"She can't swim!" Doc heard one of the Brownies yell as he arrived on the deck. *"Oh, God! No! Help! Heather can't swim!"*

He saw the screaming little girls pointing to the foamy water below. Then he spotted the top of a head and a little hand disappearing beneath the bluish-green water.

"Out of the way!" Doc bellowed, dropping his kit and taking his cellphone off his belt. "Move girls! *Move!*"

Within seconds, he'd sprung to the railing. With a quick and powerful lunge, he executed a perfect swan dive into the water.

Simultaneously, the man who had jostled the little girl spun around hearing all the screams. A second later, he also realized what had happened and, he too, climbed onto the railing and attempted the same dive. But he wasn't as physically coordinated as Doc. His body started to flip over as he dove and he landed squarely on his back with a painful slap of water.

When Doc's head broke the surface, he was aware that another adult had dove in after the little girl and that the other diver seemed injured, but his priority was the child. He took a deep breath and dove beneath the surface. A second or two later, he spotted Heather, still holding her breath and flailing her arms, but sinking nonetheless. Within another ten seconds he'd grabbed her arm, and just about the time she was going to pass out from a lack of oxygen, her head broke the surface with Doc holding her up from behind.

"You're okay, honey," he reassured the girl as she screamed and clutched his arms wrapped around her chest and under her armpits. "Just hang on. Let me do the work and I'll swim you right over to the boat."

It took a few moments for Heather to calm down, but once she was assured by Doc's firm hold, she relaxed. The engine had been cut by the time he reached the port side of the ferry and a cargo bay door had been swung open on the lake side by one of the crew members, who happened to be the same young man that had scolded the tourist earlier about smoking on board. As the little girl was lifted out of the water by the mate, Doc turned and swam back toward the dazed would-be rescuer just as the Coast Guard boats arrived.

The man was disoriented and sore from his fall, but he didn't struggle as Doc locked his hands around his chest under his arms then scissor kicked his way toward the ferry. Within another three minutes, both men were safely aboard the docked vessel while KK and the night crew firemen were overseeing the disembarking of passengers on the starboard side.

Posing as a fisherman on Round Lake and watching the downtown confusion some distance away sat Yuri, Bartholomew's European cousin. He sat in the rowboat with the outboard on the back that he had murdered Edgar Seward to obtain. As the Coast Guard boats sped by him, he slowly raised a detached riflescope up to his creased face like a spyglass. Rocking in the wake from the safe boats, he eyed the jumbled traffic and the still-raised drawbridge. Then, he turned the scope to the disembarking passengers of the *Michigan Mist* and the black curling smoke that was still pouring from the vessel. Next, he turned to his right and looked toward the gravel parking lot of the Portside Marina. He'd been watching Farren's car in the lot and noticed she was working late. He'd also seen that five minutes earlier, the police cruiser that always accompanied Farren had sped out of the marina's lot with its bubble lights blinking and its siren screaming. As he refocused his scope on the parking lot again, he caught the taillights of Farren's blue VW Beetle as it drove down a gravel lane then disappeared behind a row of Leyland Cypress trees, heading for the street.

"Police have left woman," he said to himself in his thick Moldavian accent. "They will be busy for hours."

He lowered the scope from his narrowly set eyes and hook nose and uttered one word.

"Now."

35 Belated Birthday

In August 1956, the DuMont Television Network had its final national broadcast after having gone bankrupt the previous year. Pat Boone's "I Almost Lost My Mind" was a jukebox favorite and Elvis Presley was less than a month away from making music history with his first appearance on *The Ed Sullivan Show*. Also in August of '56, Aaron and Portia Sinclair had both separately accepted an invitation from Gus and Clair Cooper. It would be the first time that Clair's parents would be under the same roof at the same time since they had divorced a year earlier.

The event was little Jackie's fourteen-month-old birthday party. An admittedly untraditional date, but Aaron had been, as usual, unavailable for his granddaughter's one year birthday because of work. Simultaneously, both Leland and Mary Cooper had been fighting colds when Jackie turned one and didn't want to risk being around the baby. So it was decided her birthday would be celebrated later in the summer, since the child was too young to know the difference anyway. This particular date also happened to fall on the day before Clair had to depart for Camp Grayling for her annual two-week training in the Army Reserve. This would be her third summer that involved reservist training.

"C'mon, Jackie, smile for Aunt Jessie," Clair's younger sibling cooed in an overly gushy voice. The child sat perched on her mother's lap on the front porch swing with Gus sitting next to them.

Everybody held their smiles for what seemed like a long time until Jessie finally got the baby to look directly at the camera.

After the camera clicked, Leland and Mary Cooper pulled up in front of the small single-story white house in their '53 Ford, smiling and waving. Gus, Clair holding Jackie, and Jessie all went off the porch, down the four front steps and down the front sidewalk to meet them. Portia also appeared in the screen door, dishtowel in one hand and waving with the other.

Mary got out of the car carrying some homemade bread wrapped in aluminum foil while Leland reached into the back seat and retrieved a wrapped birthday present with a big red bow. The scene was quite Norman Rockwell-like in its cheery mood of family coming together on an early Friday summer's evening.

"Well hello, Jessie," Mary called, having not seen her in some time. "How's the college girl? Excuse me, college 'woman'?"

"Fine, Mrs. Cooper. Thanks. It's nice to see you." Jessie answered. She was wearing her hair longer these days, and although she still wore her tomboy blue jeans and sneakers, at least she was wearing a decidedly feminine blouse.

"Dad, I told you no presents!" Clair scolded with a smile as she pecked her father-in-law on the cheek. She wore a light-colored cotton sundress with a small flower print pattern on it and had her long blonde hair bouncing freely off her shoulders.

"Nonsense," Leland waved off. "It's a birthday party."

"I told him not to," Mary said, likewise receiving a kiss from her daughter-in-law. "But you know Grandpa."

"She got lots of presents on her real birthday," Gus reminded, offering to take his mom's package. "What've you got there?"

"Homemade raisin bread," Mary grinned.

"Oooo—I love you! Thanks."

"Yes, thank you so much, Mom," Clair seconded.

Mary took the baby's hand and patted it, saying hello. Jackie, recognizing her grandma, smiled back.

Leland looked around. "I thought we'd be meeting a friend of yours, Jessie?"

"Oh, you mean Craig? I was hoping he could come too, but he

had to work."

"What's he do?" Mary asked.

"Writes poetry," Gus answered with dubious raised eyebrows. "He's a beatnik."

"A what?" his father asked.

"He works in a bookstore," Clair corrected. "Poetry is a hobby."

"Do we have a hug for Grandma?" Mary asked, extending her arms to Jackie. Clair happily handed her over.

"And what about you, dear?" Mary asked her daughter-in-law, now jiggling Jackie in her arms. "How are things going at Doctor Mortin's? Do you like it?"

"It's okay. But weighing people and taking their blood pressure isn't exactly working in an operating room. That's where the action is."

"Hasn't anything opened up at the hospital yet?" Leland asked.

"I wish," Clair answered. "But at least I'll be in a surgical setting down at Camp Grayling."

Just then, she spotted her father's red and white Studebaker coming down the street.

"Here comes Daddy," Jessie said.

"This'll go better than last time," Gus said to his parents. They hadn't seen Aaron since Gus and Clair's wedding day at the Regency, although he'd been invited to Thanksgivings, Christmases, Easters, and Jackie's christening.

"I'm sure it will," Mary agreed.

Portia came through the screen door and stepped out onto the porch. As she did, Jessie noticed something about her father's car. He wasn't alone; a woman was riding with him.

"Oh, oh," she said under her breath. "Here we go."

Everybody else noticed Aaron's passenger a couple of seconds later. She had shoulder-length red hair pulled off her forehead with a black barrette, a narrow upturned nose, large brown eyes, and breasts that were prominently pointing forward like two abnormally large missiles— 'a bullet bra' the boys called them.

From a distance, she seemed every bit as attractive as Portia, only more so because she was twenty years younger.

"He brought a 'date'?" Clair asked, surprised and indignant.

"It'll be fine," Gus said quietly.

As the Studebaker pulled over to the curb of Sheridan Street and came up behind the Cooper's Ford, Clair turned and looked at her mother. She could see the hurt in her eyes although she mustered a smile for appearance's sake.

"Hello everyone," Aaron called, climbing out of the car. He was wearing a two-tone shirt, half yellow, half brown, dark-green slacks, a white belt, and white loafers. Although his choice of wardrobe might've suggested a midway barker at a county fair, his companion's clothes made a very different type of statement. She wore a tight-fitting, dark-red blouse and a black skirt with a slit up her nylon-covered right leg. She looked more like she was going out to a nightclub instead of a one year old's belated birthday party.

As Aaron held the door open for his guest, her shapely high-heeled ankles, then long legs, then small waist came into view. Mary leaned over to Leland and quietly said, "Eyes on her face, dear."

After she was out of the car, Aaron retrieved a wrapped present from the backseat, which was three times larger than the Cooper's offering. Although it was wrapped, it wasn't in a box so the outline of the present was unmistakable. The long four legs and even longer neck was a dead giveaway for a huge stuffed giraffe.

"Bet you'll never guess what it is," Aaron joked dryly. He nodded to the redhead. "Everyone, this is Georgia."

"Of course it is," Clair muttered disapprovingly.

"Georgia, these are my daughters Jessie and Clair, Clair's husband, Gus, and his parents Leland and Mary Cooper." He then surprisingly added, "I was a total ass in front of the Coopers the first time we met."

Everyone said hello and shook hands with Georgia, although Clair's greeting was distinctly reserved. Gus and his parents, on the other hand, were both warm and genuinely surprised that Aaron's introduction would include an acknowledgement of his previous bad behavior. Gus also realized that for Aaron, it was as close to an apology as they were ever going to get for his actions at the Regency.

"And that young lady coming down the porch steps is Portia,"

Aaron continued, "Clair and Jessie's mother."

Portia smiled more broadly and extended her hand. "It's very nice to meet you, Georgia," she greeted graciously.

"Nice to meet you, too," the redhead reciprocated. "You have a beautiful family."

"And this," Aaron said, handing his large birthday present to Gus and taking the baby from Mary, "is Jackie, who was very understanding when Grandpa couldn't come to her real birthday."

"That's because she doesn't know any better," Clair quipped rudely.

"Shall we go inside?" Portia quickly gestured, deflecting Clair's comment. Everyone agreed and started walking toward the porch.

"We were also sick on her real birthday," Mary explained to Georgia. "Then between everyone's schedules—well—this was the first opportunity we've had to get together."

"I know what you mean," the redhead agreed. "Between work, college graduation parties, and vacations, summer just flies on by."

"Oh, did you recently graduate?" Clair asked.

Aaron cleared his throat disapprovingly.

"My younger sister did," Georgia continued, obvious to the intended slight. "From Houghton."

"Do they have a college for hair dressers up there?" Clair asked, lobbing another.

"Michigan Technological University," her father corrected. "It's a good engineering school."

"Yes, one of the ladies I clean house for has a son that goes there," Mary said. "The winters are frightful, though."

"They say you can walk down the shoveled sidewalks and not even see the houses because the snow is piled so high," Aaron said. "It's almost like walking in a tunnel."

"Are you a maid?" Georgia asked Mary.

"No," Clair answered for her mother-in-law.

"I pick up some extra income cleaning a few houses for ladies who either don't have the time because of their children's activities, or who are elderly and need a little help," Mary answered.

"I didn't know that you did that for elderly people," Aaron said.

"Gives them a reduced rate," Leland threw in.

"That's nice," Aaron nodded.

As everyone stepped onto the porch, Gus made a suggestion. "The house gets pretty hot this time of day—western exposure—so would everyone like to sit out here? I'll get some extra chairs, and honey, why don't you take the drink orders?"

"I just made some lemonade," Portia said. "Would anybody like some?"

"I'll have one," Mary said.

"I'll have a beer," Aaron answered.

"Me too," Jessie chirped in.

"No you won't," Portia replied.

"Beer sounds good," Leland agreed.

"And what about you, Georgia?" Clair asked. "Milk?"

"I'll have a beer too," she replied. "Uh, why would you think I'd want milk?"

"Jessie, come help me serve," Portia smiled gesturing her inside and trying to change the subject.

"Sweetie, help me grab a couple of folding chairs, eh?" Gus asked Clair, extending his hand and taking hers. He led her inside while his father asked Aaron how the construction business was in Petoskey.

Once they were in their bedroom and out of earshot of both the front porch and kitchen, Gus quietly asked, "What are you doing?"

"What am *I* doing?" she asked in an angry whisper. "What is *he* doing? How dare he show up here with someone my age!"

"I don't think she's that young. Early thirties, maybe."

"And did you see her chest? We're standing in Michigan but her boobs go all the way to Wisconsin!"

"Actually, you're about the same size as—"

"Well I certainly don't flaunt 'em with brassieres that makes 'em look like they're sitting in a rocket launcher!" she interrupted. "And why are you looking at hers, anyway?"

"Well, they're kinda hard to miss."

"My point exactly! He just brought her as an ornament, a way to say he's starting to become successful again."

"And what's wrong with that?"

"This is a family party!"

"I mailed the invitations for you," he remembered. "You wrote, 'Mr. Aaron Cooper and guest.'"

"Well I didn't mean it, Gus!" she snapped but still whispering. "Why would I want him to bring a date? Mom's still in love with him, although I can't imagine why! Did you see how hurt she was when they pulled up? It was like the light was taken right out of her eyes."

"All I've noticed is your mom being hospitable and polite. Two things you are definitely *not* being." He got down on his hands and knees and reached under their bed where two folding chairs were kept.

Clair folded her arms and fumed. "And did you see her skirt? That split? What does she think we're going to do? Have a limbo contest?"

"Clair, you've got to get over this," Gus warned getting back on his feet then picking up the chairs. "Your father brought a date, your invitation said he could, and even if he hadn't, he's not going to get back together with your mom."

"How do you know?"

"C'mon, this is supposed to be a party," he said, moving over to the closet. "Be the hostess you're supposed to be and let's go, Daddio. Here, take these chairs. I've got two more in the closet."

She took the chairs and coolly looked at him, not liking that he didn't agree with her.

The next couple of hours were, as Bette Davis famously said in *All About Eve*, "a bumpy night." For the most part, Clair contained herself, but like some witch's brew in a black caldron, cutting comments bubbled to the surface every now and again. When Jessie asked how her father and Georgia met, Clair said, "Yes, do tell us. Was my father chaperoning a Petoskey high school sock hop?" When Georgia said she didn't understand what that meant, Clair explained she simply meant that Georgia's skin was so clear and youthful looking, to which her mother quickly added, "And absolutely beautiful." This then caused the conversation to temporarily veer off into a discussion about Georgia's make-up regimen.

Aaron and Georgia really met because Georgia was a teller at a Petoskey bank where Aaron was a regular customer. She never went to college, was divorced, and was thirty-one, but truly did look a few years younger. She also explained her dress. After the early evening party for Jackie, she and Aaron were having a late supper with one of his new business prospects. She also acknowledged the age difference between herself and Aaron and justified it by saying, "He's just so knowledgeable but young thinking." Clair's response to this was a low but audible laugh that caused Aaron's face to turn visibly red.

By the end of the evening, it was pretty obvious to everyone, including Georgia, that Clair strongly disapproved of her and her father as a couple. Aaron left that evening fuming mad, but he was also apparently determined not to repeat his bad behavior at the Regency. He therefore held both his tongue and his temper, which surprised and pleased Gus, Leland, Mary, and especially, Portia. Jessie, on the other hand, was disappointed that the evening hadn't been more explosive, but enjoyed Clair's verbal bullets pinging and whizzing around the porch.

Portia turned out to be the real class act of the evening. She was the hostess her daughter failed to be—diverting sensitive subjects, being supportive of Aaron's May/December relationship, congratulating her ex on the exciting new directions in his life, being complimentary to Georgia, and being the consummate attentive grandmother to Jackie.

The entire birthday party was only a two-and-a-half-hour affair, but to Gus, and no doubt to Aaron, it felt like ten. There was still an hour of daylight left by the time the last guest had gone, and while Clair put Jackie to bed, Gus shuttled back and forth from the front porch to the kitchen, cleaning up, and mentally preparing for the inevitable fight to come.

When Clair finally appeared from Jackie's bedroom and came into the kitchen, Gus was washing cake crumbs and frosting off the last of the plates. Their kitchen was small and painted eggshell to make the room look bigger. It also accentuated its vibrant red and snow white tile counters.

"Can I do anything to help?" she asked.

"You've done quite enough already," he said tersely. "Why don't you go pack? You've got to get an early start tomorrow."

"He shouldn't have brought her, Gus," she began, ready to get into it. "Simple as that."

"Even if the invitation didn't say 'and guest,' which it *did*, you don't belittle someone who comes into our home," he fired back, jamming a plate into a dish rack so hard he nearly broke it. "You embarrassed me, your mother and father, my parents—but most of all—yourself! You were an absolute bitch to that poor girl."

"Emphasis on 'girl,'" she spat out.

"If Georgia's okay with the age thing, then it's none of our business," Gus reminded his wife.

"He only brought her tonight to spite Mom!"

"I don't think that's true," Gus said, washing another dish. "He brought her because he had another engagement tonight, a dinner that probably involved a business prospect and his wife. So bringing a date would make perfect sense. And even if he did, that's between your dad and mom and we shouldn't take sides."

"Shouldn't take sides?" she bellowed. "Are you serious? He's never liked you, he threw a drink in my face on our wedding day—"

"He never said he didn't like me," Gus cut in. "He said he wanted someone for you who could offer you more."

"And himself!" she barked.

"That might make him self-serving, and yes, his actions were atrocious at the restaurant. But remember, we blindsided him with the marriage. You can't make him hang on a cross forever, Clair. Besides, he's trying in his own way to make amends."

"Oh, really?" she asked, folding her arms while he put another dish in the rack. "How?"

"He came today, didn't he? You heard what he said about being an ass in front of my parents, didn't you? The day Jackie was born, he got me to the hospital, didn't he?"

"Too little, too late," she dismissed. "All he cares about is money!"

"Really?"

"C'mon, Gus, you *know* it's true."

He washed the final glass, put it in the dish rack, then grabbed a dishtowel, wiped his hands and turned to her seriously.

"How'd we get this house so cheaply, Clair? Ever wonder about that?"

She looked at him for a moment, not understanding. "Old man Fessler wanted the house occupied. He wanted hot water running through the pipes in winter," she answered.

"That's what we were told," Gus agreed, hanging the dishtowel on a cabinet knob. "But once your dad found out we were interested in this place, he cut a side deal with Fessler. He's been slippin' him an extra hundred every month that we're not supposed to know about."

"What?"

"He didn't want his pregnant daughter living in a crummy little upstairs apartment and going up and down those steep steps in back. He also didn't want to hurt my pride. So he's been paying part of our rent under the table while *also* trying to get back on his feet and pay your mom child support. That's why he's working all the time."

Clair cocked her head and squinted at him. "He told you this?"

"No. I got it from Mrs. Fessler. She let the extra money thing slip one day when I was dropping off the rent. It wasn't hard to piece the rest together."

"When was this?"

"Couple of months ago."

"A couple of months ago?" she asked wide-eyed, her voice rising with disapproval again. "You've been hiding this from me?"

"I've been respecting your father's wishes."

"By keeping things from me," she accused. "Just like you did after you went to his shooting club." She shook her head. "Boy, you're unbelievable."

"Why? Because I wanted to give your dad the opportunity to tell you himself, in his own way in his own time? I think he's paid for that right. Literally."

She shook her head again, still belligerent and angry. "It doesn't matter. He still shouldn't have brought that, that 'teller.' It was inappropriate and it absolutely crushed my mother!"

"Clair, your mother knew your father's bullish personality when she married him. If she didn't like the way she was being treated, there were a *lot* of things she could've done besides running out to a bar and screwing some stranger. *She's* the one who broke their marriage vows, not him!"

Almost as quickly as the words left his lips, Gus knew what he had just said was a mistake. Clair's eyes narrowed again to fiery jade daggers.

"Well, at least I didn't keep the information from my spouse." She hissed. "I gotta pack," she said, turning and leaving the room.

After a moment, she suddenly reappeared in the kitchen doorway.

"By the way, don't ever talk disrespectfully about my mother again."

"I didn't," he defended. "I simply told the truth."

36 Without Regret

Two hours after fire had broken out on the *Michigan Mist*, things were still busy in downtown Charlevoix. Firemen and members of the Coast Guard prowled the decks, corridors, and engine room of the empty boat assessing its damage. The loading dock and ticket office of the Wolverine Transport Company was closed off to the public while crewmembers stood on the pavement, wet from the fire hoses, and gave statements to officers. The streets were still packed with an unusual amount of curious tourists and backed-up traffic. The atmosphere was strangely carnival-like. Everyone was curious to see the boat that had caught fire or walk down by the Pine River to see where a young woman had been sliced to bits.

The hospital was also busy with passengers, friends, and reporters coming and going. Some of the press had come from as far away as Traverse City. The final injury tally of the evening was one passenger fatality and another in critical condition; that was the passenger who jumped off the *Mist* and was struck by the ski boat. There were also five passengers who had to be treated for smoke inhalation and another who broke his ankle while disembarking too fast and tripping. Then there were numerous cuts and scrapes while still other passengers, like Heather, the Brownie Doc had pulled out of Round Lake, had to be examined. All in all, the police, fire department, Coast Guard, and the city's medical personnel still had their hands full.

Meanwhile, out at Doc's cabin as the sun was slowly sinking and things were getting dark an old aluminum row boat with a twenty-five horsepower Evinrude outboard on the back quietly puttered its way toward Doc's beach through dead calm water. Manning the control handle was the silhouette of a lean figure wearing a flat-brimmed cap. Still several yards from shore, the silhouette cut the engine, quietly raised it, and then let the forward momentum carry the boat past Doc's aluminum dock until its bottom slid onto the sandy shore where it stopped with a subdued scraping sound.

The silhouette looked left toward a darkened house on the far side of a patch of woods about fifty yards down the shoreline, then looked right toward another house about the same distance away. It was lit, meaning people were home, but no one was on the dock, back deck, or in sight. This was satisfactory, so Yuri leaned forward and uncovered his Dragunov sniper rifle with its long barrel and six-inch silencer that was hidden under a blanket taken from his hotel. Slipping in a five-round clip, he stepped out of the boat and onto the beach. In another few seconds, he was on the path that led to the screened-in porch. It was a location he had scouted once before in broad daylight when he thought Doc would be sleeping. But it turned out he was mistaken when he peered past the screen-in porch and through a window to see the paramedic taking an online test.

His narrow eyes darted here and there, drinking in every detail of the area until his eyes settled on Farren's blue VW Beetle in the turnaround on the other side of the cabin. Then, past the porch and through one of the two windows, he saw the silhouette of a woman's figure against the thin, closed curtains. She was sitting with her back to him as if she might be reading. To an expert "mechanic" like Yuri, as his cousin called him, a silhouette was all the target he needed.

He brought the rifle to his shoulder and took aim. It was an easy shot, maybe a distance of a mere fifty feet without any wind. Yuri unclicked the safety, and a second later the Dragunov belched, "PHITT."

The head of the silhouette immediately disappeared amidst the tinkling of some broken and falling glass. With such a powerful weapon at such a short distance, Farren's skull would be split like a cantaloupe hit by a sledgehammer. The Dragunov had four shots left, but Yuri was pretty sure they wouldn't be needed.

On the off chance, however, that his target was still alive and perhaps reaching for a cellphone, Yuri charged toward the cabin. He kicked open the porch screen door and then the door leading into the living room. Having missed once before, he wasn't leaving anything to chance. He wanted to personally confirm his kill.

Coming into the house, he suddenly stopped when he saw a body of a woman sprawled across the width of the coffee table in between the two leather sofas in the living room. The shoulders, neck, and head of the woman were drooped over the far side of the table, pointing toward the floor from the impact of the shot, so Yuri couldn't immediately see the damage he'd inflicted. But he knew in an instant she was dead, her motionless bare legs and feet were testament of that.

His wrinkled face relaxed into a small smile. He could finally go home now, he thought, after ten days of stalking, waiting, and calculating potential opportunities. He lowered his rifle and took three more steps toward the body before he realized that something wasn't right. There was a knocked over desk lamp on the floor next to the coffee table with a broken bulb. It had one of those flexible, adjustable necks, which seemed to be pointed at an upward angle. He looked at the woman more closely. She didn't look right, either, even for a corpse. There was no blood on her housedress.

Within another four seconds, he realized she wasn't real. He'd been duped by Gertrude. Hearing the familiar click of a gun safety behind him, Yuri suddenly froze.

"Don't shoot, my friend," he said with his thick accent. "You have me."

He slowly raised one hand while placing the butt of his rifle on the floor, let it fall, then raised the other. Next, even more slowly, he turned around to see the open guest bedroom doorway and the man standing in it with the aimed Remington double-barrel shotgun. He recognized the man instantly. It was his target's grandfather.

"Oh, Grandpa," Yuri began in a friendly tone, "I see you trick—"
The discharge of the first barrel slamming squarely into Yuri's chest

abruptly stopped his words. Gus was only standing about seven feet away, so the impact from the blast literally lifted the hit man off of the ground and sent his body flying backward toward the kitchen. He landed on the hardwood floor with a spine-cracking thud just past the far leather sofa. He had a foot-long spray of buckshot in him and was dead before he even landed.

Gus took a couple steps forward, took aim again, then fired the second barrel. Unemotionally and without regret, he held the smoking barrels pointing at Yuri for several seconds before deciding to lower the weapon.

The back wall of the living room had a locked glass gun cabinet up against it that belonged to the cabin's landlord. It sat next to the entranceway that led into the kitchen. Now everything against that wall was covered with a fanned-out spray pattern of dark red streaks and greyish chunks. The body on the floor in front of Gus no longer had a face and not much left of what could be called a skull. The old man turned and slowly walked back to the kicked-in open door that led to the porch and stepped out onto it. He slowly set the Remington down across the arms of one of the white wicker rocking chairs, reached for the iPhone on his belt, and dialed 911.

37 The Last Time

Gus' alarm clock went off at 5:00 a.m. He slapped it off, then nudged Clair who had to be out the door and heading for Camp Graying by 6:15. But after he nudged her, he unintentionally fell back asleep. When he opened his eyes again, it was 6:03. He quickly sat up and noticed that Clair's green fatigue military duffle bag was missing from the corner of the room where she had put it after packing the night before. Worried that she had left without waking him to say goodbye, he scrambled out of bed. He didn't want her to be gone for two weeks with their harsh words from the night before hanging in the air like a virus.

He climbed into a pair of jeans, Hush Puppies loafers without socks, and a white T-shirt, and then hurried to their closed bedroom door. After he opened it, he was relieved to hear Clair's voice talking in soft low tones to Jackie in the kitchen. He walked through the living room and poked his bedhead around the kitchen doorway to see his child sitting in her pajamas in a wooden high chair with her mouth open like a baby bird. Clair sat in a chair in front of her feeding her Gerber apricots. She had her blonde hair tightly pinned up and was wearing her beige army summer uniform dress. He paused for a moment, drinking in and relishing the mother-daughter scene. Then the baby spotted him. Her blue eyes widened and she pointed to her daddy, smiling with a mouthful of food.

"There's my girls," Gus said, scratching the back of his head as he came into the kitchen. He went over, kissed Jackie on the top of her head and said, "Good morning, darlin'." Then he looked at Clair and cracked half a smile. "I was afraid you'd already left."

"I'd never leave without saying goodbye," she answered, revealing neither a good mood nor bad. "In fact, I was just about ready to get you up."

"Good. I, uh, I'm sorry we kinda fought last night."

"We didn't 'kind of' fight, Gus," she corrected. "We fought." She gave the child the last of her breakfast, then carefully wiped her mouth without looking up at Gus. He could tell by her tone and lack of eye contact with him that she was still pretty angry about the night before. She offered the baby a drink of milk from a small plastic cup, but Jackie shook her head no.

"It's just...this 'thing' with you and your dad," he tried to explain, "it's gone on for *so* long and you just get *so*—"

"Can we not do this now?" she cut in, rising out of her chair and picking up the baby. "I wanted to spend some nice morning time with my daughter before I leave for two weeks. I don't want to talk about last night and how unsupportive you are about my feelings."

Her verbal jab caused Gus to open his mouth in response, but then he thought the better of it.

"Okay," he said instead. "Do you have everything you need? Can I help with anything?"

"No," she answered. She looked at her daughter and smiled widely. "Oooo, Mommy loves her little jitter bug sooo much! You be good for Daddy, okay? I'll call you tonight and sing to you over the phone. I miss you already."

She brought Jackie close to her face and rubbed her nose back and forth against hers. "I'm kissing you like the Eskimos do. Yes, I am," she smiled tenderly, "Yes, I am."

"Got one of those kisses for me?" Gus asked.

"All you deserve right now is icicles," she deadpanned. He looked down at the floor, ignoring yet another barb. Seeing this, her face softened a little. "But give it time. Icicles melt." She looked at her wristwatch, "I've got to go. Call you from the base tonight."

"We never have good conversations when you're on base," he

sighed.

"That's because there's a two minute limit on phone calls and usually a long line of impatient women behind me wanting to talk to their kids, husbands and boyfriends."

"Great," he said frustrated.

"And that's if the phone in the booth is even working," she reminded. "Sometimes, it didn't last year, remember?"

He nodded while she looked lovingly at her daughter, gave her a hug, then handed her to Gus. She picked up her army cap in one hand and the duffle in the other. Positioning the cap on her head, she walked out the back kitchen door and into an overcast morning.

"Storm's comin'," she said, looking up. "Hope it doesn't slow me down."

He followed her outside carrying the baby. "Don't push it if you run into rain."

"I won't," she said.

Her maroon Jeep station wagon with the scratches on the side was parked behind his Chevy pick-up in the drive. She opened the driver's side door, tossed her duffle into the back seat, then turned to him.

"Love you. See you later," she said very obligatory. She gave him a quick peck on the lips then turned and climbed into the Jeep.

"Wait a minute," he protested. "You expect that kiss to hold me for the next two weeks?"

"Let's hope for better things on the other side," she smiled faintly. "Call you tonight." She looked at Jackie and her smile widened considerably. "Bye-bye, my darling. Mommy loves you! I'll see you later." Jackie outstretched an arm for her mother, but the army nurse knew she had to go, so she just rolled down the window and shut the door. "I hate this," she muttered. "But the sooner I leave, the sooner I'll be back."

Gus didn't know if she meant she hated leaving her child or leaving things still unsettled between them. He wanted to ask, but he didn't.

The Jeep groaned to life while Gus took a step back closer to the house, still holding the baby and patting her bottom as Jackie was becoming increasingly upset that her mommy was going away. As the Jeep slowly backed out, Gus walked down the driveway and followed to where the driveway and sidewalk met. Then the Jeep backed into the street. Switching gears from reverse to forward, and with a little wave to him and a blown kiss to Jackie, Clair pulled away and down Sheridan Street.

38 A Good Man

The city's boxy ambulance bounced its way over potholes as it hurried down the wooded lane to Doc's cabin. Beams of white and red lights on its front, side, and back cut through the tall pines and darkness, scattering both deer and raccoon alike. Although the lights pierced the night like a knife, KK had left the siren off. It wasn't needed because they already knew from the dispatcher that they were going to collect a dead body. Between the dispatcher's call and Doc having briefly spoken with Farren a little earlier, he had already, more or less, pieced things together. He knew that Gus was the one who had made the call and that he was reportedly alright, but he was still anxious to get to his place and make sure. Following right behind the ambulance were two police cars with BJ being in the first. Ten minutes behind this trio of city vehicles was Dr. Allen Colfax, once again representing the county coroner's office.

Pulling into the turnaround behind Farren's VW near the kitchen door, Doc and KK hopped out of the ambulance and sprinted toward the cabin. Doc retrieved his keys from his black cargo pants as they ran, but Gus met them at the door and opened it. He looked pale and tired.

"You okay?" Doc asked.

"Sure," the old man answered stoically.

"Where's the body?" KK inquired.

"This way," Gus said, turning and walking through the kitchen.

They followed him past the kitchen table and chairs, around the entranceway, and into the living room. Gus half-heartedly gestured to his right. Seeing the virtually headless body of Yuri lying on the floor in a pool of blood and more blood and pieces of his brains and skull splattered on the living room wall and glass gun cabinet, KK's mouth fell open, stunned. Even for a seasoned EMT like himself, the carnage was gruesome.

"*Jeeesus!*" he gawked. He put his hand on his stomach then quickly turned and stepped back into the kitchen. Doc, who'd been walking behind KK, stepped into the living room and surveyed the scene. His gaze fell upon a couple of trickles of blood that were still slowly dripping down the glass doors of the locked gun cabinet.

"You've redecorated," he understated.

The old man couldn't help but appreciate his young friend's attempt to lighten the tension of the moment. Doc looked away from the mess and eyed Farren's grandfather carefully.

"You sure you're okay?"

Gus stuck his hands into his pockets, looked at the body, and visibly slumped like a balloon being deflated.

"I, I really wanted to see Clair, again, you know?...I really did...I really wanted to be with her in heaven...But only good people go to heaven..." He shook his head slightly as his eyes welled with tears. "And I'm not a good person...A good person doesn't do *this*."

He raised his eyes to the paramedic as a single tear rolled down his weathered cheek. Hearing the kitchen door open and BJ's voice ask KK, "Where's Cooper?" he quickly wiped it away with his open palm and straightened up, too tough to let one of his peers see his suffering.

BJ waddled into the living room and surveyed Yuri and the bloody mess dispassionately. Tall Michael O'Hearn came in next. Just a few seconds behind them was David Wright, who'd been driving the second cruiser.

"You alright?" the chief asked. Gus slowly nodded while Michael, standing behind his boss, eyed the floor, then the walls.

BJ turned and looked at Yuri with an experienced forensic eye. "I'd say a 12-gauge at close range. Maybe six or seven feet. Both barrels." He turned back to Gus. "Where is it?"

"Out on the porch," Gus answered.

BJ turned his glance to Michael. Understanding, the big-shouldered cop walked through the living room and onto the porch. BJ pushed back the brim of his cap as he eyed the kicked-in door. He also noticed Gertrude lying across the coffee table. He took a couple of steps forward and peeked over the sofa nearest him to see that about half her head had been blown away. Then he turned around and looked past the entranceway leading into the kitchen, trying to determine where Yuri's round finally stopped. He figured it lodged somewhere in the kitchen to the right of the back door.

"Holy shit!" David Wright uttered, now in the living room and surveying the crime scene.

"Uh, David, why don't you take KK in the kitchen there outside and let him get some air. Then drive back down the lane and close 'er off except to the medical examiner. We've got a fair amount of reporters in town tonight and if anyone was monitoring the police band..."

David nodded, then turned and disappeared into the kitchen. "C'mon, KK," he said. BJ turned his eyes to Doc who was just watching and waiting as the senior officer on the scene made his decisions.

"Hell of a night, eh?" the chief said to no one in particular. "There hasn't been this much action in town since—well—ever."

"It's an old Remington double barrel," Michael reported, reentering the living room from the porch. "A *really* old Remington. Like, more than a hundred years."

BJ nodded, then sunk his hands into his trouser pockets and stepped over to Yuri's rifle on the floor. "And this?" he asked, directing the question to Michael. "Ever seen anything like it?"

"Yes, sir. In Iraq. Dragunov sniper rifle. Russian-made. Accurate up to a thousand meters. We make counterparts that are a lot better."

BJ nodded again, remembering the ballistics report. "Dragunov was on the list of possibilities. He broke in on the lake side. Go check down by the beach."

Michael turned and disappeared onto the porch again and down the path that led to the beach. BJ looked at Gus who had his eyes transfixed on Yuri's body, then at Doc.

"Got a beer?" he asked the paramedic.

Doc was a little surprised by the question, but nodded. He slowly walked into the kitchen. As he did, BJ stepped over to Gus. "C'mon, Cooper," he said kindly, gently taking him by the back of the arm and leading him into the kitchen.

Once in the kitchen, the cop gestured for Gus to sit at the kitchen table and Gus sat down as did BJ. Doc brought over a Bud Light and BJ gestured that he should give it to Gus, so Doc twisted off the cap and set it down on the table in front of him. To Gus, everything seemed to be happening in slow motion and had a surreal feeling to it.

"Whenever you're ready," the old cop prompted Gus.

"I killed him in cold blood," Gus flatly admitted, looking at the beer but not taking it.

"Wait a minute, he—he shouldn't say anything without an attorney," Doc suggested, trying to protect his friend. "Besides, I'm sure he's in shock right now and not responsible for what he's saying."

"What happened?" BJ asked Gus, ignoring Doc's comments.

"We were working late at the marina," Gus began with a vagueness in his voice. "I heard the rapid horn blasts from the ferry and knew that something was wrong. So I walked out to the end of one of the docks and took a look. I saw the smoke, people scrambling around on the decks, the tourists coming out of restaurants and shops... About a minute later, your boys watching Farren were called away. I knew it was a serious emergency. I knew everybody was needed."

Gus rubbed the white stubble on his chin, still recalling, as if sharing a dream.

"I figured, if *I* were a professional killer and missed my target, I'd still be hangin' around lookin' for another opportunity. And with all of downtown distracted by that boat, *that* was an opportunity. I also figured if this guy were any good, he probably knew where Farren was staying by now. So, I made her switch cars with me. I sent her to Ellen Mitchell's in my Accord with Doc's .38, and I went home, got my shotgun, then came out here."

"Who's Ellen Mitchell?" BJ asked.

"An elderly lady from our parish," Doc answered. "She's nearly blind. Farren reads to her."

BJ nodded as Gus continued.

"I parked her car on the far side of the turnaround so it could be seen from either side of the cabin, land or lake. Once inside, I saw that rescue dummy Doc's been carryin' around. It gave me an idea. I drew the curtains that overlooked the porch, put the dummy on one of the sofas, then put the lamp from the desk on the floor in front of it and pointed it up so the dummy's silhouette would show against the curtains. I didn't know if it would work. I didn't know which side of the cabin he'd come from, or, if he was even coming…But he did. I was waiting in Farren's bedroom. When I got the drop on him, he had his back to me. But he heard me, or maybe sensed me. He said, 'Don't shoot.' He dropped his rifle, raised his hands, and turned around slowly. He started to say something but I didn't let him finish. I just shot him. I knew the first barrel killed him…but I put the other into him anyway."

B.J. paused for a moment before asking his next question.

"Why, Gus? Why both barrels?"

For the first time since telling his story, Gus' eyes turned directly to BJ.

"Because this was the third time in less than a year that someone tried to kill my granddaughter. If that's Bartholomew over there, I wanted to end it. If he works for Bartholomew, I wanted to send a message. One he could understand loud and clear."

Finished with his story, Gus reached over, picked up the Bud Light and took a sip.

"So there ya go," he said, setting the bottle back down. "That's it…I killed a man in cold blood. With premeditation, intent, and frankly, a little bit of luck. So go ahead and arrest me, Chief. I'll tell the same story in front of an attorney."

Just then, Michael called from the porch. "Chief?"

"In the kitchen," BJ answered. Then he looked at Doc. "Why

don't you go see how your partner's doing?"

"He'll survive," Doc answered, not intending to go anywhere.

Michael came into the kitchen. "There's a rowboat down on the beach. Aluminum with an Evinrude on the back. Registration number sixteen-ten."

"Edgar Seward's boat," the chief noted.

Gus looked at BJ, surprised.

"That guy killed Edgar?"

"He wanted an anonymous way to get around on the water," BJ reasoned. "Rentals draw too much attention with the marina's phone and web painted on the hull. He probably scouted out a few lakeside places, saw that Edgar was older and lived alone, and figured he wouldn't be missed for a while if he disappeared."

"He wouldn't have, either, if those kids hadn't of found him," Michael said. "With both of Edgar's kids grown and living out of town, it could've been a long time before anyone got suspicious."

"Then I'm even more glad I did what I did," Gus decided. He brought his wrists together and presented them to BJ. "Go ahead, you old fat fart. Arrest me."

BJ leaned back in his chair and looked at Gus analytically. Then he looked at Michael, then at Doc. After a few quiet moments, he made a decision.

"What we have here is an open and shut case of self-defense," he announced.

"Hey, Dick Tracy, ain't you been listening?" Gus asked. He intended to say more, but BJ cut him off.

"You traded cars with Farren because her engine was making a funny noise and she wanted you to check it out. You brought your shotgun out here because Doc wanted to borrow it. He's recently developed an interest in..." BJ's eyes searched for a moment, "...duck hunting." When you came inside, the intruder was already in the house. He had a weapon, you had a gun, you had to defend yourself. End of story." BJ looked at Michael. "You got any problem with that, officer?"

"No, sir. None whatsoever."

BJ turned to Doc. "How 'bout you?"

"Duck hunting's my life," Doc agreed.

"Good," the chief said. Then he looked at Michael again. "Put some gloves on and see if that yo-yo in there's got any ID. If he does, it'll be bogus. But we gotta start somewhere. Then go look at the wall over there. See if you can find the slug from the Dragunov."

Michael nodded and went out the kitchen door to retrieve some latex gloves from his car. Doc saw Gus staring at BJ and wondering why he was going to cover for him. He decided these two men had things to discuss in private.

"I'm going to go check on KK now," Doc said, jerking his thumb toward the door. He walked over to it, then exited the kitchen. Once outside, he saw that the ambulance's back doors had been opened and KK sat on the edge of the doorway, his legs dangling off the back.

"Sorry, man," he said as Doc approached. "I've seen a lot of things on the job. But never a dude with no face."

"It's okay," Doc said. "Stuff still gets to me, too."

"So what happened?" KK asked. "What's goin' on?"

"We can't do anything until the medical examiner arrives," Doc answered. "Meantime, Gus and BJ are talking things over. But it looks like a case of self-defense." He spotted Michael pulling on his clear, tight-fitting gloves and called out to him. "Michael, what does BJ stand for anyway? Billy Joe?"

"You've been here going on two years and you don't know the story?" the tall cop answered, walking over. "It's legend."

"What's legend?" Doc asked.

"BJ," KK replied. "How do you think that guy has been able to hold onto the job of chief of police for, like, forty years?"

"His svelte figure and cat-like reflexes?" Doc joked.

"Once upon a time, they *were*," Michael confirmed. "BJ's the only man alive who ever ran up a leaf of the Memorial Bridge *while it was rising*, then jumped over the edge and drop into the Pine."

"At *night*," KK added.

"What?" Doc asked, not understanding.

"Ironic that something technically illegal would make him so famous in law enforcement," Michael noted, "but that stunt when he was a kid propelled him to superstar status among the locals."

"But he's a good cop, too," KK said.

"Oh, yeah. For sure," Michael agreed. "They say his father was grooming him to take over his building supply business. But he didn't want it. He wanted to be a cop."

"When was this bridge thing?" Doc asked.

"Back in the fifties," Michael replied. "It was like one of those stunts kids pull in college. I wasn't born yet, but I heard all about it from my dad."

"His real name is Derek," KK said. "BJ stands for 'Bridge Jumper.'"

The paramedic looked at KK, then at Michael, not sure whether or not to believe them.

"That is so totally weird," he observed.

Meanwhile back inside, Gus was leaned back in his chair at the kitchen table.

"Why?" he asked BJ.

The cop with the large stomach and badly died black hair folded his hands on the table. "The law is about justice, about things turning out right. You may have gone about it the wrong way, but the final result was right. It was just for your granddaughter, for Edgar Seward, and for Charlene Rogers, who'll never get the full use of her arm again. It was also just for all those other poor sons of bitches that guy killed, 'cause let's face it, this wasn't his first job."

BJ rose. "Or, maybe I just admire a guy who raised a daughter all by himself. A guy who kept it together after losing his wife when lesser men would've fallen apart. Or, maybe I never got over Clair. Or, maybe I just felt sorry for a poor slob who had to finish raising a granddaughter after losing his daughter."

"Or maybe it's because I saved your ass on that bridge and never told a soul," Gus suggested.

"It's a mystery," BJ answered evasively. "But whatever the reason, we're square now, Grease Monkey." He wrapped a meaty fist around Gus' beer and took a swig. He eyed his former competitor for Clair's affections up and down. "God, what a night. You were lucky, you know. Even at close range, he still could've survived the first barrel and put one in you. Or the kick from that shotgun could've broken your shoulder, an old shit like you."

Gus extended his arm for the beer, and BJ handed it over.

"Hey, man, it's northern Michigan," he said taking a swig, "any schmuck with a gun knows how to shoot."

39 Downed Wires

There was a line of about seven or eight Army nurses standing outside a telephone booth at Camp Grayling. It was one of only four phone booths on a military base that could house well over 10,000 soldiers. It was just after sundown and the worn wooden booth with its two long and narrow glass windows in the accordion door was bathed in the bug-filled yellow light from a street lamp sitting on a pole about fifteen feet above the booth.

This particular day, the first of the two weeks that Clair would be doing her annual training, had been especially long. There was check-in, a physical exam, barracks assignment, then calisthenics and marching, and since hundreds of reservists had arrived this day, each step took time. Then the medical personnel were divided into surgical units for training exercises. Next, there was chow. After that, there was a nurse's briefing where the nurses were told what their doctors and unit commanders expected of them. By the time they got back to their barracks and were done for day, it was already 10:00 p.m. so the nurses didn't get to the phone booth until about 10:15 and lights-out was at 11:00. That left very little time for the women to call their families, get back to their barracks, shower, then hit the racks. Revelry was at 5:30 a.m.

Clair stepped into the hot, stifling booth, slid the accordion door shut that caused a twenty-watt light bulb to flicker on above her, deposited her nickel, then made her collect long-distance call. After

Gus answered and accepted the charges, they had about two-minutes—the expected length for phone calls when there were a lot of people waiting to use the phone.

"Hi," Gus said warmly, talking from the wall phone in their kitchen, "how was your day?"

"Long."

"Did you run into any rain?"

"A few sprinkles. Nothing serious. I don't suppose Jackie is still up, huh?"

"No, sweetie. She went to bed hours ago."

"Dang," she sighed. "I told her I'd sing to her tonight, but we had this nurse's meeting after chow that went on forever."

"Well, since she's only fourteen months old and doesn't understand half of what you're saying, I think you're okay."

"She understands more than you think," Clair answered with a slight argumentativeness in her voice, Gus concluded she was still upset with him from the night before. After all, nothing between them had really been resolved. He thought that Clair had been horribly rude to Georgia and wanted to purposely embarrass both Aaron and her, while she thought her father showing up with a woman half his age at a family function was not only inappropriate, but just the latest in a long line of manipulations. The revelation that Aaron had been partially paying for their rented house wasn't as appreciated by her as Gus might've hoped. She didn't want her father to buy things for her anymore. The one thing she wanted more than anything else was an apology for his past behavior and his time.

Both Gus and Clair knew the other had valid points. But Clair didn't seem ready to extinguish her anger at her husband. At least, not entirely.

"So, what was your meeting about?" he asked, wanting to avoid any topic that might cause further conflict.

"Tomorrow morning we're going into mobile-surgical-unit mode. We're going to be receiving patients by helicopter and timing diagnosis and surgical prep. I'll actually be working in an operating room. Granted, the patients are only dummies and the walls of the

OR are canvas, but it's still surgery."

"How do you make a diagnosis on a dummy?" he asked.

"Tags that the medics in the field put on them."

"Of course. Well, I know this is exciting stuff for you," he smiled. "The OR is where you want to be, and *will* be full-time, soon as something becomes available at the hospital."

"Yeah, right," she said. "It's been more than two years. Nobody ever leaves the hospital, you know that."

"Oh, something will open up," he said optimistically.

"My father's handiwork is the gift that just keeps on giving, isn't it?"

They were interrupted by a knock on the glass of the door. "C'mon, Clair! Two minutes!" the next nurse in line called.

"I gotta go. There's this nurse named Lauren behind me and she's got, like, two hundred kids."

"Wow. Her vagina must be huge," Gus joked.

"Well, maybe it's only four kids," Clair corrected, "but she acts like the final authority on all things maternal. You know the type. Oh, tell my mom not to forget Jackie's doctor appointment, next Tuesday at 4:00."

"Why does she have to take her? I can do that."

"No you can't. Look at the calendar. You wrote, 'Lewis at one. Ring job.' Don't ring jobs take all afternoon?"

"Geez, you're right. I forgot about that. Okay, I'll call her."

"Clair?" the nurse outside the booth called again. She held her wristwatch up to the window and pointed to it.

"I gotta cut out," she said.

"Yeah, okay...I, uh, I really hate that we're going to be apart from each other for two weeks when we've still got some downed wires from last night. There's some things that need to be fixed, y'know?"

"Then fix it," she suggested, more serious than playful. "Just admit you were wrong, apologize for being such an ass, and I'll consider your request."

Her tone reminded him of her father's at the Traverse Bay Shooting Club. He expelled a heavy breath. He wasn't really sorry for his point of view, but he *was* sorry that it had obviously upset her so much. He opened his mouth to say something but heard the background sound of someone knocking impatiently.

"Lauren! Cool it!" Clair called, away from the phone. "I gotta go," she said back into the receiver. "It's like an oven in here anyway. We'll take up this apology thing tomorrow."

"Okay," he said, somewhat hesitant. He was just about to tell her that he loved her, but she had already hung up.

40 Insignificant Nobody

    Farren squeezed the honey from the plastic bear onto a tablespoon, then put it into the mug of tea and stirred lightly. While she stirred, she noted the time. It was going on 1:00 a.m. and she was feeling the day. She'd put in a full nine hours at the marina, then lost her police bodyguards due to the fire on the *Michigan Mist*, then visited with her nearly blind friend, Ellen Mitchell, then was informed her grandfather had shot and killed the alleged assassin that had been stalking her for nearly two weeks. She was also told she couldn't return to Doc's to spend the night because it was a crime scene. "Besides," Doc had said over the phone, "when the police are finished, we're going to want to have somebody come in and do some industrial strength cleaning. It's a tad messy," he understated.

    Now she was over at Gus' to trade cars and be with her grandpa just in case he needed to talk, or even not talk. She picked up the mug and walked from the kitchen, through the dining room and into the living room of the house she'd been raised in. Gus was sitting in his recliner staring at the picture of Clair sitting on his bookshelves. She noticed it before he could turn his tired brown eyes to her.

    "What's this?" he asked.

    "Chamomile tea with honey. It'll help to settle your nerves."

    "My nerves don't need settling."

    "Well, mine do," she said, offering him the mug. "Please drink it.

It'll give me the illusion that I've done something helpful."

He cracked a small smile and took the steaming mug. She stooped down on the floor by his feet and glanced at the picture on the bookcase.

"You still miss Grandma a lot, don't you?"

"Only when I breathe," he answered, appreciating the question. He blew on the mug, thinking. "It's funny. I've been a widower twenty times longer than I was actually married. When I think of us, I don't know if I'm remembering how we really were, or if it's just some romantic illusion of how I *think* we were."

She patted his knee with her small hand. "You should've gotten married again."

"Maybe I will," he answered a little spryly.

Her dark eyebrows rose in surprise. She smiled, nodded approvingly, then changed subjects. "I know what happened tonight was...difficult. But you're my hero. You know that, right? You had this pegged right from the get-go."

"Most girls want a hero who looks like he came off the cover of *GQ*. You got the poster boy for Preparation H."

"I'll take him," she smiled.

"I could've just as easily been wrong, y'know. And let's not forget, Doc went right along with me. He's a good man. You ought to get married again."

"Maybe I will," she answered, a little spryly.

He smiled and took a sip of tea, then looked at the mug pleasantly. "This is good."

"So what happens now?" she asked, still at his feet.

"With me? Nothin'. The police are calling it self-defense."

"And Bartholomew?"

"The police in Flint confirmed the guy I shot isn't him. But they're going to bring him in for questioning and try to link him to the hit man. Don't ask me how exactly, but that's what BJ said."

"Do you think it's over? Do you think I'm safe?"

He took and squeezed her hand still resting on his knee. "I sure hope so, honey. Even *I* don't think Bartholomew would be stupid enough to try something again." He was going to add, "At least, not for a while" but decided not to. He saw no point talking about a possible on-going war when a major battle had just been won.

"So where are you going to sleep tonight?" he asked. "I'd offer you your old room, but you took your bedroom furniture when you moved."

"I'm going to go home," she said, rising. "Doc's going to sleep there, too, when his shift is over. Unless you want me to stay. In which case, I'll be happy to."

"No, sweetie," he said and smiled. "I'm just gonna drink my tea and maybe read some Shakespeare. It's the perfect time of year for *A Mid Summer's Night Dream*."

"You sure? I'll be happy to stay."

"Actually, I'd kinda like to be alone for a while if you don't mind."

"You don't have to explain," she said, leaning over and kissing the top his head. "I just wanted to thank you for taking care of me."

"What goes around comes around," he said, setting his tea down and standing. "You'll be taking care of me sooner than later."

Knowing what he meant, she stepped over and gave him a hug.

"That's not going to be for a long while. Don't you worry about that."

"You're a good girl," he said, enjoying the embrace. "Now go on. Go home. Sleep well."

"For the first time in a long time, I think I will." She stepped away from him, picked up her purse, then walked over to the front door.

"Goodnight, Grandpa," she said, going onto the front porch.

"'Night, baby."

He followed her onto the porch and waited until she had gotten into her blue Beetle and driven down the street. Once she was gone, he stood there for a few moments, drinking in the night. He paid attention to the crickets. He heard a dog barking in the far distance. He looked up toward the sky, and even though he couldn't see the stars for the porch ceiling, thought about the vastness of creation. Then he thought about what had recently been revealed to him. Thanks to Doc, he knew that God, heaven, and the angels weren't quaint bedtime stories or mere theoretical possibilities, but facts. Facts that seemed to answer so many questions, yet simultaneously, left so many other questions unanswered. He thought he would be a better, more compassionate man for the gift of this knowledge. But what had he done? He'd killed somebody. Not only killed them, but intentionally disfigured them in the name of revenge. He wanted to feel bad about his actions, but he didn't. As a result, he was questioning his morality.

"If you ever wanted to say something to me...Cut me some slack, now would be a really good time," he muttered quietly.

He waited for a half a minute, half expecting to see, hear, or feel something. Nothing happened. Only the crickets answered back.

"Right," he finally said. He lowered his head and turned to go back into the house.

Later that morning, but still early, Nelson Kaiser sat at his desk reading BJ's report. His desk was one of many in an open area of Precinct Two of the Flint Police Department on East 5th Street. Kaiser was thirty-three and an eight-year veteran of law enforcement who didn't show a lot of emotion except to close friends. Although not traditionally handsome due to a high forehead and ruddy face, his taut build and penchant for Brooks Brothers knockoff suits gave him a good first impression. He was considered "a comer" in the department, was the first of his graduating class to make detective, and he didn't like, really didn't like, Gordon Bartholomew.

Normally, a local loan shark wouldn't merit much attention from a detective. Sure, a loan shark was a law-breaker, but detectives usually spent their time on murders, missing persons, rapes, and crimes more violent than people who lent money to foolish gamblers at incredibly high interest rates. But Bartholomew wasn't the run-of-the-mill loan shark. Some of his clients were visible in the community: doctors, lawyers, even a sports writer. There was also the occasional death that he might've been involved with but nothing could ever be proven. Then there were the rumors. Rumors that he occasionally helped an overseas drug operation. Rumors that part of his income went to a syndicate in Chicago. There were even rumors that he was involved in the trafficking of runaway girls who were sold to a Russian cartel.

He'd been questioned by the police so many times on so many things he practically had his own private interrogation room. But Bartholomew always bounced away from arrest and prosecution like a flat, smooth stone, skipping over the top of a calm lake; a stone thrown expertly by his attorney. Nelson Kaiser knew in his gut that it was only a matter of time before that flat stone would lose its momentum and sink, and he wanted to be the cause of it.

Bartholomew sat quietly in Interrogation Room Three with his hands folded on a laminate table in from of him. The table had its legs bolted into the floor and there was a small railing on its side where prisoners could be handcuffed if necessary. He sat wearing khaki slacks, tan Merrell loafers, a pink Polo dress shirt with a paisley ascot, and a blue blazer. His closely cropped brush-cut hair stood on his skull like a sea of brownish-grey needles. His appearance was calm and patient. He might've been picked-up by the police for questioning, but he was the one who projected control. His jowls coiled back into a polite smile as Kaiser came into the room carrying a manila folder.

"Detective. Lovely to see you," Bartholomew purred.

The cop noticed the ascot. "Off to the steeple chase today, Mr. B?"

"Only my closest associates call me that," he reminded him politely.

"Oh, you mean like Stanley and George?"

"Is that why I'm here today?" the loan shark asked hopefully. "Please tell me you've located the lads. I've been so worried about them."

"I think we both know they're not going to be found," the cop said honestly.

"Ah, the Hoffa School of Magic," the older man mused. "Tell me, has my attorney arrived yet?"

"Why? Do you think you need your attorney?" Kaiser asked, sitting down in the only other chair in the room across the table from the suspect.

"Absolutely not. I'm a Boy Scout. But like the scouts, I like to be prepared."

The detective smiled and slid the folder he was carrying in front of Bartholomew.

"What's this?" the older man asked.

"Something you might want to see," the cop answered with a hint of smugness.

Bartholomew extended a thick, short finger and flipped the manila folder open. Inside was an eight-by-ten-inch color copy of Yuri's lifeless and faceless body. The loan shark's face stiffened to a stone expression as if he'd seen Medusa, although it was subtle. He feared the corpse was his cousin but he honestly couldn't tell because of the disfigurement. He also knew that Kaiser was looking for a reaction. It took every ounce of his self-control to hold himself in check. His eyes turned up to the cop.

"And who might this be, whose end was so wanweird?"

"His driver's license and social security card said Alex Kurzenowski. But as you know, Alex Kurzenowski died thirty years ago in Salt Lake City."

"Do I?"

Kaiser tapped on the picture with the tip of his forefinger. "This is what's left of the mechanic you sent up to Charlevoix."

The suspect's worst fears were confirmed. A hand that was resting on his leg under the table and out of the detective's view tightened to a fist, yet the rest of him remained calm.

"Really?" he asked innocently. "Do I own a vehicle up north in need of service?"

"You sent this man to kill Farren Malone. But he ran into a couple of problems. Two twelve-gauge problems to be exact."

"And may I inquire where this poor soul met his demise?"

"In a cabin rented by a paramedic named Reynolds. Miss Malone's been staying there."

"'Doc Reynolds," Bartholomew acknowledged. "Yes, I remember reading about his brave exploits from statements and depositions." The loan shark closed the folder then fiddled with the cuff of his blue blazer as if he were inspecting a newly sewn-on button. "And you brought me here today to what? Extrapolate a confession? Sorry,

Detective, you're going to need more than a gory picture."

"What if I told you that after the first barrel had been emptied into him, the mechanic pleaded for his life and confessed your involvement?"

The stocky man shook his head, forcing an amused look. "You're a philosophunculist, Detective."

"A what?"

"A bluffer. Prove your accusations or let me go home."

Just at that moment, the door opened and Bartholomew's attorney, Theodore Hall, came in. He was well dressed like his client but wore a three-piece suit. Although a few years younger than Bartholomew, he sported a very similar brush-type hair cut as if it were a secret sign among wise guys. He laid his five hundred-dollar Hartman briefcase down on the laminate table with a disapproving thud.

"You're not supposed to be questioning my client without me being present, Detective," he began like a teacher scolding a student.

"Oh, he wasn't questioning me, Theodore," the loan shark corrected. "He was entertaining me with stories. Fantastic stories that even had pictures."

"You wanna fill me in, Detective?" the attorney asked.

"Last night in Charlevoix, a man took a shot through a window at the home of one Wyatt Reynolds, then broke into that home. We believe the shooter was intending to kill Farren Malone who was staying with Mr. Reynolds. After gaining entrance by kicking in a door, the intruder was killed by two shotgun blasts." Kaiser gestured to the folder. The attorney opened the folder and looked at the picture as the cop continued, "The deceased had a set of false ID papers, identification from a man who died thirty years ago across the country."

"How do you know this?" the attorney asked.

"A friend at the Social Security Commission. The deceased also carried a Russian-made rifle preferred by snipers and spoke with a foreign accent that suggested Eastern Europe. I believe we've questioned your client about his connections in that part of the world before."

"Alleged connections, Detective," the attorney corrected.

"This was the second time that this particular rifle has been linked to an attempted murder in Charlevoix since your client's release from jail," Kaiser reminded him. "It's pretty obvious Mr. Bartholomew is bent on revenge and sent someone up there to take care of business."

"Someone not very good, apparently," the suspect quipped, leaning back in his chair and folding his hands across his chest.

"Well, I'm glad you've got everything figured out so neatly, Detective, the attorney said. "Do you have anything that directly ties my client to this dead man?"

"He said that the deceased mentioned my name after being shot but before dying," Bartholomew said.

"That true?" Hall asked the cop.

"What I said was, 'What *if* the deceased confessed your involvement?' I didn't say that he did."

"Okay, we're done here," the attorney said, perturbed and gesturing for his client to rise. "If you have something concrete, make an arrest and we'll make bail in twenty minutes."

"Your client didn't get bail the last time, counselor," Kaiser reminded. "Plus, he's getting sloppy. It's only a matter of time."

"Ask yourself this, Detective," the attorney retorted. "Why in the world would my client want any harm to come to Miss Malone? Eh? After Charlie Huffman made false accusations implicating Mr. Bartholomew in one of his cons, he'd be the *last* person who'd want to see her get hurt. I know it, you know it, and he knows it. So tell the police of Mayberry-By-The-Bay to go look for bad guys in their own back yard."

Kaiser smirked and picked up the folder from the table. "Oh, I agree, hurting Miss Malone wouldn't be smart. But just because your incredibly bipolar client uses five-syllable words, that doesn't make him smart."

The loan shark looked the officer up and down, then smiled. "Ever wonder what a *real* Brooks Brothers suit feels like, Detective?" His attorney chuckled as they opened the door leading out to the hallway.

Kayla Morrison was thirty-one, brunette, and had a master's degree in economics from the University of Michigan. Although dark haired, she had beautiful pale skin and was curvaceous like Scarlett Johansson. For the past year and three months, she had been Gordon Bartholomew's live-in girlfriend.

They met in a casino in Detroit. She was working as an accountant for Arthur Anderson at the time but quit her day job four months into the relationship and moved in at his request. She knew he was a loan shark, knew he was into some other nefarious activities, knew he was prone to emotional extremes, and knew he was responsible for the death of others even if he, himself, hadn't actually pulled the trigger. There was both an element of excitement and danger around Bartholomew, which she found intoxicating. She loved his power, was drawn to his taste for the finer things, and she even liked the fact that he talked about leaving his criminal life behind. It seemed to make the unsavory things he did not so bad somehow because, after all, he intended to go straight.

They lived in a condominium that was one of two top-floor units in a five-story building in a fashionable Flint neighborhood. Their home was done in modern Scandinavian furniture that was open, sleek and angular. A low-sitting red leather sectional sofa dominated their living room, complemented by a thick glass and steel coffee table sitting on a white round area rug.

Opposite the sectional were two fabric accent chairs with wide wing-like arms that looked like they came from the set of *Star Trek*, and the focal point of the room was two large Warhol's hanging on a brick wall side-by-side highlighted by halogen spotlights. Kayla sat at a glass-top desk reading the Detroit Free Press online in an alcove between the living and dining room when Bartholomew returned. She was wearing an elegant navy blue Ann Taylor pants outfit as if she might be going off to work, although she wasn't. Hearing him come in, she immediately hopped up and hurried to the foyer.

"How did it go?" she asked, knowing where he'd been.

Bartholomew tossed his keys into a ceramic bowl sitting on a side table. "My cousin Yuri—he's dead," he announced wearily.

She wrapped her arms around him and drew him close, which

emphasized her height. She was a good four inches taller than her boyfriend.

"Oh, baby. I'm so terribly sorry," she said soothingly. "What happened?"

"Farren Malone happened," he grumbled bitterly, his anger stewing. "This insignificant nobody, this goody-two-shoes babysitter of boats has pierced my side once too often. What am I supposed to tell my mother's sister?"

"She's still alive?" Kayla asked surprised, considering Yuri was at least fifty.

"'Course she is," Bartholomew answered. "Alive and well in Moldavia."

"Tell her...there are hazards connected with being a killer."

Bartholomew gave her an exasperated look and headed for the kitchen.

Kayla immediately changed tack, wanting to be genuinely helpful. "Tell her he was involved in a horrible traffic accident and was burned beyond recognition. Then send her a box full of ashes."

He paused at the stainless steel double-door refrigerator before opening it, considering the idea. "That's not bad, actually." He got out a bottle of white wine. Next, he opened a cabinet and got a long-stem glass.

"Would you like me to fix you some breakfast?" she offered. "Eggs, toast, bacon? It'll help you think more clearly than—" she stopped herself when he shot her another disapproving glance. "Fine. Wine's good too," she conceded.

After pouring himself a glass, the short, stocky man slowly slipped the cork back in the bottle while making a decision. "It's time to deal with this annoying woman personally."

"No, baby," Kayla warned, concerned. "That's just what they want. You can't leave town, you can't be seen in Charlevoix, and you can't kill her. Especially now that they *know* someone was after her. There are threads out there already that connect you to Yuri."

"If the police had anything, I wouldn't be standing here," Bartholomew reasoned. "Maybe Miss Malone has become a bit of a cacoethes for me, but she's cost me millions, and now family, too!"

"Projected millions, honey," she reminded.

"*Yuri's death was not a projection!*" he screamed, suddenly losing all control. "*Me being incarcerated for six months was not a hypothetical. It was real!*"

"Being mumpsimus is ill advised!" she shot back. "I'm sorry but I care about you, so I'm not going to be thelemic!"

Bartholomew glared at her, so angry he was shaking. Then he took a quick swallow of wine, set his glass down on the white marble kitchen counter, and walked quickly over to a chest-high bookstand holding an extremely thick and open dictionary in the alcove near the glass-top desk.

"Mumpsimus," he muttered to himself, flipping through the pages. Is that with an e-s, or, u-s?"

"U-s," she answered.

Coming to the page he wanted, he ran a thick finger down the text until he found it. "Mumpsimus," he said, reading: "One who sticks obstinately and wrongly to their old ways."

Kayla put her hands on her hips. "Do you want the spelling for 'thelemic?'"

"No...I know that one."

He left the bookstand and returned to his glass of wine on the counter. He took a drink, thinking things over.

Perhaps you're right, dear," he said, now calm again. "Rashness and hamartithia go hand in hand. But you *do* have a master's degree in economics and you, yourself, helped me with the numbers of what we could've made with that condominium complex in Charlevoix."

"I appreciate that," she said, walking over. "What I don't appreciate is for the fifteen months we've been together, you spent six them away from me. I didn't like that. I didn't like at all."

He looked at her and smiled curiously.

"Tell me honestly, Kayla. If I had no temper, wielded no power, had no money and was a just a short, chubby middle-aged man, would you still be attracted to me?"

"Theoreticals are useless," she answered. "The truth of the matter is you *are* well moneyed, you *do* have a temper and you wielded power *long* before I ever came into your life. But if I have any sway with you, I don't want you to be arrested for this insignificant nobody. Your words, Gordon, 'insignificant nobody.' If she truly is, then why risk *your* valuable life with her death?"

Bartholomew's jowly cheeks slid back into a genuine smile. "Alright, my darling. Let it never be said that I can't be influenced. I won't kill Farren Malone. Not right now, at least. Instead, I'll dissect her life and take it apart like a biology student dissecting a frog. First, I'll destroy her business, then her grandfather will suffer a fatal heart attack, then her boyfriend will be poisoned with the slowest working chemistry money can buy. This will actually be better. I can stretch her suffering out for months."

Kayla raised a cautionary finger. "That wasn't exactly what I had in mind."

Bartholomew took another drink of wine, then set his glass down again and went into the living room. Grabbing the end of the round white area rug that held the thick glass and steel coffee table, he pulled the rug and the table toward him with considerable effort until she could see a the outline of a thin rectangle cut into the wood floor underneath.

"What's that?" she asked. "A secret compartment? That's so Sopranos."

"Where do you think I got the idea?" he answered. Once the rug was totally clear of the rectangle, he walked over to it and, carefully using his fingernails, lifted the piece of cutout flooring.

"My emergency stash," he announced.

"Stash of what?" Kayla asked.

Bartholomew pulled a brown leather briefcase out of the floor that had a combination lock. "Plastique," he answered.

"Y-you mean, as in, 'explosives?'" she asked.

"I told you, Yuri and I learned different disciplines as kids," the loan shark reminded, sliding a fat thumb over the tumbler wheel to begin the unlocking sequence. "He learned firearms and I learned explosives."

"Yes, but I didn't know you still handled them."

"On special occasions. And Miss Malone is a *very* special

occasion."

He fiddled with the tumblers for another moment, then clicked open the briefcase. Raising the lid, he smiled and produced a yellow six-by-two-inch rectangle wrapped in clear plastic.

"This is special, Kayla. Just as volatile as C4 but virtually untraceable. Put a timer on it that'll shatter into a million bits and nobody will ever know what happened. Compliments of the Israeli government."

"How did you get that?" she asked, curious.

"Doesn't matter," he said, putting it back in the briefcase. "I'll pack it inside something simple like a soda bottle. Something you'd find around a marina. Marinas have paint, varnish, gasoline—this'll cause quite a mess."

"Baby—" she said hesitantly.

"Here's what I want you to do," he interrupted. "I'm going to give you a list of names. Names of people you're going to invite to dinner here tomorrow night. People who owe me and will swear I was here all night. I'll write everything out for you—what I was wearing, what we talked about over dinner, what we ate, what wine we drank, even a call I made on the land line that you'll actually place."

"Gordon—"

"And before you wake up the following morning, I'll be back."

"Please don't do this," she protested. "The cops could be tailing you."

"Of course Detective Kaiser has someone following me," he replied. "You leave losing them to me."

41 The Worst Part Of The Job

It was late on a sunny Sunday morning when the 1956 Ford black-and-white police cruiser turned into the drive of Stu and Ernie's. Henry Sutter, the town's chief of police, was behind the wheel. He was a thin man with narrow eyes and prominent bags underneath them from years of smoking Pall Malls. As a result, he always looked tired, but he cared deeply about the community he served and was a good, honest cop.

He didn't pull up to one of the pumps, but instead went past them and pulled over to the side of the building next to the office. Seeing him arrive, Louie rose from the office desk, put on his station attendant cap and went outside.

"Morning, Chief," he said, approaching in his usual eager-to-please way. "If you're looking for Stu, he's at church, and Ernie's gone to—"

"Are Stu and Ernie ever here, Louie?" Sutter interrupted taking off his sunglasses and slipping them into the breast pocket of his blue uniform. "I mean, do they ever actually work? Pump gas? Repair cars? Change tires?"

"Sure," Louie said, not understanding the question.

"Never mind," the chief shrugged. "Where's the teacher?"

"Gus? Service Bay One, under Will Oakley's truck."

"Thanks. Give us a few minutes alone, okay?"

"Those parking tickets starting to catch up to him?" the younger man half joked.

Sutter looked at the gas jockey with his no-nonsense cop stare. "Undisturbed, Louie."

The smile faded from Louie's face. "Yeah. Sure." The chief nodded a "thank you," then went into the garage. He looked around for a moment until he spotted the radio on a shelf playing "Heartbreak Hotel" by Elvis Presley, then walked over and snapped it off.

"Hey! I was listening to that," Gus called from under a 1952 Dodge truck. He rolled out from under the engine on his mechanic's creeper with a wrench in hand and recognized the upside-down face of Sutter.

"Hey, Chief."

"Gus."

"Something wrong with the patch I did on that front tire last week? Didn't it hold?"

"No, it's fine," Sutter said. "Come on up here. I need to talk to you."

Gus climbed to his feet, tossed the wrench into an open toolbox, and then grabbed a red rag from a counter and started to wipe his hands. As usual, he was wearing his brown overalls unzipped to about the mid chest and had a toothpick dangling out of the left hand corner of his mouth.

"What's up?" he asked.

"I just got a call from a Coronel Bradley Foote, commanding officer over at Camp Grayling. They've been trying to reach you at home but finally called me because they didn't have your work number."

"What's wrong?" he asked, fearing that Clair was either ill or injured.

Sutter took off his police cap and his narrow eyes looked at Gus sincerely.

"Son, there's no easy way to say this. So I'm just gonna come out with it: there's been an accident. A very bad accident."

Gus' mouth dropped open a little while the rest of him froze. All of the blood seemed to rush out of his head. His arms and legs were suddenly a mass of goose bumps, his brown eyes fixed on Sutter's.

"How bad?"

The cop looked down at the ground for a moment before returning to the mechanic's face.

"I regret to inform you that Clair and three other souls perished about 8:00 a.m. this morning."

Gus' knees visibly buckled. His jaw dropped and the toothpick fell out of his mouth. The chief reached out to grab an arm and hold him up, but it wasn't necessary. The mechanic took a step back shaking his head in disbelief as his eyes started to fill with tears. With one sentence—seventeen words—his universe had changed forever.

"No!" he blurted. "*No!*...She, she *can't* be gone! W-w-what happened?"

"She was in an operating room in the field with two other nurses," Sutter explained, "a big tent with a wooden floor...they were doing exercises for incoming wounded. Dummies were strapped to stretchers on the sides of helicopters and they were timing responses. The surgeon wasn't in the tent at the time. He was at the landing pad about a hundred yards away from the surgical tents. One incoming chopper developed a problem. Some eyewitnesses say it was the rear rotor. Others say it was the horizontal stabilizer, whatever that is. It missed the pad, came in fast, went down at an angle and exploded on contact killing the pilot. The tent that Clair and two other nurses were in was right in the path of the resulting fireball...I was told they never knew what happened. They might've heard the crash but..." Sutter's voice dropped off when he saw Gus' wide, horrified eyes. He now had a hand clamped over his open mouth.

"I'm so sorry, Gus..." he concluded. "I'm just as sorry as I can be."

There was a long quiet pause between the two men. After about fifteen seconds, Gus' hand slowly fell away from his mouth and he looked around the garage at nothing in particular. He spotted Louie outside near the pumps, trying to casually glance inside and figure out what was being said.

The Intended Ones

"She...she's only twenty-five," Gus said in a near whisper.

"They'd, uh, they'd like you to go down to Camp Grayling and make a positive identification. One of her parents could do it if you'd rather. But, as her husband—"

"I'll go," Gus interrupted. "Her mother's watching the baby...I'll...I should go there first and...explain..."

"I can go with you if you want. I'll even drive you down to Grayling with the siren going."

"No, I'll go," Gus said, more determined. He wiped his eyes and looked around for a clean rag to blow his nose. Sutter reached into his back pocket and offered him a white handkerchief, which Gus took.

"I've been doing this for over twenty years and this is the worst part of the job," the chief said, filling the awkward silence with whatever words he could think of while Gus wiped his nose. "I'll have Louie explain things to Stu and Ernie. Do you want me to contact anyone for you? Clair's dad? Your folks? You want me to call the funeral home?"

"No, I'll, I'll talk to the parents. Thanks," Gus said. He offered the handkerchief back, but Sutter held up a hand, indicating for him to keep it.

"I, uh...I guess I better go change, first," the still-stunned mechanic decided. "Yeah. I'll go home and change, then go over to Portia's, tell her and Jessie, then call my folks and her dad from there." His eyes darted here and there, trying to think of what else to do. "Maybe, if you don't mind, maybe you could call the funeral home. We'll need to make arrangements...pick out clothes, pick out a casket..."

"You should think about cremation," the chief suggested.

"What?" Gus said, surprised by the suggestion. He knew what the process was, but he didn't know anyone who had ever done it to a loved one.

"Have you ever seen a bad burn victim, son?" Sutter asked. Gus shook his head. "Well—you should be prepared for the worst," the cop suggested. "She's not going to look like...families often decide that cremation is best for fire victims." The thin man fiddled a little

347

with the hat still in his hand. "Just remember, what you'll see in Grayling is just a shell. It's not Clair anymore. Clair's already in heaven with God."

Gus' wet brown eyes looked out at Louie again, then at the hood of the truck he was working on, then at a family of tourists that had just pulled into the station. Everything seemed different somehow. It was as if he'd never see the world the same again. And indeed, he wouldn't.

"So—are, are you saying I won't even be able to recognize her?"

"Try not to look at her face," the cop said, now starting to fight back tears, himself. "Look at the rings on her fingers. Look at her dog tags. That's what they told me to tell you."

42 The Storage Barn

It was just after 3:00 p.m. when Doc's red Jeep Wrangler with its black fabric top pulled up in front of Gus' house on West Upright Street. The sun was intermittent, peeking in and out of billowy clouds rolling in from Lake Michigan. Doc was dressed for work wearing his dark blue Charlevoix Fire Department T-shirt and his ever-present black cargo pants. Gus was wearing old jeans with kneepads over them, a tan short-sleeve Columbia fishing shirt, and an old straw hat that made him look Amish. He was weeding the flower garden under the porch in his front yard. Two considerable piles of weeds were at his left and right.

Turning and seeing his young friend approach, he climbed to his feet, although slowly.

"Hi," Gus greeted as Doc came across the small lawn. "Isn't this, like, the dawn of the day for you?"

"I have to go in early and meet the insurance adjuster for the *Michigan Mist*. KK and I were the first emergency personnel on board last night."

"Do they have any idea what caused the fire?"

"Not for sure. But we know there was a crewmember that had to speak to a passenger more than once because he was smoking cigarettes. So a quickly discarded smoke in the wrong place is a theory, but that's all I know. I suspect I'll learn more when I go in."

Gus nodded. "The cops at your place last night said you fished a couple people out of Round Lake?"

"It was no big deal," Doc shrugged modestly. "Farren called and said you were taking the day off. I just wanted to see if you were okay."

"For a man who expected to be in jail this afternoon instead of weeding, I'd say I'm doing alright."

"You talk to anybody today?" Doc asked. "The press? BJ?"

"Nope. Everything's been quiet."

"I think BJ's keeping a pretty tight lid on what happened at my place."

"When can you move back in?"

"BJ called about an hour ago and said they'd probably be finished by the end of the day."

"What're they doing?"

"Pictures, bullet trajectories, dusting for fingerprints, that kind of thing. He's going to call when they're finished. He's even got the number for a cleaning crew that specializes in crime scene cleanups. I think he said they were from around Grayling."

"Anything new on Bartholomew?" Gus asked.

"BJ said he was questioned this morning by the police in Flint and shown a picture of the deceased. But they don't have anything to hold him on."

"Well, maybe the picture put the fear of God in him."

"It'd be nice to have *him* be nervous for a change," Doc agreed.

"You want some lemonade?" Gus offered. "Made some this morning."

"Sounds good. Thanks."

They walked up the four wooden steps that led to the porch and Gus gestured to a chair as he took off his hat.

"Take a load off. Be right back with the drinks."

The front screen door squeaked open as he disappeared inside and Doc wandered over to one of two rocking chairs. He sat down and imagined a young Farren playing with her dolls on the porch, drawing chalk pictures on the sidewalk, and watching for Santa through the front window. He hoped if they ever got married, their kids would look like her instead of him.

"So, what'd you think?" Gus said a minute later, pushing open the screen door with his foot while holding a tall glass of pink lemonade in each of his still dirty hands. "That I was layin' around bemoaning what I did?"

"Well—you *did* say last night that you weren't going to be able to see Clair again."

"That's probably true," the old man said, handing him a sweaty glass. "I don't think God lets murderers into heaven. And let's not fool ourselves, I went to your place last night to kill someone. I'm just sort of amazed I got the drop on him." He settled into the rocking chair next to his guest. "No, I don't expect I'll get to see Clair when I die. But it's a fair trade, my soul for Farren's life."

They both took a drink of lemonade and were quiet for a moment.

"You're talking like what you did last night was wrong," Doc finally said. "I mean, maybe it was. *I'm* not God. I can't speak from the divine point of view. But from an earthly standpoint, I think justice was served. That guy killed Edgar Seward, shot Charlene, has no doubt killed other people, intended to kill Farren, and he certainly would've killed *you* if given the chance. That's not murder, Gus. That's stopping evil."

"Yeah, but Doc, I don't even feel bad about it. Not even the second barrel. That ain't right."

"Why don't you let God decide what's right and stop punishing yourself?"

"I'm not punishing myself."

"Sure you are. You say in one breath that what you did last night doesn't bother you. But in the next, you've already put yourself on trial, found yourself guilty and have decided you don't get to spend eternity with your wife. If that's not punishing yourself, I don't know what is."

Doc put his glass down on the small rounded table between them and turned to his friend. "Look, have you ever wondered why Clair took that sickness out of you? I mean, if she hadn't, you'd have been with her that much sooner, right?"

"I don't know about that," Gus said with hesitation. "I was

pretty angry at God for a long time. I basically hated him for years."

"You're missing the point. I asked Clair about it and she said you'd been granted more time. She said you had something important to do. Maybe last night was it."

Gus looked at him suspiciously. "Shooting someone?"

"Outsmarting a killer and defending your family. Wasn't Michael the Archangel a warrior angel? Didn't Jesus lose it with moneychangers in the temple? Didn't one of the apostles cut off a servant's ear to defend Christ in the Garden of Gethsemane? Sometimes soldiers are needed."

The old man rubbed the stubble on his chin, thinking.

"I'm just not getting any answers, Doc," Gus finally said. "I *am* asking. But the silence is deafening."

Doc nodded, understandingly.

"I get that...I really do...I only became a true believer myself because I got to meet a celestial being. But that was just at first. A deeper conviction came later. Faith's a bitch, man. You gotta keep *wanting* it. Working on it. Sometimes you feel like you've got a relationship with God and things are great, and other times you feel alone and ignored. It's like any relationship, in a way. And if all you're feeling is silence—I don't know—talk to someone. Listen harder. Read the Bible. Join a fellowship group. I'm not saying I know how, but I *do* know you can sail your soul to better waters if you give it time and *want* to."

Gus shrugged, took a drink of lemonade and looked out at the day.

"Are you gonna marry my granddaughter?" he asked.

"Don't change the subject."

"No. I wanna know. What's your intention?"

Doc smiled at Gus' old-fashioned notions, but respected them.

"If she'll have me, yes. More than anything else in the world, I want to marry your granddaughter. Is that okay with you?"

Gus tossed him a challenging look. "What if it wasn't?"

"Then I would be genuinely broken-hearted," Doc said, unruffled, knowing Gus was just being Gus. "But I'd understand because *nobody's* good enough for her. But since we both *know* that nobody's good enough for her, she might as well be with somebody you can beat at poker, eh?"

The old man hid the urge to smile and nodded slightly, then looked out at the day again.

Nearly twelve hours later, at 2:51 a.m., a lone figure walked silently across the gravel parking lot of the Portside Marina. It was Gordon Bartholomew heading for the storage barn. He was wearing a maroon Polo shirt, black sports jacket, dark slacks, loafers with black snow rubbers and clear, tight-fitting latex gloves. He wasn't dodging from shadow to shadow like a Ninja, but he certainly wasn't trying to draw attention to himself, either.

He walked quietly but confidently across the lot shifting his eyes here and there. The night was silent and still except for the occasional splash of a fish jumping in Round Lake or the squeak of a boat gently rubbing up against a rubber bumper placed between it and the concrete docks in front of the marina store.

Bartholomew had parked his neighbor's car nearly a quarter of a mile away and using that car was exactly how he had eluded the police staking out his condo. They had no way of knowing that one of his neighbors who lived in the same building was also a client who owed him seventeen grand. The loan shark forgave half of the debt in exchange for the neighbor simply pulling out of the condo building's underground garage with Bartholomew hidden in the back seat. Then, a mile or so later, Bartholomew took the car and the neighbor took a city bus to a relative's.

Coming to the access door that was next to the large airplane hangar-like doors, he pulled out something that resembled a Swiss Army knife, but instead of blades and utensils, it held numerous lock picks. He unfolded a couple of options while checking the door to see if it was alarmed. It wasn't.

"Bumpkins," he muttered, trying the first pick. With a couple of expert jiggles, the door opened easily. He slid inside and quietly shut the door behind him.

The door had a window with a venetian blind over it, and he closed the blind but kept the overhead fluorescent lights off, in case there was any light leakage that could be seen from the outside.

Next, he pulled out a flashlight, clicked it on and looked around. Since the barn was big, he walked around for at least two minutes casing the place and trying to decide where his plastique could do the most damage. He finally settled on the detailing area in the back right-hand corner of the barn where Farren had danced to Carly Simon.

In the middle of the detailing area was a twelve-foot Mirror Dinghy sailboat that sat on a trailer and had been brought in for a hull cleaning and line re-rigging. Beyond the boat against the far back wall and the wall to the right and closest to the marina store were shelves lined with varnish, paint thinner, and polyurethane. There were also some large fifty-gallon drums full of used engine oil.

"Beautiful," the loan shark smiled, liking all the flammables he saw. "The explosion will rattle windows for a half-a-mile in every direction."

He looked behind him. The beam from his flashlight darted here and there until he spotted the workbench and motor repair area. Going over to it, he saw a workbench light and turned it on, figuring it was small enough not to be seen from the outside. He found a pair of pliers and went over to one of the fifty-gallon drums. Rolling the heavy base of the drum inch-by-inch, he positioned it on the floor of the detailing area about five feet away from the right-hand side wall in between the stern of the dinghy and the workbench.

The drum was sealed with a lid that had a dozen bendable metallic tabs. Taking the pliers, he loosened the lid tab-by-tab, then lifted it off. He saw a battery-operated water pump sitting on a shelf behind the workbench, which many boats on the big lake carried as a safety precaution.

"Better and better," Bartholomew said to himself.

He retrieved the pump, set it on the floor next to the open oil drum stuck the vacuuming end of the hose into the oil, turned it on, then flicked a switch to start the pumping action. Holding the other end of the hose with one hand and his flashlight in the other, he started to spray oil everywhere—on the workbench, on the floor, against the shelves, on other boats and on the walls. The man bent on avenging his cousin's death even began to happily whistle the old tune "They'll Be A Hot Time In The Ol' Town Tonight," already congratulating himself on the havoc he'd wreak in Farren's life. Kayla was right, he decided. Not killing her, but taking her life apart piece-by-piece would infinitely be more satisfying, even though, in truth, Kayla never meant such a thing.

After a good minute's dousing of everything the hose could reach, he set his flashlight down, turned off the pump, and tossed it aside. Then he reached into one of the side pockets of his sports coat and pulled out a twelve-ounce bottle of Diet Coke that had been carefully repacked with his special plastique. There was a small green luminous timer taped to the outside of the bottle with a wire that ran down its neck and went into the plastique inside. He turned on the timer, set it at eighteen minutes, and then turned it off.

Pleased that he had eluded the police in Flint, gotten into the storage barn so easily, had found so many flammables, and that he had an airtight alibi when he returned, Bartholomew confidently took the bottle by its neck and tossed it into the air. It spun around then landed back in his hand. He was feeling cocky and knew the explosive was safe so long as the timer was off. Now that his eyes were adjusted to the dim and distant light from the workbench, he looked around, trying to decide where to place the plastique. Investigators would no doubt wonder for weeks what had caused the fire, and they might even suspect arson, but he was confident his explosive wouldn't be identified. He'd used it before and it never had. He eyed the shelves in the detailing area carefully, then turned back to the workbench. If he put the bottle on the shelves of the detailing area, there would be an immediate huge blast from all the combustibles. If he placed it on the workbench, the explosion would trigger a fire from the sprayed oil that would eventually reach the oil drum, then the shelves, meaning there would be a second and third explosion.

Decisions, decisions, he thought, playfully tossing and spinning the Coke bottle again.

This time, however, when the bottle landed in his hand, it landed on the fleshy part of his palm at just the right angle and bounced into the air again. This caused the stocky man to juggle and grab at it with his thick hands like a receiver trying to grab a nearly caught football. After a couple of clumsy fumbles with the bottle, Bartholomew's hand unintentionally swatted it away from him toward the workbench. It landed and bounced a few times across the floor, aided by the slick oil sprayed everywhere, and came to rest against the side of a sawhorse some sixteen feet away. As the loan shark started to walk toward it to pick it up while being mindful that his rubbers were now walking on an oily floor, he made a horrifying discovery. Somewhere in between the bottle bouncing off his hand, him fumbling with it, and then it bouncing on the floor, the luminous green timer had been activated and it was now counting down, but not from eighteen minutes, eighteen *seconds.*

"What?" Bartholomew cried, incensed. "It *can't* reset itself like that!"

But it had. It took three seconds to realize he was mistaken and two more seconds to decide to go after the bottle. Now the countdown was at twelve. He took a step toward the workbench and felt his feet sliding on the oil, even with the grips from his rubbers. Knowing he didn't have the time to reach it, he spun around and saw the dinghy. Maybe he could jump into it for protection from the blast. He started to walk slowly toward it so he wouldn't slip and fall. When the counter was at six seconds he'd made it to the trailer. At five, he stepped onto the trailer. At four, he grabbed the starboard side of the boat. At three, he hurled his body over the side and onto the floor of the vessel. At two, he started to crawl toward the bow to get as far away from the blast as he possibly could.

Meanwhile, about a mile-and-a-half away at the fire hall, Doc had the ambulance out on the driveway in front of the tall rolled-up garage doors. He had just finished washing it using the streetlights and building spotlights for illumination. He was drying off the front grill with a towel when he heard the blast interrupt the quiet of the night.

Also hearing the noise, KK came casually strolling out of the garage and looked at his wristwatch.

"Fireworks, at this hour?" he wondered. "Crazy tourists." They both froze for a moment, straining to hear more. After several seconds, KK shrugged and changed subjects. "Don't Lance and Charlene get home tomorrow?"

"They're actually back in the country now," Doc said. "They wanted to spend a few days in New York—" He was interrupted by the blaring of the alarm going off inside the garage, directly followed by the voice of a female dispatcher announcing the nature of the emergency and the address.

Doc recognized the address of the Portside Marina immediately.

After quickly dressing in his brown firefighter pants, heavy brown turnout jacket with the day-glow striping and his treated boots, he reached for his cell. He woke Farren out of a sound sleep while the night crew ambulance and fire truck were just rolling out of the fire hall.

"Hello?" her groggy voice answered.

"Are you at home?" he asked urgently, sticking a finger in his free ear and practically yelling to be heard above the siren.

"Yes. Why? What's going on?" she asked, becoming more alert.

"We just got a call. There's been an explosion over at your storage barn."

"What? What kind of explosion?"

"The really loud kind," he quipped. "We don't know exactly. We're still en route. Listen, call Gus, then take my revolver, go over to his place, but *stay* there! You understand? Stay there, until I know what's going on. I gotta go now, but I'll call you and fill you in just as soon as I can."

"I'll call Grandpa but I'm not staying away," she announced. "That's my business we're talking about. I've got customers sleeping on boats!"

"Remember last night at my place? This might be another attempt. Go to Gus'! Stay there!" he ordered.

"Not likely!" she fired back, disconnecting him.

A second later, even with the blaring siren, he heard a second explosion. A few seconds after that, a third.

43 At the Cemetery

"Lord, please bless and keep our sister, Clarissa Marie Cooper," the priest began, then Gus' mind started to wander as he stood at the graveside service of his wife at the City of Charlevoix Cemetery.

Clarissa Marie Cooper, he thought to himself. The only other time he had ever heard her full name spoken out loud was the day they got married in Petoskey. Now it was unlikely that he'd ever hear her full name spoken out loud again. What was he going to do with her clothes? Her make-up? Her perfumes? Her maroon Willys Jeep station wagon that was still sitting in the parking lot at Camp Grayling?

Dressed in a dark suit, he looked at the casket while he held his young daughter in his arms. He'd decided against cremation although Clair's body had been burned beyond all recognition. Chief Sutter had been informed correctly, her dog tags and wedding ring were the only ways to identify her.

"She's been burned enough," he told the undertaker. "Just lay her down gently and we'll have a closed casket." This was done as Gus had requested, although Clair's right arm had to be removed so the casket could be shut. It was outstretched, fused in place, as if to fend off the sudden and deadly tidal wave of fire that engulfed her. The undertaker never told Gus about what he had to do to Clair's arm, although Gus had already assumed that certain things had to be done to get her into the coffin.

The Intended Ones

He was surprised by how many people had come to the visitation and attended the funeral. Friends from Ferris University, friends from the toy store and doctor's office where she worked, and friends of her mother's. Then there were grandparents, cousins, aunts and uncles, people from the military, relatives from Gus' side of the family, Stu, Ernie and Louie, his pilot buddy Glen, fellow teachers, students, even Derek Worthing. It was overwhelming, but he smiled, shook every hand, and thanked every person for coming. In future weeks, he would write more than two hundred thank you notes. But for now, he just wanted to get through the day.

"She died in the service of her country," the priest continued. "She gave her life while training to save others." He'd never really thought of her being a reservist as some noble calling. He'd always thought it was a slightly impetuous decision she'd made so he could continue his education inexpensively and she could keep her OR skills in tune for a job at the hospital as a surgical nurse. Then, of course, there was the extra benefit of taking a jab at her father to prove she wasn't the princess he was counting on her to be. "She gave her life while training to save others," he repeated in his head. It gave a little meaning to what seemed to be a meaningless death. It was something he could say to his daughter when she was old enough to understand.

After a relatively short graveside service, people were invited to a luncheon at the Regency. Aaron had arranged it and insisted on paying for it, and Gus didn't argue. At the graveside service, he'd also noticed that Aaron didn't bring Georgia and stood near Portia for support. In fact, Jessie stood in between them clutching her mother's hand on her left and her father's hand on her right. Her boyfriend, Craig Berry, stood behind her. He knew the showing of family unity between Aaron and Portia was just grief and didn't mean a reconciliation, but it was still nice to see.

As people started to walk back to their cars on this beautifully sunny but incredibly sad day, Derek spotted Tommy Boil's father putting a potted flower on the grave of his son some distance away. Derek stopped for a moment to watch as Mr. Boil knelt at Tommy's grave and lowered his head in prayer. Maybe it was because he was already grieving over Clair, but he was truly moved and sorry for this father who had lost his son.

44 Egregious

"Oh my God!" Doc said, eyeing the red aluminum storage barn. Although he wasn't even seeing the worst of it yet, he could already see the orange flames and black smoke curling around and consuming the building. One of the explosions had blown one of the large airplane hangar-like doors off its tracks and it lay in the gravel parking lot with a large bow in it. Replacing the door was a billowing wall of smoke and flame.

A dozen or so of the boat owners who stayed at the marina were standing in the parking lot with more hurrying in from the docks where their boats were kept. Some were wearing robes, others aimed their cellphones for a picture, while still others were calling friends or relatives.

"We're gonna need help," Doc surmised. "Two guys in an ambulance and two guys in a fire truck aren't going to be enough."

"The guys behind get top priority," KK said.

Doc understood what he meant. With the *Michigan Mist* incident from the night before, injuries had been reported while Doc and KK were on the way. Plus, the bridge keeper had told Doc from his conversation with the boat's captain that the fire wasn't really affecting the vessel's ability to maneuver, putting the onus of the emergency on the injured and getting passengers off the boat. But tonight, no injuries had been reported, so the priority was to firemen in the truck following. As a certified fire fighter, KK's first responsibility was to fight the blaze until additional help arrived.

"What do you need?" Doc asked, letting KK take the lead as the ambulance rolled to a halt.

"Check with the bystanders to see if anyone knows how it started or if anyone's hurt. Next, call Stubigg and BJ. You're right, we're gonna need some extra help. Then set up a perimeter."

"You got it," Doc said, grabbing his helmet and air bottle with mask and getting out of the vehicle.

While KK and the firemen unloaded hoses and hooked up to a hydrant, Doc strapped on his air bottle, then called the police dispatcher to have her notify Stubigg and BJ. He then ran over to the crowd and asked if anyone was hurt. No one was, so he hurried over to the fire truck, grabbed a stack of orange hazard cones, and returned to the onlookers. Asking them to step back, he spread out the cones about ten feet apart, then took some yellow hazard tape and wrapped it around the top of each cone creating a knee-high barrier. He couldn't cordon off the entire area, but what he did certainly communicated to people that they supposed to stay a certain distance away.

He asked if anyone knew how the fire started, to which no one responded but all seemed to agree it began with an explosion. Moving over to the far right side of the barn, he could see that one of the three explosions he'd heard had ripped a 5-foot-high tear through the shelving and wall on that side of the building. Not only that, but flaming debris and half blown apart containers of flammable liquids had been blasted into the limestone veneer of the marina store, catching it on fire, too.

Farren arrived about five minutes after the night crew wearing a large Mercury outboard T-shirt that she'd been sleeping in with jeans and tennis shoes. Gus arrived about five minutes after that, just as the flames on the side of the marina store stretched up its limestone veneer and curved onto the slight A-frame roof.

"Oh, God, we're going to lose the store, too," Farren sighed, now standing next to Doc. He had done about all he was allowed to do. He stood there looking the part of a firefighter, but his air mask hung uselessly on his chest and his Kevlar gloves drooped halfway out of his overcoat pockets.

"Everyone here said it started with an explosion," he said. "Then there were two more. We even heard 'em above the sirens while en route. Did you have some combination of materials in there that could cause such a blast?"

"We've got lots of things in there that are flammable," she confirmed. "But to have things just spontaneously explode? No. I don't think so. I mean, I'm not a chemist, or anything."

They heard more sirens approaching as they watched the swirling, roaring uncontrolled flames.

"Could it be something else?" she asked. "Arson?"

"I don't know, baby," he said. "I honestly don't know...You *do* have insurance, right?"

"Yes," she answered, then she gazed at the barn and marina store and shook her head sadly. "My parents' legacy, all of Grandpa's and my hard work, it's just—*gone!*"

"It's not gone," he assured her. "Your safety is what's important and the rest can be rebuilt." He spotted Gus out of the corner of his eye talking on his cell several yards away. "Look, look at your grandpa over there," he pointed out. "He's probably talking to a contractor already."

Suddenly, they heard what sounded like someone yelling from inside the storage barn. But with all the hisses, pops and creaks coming from the barn, it was hard to tell exactly what the noise was.

"Did you hear that?" Doc asked.

"I thought I heard 'something?'" she agreed tentatively.

"Could anyone be *inside* the barn? A customer? Isn't it locked at night?"

"Yes, usually."

Farren turned and surveyed the people behind her. There were now about two-dozen people watching the fire, all of them customers who stayed on their boats. Meanwhile, Doc peered closely through the rip in the wall.

"I don't see Al Stanislaus," Farren said.

"Who?" Doc asked.

"Al Stanislaus. He owns a cabin cruiser. Middle-aged, kinda

short, overweight...I'll be right back."

She ran over to the perimeter Doc had set up to ask people if anyone had seen Al. While she was gone, Doc spotted the profile of a man inside the barn run past the rip in the wall. He was middle-aged, kind of short, and overweight. Almost instinctively, he reached for the air mask hanging on his coat. By the time Farren turned around again, she caught a glimpse of Doc now wearing his equipment at the opening in the wall. He pointed urgently inside the barn, then stooped down for clearance and quickly disappeared inside.

Farren's first instinct was to cry out to him, but she didn't. She figured he was going after someone, and her screaming wasn't going to help. So she said a prayer instead.

When Bartholomew's plastique accidentally went off, both the dinghy he had climbed into for shelter and its trailer were literally blown forward. The trailer was launched with so much force that its front hitch embedded itself into the back wall of the storage barn, causing a shelving unit to collapse and spill its contents into and around the boat. A can of varnish clunked Bartholomew on the head, and he was knocked unconscious. Nine minutes and eight seconds later, he awoke and, for a moment, believed he was dead and literally in hell. Fire and smoke seemed to be everywhere. But after another few seconds, he realized he was the victim of his own misfortune.

His head throbbed painfully as he slowly climbed out of the boat and tumbled to the floor, which was almost unbearably hot because of the burnt-off oil sprayed everywhere. He got to his feet and was still a little dazed as he began to run one way, then another. Mini explosions blasted all around him and cut off his access, causing him to yell in fear and surprise. Bursts of flames jutted into other flames as one container after another reached its temperature threshold then exploded with a fiery plume. It was like a dozen flamethrowers were in the barn and going off indiscriminately. The barrel that he had pumped the oil from was gone. A weakness in its metal caused it to explode in the opposite direction of the dinghy, throwing an airborne lake of flame that engulfed the workbench area and access

The Intended Ones

door he had come through. He finally stopped and was surveying his options when he suddenly turned to see a fireman hurrying toward him.

"Are you hurt?" the fireman asked in a voice that was muffled because of his mask.

Bartholomew shook his head, but then started coughing from the all the air being sucked away by the flames.

Doc quickly took off his helmet, slid off his air mask and placed it over Bartholomew's nose and mouth. "Breath normally," he instructed. "Not too fast. Just normal...Okay?...Feel better?"

Bartholomew nodded.

Doc lowered the mask from the civilian's sooty face. "Good. You must be Al," he said mistakenly. "My name's Doc. Let's get out of here, eh?"

"Doc?" the older man asked. "Reynolds?"

"Oh, Lord. Has Katy Perry been talking about me again?" he joked. "She's such a gossip. C'mon," he said, gesturing behind him. "We're going to go through that hole in the wall over there. Okay? Think you can make—"

His words were interrupted by a loud "pop" and a sudden burning sensation that ran through his stomach like he'd just been stabbed by a red-hot fire poker. He jerked in reaction then, wide-eyed, looked down to see the Glock 23 forty-caliber pistol the man was holding. Its barrel was still smoking. Suddenly feeling his legs give out from under him, Wyatt "Doc" Reynolds realized he had just been shot.

As the paramedic fell to his knees, his attacker—now feeling better and better by the second thanks to the adrenalin rush of revenge—put the bottom of his shoe with its half melted rubber soul on Doc's chest and kicked him backward. The air tank on Doc's back jammed into his spine as he went down. He quickly turned on his side in agony as he dropped his helmet. Even through his fire-resistant outerwear, he could feel the intense heat from the concrete floor.

"Sorry to disappoint you, Doc," Bartholomew grinned, pleased with his victim's grimacing face. "But I'm not Al. The name's

Bartholomew."

Simultaneously, outside the storage barn on the gravel parking lot, Gus hurried over to Farren as another fire truck pulled into the lane leading down to the marina parking lot.

"C'mon, girl," he urged taking her arm with one hand while raising the other from the intense heat, "Step back!" He looked around. "Where's Doc? Wasn't he just here?"

"He's in the barn," she answered, taking a few steps back. "He went in to get Al Stanislaus. But I have no idea how Al got—"

"Al Stanislaus?" Gus interrupted. "He's not in there. I just got off the phone with him. He's on his boat. He called and wanted to know if he should move it out into the lake for safety."

Farren looked at her grandfather then at the barn.

"This didn't exactly go the way I planned tonight," Bartholomew said, leaning over Doc who was going into shock. "But it's still going to turn out well. This is serendipity. That man you killed last night was my cousin, Yuri, so now, I'm going to kill you, take your fire clothes, put on your helmet and air tank and walk right out of here as a fireman."

Bartholomew straightened up and took a couple of steps back. He pointed the Glock at the Doc's head. "The last thing I want you to think about is how incredibly slowly Farren's going to die. Got that image in your head, Doc? Can you picture her tears? Her nerves twitching in pain? The blood flowing out of her? Good!" He locked his elbow to shoot as his eyes widened with triumph. "Buh-bye now."

A shot rang out. But it wasn't from Bartholomew's Glock. The loan shark jerked forward, dropped his gun and nearly lost his footing. With an expression of anger, pain and confusion, he stumbled, then spun around to see Farren standing in front of the collapsed shelves and rip in the wall about eighteen feet away. She was pointing Doc's Smith & Wesson snubnose .38 at him and had just shot him in the lower left shoulder blade.

"*You!*" the loan shark bellowed, realizing who she was. "*This is egregious!* No stupid little girl is going be the cause of Yuri's death, *and* shoot me, *and* cheat me out of millions!" He started to walk determinedly toward her, coughing as he went.

"Stop!" Farren ordered. But when she saw the obvious pain he was in, both her expression and tone suddenly turned to something more compassionate.

"*Please* stop! Don't make me shoot again!"

Bartholomew started to smile, seeing that the young woman didn't have the resolve to finish what she had started. He continued to move toward her until, suddenly, her heard a roar, or something that sounded like one. Looking to his left, a plume of fire from an outboard's melted fuel line shot out and engulfed his body. Bartholomew started screaming and walking sideways while his arms flayed wildly. Farren lowered the revolver and looked around, trying to find a blanket to smother the flames of her would-be killer. But there was nothing at hand. Still screaming, Bartholomew tripped over a gallon of paint and fell into more flames. His screaming and flaying continued for a few more seconds, then the blazing lump that had been Gordon Bartholomew stopped moving.

Knowing there was nothing she could do for the loan shark, Farren dropped her weapon and ran over to Doc who was fighting to stay conscious.

"You brought my gun," he said between gritted teeth.

"You told me to."

"I also told you to go over to Gus'."

She looked at his stomach, the hole in his coat and the dark, expanding wet blotch surrounding it. "C'mon," she said, starting to cough a little. "We've got to get out of here!"

"Take some oxygen," he urged.

"C'mon, baby!" she said, looking around and pulling on his arm. "Get up!"

She got him to a sitting position, although he painfully groaned when he did.

"C'mon, Doc," she urged, getting behind him and trying to pull him up with her hands under his armpits. "Stand up! Just get to your feet!"

He bent his legs and tried to stand, but couldn't. His air bottle was in the way of her trying to pull him up, so she unstrapped it, then put it on herself, knowing she'd need all the strength and alertness she could muster.

"C'mon," her muffled voice ordered as she began to drag him by the arm across the floor toward the rip in the wall. "Use your feet! C'mon!"

But he didn't. He couldn't. He'd just slipped into unconsciousness.

"C'mon, baby!" she called again. When she realized he wasn't responding, she yelled at him. *"Damnit, Wyatt Reynolds! Move your ass! I want a life! I want your children!"*

She pulled him a few more feet, but then her sleeve caught fire. She dropped Doc's arm and patted herself until the flames were extinguished. By the time she had put herself out, the opening in the wall was now covered with flames from a burst can of paint thinner. Looking behind her, then to her left and right, Farren realized there was nowhere they could go. The flames were closing in and Doc wasn't conscious. She paused for a moment, then slipped off the mask, resigned to the inevitable.

"Okay," she said quietly. "If that's the way it's going to be—I won't leave you." She got down on her knees and clutched one of his limp gloved hands in hers. "Father in heaven, please forgive us any sins we've committed and accept us into your kingdom. All I ask now is that you take us quickly."

As her knees began to burn from the heat of the floor, she suddenly felt raindrops striking her arm, but they were coming at her sideways. Looking to her right, she saw the flames in front of the rip in the wall were being extinguished by blasts of water. Then an ax head appeared out of nowhere and tore the rip in the aluminum wall open even wider. Then, a second ax head then did the same. A moment later, a fireman wearing an air mask bolted through the opening. Rising to her feet, Farren yelled, *"Over here!"*

"Get that air mask on!" the muffled voice of the fireman ordered. *"Grab his feet. Right now! C'mon!"*

Obeying, Farren put the mask back over her face and grabbed Doc's ankles while the fireman locked his hands under Doc's arms and around his chest. Lifting him up, the fireman quickly walked backward.

"Watch the jagged edges of the wall," he cautioned.

Once they gotten Doc outside, the fireman slung him over his shoulder and carried him toward KK and the waiting ambulance. The back of Doc's turn-out coat smoked as they went, coming very close to burning all the way through.

While gently being placed on a gurney, Doc's eyes flickered open to see the masked face of Don Stubigg, who'd been carrying him. The senior fireman took off his helmet and mask. His eyes were filled with concern.

"Still going where you don't belong, eh, Reynolds?" Stubigg asked quietly.

"I know, Captain," he moaned, smiling painfully as a trickle of blood slid from the corner of his mouth. "I'm an idiot."

Doc's head drifted to one side as he fell unconscious again.

45 All The Explanation We Get

It had been a week since Clair's funeral. Gus sat on the chain swing on the front porch of the house he and his wife had lived in for the past nine months. He wore a white T-shirt, jeans, and sneakers and hadn't shaved in a couple of days. He had a Stroh's beer in one hand and a Camel cigarette in the other. It was a couple of minutes after 1:00 in the afternoon. Aaron's red and white Studebaker pulled up in front of the house. Gus took a deep exasperated breath, then a deep drag off his Camel.

"If you're looking for Jackie, she's over at my folks' place," he said as Aaron approached the front steps. As usual he was dressed for attention, his loud shirt and pants didn't match and he wore his favorite white fedora.

"Actually, I came over to see you," his father-in-law said climbing the wooden steps. Once on the porch, he saw a six-pack of Stroh's sitting on the floor. Two of the bottles in the carton were already empty and it sat next to an ashtray full of cigarette butts.

"I didn't know you smoked," he said.

"What can I do for you, Aaron?" Gus asked curtly, wanting to get to whatever it was Clair's father wanted.

"Actually, I want to do something for you," the older man said. "I, I've been slipping your landlord a little extra money each month to keep your rent low. I just wanted to let you know that I intend to keep doing that. I mean—if that's okay with you."

"Thanks, but that won't be necessary," Gus said, not betraying that he already knew. "I don't expect Jackie and me to be staying here much longer."

"Really? Why's that?"

Gus looked around at the neighborhood. "Too many memories. It's time for a change. Change of scenery, change of towns, maybe a change of state."

Sinclair's first instinct was to react angrily, but he held his temper. He took off his hat and gestured to half of the swing. "May I?"

Gus slid over so his visitor could sit. "Look, I'm very grateful for everything you've done for us. But I can't stay in this town anymore."

"I understand," Aaron said, sitting down. "There was a time when I wanted to leave just like you. My business had collapsed, I'd alienated my oldest daughter, didn't approve of my son-in-law, my youngest daughter didn't think much of me, I'd lost my wife, and people in town were laughing not so subtly behind my back. So, yeah, I understand the need."

He helped himself to one of the unopened warm beers and a bottle opener sitting nearby. "'Course," he continued, popping off the cap, "unlike me, you've still got a job. Hell, you've got two. Plus, you're respected in town, got a built-in support system between the Coopers and Sinclairs, you've even got a jerk of a father-in-law who's still willing to help with the rent. But you go ahead. You move and take your daughter away from the only family she's got left. I *do* understand your need."

Gus shot a glance at him, seeing his reverse psychology. "You a religious man, Aaron?"

"Religious? No, not particularly."

"Me, neither," Gus said, taking another deep drag off his smoke. "Not anymore. I hate God for taking her away from me. I hate him for stealing Jackie's mother. I hate him because the last impression I'll ever have of my wife was as a charred log. I hate him because when she died we were in the middle of an argument that never got resolved. And I hate him because the last time we spoke, we didn't..." he stopped himself, becoming so emotional he couldn't continue.

Aaron started to extend an arm to put around him, but likewise stopped, not knowing how Gus would react. Instead, he took another drink of warm Stroh's. After a moment, he asked, "What was the argument about?"

"What?"

"You said you two were in the middle of an argument when she died. What was it about?"

"Doesn't much matter now, does it?" Gus said, crushing out his smoke.

Aaron looked at Gus for a moment before continuing. "Y'know, I parted on pretty bad terms with Clair, myself. I was furious at how she kept pecking at Georgia during Jackie's birthday. I've done plenty of wrong things in my life, but that day, I think *she* was the one who..." his voice trailed off. "Well, you're right. It doesn't matter anymore. Let's just say she was stubborn like her father and leave it at that."

They were quiet for a several seconds, listening to the birds and the neighborhood kids playing in the distance.

"I was wrong about you, Gus," Aaron finally offered. "Clair could've done a lot worse."

The younger man looked at his guest as his brown eyes filled uncontrollably with tears. "I'm...just...so *angry* about it!" Gus blurted. "I, I want to blame someone. But who? The pilot? Can't. He's dead. The Army? Can't. Soldiers die. The mechanic? Was there even a mechanic that morning?"

"Don't," Aaron said, now putting a hand on Gus' quivering shoulder. "Sometimes things just happen, Gus. Sometimes, that's all the explanation we get."

Gus jerked and snorted and grit his teeth doing everything he could to keep his composure.

"Look, you got a beautiful daughter you need to make smart decisions for," Aaron continued. "Don't cheat her and yourself out of family by leaving town. We're suffering too and Jackie's our only bright spot in all of this. She's a part of Clair that lives on. Don't take that away from us."

Gus closed his eyes as tears ran down his cheeks and nodded. "Okay...Okay, Aaron. Not for now, anyway."

Not wanting to overstay his welcome, the contractor set his beer down, grabbed his hat, and stood up.

"Thank you," he said sincerely. "I, uh, I know this isn't much comfort right now, but you *are* a young man. Time *does* help to heal wounds. You *will* fall in love and marry again. Clair would want that."

Gus raised his bloodshot, wet eyes to his guest. "I'll never marry again. Why would I? I've already had perfection."

The older man smiled, his eyes becoming moist. "What? You expect me to argue?" He put on his fedora and walked down the porch steps. "I'll be around," he called as he walked toward his car.

46 Heathen Ways

    Doc's parents, Marion and James, had just arrived in town after a five-hour ride. They walked up the front sidewalk and headed for the information desk in the lobby of the Charlevoix Area Hospital on Lake Shore Drive. Just at a glance, one could tell they were from the 1970s. Marion, an accountant, wore a paisley pullover top and a long denim skirt. Her hair was long—probably too long for a woman in her early fifties—but that was her preference. It was brown like her son's, but it had several strands of grey. She wasn't the kind of woman who would go in for artificial coloring. She took the Lauren Bacall view on wrinkles and grey hair and considered them the well-earned trophies of life. James was as tall as Doc, a bit pudgy, and wore clean jeans, leather sandals, and a green golf shirt that read "Reynolds's Nursery" on the breast pocket. The "O" in Reynolds had a leaf design in it that slightly resembled a marijuana sprig but James always referred to it as a fern. His hair was curlier than his son's and considerably more salt and pepper than his wife's.
    They'd been called by Farren and had been told that Doc was in serious but stable condition due to a gunshot wound and some burns on his back and right side, as well as the back of his legs. Fortunately, he'd been shot at such a close range that the bullet passed right through him, and although he'd lost a lot of blood, no vital organs had been hit. Doctor Lancaster expected him to make a full recovery, but he was less optimistic about some scarring on his

legs, side, and back. He wanted time to pass before determining whether or not skin grafts were going to be needed.

"Every time we come to this town, our kid's in the hospital," James observed. They had been there seven months earlier in December after Doc and Farren's ex-husband, Charlie, wound up in Round Lake. Charlie drowned and Doc was treated for a throat injury and hypothermia. "And it's always because of this girl, Farren," James continued. "The woman's a walking booby trap."

"She's the victim of a con gone wrong and a crazy man wanting revenge," Marion corrected. "But it's over now. Once and for all."

"You think after all this they're gonna get married?" James asked.

"Could be," she answered.

James shook his head. "I just hope the girl isn't accident prone, too."

Coming to the front desk, Marion asked the volunteer, "Could you please tell us what room Wyatt Reynolds is in?"

"Two fifteen," they heard a voice answer behind them. They turned around to see Don Stubigg in his usual uniform. "Sorry. I couldn't help but overhear as I was passing. I just came from there. He's in two fifteen. They just gave him something to help him sleep. His skin is pretty tender right now."

James extended a hand. "You must work with Doc. I'm his dad, James Reynolds. This is my wife, Marion."

"Hi," the fireman said, shaking James' hand. "Don Stubigg."

"You're Doc's captain," Marion said, recognizing the name. "Farren told us you're the one who pulled him out of the fire." She took his hand and instead of shaking it, brought it to her lips and kissed it. "Thank you, Captain!" she said emotionally. "*Thank you* for saving my son's life!"

The barrel-chested man looked at her and smiled. "Every day that he goes to work, your son makes a promise to the people of this community. A promise that says, 'If you need me, I'll be there. And if your life's in danger, I'll put mine in harm's way to try and save you.' Men like that are few and far between." He took Marion's hand, brought it to his lips and returned the kiss. "Thank *you*, Mrs.

Reynolds."

Without speaking further, Stubigg smiled and walked away, leaving behind two very touched and very proud parents.

A few minutes later, they opened up the door to room two fifteen and saw their son lying on his stomach. He was uncovered, asleep, and wearing only boxer shorts. His face was turned to the left. Cut pieces of gauze had been placed on his back here and there to help keep an antiseptic burn ointment in place. There was gauze on his right side and legs too, and one especially thick square was taped on his lower back and to the left of his spine where the bullet had passed through. This particular square was blotted with dark red blood but not too much. An IV ran into his right hand from a hanging plastic bag and a small clear oxygen hose went into each nostril.

Seeing her child in such a piteous condition, Marion drew a sharp, surprised breath. But then her eyes drank in the rest of the scene. Doc's left arm hung off the side of the bed and Farren sat in a chair next to it with both of her hands holding his in her lap. She was also asleep and was leaned over in her chair close to Doc. She wore a short-sleeve red top and her right forearm was wrapped in gauze. She had her feet propped up on another chair that was facing her and there were icepacks on both of her knees from when she knelt on the hot floor of the storage barn to pray.

Deciding to let them sleep, Marion gestured for her husband to back up into the hallway and closed the door.

"They look like they've been through a war," James observed.

"He's burned so *badly*," Marion sighed, her eyes tearing up.

"Now, don't overreact here," her husband reminded his wife, taking her hand. "We don't know that for sure. When Farren called, she said it looked worse than it might be. The doctor isn't sure about scarring or how much there'll be."

She nodded, reached into her purse and took out a tissue to dab her eyes, then the two of them started walking toward the elevator.

"I'd like to amend my statement about they 'could' get married," she said. "After everything they've been through together, I think they will."

Marion and James stayed at a motel in Charlevoix for the next three days since Doc's cabin wasn't ready to receive guests yet, but Farren had them and Gus over to dinner at her mushroom house. They also had breakfast with her and Lance and Charlene, who had returned from their honeymoon and had numerous stories and pictures to share. The Reynolds had previously met Lance and Charlene and it was good for them to get to know the people who inhabited Doc's life a little better. They even met Judith Herriman in Oleson's grocery store, who happened to be with Gus. The Reynolds had gone in to get some snacks to take back to their room when they spotted Gus talking with Judith. He was buying groceries to restock the new temporary marina store when he ran into Judith also doing shopping.

By the time the Reynolds returned to Ann Arbor, a trailer had been set up to be the new Portside Marina store, an insurance adjuster had come and gone, the cleaning crew that specialized in crime scenes was working out at Doc's, and the patient himself was still mostly bedridden but doing better. Lancaster wanted him to stay in the hospital for another week and the paramedic, realizing he might dodge painful skin grafts, didn't argue.

As the days passed, the police identified Bartholomew's body through dental records, and upon learning of her boyfriend's death from a personal visit by a smug-looking Detective Kaiser, Kayla decided it was time to move out and move on.

On the day Doc was to be released from the hospital, Farren took the day off. She did a thorough cleaning of her place, knowing that Doc would be staying with her because it was closer to the hospital should he need it. Then she went down to the marina about noon to check on the progress of things.

A dusty bulldozer was smoothing out the land where the storage barn had been and all the burnt remains of it were gone. A couple of burned but salvageable boats sat in trailers and a yellow Hyundai midi excavator was knocking down then shoveling up the still standing charred remains of the marina store. After scooping up debris, the excavator was emptying it into an awaiting dump truck. The new marina store was a plain white mobile home that had been hauled in and set up on the opposite side of the parking lot from where the barn used to be. A temporary telephone pole had also been erected so electricity and phone lines could be run into the trailer.

Farren greeted some customers who asked about her arm as they were coming out of the trailer, then went inside. The interior had open boxes of snack chips, fishing lures, sunscreen, stacked cartons of soda, and more. Gus sat at a card table in his usual golf shirt and jeans and was on the phone when she came in.

"Store hours are exactly the same," he said into the phone. "And if you need any repairs, both Ironton Cove Marina and Northwest Marine Yacht Basin are temporarily taking our customers. Just let 'em know you're a Portside Marina customer and you'll get a ten percent discount. Okay?...Good. Thanks, Chuck." He ended the call and turned to Farren. "Hey, girl. How's it goin'?"

"Good," she said, scratching her forearm.

"Stop scratching," he warned. "It means the skin's healing."

"I know, I know. But it's driving me crazy."

"Think of how Doc must feel. What time do you pick him up?"

"I'm going to head over to the hospital around three. Bob Lancaster should be finished with his rounds by then. How goes it here?"

"Well, if the other marinas in town don't steal all our customers, great."

"They won't. They're just trying to help out. Professional courtesy. We'd do the same."

"Billy Osborne called from the insurance company," Gus said, scratching the stubble under his chin. "He's trying to expedite our check. It might be here by the end of the week."

"Good," she said, looking out one of the windows at what was left of the marina store. "New beginnings, huh?"

"Yeah," Gus said, rising from his chair. "Actually, I want to talk to you about that."

"What?"

"New beginnings...I'll stay until you're well underway with the new construction, but it's time for me to pack it in, darlin'."

The Intended Ones

"What?" she repeated, surprised.

"You've got Doc, the threat of Bartholomew is gone, fall will be comin' pretty soon and I'm just too damn old to take another winter here. I've talked about retiring to warmer weather since your folks were alive. I think it's finally time for me to do it."

"But Grandpa, what if Doc gets accepted to medical school?"

"What about it?"

"Well, I might be spending time in Detroit and really need someone here to help me with the business."

"Hire a manager. Take on a partner."

"You could be my partner. I've always considered us that anyway."

"No, sweetie," he smiled, shaking his head. "The whole point of me helpin' you with the business was so it could be *your* business. It's up to you now whether you want to continue, or..."

"Or, what?"

"Aren't you always saying everything happens for a reason? Seems to me this fire has kinda hit the pause button on the DVD of your life. Maybe it's for a reason. Maybe it's time for a major change."

Farren drank in her grandfather's words and brushed her bangs aside contemplatively.

"Well, where would you go?" she asked.

"I've been thinking about Florida," he answered, going over to some windbreakers that were hanging on stick-on wall hangers. One garment had been knocked off its hanger so he picked it up and rehung it. "The Sarasota area, or maybe Venice."

Farren folded her arms with a suspicious dimpled smile. "This wouldn't have anything to do with my therapist moving down there, would it?"

"I don't know what you're talking about," Gus fibbed.

"Well, all I know is, during our final session, she asked more questions about you than she did me."

"Well, that makes sense," he said straight-faced. "I'm more screwed up than you. After all, I just shot someone."

"She's a sex therapist," Farren reminded him.

"I'm screwed up there, too. It's been so long, I don't even remember what goes where."

"Too much information," Farren declared with a raised hand. "I'm going to meet with the architect now," she said, heading for the door.

"Hey," he called after her more seriously. She stopped and turned. "You know your grandmother will always be the best thing that ever happened to me, right?"

"Of course," Farren smiled. "You don't need my permission to be with someone else. In fact, I don't think Grandma would've *ever* wanted you to be alone for as long as you have. I didn't know her, but I can't imagine she'd want someone she loved to be alone for more than fifty years."

"Fifty-seven years, one week, two days and seven hours," Gus answered. "But who's counting?"

She walked over and gave her grandfather a hug.

"I love you, Grandpa."

"I love you, too, Granddaughter," he reciprocated, patting her back. "Your mom and dad would be so very proud of the woman you've become. Despite my heathen ways."

47 Coming Forward

The doorbell rang while Clive and Erma Boil were watching the *Milton Berle Show* on NBC. Getting up from his easy chair, Clive went to the front door to see a casually dressed and nervous-looking Derek Worthing standing on their front porch. Clive was a big man, forty-eight years old, who had done both wrestling and football in high school. Erma was lean, almost anorexic. Both of the Boils knew who Derek was, although neither had actually spoken to him.

"Who is it?" Erma called, working on her needlepoint and wearing a nice blue dress.

Clive opened the front door.

"Hi, Mr. Boil. I'm Derek Worthing. I used to go to high school with Tommy. Could, could I have a word with you, please?"

"Yes, Derek. I know who you are," Clive said politely. "Come in."

Derek walked into the nice but small home. Doilies made by Erma sat on the arms of the sofa, and on the fireplace mantel were no less than half a dozen pictures of the Boil's deceased son, Tommy. There was a picture of him playing baseball in little league, another of him playing baseball in high school and still another of him wearing his high school graduation cap and gown. There were also a couple of pictures of Tommy's younger sister, Amelia, who Derek knew worked at a pizza place downtown.

Erma looked up, visibly surprised to see Derek in her house.

Both she and Clive were acutely aware that, a couple of summers earlier, Derek had been hospitalized for jumping off the Memorial Bridge while it was opening. Since their son had died attempting to do the same thing two years before that, they couldn't help but wonder if Derek was the unidentified youth who was also on the bridge the night he died. Legally, they had no recourse, but now that he was actually in their home, their curiosity and anxiety soared. Still, both played the moment with restraint, knowing that if Derek had decided to share something with them, he needed to go at his own pace.

"My wife, Erma," Clive introduced.

"Nice to meet you, ma'am," Derek smiled.

"Nice to meet you, Derek," she reciprocated. "You were friends with Tommy?"

"Well, we knew each other," Derek answered politically.

"Sit down, Derek," Clive said, gesturing to a chair then walking over to turn off Uncle Miltie on TV. "Can I get you something to drink?"

"No, sir. Thank you," Derek said, sitting on the sofa and nearly knocking off one of the doilies.

"You're Norm Worthing's son, right?" Erma asked.

"Yes, ma'am. That's right."

"I see your dad from time to time," Clive said, patting his belly and sitting down in his easy chair. "We have the same tailor." He was referencing that Norman Worthing, like him, was a large man. "You're working with your dad, right? Being groomed over there at Worthing Building Supply?"

"I was working for him, yes, sir. But, for several months now, I've been pursuing a new career direction."

"Really?" Clive asked. "What's that?"

"Uh, law enforcement."

"Really?" Erma asked. "That must've been a brave decision. I mean, it must have been a surprise to your folks."

"Yes, ma'am. Surprise is one way of putting it. My dad thinks I'm nuts to give up a lucrative future with him. But, I don't know, I just sort of like the idea of protecting other folks. Catching bad guys.

The Intended Ones

Righting wrongs. But maybe that's me just being silly."

"Not if that's what you really want to do," Clive said.

"I'd, uh...I'd like to talk to you about Tommy," Derek began, nervously rubbing his hands together. "Eh, you're right, Mrs. Boil, we knew each other. But we weren't friends. Matter of fact, we didn't like each other. We didn't like each other at all."

"Oh?" Erma said.

"What was the friction between you two?" Clive asked.

"Well, we both played baseball. We were both pretty athletic, competitive. We both thought the same girls were cute. You know how kids are in high school. Especially boys. One minute, it's healthy competition, and the next, you're mortal enemies."

Erma and Clive looked at one another as Derek continued.

"You, uh, you may not like to hear this, but, Tommy bullied me sometimes. Actually, a lot...and one night, things got out of control."

"My Tommy bullied you?" Erma said, defensively. "I find that hard to believe."

"Let the boy speak, Erma," Clive said.

"Everybody has a nemesis, Mrs. Boil. Tommy was mine...He hit the ball harder, ran faster...He always wanted to keep me in my place and that place was always second. Even after high school. Even when we saw each other when we were home from college."

Erma looked at her husband becoming impatient, but Clive wanted to hear everything Derek needed to say.

"I know this is difficult for you, Derek," he offered. "But please, go on."

Derek nodded, then continued, "The summer he—passed—we were both working downtown so we ran into each other all the time. And one day, Tommy came up with this, this crazy notion: a race to see who had the guts to run up a leaf of the drawbridge while it was opening then jump over the side and into the river."

"No!" Erma said, angrily setting her needlepoint aside. "Tommy would *never* concoct such a ridiculous and dangerous stunt!"

"Mother," Clive warned sternly, "I want to hear what this young man has to say."

Derek clasped his hands tightly together in his lap, then went on,

"We decided to do it at night, when the big sailboats would be coming in off the lake. We both wore dark clothing thinking that would be really clever...We started the race, Tommy almost got to the edge—but then—he just *stopped*. Panicked, I guess...I-I went ahead, 'cause for once I was going to beat him. But he just stayed there. Frozen...frozen until..." Derek stopped his story, knowing he didn't have to go on with the rest. "I, uh, I never came forward and said anything because I didn't want to get into trouble. It was wrong and stupid, and left both of you wondering what happened, and I'm sorry."

"Well, I think there's *some* truth in what you've said," Erma responded indignantly, "but *you're* the one who was the bully. Isn't that the truth, Derek?"

"No," Clive answered, recalling. "Tommy *could* be a bully. I remember some of his teachers telling me that, or trying to anyway."

"I admit," Derek said, "I've pushed some people around in my day, too. But not Tommy, Mrs. Boil, I swear to God."

They were all quiet for a moment. Finally, Clive asked, "Why come forward now?"

"I can't live with the contradiction. I can't go into law enforcement but sit on information about a death. I can't do that anymore...I guess another part of the reason is I recently saw someone I know bury a loved one. I—I didn't fully appreciate the pain you've gone through until I saw it on the face of someone my age." He stood up. "Look, I know not everything I've said here is pleasant. But it *is* the truth and I figured you're entitled to that. So if you wanna call the police, bring charges against me for withholding information, or collaborating in a wrongful death, I understand. I'll come clean with the authorities."

The Boils looked at one another. Clive thought for a moment before responding.

"Bringing the police into things would, I assume, pretty much end your aspirations about law enforcement."

"Yes, sir," Derek agreed. "Pretty much. Especially since I don't think Chief Sutter likes me very much. But that's your right." He looked at both of them. "Well, that's all I've got to say. Thanks for your time. Again, I'm so sorry about Tommy."

Derek walked to the front door and let himself out. Clive and Erma were so absorbed in what they had heard they forgot to say goodbye or walk their guest to the door. They were quiet for a long time after he was gone, both of them lost in their own thoughts.

"I've prayed for an answer about Tommy for four years," Erma finally said. "But this isn't the answer I wanted." She looked at her husband. "Do you believe him?"

Clive slowly nodded. "Yes, I do...So, what do you want to do?"

"What do *you* want to do?"

He rose from his chair and walked over to the front window. He looked out at the evening momentarily before answering.

"One life's already been destroyed on that bridge. Would destroying another bring Tommy back?"

48 Changes

It was a Sunday of full of firsts. It was the first time since Doc had been injured in the storage barn that he'd attended Sunday mass at St. Ignatius Catholic Church. It was also the first time that Farren had volunteered to sing in the church choir. The church's musical director, a silver-haired woman named Ruth Hertler, had been trying to recruit Farren for years having caught her singing to herself when she was cleaning the church one day, but Farren always figured she had enough committees and activities in her life already. Now, however, she seemed ready to shake things up. Take on new challenges. So, she stood with twelve other choir members wearing a teal long-sleeve blouse to conceal the gauze she still wore on her arm, singing and occasionally giving Doc self-deprecating looks because she didn't think she sang that well.

Doc and Gus sat in the second row of pews from the altar in the small crucifix-shaped church that only held three hundred people. Doc, wearing an oversized shirt and baggy pants, occasionally fidgeted in his seat because his right side, back and legs were still sore.

"You okay?" Gus quietly asked, leaning in to him.

"Long as I don't sit too long in one position, yeah," he whispered.

The old man looked at his granddaughter, then at Doc.

"You ever goin' to tell her?" he whispered again.

"About what? Clair?"

Gus nodded.

"I don't know. I don't even know if I should've told you."

"Yes, you should have," Gus affirmed. "It helped to button things up between Clair and me. At least, for now."

Doc looked at him. "Oh, so *now* you think you'll see her again at the pearly gates? Or pearly whites? Or Pearl Bailey? Whatever heaven is?"

"Let's just say, I'm quietly hopeful."

Doc glanced over at Farren who was looking at them with wide eyes and putting a narrow finger on her lips.

"Your granddaughter doesn't think you're being very quiet."

Gus rolled his eyes as the choir finished singing, then a lector got up to give the second reading. After the reading, there was the gospel for which the congregation stood, then afterward, everyone sat down for the sermon.

"In my years of being a priest," Father Ken began from behind the pulpit, "there have been a thousand times when I've referred to my congregation as 'the faithful.' But just what does that mean? 'The faithful?' I don't know about you, but there have been times when I felt like I couldn't be considered one of 'the faithful.' I've had doubts. I've had questions. I've had anger issues with the Lord. I've sat out there like you on some Sundays not getting much out of the mass. I was here only because I was supposed to be. Oh, yes, priests have doubts and questions and issues with God, too. Especially, when they've seen good men, compassionate men, men that should have gone on to do great things and live long lives, die in the mud of a battlefield. Yep, there have been times when I just flat out didn't like my Boss very much."

Doc and Gus listened attentively. For once, Father Ken was saying something that immediately grabbed their attention.

"But here's the thing," the priest continued. "I know I'm a better man with God in my life than without him. I know our world is a better place with God in it, than without him. Some people might take issue with that. Some people might say, 'But Father, look at the division, the hatred and wars that people have inflicted in the name of God throughout history. Look at how the Roman's persecuted the Christians, look at the Crusades, the Spanish Inquisition, the witch hunts of Europe and America, the always sensitive Middle East? What about the scandals? Scandals that have plagued not only the Catholic Church, but others too?' All of those are fair points. But I *still* say we're a better planet for believing in God because we're still here. Mankind not only survives but also is thriving. Again, some might disagree. But the threat of nuclear war isn't what it once was, our economy is truly global, diseases from seventy years ago are being cured and people are living longer. Meanwhile, every day, hundreds-of-millions of people do kind things, selfless things, that are no doubt inspired by their belief in God. It may not make the newspapers or the history books, but random acts of kindness are everywhere if we take the time to look. In our second reading today, Saint Paul wrote of how God uses us in different ways, even with our imperfections."

The priest briefly glanced at Farren.

"Some people are caregivers. Strong in their faith although they've sometimes had to pay a high price for it." He glanced at Doc. "Others are healers. They mend the body while lightening the heart." His eyes shifted to Gus. "Still others are protectors. Like good shepherds, they have to be vigilant for those in their charge...Then there are people like me: long-winded talkers."

The congregation laughed.

"But hopefully, not too long-winded. My point is, faith is an ebb and flow thing. Your relationship with God is similar to your relationship with your spouse, or your siblings, or your children. Instead of thinking what it isn't, think of what it is! It may not always be perfect, but you keep working on it because you need it. It helps to define you who are. And remember, God doesn't require us to be perfect, only that we keep trying. Jesus hung out with tax collectors, lepers, lowly fishermen, women of questionable repute, and he was born in a stable. So he's used to imperfection.

"So, who's 'the faithful?' We are. Just by virtue of us being here. Just by virtue of us *choosing* a relationship with God. We may not feel particularly worthy sometimes. We may not feel like God's listening sometimes. We may never have all the answers we want or see all of the rhyme and reason of things, but that's the mystery of faith. We can celebrate what we *do* know. We can revel in our choice to be here *today!* We can accept that we all serve in different ways. We can all try to listen better, be kind to one another, and we can all chill. Sometimes, just relaxing with your faith is the very best thing you can do. So enjoy it."

The following day, Doc was standing in Farren's living room looking at the black-and-white photo sitting on her fireplace mantel of Gus, Clair, and baby Jackie. He was wearing an extra-large button-up shirt and sweatpants and had been advised to wear loose-fitting clothing for the next several weeks. Farren came through the front door with a dimpled smile and a stack of mail in her hand. She was wearing a pair of snug-fitting jeans and a short-sleeve, yellow-flower print blouse. This was also her first morning without wearing gauze. Her forearm was still red and a little scabbed, but it looked like it would heal completely.

"Hi there," she said.

"Hey," he answered, turning and a little surprised. "I thought you were signing a deal with the architect and construction company this morning."

"Nope. I pushed it off. I want to talk to you about something."

"Okay," Doc said. "You want some coffee? I just made some."

"Sure."

They walked into Farren's small kitchen that was, more or less, wedge-shaped because of the circular shape of the house. It featured a small round wooden table with a MacKenzie Child-like black-and-white tablecloth on it and vase full of Black-Eyed Susans.

"My landlord called this morning," he said, opening a cabinet to get two mugs. "Even though everything at the cabin has been cleaned up with no trace of what happened, he doesn't feel comfortable with me as a tenant anymore." He shrugged as he poured the coffee. "Guess I can't blame him."

"So that means a change in your life," Farren said. "I've been thinking about making some changes, too."

"Tuba lessons?" he guessed. "Thank God, my prayers have been answered."

She smiled, opened up the refrigerator and got out the milk for him. Then she went over the kitchen table and sat down, putting the mail down in front of her.

"Actually, I'm reassessing whether or not I want to be in the marina business anymore."

"What?" he said, quite surprised as he poured the coffee.

"I got my insurance check. It's almost 600,000 dollars. Once I pay off the mortgages on the buildings—well, the buildings that *used* to be there—and settle up with my vendors, there will still be more than a one hundred fifty grand left. That's enough to move to Detroit, get an apartment, pay for some of medical school, and even enroll me in some classes at Wayne State. If we need more, I can get a job or there's always the land the marina sits on, although I'd kinda like to hang onto it if we could."

Doc set the coffee pot back down and turned to her, open-mouthed.

"Uh, that's some plan you've got there."

"I tend to think things happen for a reason. Maybe out of all this bad stuff there's an opportunity here. Maybe it's time to stop living my parents' life and start living my own."

"But, I thought you loved the marina?"

"Yes, I do. But I love you more."

He smiled at her, then turned back to the counter and reached for the milk she'd put out for him. "You're forgetting one thing. Wayne State hasn't accepted me. If they were going to, I would've heard something by now. In fact, I would've heard something a couple of weeks ago."

Farren held up an envelope with a gold embossed Wayne State Medical School University logo on it. "You mean, like this?"

Doc turned toward her, surprised again.

"I went out to your place first thing this morning and picked up the mail. It hasn't been picked up since last Thursday. The post office originally delivered this to the wrong address, so it had to be re-routed. That's why it took so long."

Doc stared at the envelope not wanting to get his hopes up. "It's,

The Intended Ones

it's going to be a no," he figured.

Farren felt the envelope. "Pretty thick envelope if they were just going to say no, don't you think? I mean, 'no' is just two letters."

She was right. It was a pretty thick envelope. Doc took a step toward her and reached out his hand, but she pulled the envelope back.

"Not so fast, Kemo Sabe. If I'm going to contribute my money and follow you to medical school, we're going to have an agreement, a legally binding document that says if we ever break up, I get my money paid back *with interest* within a certain time."

He looked at her and smiled.

"My hopeless romantic has grown up."

"I'm still hopeless," she smiled. "But maybe a little wiser."

"I wouldn't have it any other way," he said, extending his hand again. But she still refused to hand him the envelope.

"And don't think if you agree to my terms that means I don't want a formal proposal. I *do*. I want to be totally swept off my feet. I want you down on one knee, I want to be surprised, I want a church wedding, I want my grandpa to give me away, Father Ken to marry us—the whole package."

He looked at her lovingly. "That's only fair. 'Cause that's what *I'd* be getting."

She smiled as he extended his hand again.

"Anything else?" he asked.

She thought for a moment. "No. I guess not. Except if you don't get in, it doesn't make any difference. I'll love you no matter what you wind up doing."

She finally handed the envelope over. He stepped back toward the counter, opened it, took out a folded stack of papers, and read the correspondence on top. He nervously rubbed his forehead with the tips of his fingers as he read.

After a long moment, Farren became impatient.

"Well?" she asked. "Is today a new beginning?"

He didn't respond. He just kept reading.

"Doc?"

He raised his eyes from the paper and looked at her emotionless, using his very best poker face.

Timothy Best

Timothy Best is a creative director and writer/producer in the advertising business. The recipient of more than 180 advertising honors, he's written for dozens of household brands including Allstate, Walmart, Cadillac, Fifth Third Bank, Honda, and many more. He's also an adjunct professor at the University of Alabama and teaches copywriting. He has a book of short stories available on Amazon.com entitled *The Petroglyph Papers*.

The Intended Ones is the award-winning prequel & sequel to his similarly award-winning novel, *Substitute Angel*. His next novel, *A Farm In Pennsylvania*, is a historical romance set in Gettysburg, 1863. A Michigan native, he now lives in Birmingham, Alabama, with his wife, daughter and two rescue dogs.

Readers are always welcome to follow his blog on Goodreads.com, or visit his website at Timbestonline.com.

Cover design & illustration by R. Brannon Hall. Photography by Noelani.

Timothy Best

Made in the USA
Charleston, SC
06 February 2015